KRISPR

JENNIFER HANDLER

This is a work of fiction. All of the characters, organizations, and events portrayed in this novel are either products of the author's imagination or are used fictitiously.

Print ISBN 979-8-35093-592-9
ebook ISBN: 979-8-35093-593-6

Printed in the United States of America

For my parents—the third greatest carpenter
& the consummate caregiver

"Technology has no conscience of its own.
Whether it will become a force for good or ill depends on man."
John F Kennedy

"Without music, life would be a mistake."
Friedrich Nietzsche

AUTHOR'S NOTE

In this time, our time, as we witness the rapid evolution of science and technology, it should come as no surprise that there are those among us who are swiftly closing the gap between reality and what could once only be imagined. This transformation is most prevalent in the fields of neuroscience and molecular genetics, where the mystery of the human brain is rapidly being unraveled and the ability to manipulate each gene is now commonplace. This transformation is leading to promising new therapies and a deeper understanding of the human mind but is also pushing ethical boundaries further than ever before. It begets the question: Just because we can, does it mean we should?

On October 7, 2020, The Royal Swedish Academy of Sciences awarded the Nobel Prize in Chemistry to Emmanuelle Charpentier, Max Planck Unit for the Science of Pathogens, Berlin, Germany and Jennifer A. Doudna, University of California, Berkeley, USA *"for the development of a method for genome editing." KRISPR* is purely a work of fiction, as it is not a young college student who has discovered the revolutionary technology of gene editing, but rather it has been born from the extraordinary vision of Dr. Charpentier and Dr. Doudna

Table of Contents

CHAPTER 1

Daunting Decisions

"We don't kill. We sacrifice."

He had told her this.

She thought about the many times she felt life leave the warm, soft body at her own hands. It should have bothered her. But it didn't. Because that's what she was doing… not killing. She wasn't a killer. It was a sacrifice. A sacrifice for the greater good. The decision would need to be made again, only this time, it would involve human life.

Is it ever justifiable to do the wrong things for the right reasons?It was not only justified, it was justice, she had thought.

And should she destroy something so revolutionary, with so much promise for good, yet so much potential for evil, to ensure it would never be exploited—never be used for sinister purposes? Yes, that would be the right thing to do. Destroy it forever. But doing what's right isn't always easy, especially when it comes to the ones you love.

She had decisions to make.

Should she strike the match and light the fuse?

Should she depress the plunger on the syringe?

CHAPTER 2

The Early Years

Do you play basketball? How tall are you? You can't possibly still be growing? Are your parents tall?

How she hated being so tall. During grade school and high school, she was the tallest in every class, at every school. She came to despise her height—always so much taller than every girl and certainly every boy. Would she ever have a boyfriend? Her height was her whole identity … the "Tall" girl. She turned inward. She didn't want to be known only as the tall girl but felt like it was hopeless. It was too late. There was no way to shrink. Hell, even her name meant tall, she thought. Aliya: "tall, towering." How could her parents possibly have known when she was in-utero? It was a damn curse. She felt like a freak.

But then, at some point, as she moved through adolescence, a new question emerged. It began to be asked not once, not twice, but many times …

"Are you a model?"

Her mind flooded with confusing thoughts. What? Modeling. Me? Could I, the total outlier, the tree, the plain girl from the

Mundane Midwest, actually become … a model? Was this some kind of cruel joke?

She realized that there was only one way to find out. She had to do what her driven self did naturally. She had to go for it. It was a flicker of hope that might just free her from her desperate existence. In her head, she could clearly hear her dad's words: "If your ship doesn't come in, LeeLee, swim out to meet it."

"Okay. I'll pick you up as soon as school lets out, right at 3:15. At the back door. I'll be sure to get there early so I'm first in the line. We'll stop at the Kelsey's Deli that's on the way to save time. You can change there, and I'll get you a salad to eat as we drive. Sound like a plan?"

Aliya's face softened. "Thanks Mom. You're the GOAT."

The modeling agency was an hour's drive away. Each class was scheduled for three hours. Five hours would make for taxing school nights during her junior year, at the height of a schedule filled with AP and honors classes at the private, college-prep high school that her parents sacrificed to send her to. It was a big commitment.

Aliya squinted. The wall of shiny black tinted windows lining each floor of the angular modern building reflected piercing rays of sunlight. "*SMA*" was artistically etched in gray on the large glass double-doors. Her heart fluttered as they approached.

"You got this," her mom said, giving Aliya a fist bump.

The pounding beat of EDM—the unmistakable genre of music customary for fashion shows—resounded in the lobby. A large screen covering the wall behind the circular desk flashed images of gorgeous models strutting down the runway as strobe lights flashed in unison with the beat. Aliya's mouth dropped open. Although she tried her best to appear nonchalant, she couldn't help but stare at the stunning young woman behind the desk. She was damn near perfection: long lashes, sensual dark eyes, high cheekbones, sultry red lips, bright white, perfectly aligned teeth. Dangling silver earrings were the perfect accompaniment to her wavy long, ebony hair, and her well-manicured, teal nails accented the silver rings on her fingers. Her fitted, low-cut, jet black dress undoubtedly fulfilled its purpose of focusing one's attention on her voluptuous breasts. Yes, she definitely had it all going on.

"You must be Aliya. I'm Daija. Welcome to Synergistic Modeling Agency."

Aliya dutifully attended the classes. She learned about the "business" of modeling—exactly what was required of her and how unforgiving it could be. Then she worked at it relentlessly, practicing and practicing. She was consumed by it. She learned about photo movement and about poise. She mastered how to walk a runway: to pause, pivot, and flip her head at just the right moment. She learned how to emulate the look, the expression of a high fashion model: tilted head, longing eyes, lips slightly parted.

On "Prep Day," Aliya and the other aspiring models went from one station to the next to be assessed and counseled on their weight (skeletal), their measurements (the perfect 34-24-34), their hair color (tailored to each complexion), their nails (precisely manicured with a neutral color), their makeup (fresh and natural), their complexion (flawless), their clothing (always all black: leggings to define their shapely legs and hips, a crop top to accentuate their cleavage and reveal their tiny waistline, and, of course, high heels). They learned about proper "model" nutrition (carbs are evil), about hydration (essential for smooth skin), and about exercise (not building muscle but rather walking forty-five minutes twice a day to keep thighs thin and calves shapely). It was as if they were fine thoroughbred horses being prepared for sale at auction.

The agency recommended a photographer to get shots for her "comp card." She was sent to a studio on the top floor of a decrepit building in the shadiest, grittiest part of downtown Cleveland. Having no idea what to bring, Aliya and her mom entered the ancient freight elevator carrying a pile of clothing. The creaky elevator was painted a tattered red, exposing its gray metal in the many spots where the paint had chipped away.

"What on earth are we getting ourselves into?" murmured her mother.

Aliya returned a timid smile. But on the inside, her heart leaped with anticipation.

The elevator was manned by a chill old hippie. He wore black straight-leg jeans, tattered black boots, and a denim shirt that hung loosely on his thin frame. A graying, scruffy beard matched his full head of wiry gray-black hair that was quite neatly pulled back in a ponytail. Aliya felt perfectly safe, in a hippie kind of "acceptance" way.

The elevator was his personal sanctuary, filled with his prized possessions from cherished concerts and relished second-hand stores. Among his many trinkets, she noticed a small, white-washed wooden chair missing a few spindles; a sign with a red, white, and blue image that had a skull with a lightning bolt on it that read, "Have a Grateful Day"; a flag that was black and green with a yellow "X" in the middle; an old cigar box (that she surmised was used to safely keep the things he smoked); and a variety of well-used candles. Pinned to the wall was a tattered picture of a deeply distressed Black Jesus, his downtrodden body kneeling near a large boulder—his sweat, drops of blood.

For a few moments, Aliya was mesmerized by the drama of this portrait of Jesus praying his agonizing prayer in the Garden of Gethsemane. Yes, she knew of it well from her grandma, who had prayed the rosary with great diligence and read bible stories to her and her sister whenever given the opportunity. The portrait depicted the first sorrowful mystery, the night before Jesus would be tortured and crucified. "Father, if this cup cannot pass away from me unless I drink of it, thy will be done."

Aliya snapped out of her trance to ponder this funky scene. The elevator door spanned the whole front wall and was made entirely of bars, like a jail cell. The hippie operator had to hand pull a large chain to make the top and bottom halves of the barred door join in the middle, before flipping a handle upward to begin their ascent to the top floor where the photographer's studio was located. The ride was noisy, creaky. They didn't speak, just politely returned the genuine yet gnarled smile of their new acquaintance.

Despite the scary location, the studio was modern and totally *au courant* with the photography world. A wall of windows provided amazing views of the city. A single stool sat in front of a white backdrop surrounded by lights, hanging umbrellas, and a fan or two. A rack of clothes stood next to a partially folded partition, behind which served as the changing room. In the other corner was another stool which sat in front of a table with a large, well-lit mirror. The table was littered with a hairdryer, combs, hairbrushes, styling wands, sprays, makeup brushes, applicator sponges, and a large basket filled with a variety of cosmetics.

The photoshoot was a celestial encounter. The hair stylist and makeup artist deftly worked their magic, tailoring Aliya's lengthy, rich, perfectly highlighted auburn hair to softly drape her shoulders.

They enhanced her already high cheekbones, thickened her brows, augmented her lips to a brilliant red sheen, and accentuated her emerald eyes (the descriptor used by the magicians) until they glistened. They used almost none of the clothing she had brought, except for a pair of jeans and her Calvin Klein bra and panties. The team chose outfits that perfectly accentuated her figure: the consummate black dress, a form-fitting gray sweater dress, and her fitted jeans open to reveal her Calvin Kleins and tiny waistline. As was her natural disposition, she took direction well and responded innately to the photographer's kinesthetic commands detailing where she should position her hands, arms, and legs; how she should tilt her head, adjust her facial expression, and bring forth in her eyes the emotion he was seeking. As his Nikon clicked away, she felt nothing less than ethereal.

The photographer's work was pure genius. He had a gift like no other. Aliya was transformed. Seeing the photos made her realize, for the first time, that maybe she could, actually, walk a runway. She signed a contract with *SMA* and entered a modeling and talent competition held one very warm week in the summer preceding her senior year of high school. She and her mom road tripped to the Big Apple. Aliya had never been there. Her parents had gone many years before, when "*Cats*" was playing at the Winter Garden Theatre on Broadway. That, and Google, were the extent of their familiarity with The City That Never Sleeps. They checked into The Hilton on 53rd in Midtown Manhattan. It was bustling with young, talented contestants, and they were at once surrounded by "the beautiful people." Gorgeous, glamorous … downright ravishing.

Aliya met up with the other models from her agency as they prepared to compete. They turned heads everywhere. Their hair was perfectly straightened, their makeup flawless, and they donned black leggings, black crop tops, and requisite four-inch heels. They were all about six feet tall, the perfect 34-24-34. Their youth and beauty exuded.

Aliya and her mother sat with the others on the padded stackable conference chairs in the crammed hotel meeting room.

"Welcome to MMTC," said the attractive blonde at exactly 7:30 a.m. She was all business—straight black pencil skirt, collared white blouse, dark-rimmed glasses, and black heeled Gucci loafers sporting a shiny brass buckle.

"Each day of the competition, we will meet here promptly at 7:30 a.m. to review the schedule for the day."

Aliya sat up straight, leaning in and listening intently as her mom pulled out a pen and notepad.

"We'll start with the do's and don'ts. If approached by someone from a potential agency, do not give out any personal information. Collect business cards. Keep notes on everyone you meet. And always carry your comp cards, being sure not to forget to hand them out." She flipped the page on her clipboard and glanced down at her notes.

"At 4 p.m. today, there's a runway competition. Top designers will choose models for the fashion show that culminates the week's festivities. If you fit the look the designer desires and are chosen, you'll be required to attend practices throughout the week and then will be a part of the grand showcase at the final gala held at the week's end. I highly recommend you all try out for this. It is very prestigious."

It was Aliya's first taste of the grueling selection process.

"Next."

She felt the eyes from solemn faces piercing her like daggers with every stride her long legs took during the audition. She was competing with goddesses. She figured she had no chance in hell.

Early the next morning, Aliya walked alone to the area outside the hotel's grand ballroom, filled with trepidation as she approached the large bulletin board. Her body tensed as she scanned the sheets of paper posted on it. She found the sheet entitled "Fashion Show Call-Backs" and stepped closer, bringing both hands to her mouth.

There it was: #8085!

CHAPTER 3

NYC

"Mom, do you hear that?" Aliya whispered with a gentle smile as they approached the main path. Not far in the distance was a shiny black grand piano gracing the center of the walkway. An attractive young pianist, with a sturdy, muscular frame—a physique unlike that of the stereotypical scrawny musician, but rather like that of a personal trainer—so delicately pressed out the initial, unmistakable chords of "Clair de Lune." The air was crisp and clean. The sky a brilliant blue. The iconic Washington Arch welcomed them like an old friend. The locals relaxed on park benches or wandered about, savoring the long-awaited warmth and sunshine of the first days of spring. A gentle breeze caressed the fresh blossoms of the budding magnolia trees, as colorful tulips and daffodils dotted the landscape. They basked in the heavenly music, surrounded in sublimity.

This was Aliya's second visit to New York. They had just completed a tour of NYU. Cameron, their student tour guide, had stopped at the Mark and Debra Leslie Entrepreneurs Lab. Peeking in the window, Aliya was struck by the words: "A vision without execution is hallucination." She was barely eighteen with absolutely no vision for the future, but hungering for a new beginning. Hungering to one day do something extraordinary.

NYU, like most colleges in the heart of Manhattan, was too expensive for someone with such humble beginnings. But her high GPA and SAT score enabled the nearby James Franklin University to offer her a substantial merit scholarship, and it was there that Aliya began the next leg of her life's journey. She moved into a room on the twenty-first floor of the dormitory located in Lincoln Center, the quintessential hub of culture and the arts. The dormitory floors were recent additions to the top of the pre-existing library building. The modern rooms were exquisite in comparison to a typical college dorm room, with one entire wall composed of windows.

Unlike most NYC views, the room did not look directly into another building, but rather overlooked an outdoor amphitheater and an open space almost the size of a football field. Julliard, which was only about five stories high, was adjacent to the amphitheater. Then began the emblematic skyscrapers gracing the splendid skyline. If that wasn't stunning enough, to the west there was a beautiful view of the majestic Hudson. And in the distance, to the northeast, was the picturesque Central Park.

At night, she and her roommate kept the windows cracked and the shades wide open to soak up the twinkling lights of the skyline. She often drifted off to sleep to the music of the Met Opera, which gave free performances at the amphitheater below. Lying in bed, listening to the dreamy music and sensual voices emanating from a performance of "The Magic Flute," Aliya knew this was extraordinary. What eighteen-year-old lives like this?

As the days passed, her focus turned to her heavy course load and taking in everything she could about NYC. Free days were spent at the Met, the Whitney, the boutiques of SoHo, and the concerts in

Central Park. The friends she made were all like-minded: hard-working in school (to keep those scholarships) but also with a carefree spirit, wanting to explore and experience everything that NYC had to offer. As with thousands of young New Yorkers, they all dreamed of getting into the studio audience for SNL but usually just ended up at the Wendy Williams show, which they agreed had to be as much fun.

She was, by nature, inquisitive. She loved the French language and had taken four years of French in high school but realized the job market for French majors was virtually non-existent. She decided to opt for a French minor and found herself gravitating to her science classes. Science—in particular, the study of life itself—was becoming very seductive. Etched in her memory was the day she learned about the First Law of Thermodynamics: processes are subject to the principle of the conservation of energy. Hence energy cannot be created or destroyed. She and her friends spent hours lying on blankets at Sheep Meadow in Central Park discussing this vital topic.

"So, like, when you die, the energy in the body doesn't just disappear?" asked her friend, Adam.

"Right. It has to go somewhere," Aliya replied.

"So, like ... there really is heaven and hell?"

"There must be. Where else could the energy go?"

Adam raised his eyebrows and folded his arms across his chest. "Wow! That's deep."

She enrolled in more and more science courses, searching for her passion. Because the elderly departmental chairman was once a successful bacteriologist, he insisted that the core curriculum for all Bio majors included courses on bacteria and archaea. This topic was as antiquated as the chairman, painfully boring, and, frankly, just plain pointless. When would she ever use such useless knowledge?

Having to take these courses almost derailed her interest in the life sciences, until she began to learn about other disciplines and realized that passing these courses was nothing more than just another hoop to jump through.

Genetics and Neuroscience, on the other hand, were at the cutting edge. She was intrigued by the notion of understanding the genetic code: the entire blueprint for every single living thing in the universe (that would be both the "known" and "unknown" universe, as Dr. Gustaffason would never fail to remind his students). She was enchanted by the thought of elucidating the life story of every being, every ancestry, with all its profundity, with all its faults, with all its successes, with all its secrets, and above all, with all its messiness!

And Neuroscience, the study of the brain, that three-pound mass of gray and white matter that embodied the mind: every thought, every feeling, every memory. The good, the bad, the ugly. The entire spectrum, from the altruistic and the geniuses, to the feeble-minded and the psychopaths. The "Me" of every soul. Still, such a mystery, with so much not understood and left to be learned.

Sure, to the erudite student of neuroscience, brain anatomy is well known (perhaps even committed to memory). Every fold, every sulcus, every gyrus, every nucleus. Every structure is given a funky name like "pyramadus," "amygdala," "hippocampus"—but its connections, by which it integrates all that gives rise to the "Me," were an intricate conundrum for sure.

In those days, Aliya's "Me" was intensely driven, intensely curious, but also intensely adventurous and fun-loving. In addition to running and yoga, she felt strongly that partying with friends was equally worthwhile. Her motto: Work hard, play hard. Her life was pretty awesome. But like what often happens to the complex connections in the brain, it got tangled … fast.

CHAPTER 4

The One

Nature versus nurture. Yoga and going for regular runs begot her fit body, but her long, shapely legs, tiny waistline, full breasts, and luscious hair must have come from her genes. Her fun-loving disposition and inquisitiveness likely came from both—nature and nurture. And the question: "Are you a model?" was still being asked, even though she had concluded after high school that modeling was a bit too vacuous for her. Still, these things were all good.

Sex was good too. Especially as a young, pseudo-independent, highly attractive woman surrounded by predominantly eighteen to twenty-two-year-olds, living the dream in college … when Mom and Dad paid for all the necessities (food, housing) and many non-necessities (Starbucks, Netflix). Each week was highlighted by Thirsty Thursdays, No-class Fridays, weekend campus parties, and, of course, since it was Manhattan, dancing and karaoke at local clubs until closing time, as fake IDs were easy to come by. Nights like these were usually followed by hearty breakfasts in the wee hours at local diners.

Work hard, play hard.

It was around this time that Aliya observed that guys who played soccer called each other "boys." It was kind of a thing. He was a soccer player, a right midfielder to be exact. Lean and lithe, six-pack abs (actually, as she delightfully learned later when they consummated their relationship, abs so defined they were more like an eight-pack), and at six foot four inches, taller than her. To top it off, he was smart—pre-med at Columbia.

Aliya and her roommate had headed to The Valencia in NoMad for a few drinks and to hear a band they both liked. Per their usual routine, they had some very strong cocktails in their dorm room before venturing out. The bar was packed. Apparently, the Met Gala was going on, and many celebrities were in town, although they saw no one they recognized. Only two stools were left open. He had his elbows perched on the bar, his chin resting on his folded hands. Aliya expected him to be "Creepy Guy Number 22," as that was what she and Julie affectionately labeled most of the guys they met at bars, and they were now getting up there in numbers.

He turned to look at her, at first a nonchalant glance, then his expression softened. A gentle smile came across his face as he said, "I knew you would come."

Aliya shrugged her shoulders and cocked her head, bemused by his words. "What? Who are you? "

Just then something utterly crazy happened. The lead singer invited his "old friend" up to the stage to perform a few songs with them. Julie and Aliya's mouths dropped open when the legendary Bruce Springsteen sauntered onto the stage. Once the astounded crowd quieted, The Boss began playing a rousing rendition of "Rosalita." The place went berserk. Julie, like everyone else, instinctively grabbed her phone to get a video of this miraculous moment in time. But Aliya instinctively jumped up to dance. She grabbed Julie's hand."Come on. Put the phone down. Live the moment!"

The two hit the empty dance floor and immediately got lost in the rapture of music. This made Mr. Springsteen positively elated. "Come on everyone—dance!" he shouted.

With that, the dance floor immediately filled. After this otherworldly performance, Mr. Springsteen chatted with the audience, saying he was here in his favorite city working on his upcoming Broadway show."Who would have ever thought I, of all people, would make it to Broadway?" he quipped, eliciting laughter and cheers from the audience. He had stopped by The Valencia to see his buddy's band. He was going to grab a beer then would take requests and do a few more songs. Aliya and Julie looked at each other in awe, intuiting each other's thoughts: Could this really be happening?

Aliya had, in fact, completely forgotten about the smiling guy seated next to her. He looked directly into her eyes and placed his hand on his now noticeably attractive, sharp jawline. "So, what's your favorite Springsteen album?"

"That's easy. His second."

The smiley, now somewhat appealing dude responded, "If I guess your favorite song off that album, will you dance with me?"

"Sure," she said, without an ounce of hesitation. She looked directly into his eyes and returned her best smile, knowing full well he would never guess it. First, he had to know what the prolific Mr. Springsteen's second album was, which sadly wasn't one of his more popular hits upon its release, although a true Springsteen fan would certainly know it well, and second, even if he did, everyone and their brother (except for her, of course) would pick Springsteen's masterpiece: "New York City Serenade." With that, the now undeniably gorgeous, smiley guy got up from his seat and approached the stage. He slipped one of the brawny stage managers what looked to be a crisp one-hundred-dollar bill and said something Aliya couldn't hear. The guard walked backstage, and her new acquaintance returned to his seat, now with a very confident smile.

The magnificent Mr. Springsteen returned, and after several minutes of extreme euphoria from the crowd, shouted, "How y'all doing, Manhattan?" The crowd roared yet again. "We've had some great requests, but I like this one the best. It's off my second album, *The Wild, The Innocent, and the E Street Shuffle*, something the boys and I did when I was just a youngster."

As the skilled pianist played the opening notes, the room fell silent. She shook her head in disbelief as her eyes met his. His smile grew wide. He swept her to the dance floor, pulling her as close as could be. The masterful Mr. Springsteen joined in with his guitar and soulful voice. As their bodies swayed, they became lost in the dreamy melody of "Incident on 57th Street."

Drink after drink, they divulged their stories … and she crashed into him and he into her. She would have gone anywhere with him that night. But Julie, her trusty roommate, who protected her like a mother grizzly, saw that Aliya was next to incoherent in drunkenness and insisted that they go home. As typical college students, they felt they were too poor to take an Uber. Bad decision. The jerkiness and stench of the subway was a nightmare for a skinny, queasy, underage drunken girl. Thank God Julie always carried plastic grocery bags in her enormous fake (although she had long ago convinced herself of its authenticity) Michael Kors purse that she had purchased from a shady Times Square vendor.

"This is the fourth time he's called," Julie remarked the next day. "Clearly, he is not buying me telling him that you left your phone here and are at the library."

"I know," Aliya groaned. "But my head feels like a football, and if I move from this bed, I'll puke again." He is persistent, though, she thought with an inner smile, knowing that moving her facial muscles would surely enhance the pain in her head. "Why doesn't he just text, like normal people?"

"Probably because it's too easy to get blown off from a text. He must be an omega male, continuing to call you, even though you continually reject him. He's either a wuss or just plain stupid. Who would actually believe you've been down at the library all this time anyway? Especially after a night like last night. And what was that cheesy line he said when he first saw you? 'I knew you would come.'"

As Julie chattered on, Aliya couldn't help but think: Oh my God, I'm gonna puke again.

"Aside from Springsteen, which I will never, ever forget, I can hardly remember last night. Was he cute?" Aliya inquired in a weak voice.

"Oh God, yes! A cross between Leonardo DiCaprio and a young David Beckham, without the tats. Awesome smile. And you two were totally into each other—slow dancing and sucking face on the dance floor. Very romantic," Julie replied sarcastically.

Aliya did not pick up on the sarcasm. Romantic. That's so nice, she thought with a peaceful smile before drifting off to sleep yet again. She woke at dusk and was actually beginning to feel a bit better. Julie's relentless badgering for her to hydrate, take Advil, and sleep worked miracles. If Julie ever switched from her business major, she would make a fine nurse.

Aliya's cell chimed yet again. This time, she answered, and it was a good thing she did, because he told her later that was the last time—he would have given up had she not answered.

Columbia was only 2.8 miles from Lincoln Center. They were together every possible minute. They were both old souls. They shared an eclectic taste in music, everything from vintage rock to The 1975 to Kendrick Lamar and Frank Ocean. They loved being together and doing the same kinds of things, like making the short trek to MOMA, taking the train to the Bronx, or spending an afternoon riding Citi Bikes along the Hudson River Greenway.

They frequently took the quick subway ride to meet with friends at NYU and get the absolute best New York-style pizza at Napoli's. Many Thursday nights were spent grabbing a bite at the authentic eateries in Hell's Kitchen, enjoying Peruvian, Thai, or Mid-Eastern meals before seeing their favorite improv show. In warm weather, they would attend just about every free outdoor concert New York City had to offer, lounging on a blanket in the grass, shoulder to shoulder.

They often met at a convenient midway point—Sheep Meadow in Central Park. They spent countless hours enjoying the expansive, open green space, hanging with friends, picnicking, playing spike ball, or just watching the cosmopolitan world unfold around them. He usually walked her back home and stayed in her dorm room, as Julie was often at her boyfriend's place. Aliya could hardly believe how quickly and how hard she had fallen for him. The feeling was mutual; there was no doubt about it. She came to realize that sex could be whatever it wanted to be, like the shape of water in a container. It could be crazy fun, hot and physical (which was what it was like for them most of the time—in their youth and virility), or intensely emotional. As time went on, after they made love, he sometimes gazed directly into her eyes.

In earnest, with passion and unbridled devotion, he would say, "My God, Liya, you're so beautiful. You are the love of my life."

He would then give her the sweetest, most tender kiss, as she whispered, "You are the love of my life too, Aaron."

They shared their dreams—how he wanted to be a doctor and travel the world with Doctors without Borders, working for the people who would need his skills the most. He spoke of how he loved his A&P course, where he learned about the incredible design of the human body manifested by evolution, how form (anatomy) and function (physiology) were so interconnected, how the exquisite architecture of the body's organ systems was optimized for maximum efficiency and was derived from ongoing natural selection as animals adapted to their environments. He was truly amazed by the interdependence of physiological systems and how the integration of the functions of these systems was vital for maintaining homeostasis, which, when not maintained, led to the pathophysiology underlying human disease.

She told him all about her fascination with Genetics and Neuroscience, and her desire to someday pursue a Ph.D. They were living a pretty blissful existence. As the saying goes, "The college years are the best years of your life."

CHAPTER 5

Plaques and Tangles

"Can you count back from one hundred by sevens for me please?" the pleasant physician's assistant politely inquired.

"Sure," Matthew replied, immediately saying: "ninety-three." He paused briefly, then said, "eighty-six." The next pause was more prolonged. He rubbed his neck and glanced at Ellie in earnest, silently imploring her help. She said nothing but returned a hopeful look. He bit his lip, concentrating hard. "Seventy-nine?"

"Yes, that's correct. Please continue."

"Seventy-two," he said confidently. Then he paused again, this time for a long while. He was visibly flustered. "I, I … can't. I don't know," he agonized.

"That's no problem, Mr. McKenna. No problem at all. How about this?" she said with a warm smile, as she handed him a sheet of paper and a pencil. "Can you draw a clock for me?"

His weathered, yet once highly skilled hand trembled as he slowly drew a circle, then one arrow, then another. He grimaced as he realized it just wasn't quite complete.But he couldn't for the life of him figure out what was missing—too much fog.

"Ok, thank you. Now, can you please spell the word 'world' backward?" she again very politely inquired.

The tests seemed endless, each one more difficult than the last. His mind grew more tired as he struggled to put things together, to recall even the simplest concepts. When they were finally done, the young lady left the room, promising to return shortly with the neurologist. Matthew felt drained, defeated. Ellie gently grasped his hand in hers.

Looking into his eyes and with a warm smile, she reassured, "It will be alright, Matt."

His face softened. Her loving smile and gentle voice always calmed him.

The physician's assistant returned with a bespectacled, bearded older gentleman in a white coat.

"Mr. and Mrs. McKenna, this is Dr. Lander."

He greeted them warmly, and although try as he might to appear genuine, it was clear that what he was about to say, he had said to many, many others. He was an expert at delivering devastating news, without skipping a beat. He kept his fact-laden oration brief. Most of it went right over the McKennas' heads, as if he were speaking a foreign language: MMSE rating, CDR scale, beta-amyloid plaques, tau protein tangles, the hippocampus, Presenilin-1, cholinesterase inhibitors, Donepezil, Rivastigmine, Galantamine.

What they did hear loud and clear was that although there was a tremendous amount of research being conducted, the cure was nowhere in sight. The McKennas' expressions were ashen. Dr. Lander's aloof behavior was perpetuating despair. As he left the room, the physician's assistant took both of Matthew's hands in her own and gave them a gentle squeeze. "Know that we will do everything and anything we can for you."

Matthew's eyes met hers. His pain was palpable. He knew things had been changing ever since that god-awful day when he became lost in his own neighborhood, the neighborhood where he had lived the last twenty-five years of his life. Since then, his life was growing more discombobulated. But he was in denial. And he never once considered the culprit to be Alzheimer's Disease.

Ellie always was, by nature, the consummate caregiver, and although her own heart was breaking, her thoughts immediately turned to Matthew. How would he ever cope with the anguish of what they were just told and the realization that this dreadful, irreversible process was already in motion? Matthew was about to lose all that was rooted in his memories, the most precious treasures he had: his personal history, his knowledge of loved ones … of himself.

Ellie pleaded in a silent prayer: "Merciful Father, take away this cup that is before him."

"Matt," she said, summoning up as much positivity as possible as they climbed into their SUV. "It's a beautiful afternoon, why don't we stop for a drink and try to make some sense out of all of this."

Her warm smile and outstanding suggestion lifted his spirits. Going straight home would be depressing. Their house was so quiet these days. He needed to think this through. And a stiff drink certainly wouldn't hurt. They headed to one of their favorite taverns, The Erie Island Eatery, and seated themselves outside. The outdoor patio abutted Lake Erie, with a marina full of boats, and had a small, canopied stage surrounded by picnic tables topped with vibrant red umbrellas that shaded them from the bright sunshine. It was a perfect late afternoon at the end of summer. The blue of the sky matched the blue of the water. They ordered their signature drinks: he a CC and Seven, she a glass of rosé wine. Once free from the sterile doctor's office and in familiar surroundings, they began to relax.

Band members took the stage. A drummer, guitarist, keyboardist, and female vocalist began playing an old favorite, "Silver Springs" by Fleetwood Mac. They wordlessly basked in the warmth of memories of their youth.

As the song ended, Matthew's eyes filled with tears. "How will we ever tell the girls?"

CHAPTER 6

Friendship

Aliya's stomach growled. She had been so absorbed in her work that she hadn't eaten all day. She rubbed the tight muscles on the back of her neck as she leaned back in her chair, thinking how good a massage would feel right about then. She had been crouched over her laptop for hours, running BLAST searches on the GenBank website.

Dr. Gustaffason entered the lab, not surprised to see that she was still there, working diligently.

"Still at it. It's been a long day for you, hasn't it?" He peeked over her shoulder, squinting as he looked closely at the strings of A's, G's, C's, and T's on her screen.

"I see you have become an expert at using the Basic Local Alignment Search Tool. Looks like you found some highly interesting sequence comparisons. This technology is so amazing," he said, shaking his head. "To think we now have an easily searchable database of all of the known genetic sequences, as well as tools like BLAST to readily compare new sequences to them. Well … it just blows my mind." He waved his forefinger in the air as he continued,

"I remember when I had to do this the old-fashioned way, with pencil and paper. Took forever!"

Aliya couldn't help but smile. Dr. G's "I remember when" stories definitely contributed to his reputation of being past his prime. But after working closely with him for a few years now, she had no doubt that his experience had honed his intellect, and it was sharper than ever, regardless of how hokey he came off at times.

He patted her shoulder. "Keep up the good work. We're almost there," he said, with a twinkle in his eye, then left the lab.

"Hey, remember me? Ur OG, ur rock, ur confidant? The 1st person u got stoned with, the only gfriend that u divulged all ur sexual exploits with, the..." Aliya stopped reading the text from Julie.

"Enough already. No need to go any further. I get it. Miss u 2," Aliya texted back.

"Meet me at SM in 30," Julie's next text read. "Need to get a handle on this situation."

"K" Aliya texted back reluctantly, knowing she had far too much to do to waste time at Sheep Meadow. But it was Julie. And she was indebted to her for her unwavering support and loyalty from the moment they moved into their dorm freshman year and commenced their immortal friendship.

Aliya had not been to Sheep Meadow in a very long time. She had forgotten how much she loved it there. It was always so green and lush in the spring. New Yorkers came out in droves to enjoy the warmth and sunshine after the cold winter. Their spirits were as light as the springtime air.

Aliya found Julie lounging on a blanket at their usual spot. Of course, she brought cocktails in her well-worn personal cooler.

"Drink of the day!" Julie said with a wide smile and eager eyes, as she poured each of them one of their favorite spring concoctions—Grey Goose, cranberry, and a touch of pineapple juice.

"Prost!"she said, which was one of her favorite ways of saying "Cheers" (although she had many).

Aliya attempted to push the red plastic cup away. "Thank you, but I can't. I've got a PCR reaction running. It will be done in about an hour. Then I have to get back to the…"

Before Aliya could finish, Julie shouted in exacerbation. "Aliya! You have no life! You are consumed with that damn laboratory. What the hell has gotten into you?"

"It's just that … we're on the brink! This is big, Jules. Really, really big. It's totally under the radar. Nobody else gets it but me and Dr. Gustaffason. He found this crazy system in bacteria, an immune system of all things. And I know we can manipulate it to make it useful in mammalian systems. It's got so much potential."

Julie shook her head and rolled her eyes as she took another big swig of her drink. "Okay, whatever. How's Aaron? Any hot romance I need to be informed of?"

"He's so awesome. I love him so much," Aliya gushed.

"So, like, what's the plan? We've only got a year left. Then what?"

"So, he's applying to a ton of med schools, but he wants Columbia or NYU so we can stay in the city. He's worried he won't get in, so he is applying all over. But I know he will. He's so freakin' smart."

"And gorgeous," Julie added. "So, you'll stay with the crazy old professor here at FU?"

"Hey show some respect. It's JFU! And soon to be your alma mater. Yup. I'm staying with Dr. G. for my Ph.D. We're headed for the Nobel! Everybody thinks he's basically senile, but actually, he's a genius. And so inspiring. We found these unique palindromic DNA sequences in the bacterial genome that are flanked by foreign DNA..."

"Okay, okay. Enough already." Julie groaned. "This is making no sense at all to me. Recall I am a business major, at the renowned Carnegie Business School, I might add. Let's talk about something more interesting ... like me for example. I've got great news. I landed an internship at the Chicago Board of Trade this summer. It pays big bucks. And I get to live in Lincoln Park, with all the other Yuccies. Maybe I'll find my soulmate this summer."

Aliya began to realize how much her preoccupation with her research had really detracted from her "Julie time."And she missed it. She filled her cup to the brim then clinked it with Julie's."Congratulations. I'm so happy for you!" Tilting her head, Aliya continued, "What the hell is a 'Yuccie'?"

Julie paused so they could both drain their cups, immediately feeling the effects of the stiff drinks. "It's a blend between yuppies and hipsters," Julie replied, as she refilled both their cups.

"Okay then, what the hell is a yuppie?" Aliya said, finding the term vaguely familiar.

Julie let out an enormous sigh. "Ahh my God," she said, in her best valley girl voice, one that Aliya had heard so many times before. "A 'yuppie' stands for 'young urban professional.'"

Now it was Aliya's turn to shake her head and roll her eyes. "You're such a throw-back to the '80s."

"I get it all from Joanie and Dale," Julie proudly replied, referring to her parents. "They taught me everything I know, and, of course, fostered my impenetrable love for Madonna," she added with the utmost sincerity.

"Ok, so then what's a 'yuccie' again?" Aliya asked.

"It stands for 'young urban creative.'"

As the afternoon wore on, the two friends basked in the warm sunshine, sipping their endless supply of refreshing cocktails (Julie always came prepared), people watching, and exchanging playful banter. It was just like old times … a great respite. The alcohol, friendship, and exquisitely chill surroundings lightened Aliya's mood. She no longer felt the need to return to the lab that day, happy to know that PCR machines had built-in refrigeration systems. Once the reaction concluded, the machine would cool to four degrees Celsius, keeping the products of her reaction stable until she returned to run them on a gel and analyze the results.

As evening descended, their hunger grew.

"Let's head to Napoli's in Greenwich Village then go clubbing," Julie suggested.

"I'm down," replied Aliya.

Julie grabbed her phone. "I'll send a text to the group to meet us there."

Aliya's phone chimed. "Hey," she said softly, with her gorgeous smile. Julie knew at once who the call was from.

"I've been at Sheep Meadow with Jules," Aliya said, with a bit of a slur. "Meet us at Napoli's in thirty." Then she whispered something so quietly that Julie could just barely hear it.

"Oh my God. Give the girl a few drinks, and she becomes so freakin' horny!" Julie teased.

"What? I miss him," Aliya replied sheepishly, but with no attempt to conceal her excitement about seeing him.

CHAPTER 7

Hearts Beat as One

Aliya awoke slowly, luxuriating in the comfort of the cozy bed and the warmth of his body. With her emerald eyes, she drank him in as he slept so serenely beside her. She studied his seraphic features, noticing his chest rising and falling rhythmically, quietly. He was so peaceful. They were so peaceful. So in harmony with one another. They were soulmates. This, she knew for sure. She awoke him with her gentle kisses, and he drew her in without hesitation, making passionate love to her. Then, as often was done on Saturday mornings, they lay together for a long time, sharing their thoughts, confiding in each other.

"So, you're headed home next weekend?" Aaron asked.

"Yeah. Mom and Dad have been saying how much they miss us and asked that both their daughters pay them a visit. Mark is coming too."

"I'll miss you."

"Well, you know you can come, but I know you have so much to do here."

"Yeah. I do. It's best I stay put and get my shit done."

"Sara thinks something is up," Aliya said quietly.

"Like what?"

"She thinks Mom and Dad have been acting differently. I've noticed too. They're kind of …" Aliya searched for the appropriate word. "Melancholy, I guess. I'm worried about them."

"I'm sure they're okay. I bet they are just going through empty nester syndrome. It's got to be a lot different not having you and Sara around to drive them crazy all the time."

Aliya felt some relief. Aaron always knew the right thing to say.

"Come on, I'll race you to the shower," Aliya said playfully. And with that, she jumped out of bed and ran toward the bathroom. Aaron chased her, following close behind. As was customary, when they reached the shower, Aaron joined her, unable to resist the temptation to make love yet again.

After their shower, they nestled together on the couch in Aaron's tiny Harlem apartment, sipping coffee and eating New York's finest bagels, with the mellow music of the Acoustic Sunrise morning program playing on Sirius Internet Radio in the background. Aliya had chosen the channel. She and Julie had often listened to the soothing acoustic music in the morning after a big night out. This, as well as mindlessly binge-watching "The Office" or "The Joy of Painting with Bob Ross" were great treatments for hangovers.

Aliya couldn't help but notice how both of their hair, still damp from the shower, became wavy as it dried. She was wearing one of Aaron's light blue button-down dress shirts that just barely reached to her upper thigh, comfortably unbuttoned to her mid-chest. She had not thought to bring a change of clothes, although she did have an extra toothbrush that lived at his apartment.

"So how did Julie ever get you away from the lab yesterday?" Aaron asked.

Aliya smiled. "Good old-fashioned guilt. It was so fun. So needed."

"Yeah, you've been working like crazy lately."

"Aaron, it's so cool. We are really onto something."

"Tell me about it," Aaron said with sincerity. He loved hearing about cutting-edge science. It was invigorating. He was even considering going the MD-PhD. route. But even more so, he loved hearing Aliya speak, in her soft yet confident voice. She was so intelligent. And so very beautiful. She was fun-loving and carefree. She was always there for him … to listen, to offer advice, to support him. He loved her so very much, and he knew she loved him the same. They would grow old together, he thought.

"Well, you know how Dr. G works on bacteria, and everyone thinks what he does is totally antiquated, because it's not 'translational.' People seem to forget that so much of what we know today in science and human disease was originally discovered using model organisms, like bacteria, Drosophila, zebrafish, *C. elegans*, and mice."

"Okay, so I know Drosophila refers to fruit flies, but you stumped me on *C. elegans*."

"Right, fruit flies fueled insanely powerful genetics. *C. elegans* stands for *Caenorhabditis elegans*. A nematode," Aliya replied matter-of-factly.

Aaron returned a confused look as he took a big bite out of his bagel. "Still not getting it," he said, with a mouthful.

She handed him a napkin, feeling compelled to have him wipe the cream cheese from the corner of his mouth before continuing.

"So, nematodes are a species of roundworms. They're only about one millimeter long."

"Roundworms! You mean the disgusting human parasites that cause all kinds of nasty diseases?"

"Well, they are sort of creepy. But they're phenomenal as a model organism. Brenner and his colleagues got the Nobel using *C. elegans* to elucidate the underpinnings of development and programmed cell death."

"Ah. Programmed cell death, you mean 'apoptosis,'" replied Aaron, trying to sound as smart as his girlfriend.

"Right again," she said, shooting him her million-dollar smile. "Plus, in 2003, when the space shuttle Columbia exploded and literally disintegrated during reentry into the atmosphere, all seven of its crew members died. But they had been conducting experiments with *C. elegans*. And *C. elegans* was the only life form that survived."

Aaron slurped his coffee noisily.

"Wow. That's intense. How do you know all these obscure factoids? Remember that game show CA$H CAB? If they are still doing it and I ever get in one, I'll be sure to call you for my mobile shoutout. Okay. So, like, what are you doing that is so great? Will I be married to a Nobel laureate someday?"

"Well, if you're lucky you will. Because Dr. G thinks this is on that level."

Aaron rolled his eyes, thinking to himself that Dr. Gustaffason did come off as a bit of a looney old professor, although he would never confess this to Aliya. "Nobel or not, I hope I'm lucky enough to spend my life with you."

"Same," she said, giving him a sweet kiss.

"So, go on."

"So, Dr. G has been studying bacteria forever. Once next-generation sequencing became commonplace, he was able to rapidly compare DNA sequences from tons of different strains of bacteria. He kept finding these short, palindromic repeats at regularly spaced intervals in almost all the bacterial DNA he analyzed. Then he realized that each repeat was followed by intragenic spacer DNA. He figured this configuration had to be important because it was so prevalent. Why would something like this be so strongly conserved throughout evolution if it didn't provide a significant advantage?"

"Survival of the fittest, eh? So let me see if I'm getting this right. Bacteria have this weird stretch of DNA sequence that's a palindrome. What's a palindrome again?"

"It's something that reads the same backward as forward, such as the word 'racecar,'" Aliya replied.

"Ah yes, I remember now. I think that word was on the SAT exam—and I got it wrong. So, all the palindromes always have, what did you call it? Some kind of spacer DNA next to them?"

"Right. IGS: intergenic spacer, a region of non-coding DNA. When I started in the lab, Dr. G gave me a project to try to figure out what, if any, connection there was. I started conducting boatloads of bioinformatics analyses. What I'm finding is that the spacer DNA sequence is frequently derived from foreign DNA, very often viral DNA," explained Aliya.

Aaron rested his chin on his hand. "So, when a virus infects the bacterial cell, it can leave some of its DNA behind. Just like when some viruses infect human cells?"

"Precisely! A virus that infects bacteria is called a bacteriophage. And how do humans fight off viral infections?"

"With the immune system," Aaron replied confidently. "But wait, bacteria are single-celled organisms. They don't have immune systems."

Aliya tilted her head and took a sip of her coffee. "Well, certainly not like ours—with antibodies and the huge variety of cell types: B cells, T cells, neutrophils, eosinophils, dendritic cells, macrophages... So now I'll ask you the exact question Dr. G asked me: Could something like this, in the tiny bacterium, be a type of immunity?"

Aaron thought very long and hard before saying, "I have absolutely no idea."

"I didn't either, nor did Dr. G. But something he once said to me really stuck with me. It's a quote from Isaac Newton: 'If I have seen further, it is by standing on the shoulders of giants.' So, I delved into the scientific literature, reading everything I could find that was even remotely related. Maybe someone else discovered something that would help me make sense of this. And guess what? Our favorite model organism, *C. elegans*, gave me the clue I needed, not to mention another Nobel prize—this time for two scientists by the names of Fire and Mello. These two researchers discovered RNAi: RNA interference. It turns out small stretches of RNA can direct enzymes to destroy messenger RNA, which as you know, are the direct precursors to proteins."

"A light bulb went on when I read that RNA interference is involved in defending cells against parasitic sequences, such as those from viruses. So, it seems that in the host cell, enzymes are targeted to specific foreign sequences and can degrade the RNA of the infectious agents. If there is something like this going on with the sequences we are studying, there must be a similar enzyme in bacteria. I just needed to find it. And this past week ... I think I may have!"

Her eyes sparkled as she shifted in her seat, finding it hard to contain her enthusiasm. "I discovered particular sequences in the DNA that surround the repeat sequences. These sequences encode for enzymes. Here's how I think it would work as an immune system in the bacteria: the enzyme would be 'guided' to the exact target sequence, which is the invasive viral DNA, by a piece of 'guide' RNA that can attach to the enzyme at one end and also has a sequence that is complementary to the target, viral DNA—so it could form chemical bonds with the target DNA. Once associated with the proper target, the enzyme could cut the DNA like molecular scissors, damaging the DNA, but also leaving some of the viral sequence intact, not enough, though, to make a functioning virus. If the same virus were to infect the bacterium again at a later time, the bacterium would be able to recognize the viral sequence, due to its previous association with it, make complementary RNA to it, and use this 'guide' RNA to direct the special enzyme to cut and disable the new viral sequence, preventing a second infection."

Aliya's face lit up as she lifted her mug. "Voila'! An adaptive immune system in bacteria."

Aaron clanked his mug with hers. "Wow. That … that's really something," he said, a bit hesitantly.

Aliya rested her chin on her hand. "Are you sure you're getting this?"

He shrugged. "Uh, it is a little hard for me to follow."

"Let me refill our coffee," she said, as she grabbed their mugs and headed for the kitchen. She returned with the fresh coffee, as well as with a multi-color pen from her purse and a piece of paper. "I'll draw it out for you."

Aaron's eyes followed each stroke of her pen intently. “Okay. That makes a lot more sense now. It’s awesome!”

“It is totally awesome, but the true awesomeness lies in the versatility of its application.”

Aaron wrinkled his forehead. “What do you mean?”

“Well, since the human genome, as well as the genomes of model organisms, have been entirely sequenced, we already have the genetic code for just about everything. Once I isolate and purify this special enzyme protein, I can associate it with a ‘guide’ RNA sequence that can be made in a lab, which is complementary to a target DNA, and cut practically any DNA sequence with virtually 100% accuracy.” She paused, raising her eyebrows. “And what does DNA make up?”

“Genes!” Aaron responded, with his signature grin.

“Right. I can target the enzyme to disrupt a specific DNA sequence that encodes for a specific gene, thereby disabling the gene. No gene, no RNA, no protein! Plus, with a little ingenuity, the enzyme complex could be manipulated to not only disrupt a given gene, but to add genes at specific places, or turn on genes that are already there.”

“Okay. So that’s cool for molecular biology. But how is this going to help mankind?”

“You meant to say ‘humankind,’ not just ‘man’-kind, right?” Aliya asserted.

“Yes, of course. Just a slip of the tongue.”

“The possibilities are endless. The most obvious stuff it could be used for is to cure single-gene disorders, like cystic fibrosis, muscular dystrophy, hemophilia, sickle cell anemia, Huntington’s Disease, and Fragile X Syndrome. But I'm sure it could also be used explore the causes of and hone in on the treatment for multi-factorial disorders like cancer and infectious disorders, such as HIV."

"Wow! That's over the top, Aliya. I'm really stoked for you," Aaron replied with genuine sincerity, then added, "It's kind of crazy to think how psyched you are about this now, when you initially had such a disdain for learning about bacteria and no intention of ever working for decrepit old Dr. G."

Aliya nodded. "Ain't that the truth."

They sat in silence for a long while, both lost in their own thoughts as the soothing music continued to play in the background. Aliya lay her head on Aaron's shoulder. Aaron caressed Aliya's hair, now no longer damp, and began to gently kiss her. One kiss led to another, each becoming more passionate. Aliya climbed onto Aaron's lap and onto her knees, straddling him as he sat, throwing her arms around his shoulders. With her half-unbuttoned shirt, her chest was at his mouth, her lips at his forehead.

"On the shoulders of giants. I like that," Aaron said, as he moved his hands up her soft thighs, reaching under her shirttails. "Hey, you're not wearing any underwear."

Aliya raised her eyebrows and slowly shook her head while smiling playfully, as if to say, "I'm not … and what are you going to do about it?"

CHAPTER 8

Raindrops and Teardrops

Aliya boarded the plane at JFK for the short flight from the East to her home. Her sister, Sara, and new brother-in-law, Mark, took the quick flight from the West, Chicago. Aliya arrived a bit earlier but agreed to wait so that their mom and dad could pick them all up at once. She was happy to enjoy a couple of mimosas while she awaited their arrival. She still felt some trepidation, wondering if her parents had an alternative reason for having them both home.

The drinks worked their magic, taking the edge off. Aliya's delight spilled forth as she was reunited with her only sibling. The two were close, even closer now that they were older. And Aliya felt so very happy for Sara. She had found her soulmate in Mark. They were good together, good for each other. Aliya knew they would have a long and happy marriage. The three walked to the arrival area, Aliya and Sara arm in arm, chatting away as Mark followed behind, pulling a suitcase. Matthew and Ellie were standing by their black SUV, anxiously scanning the crowd. The family's embraces were tender and long-lasting. It was a joyful reunion.

But the joy was ephemeral, disintegrating into the gray sky as the raindrops fell. This usual dismal Cleveland weather descended upon Aliya unforgivingly, as if to foreshadow what was to come.

When Ellie, not Matthew, climbed into the driver's seat, the sisters exchanged confused glances. They had never seen this before. If Dad was with them, he always drove.

They passed through the gritty, downtrodden neighborhood that enveloped Hopkins airport, driving by the chain-link fences that surrounded a railroad depot replete with abandoned, heavily graffitied boxcars. They drove by sleazy adult-only video stores, dingy mom and pop food marts, and a gloomy cemetery. Ellie did most of the talking, indifferent to their surroundings, cheerily inquiring about their daughter's lives. Aliya couldn't help but notice that her dad was unusually quiet.

As they pulled into their development, with the mature trees, landscaped lawns, and flowerbeds dotted with brightly colored vegetation, Aliya's mood began to lift. Their home sat on a cul-de-sac in a convivial suburban neighborhood. It was the kind of community where the moms lingered at the bus stop each morning, sipping coffee, chatting with each other long after the children had left, planning their next selection for their book club (a.k.a. "wine club"), while the dads in the neighborhood met every other Wednesday at nine p.m. for pick-up basketball games at the local middle school gym and gathered regularly for euchre tournaments (a.k.a. "craft beer club"). And of course, entire families gathered together for the big sporting events: the annual Ohio State-Michigan football game (Buckeyes only welcome), the Browns vs. the Steelers, the Cavs vs. the Golden State Warriors in the play-offs, or the Indians vs. the Cubs in the World Series.

As they entered the home of their childhood, Aliya absorbed how wonderfully warm and inviting it was. Everything was exactly the same, the walnut dining table that her dad had custom made himself, the faded cream and sage curtains framing the kitchen window, the large painting of the Grand Tetons hanging above the fireplace, and Mom's potted plants on the stand by the sidelights of the front door. This was enormously comforting. Home had always been her safe harbor. She knew that whatever choices she made, even those that led her astray, or whatever happened to her that was out of her control, she could always return to this place for unconditional love, support, and acceptance. This she knew for sure.

They sat around the kitchen table, which had always been their public square—where ideas were discussed and opinions challenged, hopes and dreams revealed, plans for the future devised. Knowing that they must be hungry, Ellie began making one of their true Midwestern favorites, steak sandwiches on toasted Kaiser rolls, complete with au jus, melted mozzarella, sautéed mushrooms, and a bit of spicy horsey sauce to add a touch of heat.

She melted butter and added sliced onions to a large frying pan, where she cooked her specialty, homemade pierogies, chock-full of bacon, cheddar, and creamy potatoes. When they were nicely tanned on each side, she would serve them with a dollop of cool sour cream and a smattering of chopped chives.

Dad was more himself once back in familiar surroundings, placing a bag of pretzel sticks and a container of cream cheese on the table, and offering everyone a beer while Ellie cooked.

"What's the cream cheese for?" asked Mark.

Aliya and Sara looked at each other in utter disbelief.

"Duh," said Sara. "It's to dip your pretzels in" (not realizing this was a tradition exclusive to the McKenna family).

"It's been really quiet around here without you girls. Mom and I aren't quite sure what to do with ourselves these days. We're looking for projects … like grandchildren," Matthew said with a smile, shooting a glance toward Sara and Mark.

"Oh, Matthew! Stop. Give them some time," Ellie chided.

"Hmm, feeling like holding off on the grandchildren for a while. Maybe I'll let LeeLee go first," Sara remarked, returning the smile. "But I'll gladly contribute to a puppy fund for you."

Aliya's previous concerns faded away completely as they all laughed and reminisced while devouring their scrumptious meal. Time flew by, and minutes turned into hours. The sun went down, and evening descended. Initially, no one noticed the subtle changes in Matthew's behavior, until he slammed his hands loudly on the tabletop, clearly agitated.

"You all need to quit your noisy jabbering. I need to get to work. Right now!" Matt grumbled, in a manner that was utterly foreign to his usual demeanor.

"Dad, it's a Saturday evening. You don't work today," Sara responded, in a confused voice, astonished by his sudden outburst and outlandish behavior. Aliya's eyes grew wide, and her mouth dropped open. She had no words. Matthew paid no attention to them and headed for the cupboard where the car keys were kept.

"Matt," Ellie said calmly. "Let me go with you today. I can help. You should let me drive, so you can plan out the work schedule on the way. It will be more efficient that way. You won't waste any time."

Matt gazed at her, and although he did not recognize her as his wife, his mind was still capable of the most basic of instincts: friend or foe. For reasons he could not comprehend, he knew she was a friend.

"Well, okay," he agreed. "It will be more efficient. I can't be wasting time. This job has to be done right. It has my name on it," he said, repeating a line he had said since he was a young foreman.

The two headed to the door. "It will be okay, kids. We'll see you soon," Ellie reassured.

Aliya was in a daze. Sara and Mark were shocked.

"WTF?" Sara said, utterly baffled.

"Jesus," Aliya replied, as she buried her head in her hands. "He's got Alzheimer's."

Ellie and Matt returned about an hour later. Matt was no longer agitated, just confused and exhausted. Ellie had no trouble convincing him to turn in, and soon he was fast asleep. She prayed he would sleep through the night. She returned to the kitchen where Aliya, Sara, and Mark were quietly seated. Her tiredness and heavy heart were apparent to all. While Matthew and Ellie were gone, the other three had cracked open a bottle of Matthew's whiskey, making CC and 7s, all very much needing a stiff drink.

Aliya drew from all her expertise in neuroscience to carefully explain the signs, symptoms, and dire prognosis of early-onset Alzheimer's Disease. Matthew's behavior was a textbook example of "sun downing."

"Would you like a glass of wine, Mom?" Sara gently offered, as Ellie joined them at the table.

"No. I seldom drink any more. I need to sleep lightly in case Dad gets up and wanders."

"How long has he been this way, Mom?" Aliya asked.

"Well, it was gradual. I think he may have been in the early stages for quite a while but was really good at hiding it from us."

Guilt set in immediately. Or was I just too wrapped up in my own life to not recognize it, Aliya thought, with profound regret.

"I begged him to tell you all as soon as we received the diagnosis, but he just wasn't ready. And I wanted to respect his wishes. I'm sorry you had to see that tonight and find out this way. We meant to break the news to you together, before things started to get bad," confessed Ellie.

Sara's expression was pained. "Where did you go with him just now?"

"I just drove around, trying to distract him. Grayton's was still open, so I convinced him to go in and get a milkshake. After a while, he forgot all about needing to go work and agreed it was time to go home."

Aliya looked at her weary mother lovingly. She was so disheartened. This had to be incredibly difficult for her. "You did exactly the right thing, Mom. You de-escalated the situation and handled everything perfectly. But..." she continued, reluctantly, afraid of the potential answer. "Does this happen a lot? Does he ever get really agitated?"

"No," Ellie responded, truthfully, realizing what Aliya was asking. "What you saw is usually the way it happens. He can get very confused, which leads to frustration, but he never gets abusive."

Aliya sighed in relief as all three took a big gulp of their drinks.

"How can we help?" Mark asked with genuine concern.

"You can live your lives to the fullest. Be the best you can be. That's all he and I ever wanted for you all."

"But Mom, you'll need help," Sara said. "You'll burn out."

Ellie frowned, knowing she spoke the truth.

"It will be all right," Aliya said, not really believing this in her heart, nor in her mind. "We'll make a plan. And we'll work through this together. It's our turn to be here for you and Dad, just like you've been there for us all these years."

"I'm exhausted," Ellie admitted. "We can talk more in the morning."

They exchanged heartfelt embraces before heading to their rooms. Aliya thought about calling Aaron, but couldn't bear to, knowing she'd go to pieces upon hearing his voice. Tonight had been such a shock. Instead, she sent a quick text to tell him goodnight, saying all was well and that she missed him and loved him very much.

Usually, after a few strong drinks, Aliya would have drifted off to sleep easily. But tonight, her mind raced; her body was awash with adrenaline. She was surely experiencing first-hand, the sympathetic response that she had learned so much about in her Physiology course.

She grabbed her laptop and scoured the internet for recent information on early-onset Alzheimer's Disease. Knowing that there was no cure, she was particularly interested in any open clinical trials. Luckily, she thought, we're in Cleveland, home to the world-renowned Cleveland Clinic. She immediately was struck by the irony of this thought. She and Sara had always viewed Cleveland as the Mundane Midwest and couldn't wait to leave it. But with the Clinic's outstanding hospital facilities and cutting-edge research programs, it was probably one of the best places in the world for her dad.

She sketched out her plan of action. She would meet with all her dad's doctors and assess them fully to determine if he was getting the best care available or if changes would be needed. She researched caregiver support programs for her mom and day programs for her dad to give her mom a break. She also looked into in-home nursing care services, knowing full well her mom would never put him in a facility. She researched veteran's benefits and government assistance programs, such as Medicaid. Tomorrow, she would talk to her mom directly about their finances as well as their health insurance coverage. Alzheimer's Disease was often called the long goodbye, and Aliya knew that the cost for medications and nursing care for Alzheimer's patients added up all too quickly. When she was younger, she had witnessed the devastation her best friend's family went through when their grandmother suffered and died from Alzheimer's.

Aliya halted the onslaught of her thoughts, pausing to listen to the soft pitter-patter of the raindrops that had been falling all day. As she hovered over her laptop, her shoulders slumped. Her staunch academic nature began to wane as her emotional side took hold. The sky cried that night, but Aliya cried more.

CHAPTER 9

Cas

Aliya's spent the flight back to New York lost in thought, vacillating between feeling empowered to take control of her dad's health situation, as she was the science expert in the family, and feeling pure hopelessness. As the plane neared New York City, her melancholy mood began to lift. She always treasured this part of the return flight. She pressed her forehead against the window as the pilot cruised over New York Harbor, intentionally providing an unblemished view of Lady Liberty. The Manhattan skyscrapers crammed the rectangular strip of land, poking into the crisp blue sky.

The Hudson meandered below, dotted with boats that left streams of white foam in the water. The flight arrived on time but sat on the clogged runway for almost an hour, par for the course at JFK. Aliya texted Aaron to let him know she would be late. The two had agreed to meet at Sheep Meadow, as Aaron had mentioned that he would be coming directly from his evening lab class, which wasn't entirely the truth. Aaron had, in fact, arrived earlier so he could pick the perfect spot to set up. He sat on the blanket, anxiously awaiting her arrival. The small, warm, furry golden body lay fast asleep next to him, finally exhausted from running around the meadow all evening.

The days were definitely getting shorter, and it was dark by the time Aliya arrived in the city. The night air was warm and humid, as it always was at the late summer's beginning to the fall semester. All she had brought with her for the weekend visit to Cleveland was her backpack, so she headed directly to Sheep Meadow to meet Aaron, sad about the news she was about to tell him. Aliya scanned the meadow as she walked, looking for Aaron and getting ready to text him to ask where he was.

Aaron also scanned the grounds, knowing Aliya should be arriving at any moment. Before Aaron could react, the little fur ball beside him jumped up and made a beeline toward the speck walking toward them. Aliya dropped to her knees as the golden retriever puppy joyously leapt, yelped, and licked her face.

"Well, where did you come from, little one?" Aliya said in surprise, grabbing hold of the puppy's leash as she rubbed her soft fur.

Aaron arrived, breathless from his sprint. "Happy two-year anniversary!" he said, as he moved toward her to kiss her but was impeded by the jubilant youngster.

Aliya's eyes met Aaron's, and tears began to well up. It was two years ago. Two years, on this date, that they had met. She had completely forgotten.

"Aliya. What's wrong? What is it? Don't you like her?"

She picked up the adorable puppy. "Oh no. No. She's beautiful. Absolutely beautiful."

They walked back to the blanket, and Aaron gave the pup a large rawhide, which kept her occupied the rest of the night. Aliya took it all in, the soft blanket, the fresh cut flowers, the wine and cheese from their favorite deli, and the wireless speaker playing, of course, Springsteen's "Incident on 57th Street." Her tears flowed harder and faster.

"Liya, what is it?" Aaron asked, his face pained with concern.

"It's just … It's just." Aliya stuttered, trying to get the words out. "I'm just overwhelmed," she said, in a barely audible voice.

Aaron held her close, and she melted into his arms as they sat together on the soft blanket. Aliya began to relate all that had happened over the weekend. Aaron listened silently, but intently.

"Why do these things happen to such good people? My dad always took such great care of his health. He's still young. He's being robbed."

"Why does any disease happen? The best we can do is help and support your dad and mom as much as we can. And it may be too late for your dad, but with you as a scientist and me as a physician, we can try to figure out a cure, so others won't have to go through this."

"I can tell there are times he doesn't know us. Sometimes, he doesn't even really know who Mom is. I can hardly bear the thought of losing him. I know this sounds so selfish, but ever since I was a little girl, I always envisioned him walking me down the aisle, our arms interlocked, he looking so handsome in a tuxedo."

Aaron's forehead wrinkled as he thought about what Aliya had just told him. From the sound of it, that ship may have already sailed. Soon, Matthew might not be capable of accompanying his youngest daughter down the aisle.

They stretched out on their backs and gazed up at the stars, a rarity to see in the concrete jungle of midtown Manhattan, as the twinkling lights from the skyscrapers usually concealed the stars. But that night, the sky was just clear enough for a few of the brightest constellations to be discernible. They lay quietly, lost in their thoughts.

"The big dipper is easy to see," said Aliya in a pensive voice. "But what's that one? The one that looks kind of like a 'W'?"

"That's Cassiopeia," Aaron said with pride. "It's named after a queen in Greek mythology. She was very beautiful. But also very vain."

"Wow. I'm impressed," Aliya said lightheartedly. "I want you in my CA$H CAB!"

Just then the puppy leapt onto Aaron's chest and gleefully licked his face.

"Oh my gosh, she's been so occupied and quiet, I had forgotten that she was even here. You actually got a puppy!"

"Yes, she's awesome, isn't she?I never knew it, but my apartment allows pets, and I figured she'd be nice for you to have around when I have to stay all night at the hospital."

"It just seems so soon," Aliya hesitated. "I mean, I know I'll be here working with Dr. G, but you're not even sure where you'll end up for med school next year."

"No, actually, I am," Aaron said, as his smile grew wide. "I just found out, while you were gone. I was accepted, early admittance, to Columbia!"

"Congratulations! That's awesome! I knew you'd get in." Aliya leapt on top of him kissing him fervently. Seeing this, the puppy yelped excitedly, jumping on them to join in on the fun. "By the way…" Aliya said, as she pulled herself up, still straddling Aaron as he lay on his back. "What's this little girl's name?"

"She doesn't have a name yet. We have to name her."

"Hmm," Aliya said, glancing at the W in the sky. "How about Cassie?"

CHAPTER 10

His Blessing

"Stay with me tonight, Aliya," Aaron said, as he looked into her eyes and squeezed her hand.

She sighed deeply and pulled away. "I can't. I need to be at the lab too early tomorrow. Being gone all weekend really put me behind in my work." She paused and smiled at him softly. "I really am so happy for you, and I loved everything tonight. It's been the best anniversary ever." She shook her head slightly before continuing, "But, with everything going on with my dad, I just need some alone time. You understand, don't you?"

"Of course."

On the long trek back to the apartment, Cassie inevitably conked out, so Aaron had to carry her most of the way home. When they finally returned, Cassie headed directly to her water dish, eagerly lapping up the delicious cool water, and Aaron went directly to his laptop. After finding the information he needed, he picked up his cell phone, hoping it wasn't too late to call.

A few days later, Ellie led Aaron through the large mahogany-stained front door to the family room.

"We're delighted to see you, Aaron." Ellie said, as she wrapped her arm around his. "We were both so excited when you called to say you wanted to pay us a visit. Matt, look who's here! Look who has come to see us."

Matthew was sitting comfortably in his recliner chair, dozing. He looked up and smiled pleasantly, immediately sensing that this stranger was a friend, not a foe. Aaron could tell by the look in Matt's eyes that he did not recognize him. His heart sank.

He took Matt's hand in his own and said, "Hello, Mr. McKenna. I'm Aaron, LeeLee's boyfriend."

Ellie brought out some lemonade and conversed pleasantly with Aaron. Matt didn't say a word but perceived the congeniality of his surroundings and felt at ease.

Aaron took a very deep breath. A lump started to form in his throat.

"Mr. and Mrs. McKenna," he said, in a shaky voice that he had not expected to have. "You are wonderful people and have raised two wonderful daughters. I am so grateful for how you have welcomed me into your lives. I love Liya more than words can say … with all that I am. I want to spend the rest of my life by her side. I would like to ask Liya to marry me, and I would be honored to have your blessing."

Ellie jumped from her chair and embraced Aaron with unbridled excitement."Of course! Of course! How wonderful!"

Matt leaned forward on his elbows that were resting on the arms of his chair and folded his hands by his mouth. He stared blankly, looking as if he had not quite comprehended what had just transpired. Ellie and Aaron both looked at Matt, hoping for a response, but Matt said nothing. Non-verbal, Aaron thought with disappointment.

The disease had definitely progressed. Seeing Matthew in person was much more impactful than just hearing about him and his illness. Aaron could understand why Aliya was so driven to advance her research, knowing it may be able to help him.

"He's a bit tired today, Aaron. He often likes to take a little nap at this time in the late morning. Perhaps we should let him rest. We can sit at the kitchen table, and you can tell me all about your plans," Ellie said warmly.

The two conversed for quite a while. They were very fond of each other and shared a mutual respect, as well as an ardent love for Aliya.

"Mrs. McKenna," Aaron said soberly. "Aliya told me about Mr. McKenna's condition. Know we will do whatever we can to help you both. Please don't hesitate to let us help you."

"Please, call us Ellie and Matt. I already feel like we're family."

Ellie was grateful for the support, knowing she would likely need it, but would not likely accept it. They were both so ambitious and had so much ahead of them to accomplish. She would not delay their progress.

"I know this marriage proposal is probably a bit unexpected at this time, but I was hoping that Mr. McKenna, I mean Matt, would be able to celebrate the wedding with us and walk Aliya down the aisle, before he … uh ... he … well, while he could still really enjoy it," Aaron said, struggling to find the appropriate words.

"Yes. Yes. I understand," Ellie replied in a dispirited voice.

Aaron felt deeply discouraged as he glanced to the family room, where Matt still appeared to be asleep.

“Well, it’s time for me to go. My Lyft is here. I contacted one of my professor’s colleagues at the CWRU Med School this morning and arranged to meet with her at 1:30 to discuss a potential research collaboration. Then I have a flight back to New York later this evening.”

“Give Aliya my love,” Ellie said with genuine affection. She gave Aaron an endearing hug and then accompanied him to the door.

“Will do.”

“Ahem,” Matt uttered, clearing his throat loudly enough to get their attention.

As they turned, both were astonished to see Matthew standing at the entrance to the kitchen.

“Take good care of my little girl, Aaron,” Matt said with a warm smile and a familiar twinkle in his eyes. Aaron’s eyes met Matt’s and filled with a tear.

“I will, sir. I promise.”

CHAPTER 11

An Augury

The cool air and constant breeze were both signs that the fall semester was nearing its end. Aaron had just finished class and was headed home to let Cassie out when his phone chimed.

"Hey," read the text from Aliya. "On way to VEC for seminar. Join me? Then can grab a bite. Missing u, and Cas."

"Speaker? Topic?" Aaron texted back.

Aliya forwarded the information she had received in her inbox. Keynote Address: "The Promise of Molecular Genetics for Treating Neurological Disease" by Dr. Andrew Lux. Then she typed: "Big shot from NINDS."

"Interesting. Time?" texted Aaron.

"5"

"No can do. Frat mtg. Down for sushi later?"

"K"

Aliya had no problem locating the state-of-the-art Vincent Education Center. The lustrous glass tower with handsome white trim emerged supremely from its surroundings, far exceeding the height and beauty of any of the drab buildings nearby. Its angular floors and staircases were illuminated with bright light. Aliya took her seat in the pristine lecture hall that was more the size of a movie theater than a college classroom. She slid the small wooden table up from the side of her chair to provide a spot for her notebook just as Dr. Lux was being introduced.

Wow, he certainly wins the prize for best academic pedigree, she thought, as she listened attentively while his degrees and fellowships from extremely prestigious universities were broadcasted.

As he approached the podium and shook the hand of the prolocutor, the capacity-filled hall erupted with applause. Dr. Lux smiled and nodded, clearly taking pleasure in the accolades bestowed upon him. He was lean and fit, with well-coiffed dark hair. He was dressed meticulously in a tailored blue suitcoat and skinny jeans, complemented by a crisp white button-down. He most definitely possessed an air of confidence. Aliya couldn't help but find him attractive.

He's certainly one of the "beautiful people," she thought.

She was equally attracted to what she heard and how he delivered it. He was a skilled orator … polished, succinct. His explanations were crystal clear. His body language—facial expressions and gestures—were flawless and perfectly timed. He would tilt his head slightly to the side, raise his eyebrows, and make prolonged eye contact with his audience when posing questions, then throw his head back and smile widely when providing answers. He captivated his audience.

He showed a video of a boy who could barely hold his head up, not take a step, or turn the page of a book without assistance, due to very poor muscle control. Aliya, as well as the rest of the audience, couldn't help but be moved with emotion at the desperate sight of this young boy, who clearly was trying so hard.

"This boy has familial HSD, Hallervorden-Spatz Disease. It is a neurodegenerative disorder characterized by spasticity or muscle stiffness; dystonia, which refers to involuntary muscle movements; and choreoathetosis, which is characterized by involuntary twitching or writhing. Additionally, patients with HSD also present with appreciable dementia. HSD is a relentlessly progressive genetic disease that is due to a mutation in the *PANK2* gene. This boy displayed symptoms of this dreadful disease as an infant and, after a tumultuous life and much suffering, died at the tender age of seventeen."

Dr. Lux paused and looked down for a long moment before returning his gaze to the audience. "This boy's name was Jason Lux. He was my brother."

Aliya brought her hand to her mouth as her eyes widened. Dr. Lux continued, saying witnessing his brother's suffering at such a young age was his driving force each and every day of his life. He then expounded on the urgent need to develop genetic therapies to address diseases like these before beginning his discourse on yet another devastating disease, Alzheimer's. Aliya paid attention with razor-sharp focus, furiously taking notes so that she would not miss a thing.

"What if we had the technology to target and activate or even 'knock-in' those genes that stimulate neurogenesis, that escalate myelination, that inhibit neuronal cell death, and that can even activate a specific memory? And what if we could do all of this in specific brain regions, such as the dentate gyrus and the prefrontal cortex. Could we enhance memory and executive function? Or alternatively, could we prohibit memory loss and the deterioration of executive function? Could we prevent dementia?"

As Aliya listened, her sharp young mind matched his terminologies with her prior knowledge, enabling her understanding. Neurogenesis: the growth of neurons. Myelination: the formation of myelin around nerve cell axons, enabling the rapid transmission of neuronal impulses. Dentate gyrus: part of the hippocampus, a region in the brain involved with memory formation. Prefrontal cortex: location in the brain involved in planning, decision making, expression of personality, and complex social behavior.

Dr. Lux then went on to elucidate the intricacies of the molecular biology underlying current methods of genome editing, discussing ZFNs and TALENs, the Cre-Lox system, and optogenetics. Aliya was vaguely familiar with these terms, remembering only that ZNFs and TALENS were nucleases, enzymes that can cut DNA or RNA. She would definitely need to look into this more later. As he continued to elaborate, his enthusiasm intensified as he explained how aspects of this technology could be married to his true passion, DREADDS.

Aliya had never heard of DREADDS. She quickly scribbled, "designer receptors exclusively activated by designer drugs" in her notebook. She thought Dr. Lux's seminar was masterful. But when the question period began, she quickly realized that as an undergrad, she was still quite the neophyte.

Attendees who were much more astute were able to poke holes in his methodology. How would he "precisely" target the involved genes? His procedures had too many "off-target" effects, lacking the required specificity that was of the utmost importance. Plus, his experimental design necessitated a multistep molecular engineering protocol with many custom-made components, which was time-consuming and expensive, thereby making it cost-prohibitive.

There were so many caveats. He needed a method that was cheap, easy, and highly precise.

Still, he was definitely onto something. Aliya was sure of it. She found his research so fascinating, so promising. She desperately wanted to approach him after the lecture and say something to him—although being a bit star-struck, she wasn't exactly sure what she would say. But his celebrity was irresistible. Within minutes, he was surrounded by crowds of professors and students who were eager to meet him. Aliya decided to forgo the long line and head directly to the Upper Westside. Once at Sapporo, she requested a quiet corner table. There she scoured the internet, learning more about Dr. Lux and his research as she awaited Aaron's arrival.

It wasn't long before she tingled all over, arching her back as Aaron approached from behind, smothering her neck with kisses.

"You smell so good," he whispered, taking in a deep breath through his nose. He moved to his chair across from her. His smile, ever so radiant, was matched with hers, as their eyes met for a moment.

"I'm starving." He grabbed a menu. "What are you feeling tonight?"

They settled on the *Chirashi* and *Tekkadon* entrees, complemented by their usual, the *Bakudan* and Greenwich signature rolls and, of course, the plum sake.

"So, how was the talk?" Aaron asked, with a mouth full of food.

"Uh-maz-ing!" replied Aliya, as she took a bite of the succulent tuna. A drop formed in the crevice of her mouth. Aaron reached across with his napkin to gently blot it up. Such a small gesture, yet so very sensual. She basked in the moment before speaking.

"He's doing this incredible work in mice: knocking-out bad genes, knocking-in good genes, upregulating genes at specific times in the neurons of distinct brain regions. His experiments are revolutionizing the field of neuroscience. It blows my mind!"

"Like the brain regions involved in Alzheimer's?" Aaron inquired, as he crammed more food into his mouth.

"Precisely," Aliya said with a smile, impressed by Aaron's intuition.

"He works with mice, right? Is his research translational? Can it be adapted to treat AD in humans?"

"Not quite yet. But I truly believe he is on the cusp. It's just that his methodology is way too complex and not full proof."

"Meaning…?" asked Aaron, as he continued to devour his food.

"Well, first he talked about using ZNFs and TALENs, which are both nucleases that cut DNA—ZNF: Zinc Finger Nucleases; TALENs: transcription activator-like effector nucleases. The problem is this method relies on protein/DNA interactions. For each targeted sequence, you have to make a custom protein to interact with it, which can be challenging, time-consuming, and expensive." She took a sip of her sake before continuing. "Then he got really excited when he talked about DREADDs, designer receptors exclusively activated by designer drugs. He mutates certain receptor proteins so that they can only be activated by the binding of a specific drug, one that he can give the mice when he chooses to. But he has to use an inactivated virus to get the DNA for these 'designer' receptors into the mouse genome, where they then can be expressed and made into receptor proteins at the location of his choice. Here's problem number one: even under the best circumstances, viruses often only infect a small percentage of targeted neurons. Secondly, this method necessitates additional steps, namely the Cre Lox system, which entails even more precise and laborious manipulations," Aliya explained, ever so clearly.

Then she paused, and with a tiny, yet knowing smile, said, "Basically, he needs a system that is more efficient. It has to be able to target genes with precision, be less time consuming to execute, and be highly cost-effective."

"Wow! Those molecular geneticists sure do like their acronyms," Aaron said, with his winsome grin.

Aliya's face dropped in disappointment. "Really? After my brilliant explanation of these highly complex methodologies, all you got out of this is that genetic engineers use a lot of acronyms?"

Aaron set his chopsticks down, smiled again, and looked directly into Aliya's eyes.

"No, what I got out of your truly brilliant explanation is that the stuff you're doing in Dr. G's lab could be the ticket that blows this revolutionary field right out of the water."

"Precisely!" Aliya said, with sparkling eyes and an enormous grin. "And if my experiments work the way we think they will, this methodology could be applied to so many illnesses, not just neurological disorders. It's so versatile. It has so much promise. But most importantly, it may be able to help my dad." That is, she thought, if I can get it working before it's too late for him. Her thoughts took her back to when she began modeling—to the night she walked her first runway at the competition, when she learned if she really worked hard at something, great things could happen. She was as driven now as she was then.

The two walked arm in arm through the lively streets of New York, both a little tipsy from the potent sake. When they arrived back at the apartment, Cassie greeted them with her usual rapturous tail wagging, yelps, and licks.

"I'd better take her out for little exercise or else she'll never settle down," said Aaron.

"Take your time," replied Aliya with a sensual smile, as she slowly unbuttoned her blouse in front of him. "I'll wait."

Aaron's eyes grew wide as he watched Aliya. "Come on, Cas. Let's go!" he said hurriedly, knowing the sooner he wore this little puppy out, the sooner he could return to Aliya.

Later that night, Aliya awoke. She marveled at Aaron's warm body next to her own as he peacefully slept. I'm the luckiest girl alive, she thought, as she gazed at his muscular physique and angelic expression. She lay back and thought about the previous evening, about the prestigious Dr. Lux and his innovative research. She thought about her own research and how close she was to purifying the elusive, but crucial, enzyme. Once she got it, if she could incorporate her novel technology with Dr. Lux's research, well, the possibilities would be limitless! It could be applied to virtually any gene in any organism. It would be so much more direct than the gene knock-out protocols that were currently being done, and it would be easier and cheaper to do.

She quietly slithered out of bed. In the darkness, she could barely see the articles of clothing that had been fervidly ripped off and strewn all over the bedroom floor in the heat of playful passion. She grabbed the first thing she saw, Aaron's t-shirt, slipped it on, and headed for her laptop in the other room. She googled Dr. Lux and, finding his email address, began a concise explanation of the work she was doing and how perfectly it would augment his research.

That morning, Aliya could hardly wait to get to the lab to tell Dr. G all about Dr. Lux's seminar.

"I see you found him to be very charming, Aliya," Dr. G said. "Frankly, many people do. I hate to burst your bubble, but he is very egotistical—a narcissist. He is not entirely respected in the scientific community. I'd tread lightly around him. He's not to be trusted."

Aliya's face went ashen. "What do you mean?"

Dr. G's face softened as he recalled when he was a young, aspiring scientist. He was naïve, just like Aliya, thinking that all scientists were in it solely for the "Greater Good."

"I wouldn't tell him anything about what we are doing. I wouldn't put it past him to steal our work and claim it as his own. And God only knows how he might use it. Money and fame are his driving forces, not the betterment of humankind." Dr. G paused and shook his head, frowning. "I just have a very bad feeling about that guy."

"Oh God," Aliya fretted. "I already emailed him."

CHAPTER 12

The Die is Cast

Drew Lux gazed out at the picturesque New York skyline from the enormous window in his elegant grand suite. It was day-break, and the view was magnificent. Columbia had spared no expense with his accommodations. The Manhattan Isle Hotel was exquisite indeed, he thought, as he poured fresh-brewed coffee into a porcelain cup rimmed in sterling silver.

He had already completed his daily pre-dawn work-out routine, this time including several laps in the inviting, pristine indoor pool. Setting his coffee on the immaculate glass table, he seated himself on the expansive, plush ivory couch and powered up his laptop. He quickly scanned his myriad of emails, mentally triaging them. An email from James Franklin University-Lincoln Center immediately drew his attention when he noticed its timestamp: 3:18 am. His years of training in Neuroscience and the related fields of Cognitive Science and Psychology taught him to be an astute observer of human behavior.

Why so urgent, he thought, as he opened the email entitled "Vital collaboration?" He rested his chin in his hand, crinkling his brow as he pensively read the email, cocking his head at times when he paused to ponder his thoughts.

"Could this be?" he thought aloud, somewhat incredulous at the mere prospect of it all. "A simple system in bacteria that can target DNA sequences with unparalleled precision?"

He googled: "James Franklin University NYC" and in the website search engine entered, "Department of Biology." Selecting the "People" link, he located Dr. Charles Gustaffason and opened the webpage for his laboratory. The synopsis of Gustaffason's research wasn't very impressive, nor very current. It didn't seem to be updated with the research that was so meticulously explicated in the email he received from the undergraduate student, and there were almost no recent publications listed.

The photo of Gustaffason was one of a rather elderly man, well past his prime, thought Lux. He scrolled to the sub-heading entitled "Lab personnel" and clicked on it. A photo of an exceedingly attractive young woman popped up. Wow, Lux thought, lustfully. Why would a babe like that work with a curmudgeon like Gustaffason? He reached for his cell phone, saying, "Hey, Siri, call Meredith." The typical businesslike voice of an administrative assistant promptly responded.

"Good morning, Dr. Lux. How is your stay in New York going?"

"Quite well, Meredith," Lux replied. "But I need you to make a change to my return flight to Bethesda. I need to pay a visit to some colleagues here at Franklin University today."

CHAPTER 13

Superposition

Aliya rubbed the muscles on her lower back, which were stiff from being hunched over her lab bench all morning. She had been painstakingly performing protein extraction and purification experiments for hours without a break. Dr. G accompanied her that morning, working on his laptop in his office, which adjoined the small, antiquated lab space. He had been scouring the literature for clues that could illuminate the characteristics of, and thereby direct them to, the type of protein that would be strictly associated with the short palindromic repeat sequences that they had previously identified.

Aliya glanced his way, noticing his relaxed posture as he sat in his chair, his hands resting gently on his lap, his head and shoulders comfortably slumped, and the rhythmic movement of his chest. Sweet dreams, Dr. G, she thought, as he napped peacefully.

Aliya was far from peaceful. For a long time that morning, she had ruminated over her rash decision to email Dr. Lux without first consulting with Dr. G. What a dumbass she was, she thought, as she sighed in distress. Then she remembered what her favorite yoga instructor often said: "You are in control of your thoughts. Let go of what doesn't serve you. Let go of the past. Live in the present."

She put in her AirPods and tapped her favorite playlist on her phone. The music soothed her soul and lightened her spirit. The song changed to one of her favorites: "Superposition." As she listened to the lyrics, she thought of Aaron, of how he would always be there for her, and how much she loved him. She thought of their future. Graduation was right around the corner. Then she would move in with him and Cassie and pursue her doctorate with Dr. G while Aaron attended med school at Columbia. They would be together each and every day and night. She could hardly wait.

Aliya thought more about what had transpired the previous day. She had been so enthralled with Dr. Lux's seminar. Hell, just about everyone in the lecture hall was too. He truly was at the cutting edge of paradigm-shifting, transformative research. As much as she admired Dr. G, he was pretty damn old and perhaps was getting a bit paranoid. Having a "bad feeling" about a person is far from being "evidence-based," which is the foundational principle of science, Aliya reasoned. She was very close to isolating the key protein that was crucial to the targeting system she had discovered. It would be phenomenal to join forces with Dr. Lux. He was young and idealistic … the Elon Musk of the world of genetic engineering, the polar opposite of Dr. Gustaffason. Dr. Lux was already in the process of translating his work to human disease—to Alzheimer's.

What was she thinking when she emailed him? Lux was so huge! A prominent scientist like him would never respond to an email from a lowly undergrad like her. But maybe if she talked to Dr. G some more, she could convince him to at least consider contacting Dr. Lux. Maybe Dr. Lux would respond to an email from a fellow scientist.

Thinking of email, Aliya realized she hadn't checked hers in a while. She swiped and tapped her cell phone screen with her left hand as she continued pipetting with her right. "Holy shit!" she exclaimed, dropping her pipettor as she read the subject line: "Meeting in person to discuss potential collaboration?" She grabbed her phone and read:

> Dear Ms. McKenna,
>
> I am delighted that you could attend my seminar yesterday. I am truly intrigued by the eloquent experimentation you and your PI, Dr. Gustaffason, are currently engaged in. I wholeheartedly agree that a collaboration could be a tremendously worthwhile endeavor. I have managed to book a later flight back to NINDS tonight and would greatly appreciate it if we could meet this afternoon. My hotel is only about a mile from JFU, and I would very much enjoy the walk to your lab. May I pay you a visit?
>
> Kind Regards,
>
> Andrew Lux

"Dr. G, Dr. G!" Aliya shouted, as she ran into his office, thrusting her cell phone in front of his face. Rubbing his eyes, it took him a moment to compose himself before reading the email.

"Ah," he said. "This is what I was worried about." Nodding his head slowly, he quietly uttered, "The die is cast."

A short time later, the distinguished Dr. Andrew Lux appeared at their door. He pleasantly introduced himself to Dr. Gustaffason. Shaking his hand and looking Dr. Gustaffason directly in the eye, he said, "It's a real pleasure to meet you, sir. I've been reading up on your life's work all morning, and I can truly say, I have never been so incredibly impressed."

Dr. Gustaffason responded by nodding politely.

"And you must be Aliya." Dr. Lux said, with a look that was not entirely appropriate for an exchange between two professionals. Julie would have definitely classified it as "creepily inappropriate and deliberately provocative."

"It is a pleasure to meet you too," continued Dr. Lux. "Your email treatise on gene editing and the exciting potential contribution from your research findings was exceptional. It was very well elucidated. Thorough, yet concise. Extremely convincing. You are an excellent scientific writer, which will serve you well in grad school when you have to write grants, journal articles, and your dissertation."

Aliya was awestruck, hanging on his every word. As he spewed all of this, Lux sized up the pair in his mind. To him, Gustaffason was nothing more than an ineffectual old man. Aliya, on the other hand, was most definitely a bright, talented student with tremendous potential. But, Lux thought, she was also quite young and naïve. She could easily be manipulated. And he couldn't help but notice that she was even hotter in person than in her photo.

The three moved to the conference room where they had an in-depth discussion about their exciting work. Lux was incredibly brilliant, gregarious, and persuasive. As their conversation drew to a close, his tone became serious.

"I'm not the kind of guy that beats around the bush. I think we need to have a plan of action and, when the time comes, move on it … fast. With something this promising, there are likely others that we don't even know about who are pursuing this line of research, and we could get scooped at any time. What is your timeline, Aliya? When will you have the protein purified and tested in the bacterial model system?"

Aliya paused, deep in thought. "I think I can get it purified by the end of next semester and tested over the summer."

"Charles, do you concur?" Lux asked.

"Yes, I think that is entirely doable."

"Once it is proven to work the way we anticipate in the bacterial system, we'll need to take it to the next level and test it in a mammalian system. At that point, our collaboration will be imperative. The research will have to move to my laboratory at NINDS. I am exceptionally well-funded, with state-of-the-art facilities, and have access to any and all the resources we will need to catapult our research into the mainstream. It will be an extraordinary undertaking, a prodigious feat! It will change the course of the future—for the betterment of all!" Lux exclaimed triumphantly.

Jesus, thought Aliya, he really is the Elon Musk of the science world. But Dr. G's furrowed brow spoke volumes. Lux's extravagance gave him an uneasy feeling. What he had learned from all the many life experiences he had both lived through himself and witnessed others go through was a distinct benefit to being older. And it made him remarkably wise. He was a good judge of character; he simply did not trust Dr. Andrew Lux. But his research funding had all but dried up. He did not have top-notch facilities (not even close). And he wasn't getting any younger. This collaboration was his only way to make one final, meaningful contribution to society. It could be the culmination of his life-long pursuit, the climax of his entire career. His thoughts then turned to Aliya. He knew her all too well. She was clearly enamored with Lux as a scientist and intensely driven by the overwhelming notion that she just might be able to find a cure for, or at the very least, stop the progression of Alzheimer's Disease in time to help her father. He feared Lux was the type of person who would use Aliya's passion and skill to advance his own ambitions, casting her aside the moment she was no longer useful to him. Dr. G cared too much for Aliya to allow this to happen. He would need to stay with her, to ensure Lux treated her fairly. They had already passed the point of no return.

"So, do we have a deal? Aliya? Charles?" Lux eagerly inquired.

"Absolutely!" Aliya exclaimed, without one ounce of hesitation.

"We do," said Dr. Gustaffason decisively, nodding in agreement.

"And one more thing—not a word about this to anyone," Lux said firmly. He shook hands with them both. "It's been a pleasure," he said with a smile, as he took one last glance at the outdated lab and headed to the door.

"Well, it's been quite a day, hasn't it Aliya?" remarked Dr. G. "I need to head out too. Are you at a good stopping point in your experiment, so you can leave soon?"

"Yes. I am. I just need to clean up a bit. It won't be much longer."

"Okay then, I'll see you tomorrow?"

"Yes. For sure," Aliya said enthusiastically. Before he could turn to leave, Aliya couldn't contain her excitement any longer. She gave him a huge hug, thanking him profusely, knowing full well that the decision of whether or not to collaborate with Dr. Lux was entirely up to him, as he was the principal investigator of the lab.

"I know this collaboration goes against your better judgment, Dr. G. I'll be careful, I promise."

Dr. G produced a fatherly smile and, with his usual nod, said as he departed, "I know you will, Aliya."

Aliya had so many emotions, she hardly knew how to feel. For the most part, she was beyond excited. So much had transpired so quickly. She could barely believe it. She needed time to process all of this. She put in her AirPods and began cleaning up her lab bench. Her playlist had run through its entirety and began to repeat. The song, "Superposition" was replaying. As she listened, she couldn't help but think that everything seemed to be falling into place.

CHAPTER 14

The Fort

Throughout the semester, Aliya and Aaron were swamped with work, engrossed in their studies, research projects, and extra-curriculars, a narrative typical of the twenty-first century, high achieving college student. Aliya barely found time to run or go to yoga classes, which was terribly disappointing. At least having Cassie provided them with a valid excuse to regularly take long walks together in Central Park. They decided to drive to Cleveland over winter break, spend Christmas with Aliya's family, then leave Cassie with her parents and head to New Orleans for New Year's. On their way back, they would spend a few days at Julie's parents' vacation beach home in Florida. It would be a much-needed break. Aliya's dad and mom were always on her mind. Texting and Face Timing were one thing, but being home with them for a while would give her a real sense of how they were doing. And the warmth and sunshine in the South would do them a wealth of good.

When finals were over, before traveling to Cleveland, Aliya and Aaron spent a few days doing their all-time favorite thing: Christmasing in New York City. Manhattan Island became magical at Christmastime. The window displays at Macy's were as stunning as the resplendent storefronts on Fifth Avenue, aglow with myriads of Christmas lights.

They shopped at the Winter Village Holiday Market at Bryant Park and attended the tree lighting ceremony at Washington Square Park, singing along to holiday songs played by the brass quartet with the throngs of spirited spectators. Their next outing was at Radio City Music Hall.

"That was by far, the best Christmas show I've ever seen," said Aliya as she reached for Aaron's hand.

Aaron put his arm around her and pulled her close as they walked down West Fiftieth street in the frigid evening air.

"No doubt. Seeing the iconic Rockettes at Christmas is about as good as it gets." He squeezed her in closer, unable to resist kissing her.

"It's still kind of early. Where should we go now? What haven't we done yet?"

"Hmm. I know. Let's get some exercise," said Aliya as she playfully bumped him to the right, heading them in the direction she wanted to go.

The Rink at Rockefeller Center was bustling with people.

"Ice skating? Oh no. Not me. That is one thing I just never got the hang of. There's not a whole lot of ice skating that goes on where I come from, but I did try it once at a ski resort and about killed myself. Took a nasty spill. Landed right on my tailbone. My ass hurt for weeks."

"Wait. So, there's an athletic activity that I can actually do better than you? Then we are going ice skating for sure."

Aaron rolled his eyes and reluctantly followed her to the skate rental. When they hit the ice, Aliya took off, showing off her skill and grace by skating backward, pirouetting, and making a quick stop on the sides of her skates that shot ice crystals onto Aaron's legs.

"Well, you certainly have the hockey stop down," Aaron said as he clung to the side rail. "But you are much more beautiful than any hockey player I've ever seen." She was gorgeous he thought, in her fitted red jacket, skinny jeans, and beige-colored scarf that matched the highlights in her luscious long, brown hair. Her eyes twinkled under the lights.

"Come on, take my hand. I'll show you how to glide."

After stuttering around the rink a few times, Aaron started to feel more confident.

"See. This is fun, right?"

"Actually, it is kind of the same motion as skiing. I think I'm really starting to get the hang of it."

They stopped at the rail, directly across from the magnificent, golden statue of Prometheus.

"Very impressive," said Aaron.

"Yep. That's Prometheus, a Greek God. I remember learning about him in my Physiology course."

"What the heck does Prometheus have to do with Physiology?"

"Well, apparently Prometheus was punished by Zeus. Zeus chained him to a rock in the Caucasus Mountains. Each day, an eagle came and ate part of his liver. But each night, his liver would regrow, which meant he had to suffer this punishment for eternity. The story of Prometheus depicts how amazing the liver is. It can fully regenerate."

"How on earth did the ancient Greeks know this about the liver?"

"No clue," said Aliya.

Aaron read the inscription on the granite wall behind the statue: "Prometheus, teacher in every art, brought the fire that hath proved to mortals a means to mighty ends."

"What does that mean?" asked Aaron.

"Hmm. Not sure. I'm going to google it," said Aliya, as she pulled out her phone. "Prometheus is the God of fire. He upset the other gods by stealing fire and giving it to humanity. He is known for his intelligence. It says here that Prometheus represented human striving, particularly the search for scientific truths and knowledge, at the risk of reaching too far, resulting in unintended consequences."

The two gazed at the statue.

"Hmm. Maybe your new technology will be like the fire that gives mortals a means to mighty ends."

Aliya tilted her head and smiled. "Maybe it will."

The following day, they made the seven-hour drive to Cleveland, arriving on Christmas Eve right around dinnertime. When they pulled into the driveway, Ellie, Sara, and Mark came out to the car, greeting them warmly. Cassie was an immediate hit. She bounded directly to Ellie.

"Look at this beautiful baby. Dad will love her!"

Mark offered to help with their bags, but Aaron suggested that they get the bags later. With Cassie being cooped up in the car for so long, he decided to take her for a walk before going into the house and invited Mark to join him. This would also give the girls some personal time to be together with their parents, he thought. Plus, he wanted to run a few things by Mark.

As the girls headed to the house, Aliya couldn't help but notice the odd objects hanging from many of the tree branches in the yard. Were they supposed to be some kind of Christmas ornaments? She traipsed through the snow, moving closer to one for inspection. It consisted of the cardboard tube from a roll of toilet paper with a piece of yarn looped through the middle and tied, enabling it to be hung on a branch. The tube was slathered with peanut butter, to which birdseed was stuck. They were very primitive bird feeders, concluded Aliya.

"Mom?" Aliya asked, as she cocked her head in bewilderment. "Why the heck do you have all these? Was some crafty neighborhood kid selling them or something?"

"Oh no, honey," Ellie said with a genuine smile. "Your dad made those at Senior Club. Aren't they wonderful?"

Aliya and Sara exchanged glances.

"They're totally awesome," Sara said, with a feigned affection that only Aliya picked up on.

Aliya's heart sunk. Her dad was once a highly skilled carpenter. Actually, his talents went far beyond carpentry. He could draw up building designs as well as any architect. He would build homes at his own pace as an extra job, doing all the masonry, plumbing, heating and cooling, and electrical wiring himself, always meticulously performed, and in strict adherence to building code. His mastery of the building trades was paralleled by his creativity, which was manifested by the exquisite landscaping that always accompanied the home. And now, thought Aliya, the best Dad could do was make bird feeders out of cardboard toilet paper tubes at an adult daycare center?

She could tell from Sara's expression that Sara was thinking the exact same thing, but realized that her mother had already acquiesced, resigning to the sad reality that this was the new normal.

Matthew was dozing peacefully in his favorite chair.

"Does he sleep a lot, Mom?" Aliya asked, knowing this could be a sign of depression.

"Kind of," replied Ellie, in her perky voice. He's certainly not the best sleeper at night, she thought, but decided not to verbalize this to the girls. "Let's let him sleep. I'll get some hot cocoa, and we can sit by the fireplace in the other room and catch up, like old times."

"Hot cocoa ain't going to cut it, Mom," Sara said with a smile, as she followed Ellie into the kitchen. "We're officially on vacation, and besides, it's Christmas! I'll make us some festive poinsettias: Prosecco and cranberry with a lime slice to go with the colors of the season."

When they were gone, Aliya knelt down by her slumbering father, drinking in his peaceful presence, noticing his crisp red corduroy button-down, comfy black Dockers, well-trimmed dark head of hair (with just the right touch of gray), lean body, and beautiful ruddy complexion. He always was a good-looking guy, she thought. She brought her face closer to his and was overcome with emotion, with a deep sense of love.

Slowly, his eyes opened. "LeeLee," he said, in a tender voice, as his mouth curved into a gentle smile. "You're home."

She grasped his hand and kissed his cheek ever so delicately. "It's so good to be home, Daddy," she said, as her eyes welled with tears.

Aaron and Mark returned with Cassie, now a bit tired out. She went right up to Matthew, in a relatively subdued manner (at least for her), let him pet her, and then lay contently by his feet. It was as if she somehow knew, instinctively, that he was ailing.

The family gathered for one of Ellie's delicious dinners, which all but Matthew, whose appetite was steadily diminishing, enthusiastically devoured. Although Ellie did a noteworthy job of keeping the conversation going by chiming in for Matthew regularly, it was clear that Matthew was unusually quiet during dinner. Or was this the "usual" nowadays, thought Aliya.

"So, what do you plan to do in NOLA?" asked Mark, shooting a very brief, teasing glance at Aaron.

"Probably going to flash your boobs for beads on Bourbon Street, right Aliya?" joked Sara.

"Sara!" Ellie chastised, albeit while giggling. "That's not appropriate talk for the dinner table, even if you are twenty-six."

"Yeah, Sara," said Aliya in the stereotypical pompous tone of a little sister. "Listen to Mom. And besides, I believe the correct term for these beauties in New Orleanian lingo is titties," she said, as she quickly lifted her shirt and burst into laughter.

"Oh my! I do believe y'all have had a tad bit too much to drink tonight," said Aaron in his best New Orleans accent. Their uncontrollable laughter was infectious. Aliya looked up at her dad to see that he too was smiling and laughing along with the family, even though she wasn't quite sure if he knew why.

As they cleared the table, they gradually regained their composure.

"Well, what shall we do after dinner?" Mark said, anxiously recalling the enjoyable family times in the not-so-distant past, when he would visit Sara before they were married. "Perhaps a friendly little euchre tournament?"

Aliya's face dropped. She knew there was no way her dad would be able to play even a simple card game like euchre. At this point, it would likely be hard for him to follow it, even if he only watched the others play. Ellie, ever so thoughtful, had prepared for this.

"Let's save the euchre tourney for tomorrow. I've got a better idea," she said, as she finished loading the dishes in the dishwasher. "Last night, I baked a boatload of cut-out Christmas sugar cookies that are in dire need of decoration by all you masterful artists." Ellie knew this would be something Matthew could do, even in a rudimentary way.

"Great idea," said Aaron. "I haven't decorated Christmas cookies in like … forever."

Just like old times, thought Aliya. This was a long-held McKenna family tradition. Dad would enjoy it. It was a great idea, she thought, as she smiled at her mom in admiration.

When the creative cookie decorating was completed, Aaron brought the luggage in from the car, putting his bag in the guest room, and taking Aliya's to her bedroom. Aaron had always stayed in the guest room when he visited and had not been in Aliya's room often. It was still kept exactly as it was in her teenage years. Aaron relished the opportunity to get this special glimpse into Aliya's past. Hanging on her walls were posters of bands and ticket stubs from concerts she had attended, pictures from family vacations to national parks out west, playbills from favorite musicals she had seen, and best of all, glamorous professional pictures of her from her stint in the modeling business. God she was incredibly beautiful—and still was, he thought.

Hanging next to her comp card was what looked like a race bib with the number 8085. He knew she was on the track team in high school. Her long gorgeous legs were perfectly suited for running. But this didn't look like a race bib exactly, as it also had the letters: MMTC on it. Next to this was a picture of Aliya on the red carpet, exquisitely dressed in a fitted, shimmering sapphire blue sequenced gown. She was striking. A short Chinese man, dressed in a traditional-looking red and black Asian outfit, had his arm around her. As Aaron contemplated these things, he realized he wanted to learn more about Aliya's colorful past experiences, knowing that they contributed to the amazing woman she had become.

Aliya approached from behind, wrapping her arms around Aaron and gently kissing his neck. He turned and kissed her on the lips.

"I see you're checking me out," Aliya said with her arresting smile, while still in Aaron's arms. "I had my mom get rid of all the pictures of old boyfriends before you came."

"You … had boyfriends?" Aaron said sarcastically, knowing full well she probably had armies of guys falling all over her.

Aaron pointed to the photo of her in the sapphire gown. "Who's that guy?"

"Oh. That's Hai Pei," Aliya said with a warm smile. "He's a famous high-fashion designer. I got to know him in New York when I competed at the Multi-National Modeling and Talent Competition. He's such a great guy. You would really like him. Next time he's in New York, I'd love for you to meet him. It's just that you and he are always so busy. It's hard to find a time that would work for you both."

Aaron smiled and glanced around the room.

"Will you tell me about the stories behind all these things? Like this, with 8085 on it. Is it a race bib that you wore when you ran track? Maybe from an important race you won?"

Aliya's face softened as she gently touched the shiny paper. Her mind flooded with rich memories. "That's from the modeling competition, MMTC, when I was seventeen."

"What kind of competitions were you in?"

"Swimsuit, jeans, formal dress. But the best was when I was selected for the fashion show held at the end of the competition. It was really spectacular."

Aliya recalled how she dutifully attended every rehearsal for the fashion show. She religiously followed the authoritative instructions dispensed by the renowned director, Kate Newhouse, as she practiced synchronizing her steps, dressed in the stunning attire of the illustrious Chinese high fashion designer, Hai Pei. When the night of the show arrived, it was as surreal as it was divine. The grand ballroom overflowed with an audience of hundreds of stylish attendees: talent scouts, agents, and Gen Zers who were aspiring actors, singers, and models.

All at once, the house lights went from dim to a burst of bright light as piercing music with a rousing beat began to reverberate the opulent space. The raucous crowd wildly cheered when the spotlight illuminated her as she stepped onto the stage … as the lead model! She strode down the runway in stilettos and a stunning gown, adorned with the silhouettes of swans on rich sable fabric that was created by the so very talented Hai Pei, who had by now become her friend. As she turned at the end of the runway, she swept the train of the gown around in a kind of a pirouette, a twirl, just like the director had taught her. The crowd loved it, reacting with boisterous applause. That night, she, Aliya McKenna, the tall girl, was a high fashion runway model.

The experience was metamorphic. Her confidence level changed. Her attitude changed. Her life changed. Her height was no longer a curse … it was a gift. And Aliya learned that sometimes, when you put yourself out there, when you just go for it and try something that seems impossible, and then really work hard at it, great things can happen. She did not know then that this valuable lesson would make such an impact on her future.

The week in New York for the competition was transcendental. Wide-eyed young girls excitedly approached her, beseeching her to take selfies with them, whilst older people demurely requested autographs. She loved the attention. She loved the celebrity. She loved how all heads would turn as she strode with the other fabulous young models, all dressed from head to toe in black, flaunting their perfect physique. She was one of the "beautiful people." And she loved being tall.

That week, she fell in love with New York. When they had free time from the competition, she and her new model friends drank in the sights and sounds that can only be found in the Big Apple. They walked the entire High Line, splurged on knishes and chicken kabobs from the vendors in Central Park, made a special trip to Greenwich Village to delight on Karlie's Kookies (no surprise, as she was their favorite supermodel), spent evenings people watching at Times Square (as they were a little too young to get into clubs yet, although they attempted), and of course, went into every store on Fifth Avenue. Saks was a phenom. It was her first time out of Cleveland. NYC was sumptuous.

By the time she and her mom returned home, the number of followers on her Instagram account had skyrocketed. But as she completed her senior year of high school, it didn't take long for her to learn that she was a dilettante. As much as she enjoyed the ride, in truth, she had no real passion or commitment to modeling. The glamour and lure of it began to fade. She realized she had no desire to work out at the gym each and every day, or to eat a constant diet of plain Greek yogurt, bland nuts, and tiny seeds to remain a perfect 34-24-34. She missed carbs too damn much, and it was a nightmare trying to refrain when surrounded by the preferred diet of the Mundane Midwest, with staple foods like pizza, pasta, and white bread. The regular late-night trips with friends to Taco Bell or Steak N Shake for burgers, fries, and milkshakes also didn't help.

As she finished high school, even though she was no longer pencil-thin, (she was just normal thin … nicely lean, at that point), she was still blessed with an awesome figure and, in particular, great legs—fit and shapely. Sexy, in fact. Her tanned skin, the natural highlights streaming through her thick, luscious long hair, playful skirts and dresses, heels (not too high for her non-high fashion model self, just enough to accentuate the shape of her well-formed calves), and black leather jackets, were all good too. They all contributed to the vibe: young and very attractive (still head-turning, most would say).

And she just happened to be pretty smart. Perhaps all those adolescent years of being on the sidelines (certainly not one of the "cool" kids, since she was so tall and awkward), had paid off because her focus had been on her schoolwork rather than on all the emotional drama that monopolized her normal-sized peers.

That was her young self. College-bound and ready to take on the world—with the gift of self-confidence given to her that wondrous week in Manhattan, when she was one of the NYC elite, one of the beautiful people that most Midwesterners could only dream of becoming. From those magical moments at the MMTC, she was drawn like never before to "The City that Never Sleeps."

Aaron looked into Aliya's eyes and kissed her gently. " I love that you just told me that."

As the evening became nighttime, Ellie mentioned it was time for her and Matthew to call it a day. Sara and Mark also headed to bed. Aaron and Aliya decided to take Cassie for a walk. It was a beautiful night, with bright moonlight, no wind, and not all that cold. Aliya grabbed a couple of old blankets to take with them.

"What are those for?" asked Aaron.

"Oh, I thought if it's not too cold, we might sit for a while in the backyard, like we do at Sheep Meadow, and check out the stars," Aliya replied (although she actually had a much better idea in mind).

They strolled through the quintessential suburban neighborhood, taking in all the lovely homes with their soft, glistening lights, wreaths made from pine branches that smelled of Christmas, and tranquil manger scenes. They returned to Aliya's deep back yard, which was surrounded by a large, wooded area.

"How much of this land is yours?" asked Aaron.

"It goes to that stake over there," Aliya said, pointing to a stick jutting up from the ground that was wrapped with a piece of fluorescent orange tape. "But really, we are allowed on all of it. The rest of the wooded property belongs to an old neighbor of ours who lived here a while ago, before the adjacent land was developed into a residential community. He's retired now and has moved to Florida. He was a bit reclusive, but he and my dad really hit it off. His name was Ralph, but Sara and I always called him 'Ralph the Malph' just because we liked the way it sounded. He still sends my parents a Christmas card every year. He's got to be pretty old by now. Apparently, back in the day, the developer did something that really pissed him off. Dad never told us what it was, just that Ralph thought the guy was a rich, cocky bastard and said that hell would freeze before he sold him any of his property. Anyway, Ralph told us we could play on his land whenever we liked. He even helped my dad build this cool fort for us in the woods. Come on, I'll show it to you."

Aliya led Aaron down a homemade path in the woods. The bright moonlight penetrated the sparse winter canopy, illuminating the night sky. And there it was … an exquisite miniature cabin.

"Whoa! This is the Taj Mahal of 'forts,'" said Aaron, as he approached the wooden door without hesitation.

"Wait!" said Aliya, as she turned on her cell phone flashlight. "We'd better check inside first to make sure no animals have taken up residence in there. When Sara and I were little, we used to play here daily for hours at a time. Then, when we got to be teenagers, we didn't come as frequently. When we did, it wasn't unusual to find that a family of critters had moved in. Raccoons, possums, skunks—you name it."

"Good idea, Sacagawea."

They shined their lights through the windows, and everything looked clear. Even so, they decided to let Cassie enter first.

"This is freakin' amazing! You guys must have loved to hang out in here."

"Oh yes. We did. A lot of 'truth or dare' was played within these walls," Aliya said, as she spread out the thick blankets she had brought. "Why don't we play some now? For old time's sake?"

“Okay, I’m game,” replied Aaron, as they sat facing each other. “I’ll start. Truth or dare?”

“Truth,” said Aliya, as she perched her chin in her palm and smiled her radiant smile.

“Am I the love of your life?” asked Aaron, sweetly.

“You are,” replied Aliya, as she moved toward him and gave him a passionate kiss.

“Now your turn,” Aliya said, with her body still pressed up against his. “Truth or dare?”

“Dare.”

Still in close proximity, Aliya sat back on her heels and rose to her knees. “I dare you to kiss me right here,” Aliya said seductively, as she pointed.

CHAPTER 15

The Long Goodbye

The next morning, Aliya awoke early to the scrumptious smell of homemade cinnamon rolls and freshly brewed coffee. She headed to the kitchen, where she found Ellie sitting at the table.

"Merry Christmas, Mom," Aliya said, as she warmly embraced Ellie's shoulders, kissing her on the cheek.

"Merry Christmas!" replied Ellie, delighted by Aliya's affectionate greeting.

"So, how was your walk last night?" Ellie said, with a playful smile.

"Uh, fine," Aliya responded, somewhat horrified. Shit, she thought, did her mom somehow see or hear them in the fort last night? Then Aliya noticed that Ellie was glancing at her ring finger.

"Oh Mom, did you think we were going to get engaged? Sorry to disappoint, but we are a couple of broke college students, about to go even further into debt. We can hold off on marriage until we get our act together," Aliya rationalized. But deep down, she did long for the day she would marry Aaron.

Aliya examined her mother closely. She had aged significantly, even since the last time Aliya was home. She looked tired. Maybe even frazzled.

"Did you sleep well last night?" Aliya gently inquired.

"Not too bad. Actually, your dad was up quite a bit. He's been more agitated lately. I think it's due to all the hustle and bustle of the holiday season. I'm sure things will settle down."

"He looks good, Mom. Really well, really healthy. He doesn't look like he has lost any weight. You are definitely taking great care of him."

"Really? You think so?" asked Ellie, sounding greatly relieved by her daughter's kind and sincere words. "At times, it can be really hard, LeeLee."

"I know, Mom. One day at a time," Aliya said tenderly, repeating a phrase her mother had said to her so often over the years.

Aliya glanced at the book that rested on the table next to Ellie. She was delighted to see that her mom had at least some time for relaxation.

"What are you reading?"

"It's called 'Rebecca' by Daphne du Maurier. It's an old classic. My book club is reading it. Usually, we read the works of contemporary authors, but this time my friend Laura decided to change things up a bit. Dad takes a lot of naps, which gives me time to catch up on my reading. Well, I should go get him up. It's getting late, and I want to keep him on schedule for all of his meds."

"Can I help?" offered Aliya.

"No, but thank you, dear. He's more comfortable with me. You understand, don't you?"

"Of course."

Aliya realized that the day was fast approaching when they would need to hire a home health care aide to assist Dad with his daily living activities and give Mom a much-needed break. After Ellie left, Aliya picked up her book and perused it. She went to the book-marked page, first noticing the actual bookmark. Written on it was the serenity prayer: "God grant me the serenity to accept the things I cannot change. The courage to change the things I can. And the wisdom to know the difference. Living one day at a time. Enjoying one moment at a time. Accepting hardships as the pathway to peace."

Aliya then glanced at the page, noticing a few lines that Ellie had underlined: "If only there could be an invention that bottled up a memory, like a scent. And it never faded, and it never got stale. And then, when one wanted it, the bottle could be uncorked, and it would be like living the moment all over again."[1]

When the rest of the family arose, they all enjoyed a delicious, classic Midwestern breakfast: cheesy eggs, bacon, sausage, white toast slathered with butter and grape jelly, cinnamon rolls, and orange juice. It was loaded with cholesterol, fat, and carbs. Not at all like the avocado toast Aliya was accustomed to as a trendy young New Yorker. With full bellies, they gravitated to the living room to open presents. Dad sat in his favorite chair and said very little, just smiled pleasantly. Once again, Cassie relaxed at a spot by his feet. It seemed to Aliya that he and Cassie had something in common. They both were very content, sensing that it was a joyous occasion and that they were surrounded by loved ones.

---

1 From *Rebecca* by Daphne du Maurier, copyright © 2023. Reprinted by permission of Back Bay Books, an imprint of Hachette Book Group, Inc.

The family spent the day relaxing and reminiscing, with the TV tuned to whatever football games were being shown. As evening began to descend, Ellie was reminded of Mark's idea of a euchre tournament and suggested that the kids play. She set a bowl of pretzels on the kitchen table with a tub of cream cheese, and the guys brought out bottles of the special edition of Lake Erie Brewing Company Christmas Ale. Good-natured banter and laughter emanated from the kitchen as the couples enjoyed some healthy competition.

At a recent caregiver support meeting, Ellie had mentioned that Matthew often became more confused and agitated in the evening hours. The other attendees at the meeting could definitely relate, having experienced the same. A friendly woman by the name of Claire suggested a DVD called "Let's go to the Zoo" featuring Barney, a big purple dinosaur character that hosted a TV show for preschoolers in the earlier 2000s. Sometimes in the evenings, she would play it for her husband to watch. As it was pretty benign, it would both entertain and occupy him.

Ellie was able to order the DVD on Amazon. In the episode, Barney visited the zoo accompanied by a bunch of lively children. Lighthearted kid's music played in the background as the group stopped at each exhibit to take pictures of the delightful animals. Ellie focused on Matt as he watched the program. He seemed to be settled and quite content, which brought Ellie relief, as she was very tired. In one scene, Barney and the youngsters approach the lion exhibit, which was separated from the visitors by a deep trench. A fierce male lion slowly paced back and forth, eyeing the children as they safely frolicked around the enclosure. In an instant, Matthew unexpectedly arose quickly from his chair and began shouting uncontrollably.

"They got to get those little kids outta there! That lion's gonna rip them all to shreds!" He was totally disconcerted. Cassie reacted, barking loudly, confused at this sudden change in behavior. Matthew lunged toward the TV screen as if he planned to reach into it. Ellie reacted and quickly positioned herself between Matthew and the TV in an attempt to diffuse the situation. Aliya, Sara, Mark, and Aaron ran into the room just in time to see Matthew violently thrust Ellie to the ground. Aaron and Mark immediately grabbed Matthew, one on each side to contain him, as Aliya rushed to her mom.

"Turn off the TV, Sara!" she shouted.

Matthew paused and looked around the room. And in a moment of lucidity, fell to his knees and began to cry. Aliya clasped her hands in front of her mouth, terrified by what they all had just witnessed. Ellie quickly went to Matt and knelt down beside him.

"It's all right, my love. It's going to be okay."

Ellie helped Matt to his feet and said it was time for bed. Although still clearly confused, Matthew's docile persona returned, and he calmly took Ellie's arm as she escorted him to their room. Aaron grabbed a rawhide for Cassie, who was still whining, in order to settle her down, while Mark got their drinks from the kitchen, knowing everybody could use one after what had just transpired. Sara was so shaken up. She sat quietly in the corner, trying to make sense out of what they had just witnessed. Aliya sat slumped in her chair, holding her head in her hands. They all sat in silence for quite some time.

Aaron was the first to speak. "It's his parietal lobe," he said, as he rubbed his forehead. "He likely had a mini-stroke, at some point."

"What?" said Mark. "What's a parietal lobe?"

Aliya looked up. "Aaron's right," she said. "The parietal lobe is a region of the brain that is responsible for the perception and integration of stimuli from the senses. Dad couldn't tell that the children and the lion were just in a video on TV. He thought the lion could really get to them. It all makes sense now. One time when I was talking to Mom on the phone, she told me about how she was doing laundry in the other room and Dad was sitting in his chair, watching the evening news. When Mom returned, Dad kept asking her what happened to the nice-looking young man who had been there, talking with him. He was so persistent that Mom actually thought someone had come into the house. A salesman perhaps? But now I get it. In Dad's mind, the newscaster on TV was the nice young man, and Dad perceived him to be sitting right in the room with him."

"Jesus," Mark replied. "What the hell are we going to do? He could have seriously hurt your mom. What if we hadn't been here?"

After a few moments, Sara spoke. "Aliya and Aaron, you continue with your plans to go to New Orleans tomorrow. Mark and I had planned to stay through New Years' before returning to Chicago anyway. We'll figure this out. We'll get Dad in to see his neurologist right away. And then we will contact the in-home nursing service that has been recommended to us. We'll make sure he has a home health care aide here before we leave."

Although Aliya knew she should have felt reassured by how adeptly her big sister was taking command of the situation, she was still overcome with worry and awoke in the middle of the night. The evening had been going so well. She loved being with her family and especially loved getting to spend time with her sister. She couldn't help but think not only about the toll that Alzheimer's was taking on her dad and mom, but also about Sara and herself, and their futures.

Her dad suffered from familial early-onset Alzheimer's, which presents earlier in life, often during one's fifties. It is known to have a strong hereditary basis. Would she and Sara end up like her dad? Would Mark and Aaron have to care for them? Her research was more personal and more important now than ever.

The day had just been too much. She crept downstairs to the guest room and slipped beside Aaron, resting her head on his shoulder. He held her in his arms for a long time as she quietly wept.

CHAPTER 16

NOLA

Aliya and Aaron started their road trip bright and early, knowing they were in for a long day. If all went well, the drive should take about seventeen hours, and they would arrive in New Orleans around midnight. Ellie sent them on their way with a thermos of super-strong coffee, a take-out breakfast of freshly baked banana-nut muffins, and a cooler full of sandwiches, drinks, and snacks. As they pulled away, she smiled and waved.

"Have a great time, and don't worry. We'll take good care of Cas."

As they drove, Aliya fidgeted then sighed and stared silently out the car window. She lowered her head and rested her hand on her forehead.

"I've just never seen him that angry … or that broken," she said, shaking her head ever so slightly.

"The best thing for you now is sleep," Aaron said.

"I'd give anything to be able to sleep. I'm still just too worked up. My mind is racing."

"I've got it. I have just the thing!"

"What?"

"Bob Ross. You can stream it from YouTube on your laptop."

Aliya loved "The Joy of Painting with Bob Ross." It was a great distraction that soothed her mind and always ended up putting her to sleep."That's an awesome idea."

She decided to use headphones so that the calming voice of Bob Ross didn't make Aaron sleepy too. It wasn't long before she was in a deep, peaceful slumber.

Even though the Crescent City was bustling with activity, by the time they pulled up to their Airbnb in the French Quarter, Aliya and Aaron were exhausted from the long day of driving. They checked in and crashed immediately, getting a much-needed full night's rest.

When the morning sun burst through their window, they felt refreshed. The anxiety from the past few days had begun to melt away.

"Hey, I forgot," said Aaron, noticing that the time on his watch was an hour later than the time on the clock in their room. "We gained an hour."

"Hmm. What shall we do with our extra time?" Aliya flirted.

Aaron smiled broadly as he pulled her onto him. "How about another round of truth or dare?"

The warmth and sunshine of New Orleans were restorative. They started their first day off with freshly baked beignets and delicious coffee at a local cafe, then strolled the pristine grounds of City Park before touring NOMA, where they saw a magnificent exhibit by Lesley Dill, one of their favorite contemporary artists. They spent the afternoon tooling around The French Quarter and Jackson Square, lunching on delicious Cajun cuisine: gumbo, crawfish, and jambalaya, people-watching and wandering through shops.

"*Magnifique*! These pieces are exquisite," Aliya said, as she ran her fingertips along the top of the nineteenth-century French empire mahogany desk. "It's so ornate."

"Yeah. Very cool. All the antiques in here are cool. I like all these massive chandeliers. And this 'Louis XVI Mantel, adorned with bronze mounts, featuring ribbons and flowers' is also quite nice," Aaron said, reading the description from the accompanying sign. "Someday we'll have to go to France."

"*Oui, oui*! That would be a dream come true. I've always wanted to go to Paris."

They crossed the street and entered a touristy gift shop.

"I think we'll need a basket for this store," Aaron said, eyeing the brightly colored New Orleans t-shirts and Saints baseball caps.

"For sure," Aliya replied, as she examined the shelves filled with bags of pecans, beignet mix, and decorative NOLA coffee mugs.

And we can't leave without these," Aaron said, grabbing a handful of gold, purple, and green beads.

"And these," Aliya replied, holding a flamboyant, feathered Mardi Gras mask to her face. "Oh, and I'm definitely getting this Hurricane drink mix. Julie will love it."

Aliya sauntered over to another shelf and picked up a ghastly-looking voodoo doll. The small human effigy had sprigs of straw-like hair jutting out from its pitch-black burlapped head, creepy button eyes, and a sharp pin protruding from its chest.

"Now this is exactly what I need. According to Dr. G, I might have to use this on Dr. Lux someday."

Next, they visited the majestic St. Louis Cathedral. Aliya's face softened as they entered. They both paused in awe, taken aback by the grandeur that enveloped them. Not a word was spoken as they gazed at the lofty, arched ceilings, the magnificently detailed marble statues of angels and saints, and the vivid stained-glass windows that shimmered with soft tremulous sunlight. Ornate paintings and mosaic artwork adorned the pristine, cream-colored walls and cathedral ceilings. Inscribed on the vault of the cathedral was: "Sanctus. Dominus. Deus. Sabaoth."

"It's stunning," whispered Aliya. "I wonder what those words mean?"

"Lord God of Hosts," replied Aaron, still a bit mesmerized.

"You know Latin?"

"I took four years in high school. My guidance counselor told me it would be helpful for my career, as Latin is the root language for the vast majority of medical terms."

"Hmm," nodded Aliya, realizing there was still much she didn't know about her boyfriend.

Aliya walked quietly to the side altar that was covered with flickering votive candles held in red glass containers. She lit one and knelt. Bowing her head, her eyes became teary as she offered a heartfelt prayer for her dad.

They returned to their rental to freshen up and make plans for the evening. Aliya called home for an update, speaking at length with her mom and Sara. Dad's neurologist had ordered a scan, and Aaron's diagnosis had been correct. There was a lesion on Matt's parietal lobe, which was the most likely cause of the behavior they had witnessed. They also had started interviewing home health care aides and had selected two that they felt would be a perfect fit.

While Aaron was in the shower, Aliya lounged on the bed, scanning the brochure that was left in their rental. "All the restaurants advertised in here look really touristy. I'd like to go somewhere authentic," Aliya said to Aaron, as he entered from the bathroom, wearing only a towel wrapped around his waist.

"Why don't you text Mark? He told me he has to come to New Orleans frequently for business and knows a lot of the hot spots. I was talking with him about it when we took Cassie on a walk the other day."

"Great idea," Aliya replied as she pulled up her contacts on her cell phone.

"Hey! Advice on 'New Orleansy' places for dinner?" Aliya texted.

"Where r u?" responded Mark.

"French Quarter."

"Where in the French Quarter? What street?"

"Aaron, do you know where we are?" asked Aliya.

"Uh, New Orleans?" Aaron answered, somewhat confused by the question.

"No, like the street?"

"Oh. Iberville," replied Aaron, which Aliya promptly texted.

"At what cross street? Iberville is really long."

"No idea," said Aaron, as he glanced over Aliya's shoulder to read the text. "Just send him our location."

"Go to the Crawfish Grill," was Mark's reply.

Knowing it would be a late, likely drunken night, they Ubered to the Crawfish Grill.

"Oh my," said Aliya, perusing the menu. "One of us has to order the Homemade Turtle Soup Au Sherry. I've never had turtle before."

"You should get it," said Aaron. "I heard turtle meat makes people horny."

"It's turtle eggs that are an aphrodisiac," clarified Aliya. "It's a Mexican thing."

Aaron was unconvinced. "I'm going to google it." He typed in: "turtle eggs- aphrodisiac" and read aloud: "Turtle Eggs. Mexican folklore attributes the ability to inspire love and desire to turtle eggs, believing they stimulate sexual instinct and prompt male turtles to stand at attention. Unfortunately, this belief has led to a significant rise in poaching, and is one of the reasons that sea turtles are on the endangered species list."

"How on earth do you know all these trivial factoids?" Aaron asked.

"I guess I'm just smart."

Aaron took a satisfying drink from his craft IPA. "Does New Orleans have a CA$H CAB like NYC? If so, maybe we should try to find it tonight?"

"I don't know if they have a CA$H CAB," said Aliya. "But it is legal to walk around with drinks. And if you haven't finished your drink when you're ready to leave a bar, they will give you a 'to go' cup."

"What? That's brilliant. That should be written into the U.S. Constitution. How do you know this, Einstein?"

"I read about it in the brochure at our Airbnb. Waste not, want not."

"Then I'm ordering the 'Venti' sized Hurricanes tonight!"

After an incredible meal of shrimp remoulade and catfish meuniére, they headed to Bourbon Street.

"Let's go in this one. Sounds like they're playing vintage jazz," Aaron said, peaking in the entranceway. "I think I see an open table."

With its art deco styling and authentic photos of musicians from the 1920s New Orleans jazz boom plastering the walls, they couldn't help but feel like they were on a movie set. The room was crammed with rowdy patrons, dancing and drinking heavily.

Aliya and Aaron joined right in, trying every creative signature cocktail on the menu and hitting the dance floor in between drinks.

"If you order the Sazerac, I'll try the Vieux Carre. It means 'Old Square,' which was the original name for The French Quarter," Aliya said, as she scanned the massive drink menu.

They stayed until closing time, returning to their rental in the wee hours of the morning. The next day, their hangovers were unrivaled. They almost didn't make it to the "Ghost, Voodoo, and Vampire Tour" that they had booked. As it got closer to New Year's, New Orleans became even more enlivened. There were street festivals, parades, and live music everywhere. Aliya and Aaron decided to forgo the swamp tour they had planned and instead to just hang out in the city, reveling in all the activity. They wore crazy hats, brightly colored shirts, and plenty of beads as they enthusiastically joined in on all the debauchery.

Aaron had mentioned that he really wanted to ride on a paddleboat on the Mississippi, so they booked the dinner jazz cruise on The Creole Princess for New Year's eve. It was yet another magical evening. The tuxedoed band played classic jazz while Aliya and Aaron savored their divine Creole dinners: oysters on the half shell, étouffée, and redfish. Aaron suggested ordering the "king cake for two" for dessert.

Aliya took a sip of her delicious Ramos Gin Fizz. "What's a king cake?"

"Ah, finally I know some trivia that you don't," Aaron said proudly. He launched into his disquisition as Aliya listened intently, with her chin in her hand. As she gazed into his eyes, she couldn't help being charmed by his story and smitten with his good looks.

"Well, the king cake tradition originated in France to commemorate when the three kings visited the baby Jesus."

"You mean the Feast of the Epiphany?" interjected Aliya, recalling having heard this from her grandmother.

"Yeah, right. I guess that's the name of it. Anyhow, the cake is usually decorated with the colors of royalty: purple for justice, green for faith, and gold for power. They use these colors and make the cake into a circular ring to resemble a crown that a king would wear. And here's the best part. There is a little figurine of the baby Jesus hidden in the cake. The person who gets the piece of cake with the baby Jesus gets to be the king for the day."

Aliya tilted her head and smiled as Aaron beamed with pride. "Hmm. I'm impressed."

While they awaited the arrival of their fascinating dessert, the band began to play an old favorite, Louis Armstrong's classic, "Give me a kiss to build a dream on."

"Dance with me?" asked Aaron, taking Aliya's hand into his own.

As they swayed to the entrancing music, so deeply in love, the other patrons couldn't help but notice the beautiful young couple.

Aliya's wavy hair fell gently to her bare back, her natural highlights perfectly accenting her fitted, off-the-shoulder cream-colored dress. Aaron pulled her close, drinking in her celestial scent and the softness of her skin.

Upon returning to their table, they found that their king cake had arrived. It was smothered with sugary sprinkles and colorful frosting. Aaron cut the cake carefully, giving them each a piece.

"Bon appetite," he said, with his most gorgeous smile yet, as he intently watched Aliya take her first bite.

"This is fabulous! Aren't you going to try yours?"

"Oh yeah, right," Aaron responded nervously, as he awkwardly shoved a huge piece into his mouth.

"Oh, my fork is hitting something," Aliya said excitedly. "Could it be … will I be the king?"

Aliya pulled out the small plastic baby Jesus figurine. Attached to it was the most stunning diamond ring she had ever laid eyes on. Aaron moved next to her, knelt on one knee, and took her hands into his own.

"Aliya, the best night of my life was the night we met. And we met because of our shared love for music. That night, when we danced, you came into my heart, and it has never been the same. When I look into my heart now, I only see you. I wanted to bring you here, to the city of music, to ask you if you will share your life with me. Liya, will you marry me?"

Aliya's expression softened as she gently leaned her face toward his. "I will," she whispered then kissed him tenderly.

The room erupted in applause. Apparently, when they were lost in the moment, everyone else had noticed what was transpiring.

Aliya slouched her shoulders, a bit embarrassed. Aaron stood and bowed to the crowd, not knowing what else to do. The band began to play, and the vocalists performed an impassioned rendition of Ella Fitzgerald and Louis Armstrong's "Love is here to stay." The maître d' approached the young lovers' table with two glasses of champagne. "Enjoy. This night is on us," he said, with a warm smile.

They walked to the balcony of the Creole Princess and, holding each other close, counted the year down, welcoming in the new year as the sky went ablaze with colorful fireworks.

CHAPTER 17

Seaside

The drive to Julie's parents' beach house took fewer than five hours. Aaron and Aliya entertained themselves on the way by listening to Tim Ferris podcasts. They particularly liked hearing his guests answer his signature question: "What message would you put on a billboard for millions to see?"

"Okay, so what would be your billboard quote?" asked Aaron.

"I like the one: 'If it's to be, it's up to me.'"

"Very nice."

"How about you?"

Aaron glanced at the ring on Aliya's finger. "I'm the luckiest man alive," he said, with a tender smile.

They arrived in Seaside right on time. Julie greeted them warmly. "Hooray. You made it! Are you hungry? Thirsty? We can walk into town when you're ready. There are a bunch of great little eateries."

"I'm starving," said Aaron. "Let's go."

"Follow me," said Julie as she motioned them down a white brick pathway lined with palm trees.

Aaron glanced around at the locals mulling about the quaint town square as the three friends enjoyed happy hour on the patio at the Seaside Bistro. “What? You can walk around with drinks here too? I love the South!”

It was even sunnier and warmer on the Panhandle than in New Orleans.

“Seaside is so charming. I love it here too, Jules,” Aliya remarked, delighting in their surroundings.

“Yeah, it’s great for old people and families, and people like me, who need to dry out a little after Spring Break in Panama City. This time of the year is awesome too—just because it’s still so much warmer than NYC,” replied Julie, as she sipped her coconut-melon mojito.

“Your parents’ place is gorgeous. And the Gulf is so beautiful. I’ve never seen water quite that color. It’s so—”

“Turquoise,” Julie said, finishing her friend’s sentence.

“Yeah, that’s it. A far cry from dingy Lake Erie. And the sand on the beach is so white and soft,” Aliya said, taking a bite of her ceviche-stuffed avocado.

“I love the architecture,” said Aaron. “There are so many different home designs—Victorian, Neoclassical, Postmodern. The whole community looks to be formulated on the principles of New Urbanism.”

Aliya and Julie both looked at Aaron, dumbfounded. He smiled sheepishly and shrugged his shoulders. “I took an Intro to Architecture class as one of my gen eds.”

“The homes are all painted so colorfully. Love the pastels,” said Aliya.

"Yeah, Joanie and Dale love it when they come. Dale loves to fish right off the beach, and Joanie is really into all of the stuff here. She never misses the Saturday Farmers Market, and she's always going to artist exhibits, wine festivals, and theater productions. And they both really enjoy the annual songwriter's festival."

It all sounded so awesome, thought Aliya. She was happy for Julie's parents. Still, she couldn't help but think of her own. They would love a community like this too. But it was too late for them. Or was it? She still held out hope that her research could help reverse her dad's disease.

The next day, the girls sat on their blanket, drinking cranberry mimosas as they watched Aaron disappear down the beach for his morning run.

Julie clinked her glass with Aliya's. "Saluti! I'm so happy for you guys. You two are awesome together. You're going to have a great life."

"Thanks, Jules. I really love him."

"And he really loves you, Lee. I see it every time he looks at you."

"We haven't figured out the details yet, but when the time comes, we want you to be in our wedding."

"I'd be honored," Julie replied then laughed and said, "Jesus! What's gotten into me. I sound so sappy. By the way, your ring is freakin' stunning. How the hell could he afford that monstrous rock?"

Aliya glanced at her new ring. It was absolutely gorgeous: a large central diamond surrounded by several smaller ones, set in a thick silver band. "I don't know. We really never talk much about money. He just always seems to have it. I guess I just figured he was pretty much like most other college students in NYC. You know, like always trying to find the free concerts and going to campus events only for the free food."

Julie looked out at the shoreline, noticing a couple of adorable young children gathering seashells with their parents.

"What's his family like?" asked Julie, as she poured a couple of fresh mimosas.

"I only met his parents once, when they came for a weekend to visit him on his twenty-first birthday. Come to think of it, they did take us to a nice restaurant, the Marble Room, in the Theatre District, then to see *Hamilton*."

"That had to set them back a pretty penny," Julie mused, doing the math in her head.

"Yeah. And we had great seats at *Hamilton*. And the next night, we all went to a Knicks game, and we were in this big party suite that had every kind of food and drink imaginable."

"Wow! What do his parents do, like for work?"

"Well, he's from NorCal. He said they own some ski place. I can't quite remember the name. Something like 'The Swiss Alps,' or something. You know guys, they really don't talk much about the important stuff, like their families and when they were kids. Aaron talked more about how the Tesla Gigafactory wasn't too far from his parents' place and how they knew someone who worked there, so they got a private tour. Then he rambled on and on about how cool it was."

Julie started putting the pieces together. In one of her business classes, she had to write a paper on Tesla's rise to the top of the clean energy automotive industry. She knew Giga Nevada was in

Sparks Nevada, near Reno, which was only about an hour away from Lake Tahoe.

"Did the name of the ski 'place' happen to be 'Sierra Alps Mountain Resort'?" Julie said, astounded by where this conversation was headed.

"Yeah. That's it."

"Oh my God. He must be filthy rich!" Julie said, then promptly chugged her drink down. "Does he have a brother that you could hook me up with—or even a sister, for that matter? I'm not picky."

The two friends were overcome with laughter, clearly feeling the effects of the alcohol in their drinks and invigorated by the bright sunshine, picturesque beach, and crystal-clear gulf waters.

CHAPTER 18

The Greatest Carpenter

Aaron and Aliya made the fifteen-hour drive from Seaside to Cleveland in one day. They listened to season three of the Serial podcast in its entirety. Set in Cleveland, Aliya found it to be particularly interesting. They finished the last few hours of their drive listening to another favorite, episodes from The Huberman Lab podcast.

"Hello. Anybody home?" called Aliya, as she and Aaron entered her parents' house. Cassie jumped up from her perch at Matthew's feet and ran to greet them.

"Hello, Cas! I've missed you so much," said Aliya, bringing her face to Cassie's as she vigorously petted the soft fur at her sides. "Aw, you're such a baby. I love you so much."

"Hello! How was your trip?" Ellie welcomed, in her usual cheery voice.

Aliya gave her mom a big hug. "It was awesome." She entered the family room to greet Matthew. "Hi, Dad," she whispered, planting a soft kiss on Matthew's cheek as he dozed in his favorite chair.

"Hey, Sis, you look good. You got some sun," said Sara, as the two embraced. Sara happened to glance at Aliya's left hand. Her mouth dropped wide open. "Oh my God," shouted Sara, holding Aliya's hand up. "You got engaged!"

"Ah, congratulations," Ellie said, hugging Aliya and Aaron.

Cassie looked up and began wagging her tail profusely. Matthew, now awakened, smiled broadly. Both recognized a joyous occasion.

Mark shook Aaron's hand. "Way to go, man."

"Yeah, thanks for the help. The paddleboat cruise was an awesome idea."

"Why don't we all have a drink to celebrate?" said Ellie, as she headed for the kitchen. They took their seats at the kitchen table. Ellie got out beers for the guys and wine for the girls. Matthew smiled when the cold bottle was placed before him.

"Mom, I thought Dad wasn't supposed to have alcohol—you know, with all the meds he's on," said Sara.

"Oh, one won't hurt him. Besides, I bet he'll hardly drink it. And it's such a special occasion. I want him to be a part of the celebration."

They all enjoyed hearing Aliya and Aaron tell them about their trip to New Orleans.

"I love NOLA," said Aliya. "It's a really cool city. Great food, music and culture—how the waitresses call me 'baby', and especially the impromptu parades!"

"And your engagement was so romantic," said Sara, glancing at Aaron. "What about the wedding? Any plans yet?"

"Well, we don't have it completely figured out. But one thing we know for sure is that we would like you both to be in it," Aliya said, glancing at Aaron.

"It would make us really happy," added Aaron.

"Of course," said Sara. "We'd be honored."

"I also asked Julie to be in it when visited her at Seaside," said Aliya.

"How is Julie?" asked Sara. "Still as crazy as I remember?"

"Yes. For sure!" answered Aaron with a laugh.

Ellie smiled. "How was Seaside? I hear it's lovely there."

"It is, Mom. Absolutely gorgeous. Wait. Aaron, did you bring back any of those brochures they were handing out?"

"Yeah, I did. I'll go grab it."

Ellie, Sara, Mark, and Aaron gathered around Aliya as she paged through photos in the brochure, describing all the attributes of the meticulously planned community. The centerfold was a large blueprint of a sample house plan, which Aliya set aside.

When they were done admiring the brochure, they noticed that Matthew had unfolded the blueprint and had been examining it for several minutes.

"What do you think, Dad?" asked Aliya.

They all expected him to just shrug his shoulders, which was pretty much how he answered most questions these days. Instead, he pointed at the roof and, shaking his head, said assertively: "This is problematic. The pitch of this roof will never work with the design of the front elevation." Then Matthew smiled and continued with, "If you want something done right, you got to do it yourself!" He took the last swig of his beer and set the bottle on the table, saying, "I'm getting a little tired now. Going to call it a night. Goodnight, kids. See you in the morning."

As he headed for the bedroom, Ellie followed. She glanced at the others, smiling in both astonishment and delight. The four others looked on in amazement.

Aaron nodded. "Beer does him good. He should have it more often."

A short time later, Ellie returned to the kitchen. "He's sound asleep," she said, as she refilled her wine glass, feeling both pleased and relieved.

"What time are you heading out tomorrow?" asked Mark.

"Bright and early," replied Aaron. "The vacation is over. We've got to get back. We've got a lot to do."

"Yeah! Like make wedding plans," said Sara. "So, what are you thinking?"

"Well, we were talking about that on the drive here from Seaside," Aliya replied. "Since Dad is, uh I mean, with Dad's illness, we think it's best to have the wedding sooner, rather than later. We think the best time would be right after graduation, like in late May. Aaron's med school classes start in June, and even though I don't technically start grad school until August, I want to keep my research project moving."

Ellie gave them a hopeful look. "Will we see you at spring break?"

"Actually, Aaron's parents have a place in Miami Beach and have invited us to spend spring break with them. It would be good if I could get to know them a little better since I am marrying their precious son," Aliya said, shooting Aaron a smile.

"Of course," said Ellie. "That makes perfect sense. You'll have a lovely visit."

"And I'm sure the weather will be great then," said Sara. "Much better than where we'll be—freezing in Chicago!"

"You know, our old neighbor Ralph moved to Florida, to one of the keys. We still exchange Christmas cards every year," said Ellie.

"You mean Ralph the Malph? The guy who let us play on his land? He was kind of weird," said Sara.

"Aww. He was a good man. Just liked to keep to himself. He and Dad always hit it off," Ellie replied.

"Which key does he live on?" asked Aaron.

"Let me get his card. I can't quite recall," said Ellie, returning shortly with his Christmas card. "It's from Key Biscayne, although I'm not sure where that is."

"Oh, it's very close to Miami Beach. My parents use to take us to a big tennis tournament on Key Biscayne every year. It's a beautiful barrier island on the coast. I can see why your friend would like it there if he is kind of reclusive. Parts of it are pretty secluded, with lots of tropical forests, mangroves, and hidden beaches."

"Hmm. If you have time, you should stop by and see him," said Sara, reading the Christmas card. "It says here he is still running the 'Iguana Inn.' Sounds pretty skanky!"

"Oh, come on now, Sara. Remember, he did help your dad build a really nice playhouse for you girls," said Ellie.

"Yeah. That fort is impressive!" Aaron marveled.

"Oh. You've been to the fort, Aaron?" asked Sara.

"Yeah. Aliya took me there on Christmas Eve. It was awesome."

"Uh-huh. I bet it was," said Sara, slyly, raising her brows and nodding.

"Okay. That's enough Sara. Do you not remember our sacred pact?" interjected Aliya.

"What pact?" Mark asked, highly interested to learn about his wife and sister-in-law's childhood secrets.

"It's like Las Vegas. What happens in Vegas, stays in Vegas," declared Sara.

"Right," Aliya agreed. "And also remember, what goes around comes around."

Sara slumped in her seat and sheepishly replied, "Good point."

"Ah. Do tell," said Mark. "This all sounds very titillating!"

"Not to me," added Ellie. "Even though you girls are older, I still consider myself to be on a 'need to know basis,' and from the sounds of it, I don't think I need to know about all the goings-on in that fort. I prefer to picture you two playing with your Barbie dolls in there when you were little."

"Yes. I agree. The only thing I want to remember about the fort is the pleasant time Aliya and I spent reminiscing about the games she used to play in there," Aaron quipped, winking at Aliya.

The next morning, as Aaron packed up their SUV, Cassie jumped right in, excited for a new adventure.

"I'm going to miss Cas," said Ellie. "She was a lot of fun to have around. And Dad really enjoyed her too."

"Where is Dad?" asked Aliya.

"Oh, he's resting in his chair. He seems more tired than usual this morning, so I thought it best to just let him rest instead of having him come out here in the chilly air. I'll be sure to tell him you said goodbye."

"I'll go in and say goodbye."

Matthew was sitting quietly in his chair. Aliya knelt down by her dad and took his hand into hers.

"You always told us you wanted to be the third greatest carpenter. Here's the first," she said, as she placed the plastic baby Jesus in his palm and tenderly kissed his cheek.

"I love you, Dad."

CHAPTER 19

Immense Zeal

She sat slumped at her computer, leaning her forehead into her hand. When they returned to New York, Aliya was anxious to get back to her research work. But contrary to what she expected, the long hours and late nights at the lab didn't seem to help further her task of identifying the elusive protein—a protein that could be bound to guide RNA and targeted to cleave a specific DNA sequence. Progress was so painstakingly slow that it seemed virtually non-existent.

"Hey. Dinnertime. I went all the way to Napoli's in SoHo for this delectable pizza," Julie said, grinning widely.

"Shit, Julie. Get that out of here. You can't bring food into the lab."

Julie was taken aback. "Whoa. You are really pissed. Chill out. I guess we'll just have to eat in the hallway," she said, rolling her eyes.

"Don't fucking tell me to chill out. If we got caught with that in here, they could shut down the lab!"

Julie's eyes grew wide. "Okay," she said, as she backed out the door and set the pizza on the floor in the hallway before reentering. "Lee? You okay?"

“Even if I did have time for dinner, I’m not hungry. Please just let me work. I need to get this done.”

“Liya. This is bad. You’re really messed up. I’m worried about you. And Aaron is like out of his mind worried. You gotta lighten up. This shit’s gonna kill you.”

Aliya glared at Julie with her lips pursed. “Thank you for your concern. I appreciate it. But please go. Now. I have work to do.”

Julie shook her head. “Un-fucking-believable. But I’m gonna let it go, just this one time, because you’re cray-cray these days.” Then she turned and left.

Aliya dropped her head into her hands, breathing heavy, shaky breaths. What just happened, she thought. She looked back to her computer screen and began to doubt everything. What if her hypothesis was all wrong? Would she let Dr. G down? Would Dr. Lux think she was an inept fool? Even if she was right, would she be able to decipher this system in time to help her dad? She was spending less and less time with Aaron. And she practically never saw Julie. Where did the time go? Spring semester was flying by. If things didn’t change soon, she would not be able to attain her goal of working out the methodology by the time she graduated.

She closed her eyes for a long moment and began taking deep breathes, a calming technique she learned from her yoga classes.

Dr. G entered the lab. She looked up at him and sighed. Her eyes were tired and bloodshot. Her cell phone chimed. She picked it up with apprehension.

“Another text from Dr. Lux,” she said, wearily.

“Dr. Lux texts you personally?”

"Yes. Frequently. He's very concerned. He wants to 'keep the project moving.'"

"Why the hurry? He, of all people, should know great science can't be rushed."

"He said something about all the potential uses for the technology and how he could market it."

"Hmm. He has never mentioned this to me before." He frowned. "And I don't like him pressuring you like this. I think I'll have a word with him."

"Oh no. Please don't. That would be so embarrassing for me. And he's not really 'pressuring me.' He's just … encouraging me strongly."

Dr. G realized how worried, and utterly spent, Aliya was. He rolled a chair over and sat down next to her.

"Have you ever heard of Santiago Ramon y Cajal?"

Aliya shook her head slightly, quietly saying, "No."

"He said something that you might find helpful."

"Is he a bacteriologist?"

"No. Actually, he is considered by many to be the first true neuroscientist. He was awarded the Nobel Prize in 1906 for his brilliant elucidation and drawings of the microscopic structure of the brain."

"How can what he has said help me? I've got to figure this system out in bacteria before we can try to apply it to the nervous system of more complex organisms."

"Well, it's just something to keep in mind. He said: 'All outstanding work, in art as well as in science, results from immense zeal applied to a great idea.'" He gently placed his hand on her arm. "Have faith, Aliya. You'll get there," he said, with a fatherly smile. "But first,

I think you should go home. Spend time with friends. Get some much-needed rest. You need to recharge. Tomorrow is a new day."

Aliya followed his sage advice. And she did not give up. One late night, a week before spring break, she tested her most recently purified protein. She looked at her PCR results, not expecting anything from them. Then she examined the data intently, sitting up straight in her chair. She bit her lip and re-checked, making sure the expected result was, indeed, indicated. Finally, her mouth dropped open. She smiled and let out a giggle, bringing both hands to her lips. Her body flooded with emotion. She stared at the results for some time, taking it all in, almost in disbelief. Then she reminded herself that she needed to remain cautiously optimistic. Like any good scientist, she knew that results had to be reproducible to be credible.

She would need to repeat this reaction again (and again) to validate her results before she would tell anyone. Then she would be ready for the next step, which was to test her system in mammals. Thank God, she thought. She had been on the cusp of burnout—mentally exhausted. She knew Aaron and Julie had been incredibly worried about her. She realized that she needed to take some time off. And now she felt like she could. The spring break trip she had planned with Aaron came at exactly the right time. She would be able to go, and she would be able to thoroughly enjoy it.

CHAPTER 20

El Acuerdo

Andrew Lux found the sweltering afternoon heat oppressive as he exited the air-conditioned jet black Mercedes. His car door was opened by a muscular, middle-aged man whose dark black hair and thin mustache perfectly accompanied the roughness of his weathered, pockmarked face.

"*Buenas tardes*," he said in a monotone voice, as he sized up Lux and made no attempt to formally introduce himself.

Lux glanced at the highly fortified, luxurious villa as he was led up the meticulously crafted stone pathway. A large Grecian water fountain resided on the freshly cut lawn, surrounded by lush plants and exquisite landscaping. As he entered the mansion's grand open foyer, he admired the richness of the traditional Mexican décor in the expansive rooms. Walls were painted bright yellow with royal blue accents and were laden with tapestries and authentic Aztec artwork. Curved archways divided the rooms, many with massive windows that enabled the bright sunshine to reflect off the colorful walls. Beige and white marble floors were accented by vibrant red, orange, and gold area rugs. Overflowing floral arrangements graced every table. A large shrine to the Virgin Mary, surrounded by lit candles, occupied its own room. The irony couldn't be missed.

Lux was led into a sunlit atrium and offered a seat on a plush chair.

"Would you like a drink while you wait?" Immediately noticing Lux's hesitation, he continued, with some disgust, "Don't worry, it is safe to drink our beverages here."

"Of course," said Lux, pretending as if that had never occurred to him. "Water would be great."

He returned, handed Lux a glass of ice-cold water, and looked directly into Lux's eyes."I certainly hope, for your sake, what you have to say to Señor Cristof is extremely valuable. He is a very busy man. He will not appreciate it if he feels his time is being wasted."

"Absolutely, mi amigo," Lux said, trying not to sound intimidated. "I would not have journeyed all this way if it were not."

The man, who by now Lux had surmised must be Cristof's personal assistant, a higher up in the cartel, nodded slightly as he exited. Lux couldn't help but notice the two other imposing men stationed at the door to the atrium as he waited. And waited. Lux's natural impatience gave way to annoyance. It crossed his mind to ask the goons guarding the door how much longer he must wait, but then reminded himself that now he was on Mexican time, where punctuality is virtually nonexistent, and noted that asking them would probably not go over well.

Lux sighed. He stood up and walked to the window, then sighed again. He sat back down and folded his hands on his lap, tapping his thumbs together. About an hour later, Lux's earlier acquaintance returned with a well-dressed man who looked to be about his same age. Lux recognized him right away. He had an air of intelligence about him that certainly must have contributed to his success.

"Dr. Lux, it's a pleasure to see you again." Vicente Cristof said as he extended his hand in greeting.

Lux firmly shook his hand."Señor Cristof, the pleasure is all mine."

"Please, call me Vicente," he said as he motioned Lux to sit. "It's been, what … five years since I heard your brilliant talk at UNAM?"

"That sounds about right. I'll never forget the fabulous dinner you and your colleagues treated me to after my seminar. Truly, one of the most excellent meals I have ever had."

"Well, we were intrigued by your research. We are always interested in new technologies that may be put to good use in the business world. And ever since I was a young boy, I've always found the life sciences particularly fascinating, even though that is not the … occupation I chose to pursue." Cristof tilted his head and paused. "You look surprised. Do you find this surprising?"

"Not at all. I too feel that the life sciences are exceptionally fascinating. And I'm sure a successful entrepreneur like yourself realizes that revolutionary discoveries, when applied intelligently, can lead to extremely lucrative endeavors."

"Yes indeed. And that is why I am anxious to hear more about what you mentioned when you contacted me."

Lux leaned in and launched into his soliloquy. "I am certain our collaboration will pay enormous dividends. We will be the first to market. Then, with my expertise, and your, shall we say, unique business prowess, we will corner it. You will invest in me, and I will be loyal to you."

"Of course you will. You have no choice. If you enjoy living, that is. So, tell me, what is this new, mysterious product that is so irresistible, so easily produced and so much more lucrative than the business I am in? You are a scientist. Is it a new narcotic, perhaps? Something synthetic that is highly pure?" There was a steely edge to his questions.

"No. It is not a drug. It is so much more far-reaching than any one drug. It is derived from the ingenuity of modern science. We shall be the first to exploit the genius of an old dotard and a naive girl."

Cristof leaned forward in his chair. "You've piqued my interest. Does it involve artificial intelligence? Scientists have been working on that for years but are still nowhere near to producing the desired results."

"No. AI will never be able to match the complex and ever-evolving human mind and body. Nerve cells are highly diverse. They have an exclusive morphology, physiology, and neurochemistry. They are uniquely designed for the simultaneous transmission of an infinite number of messages. And they are constantly being remodeled to achieve optimal functioning. Because of this, AI will never be able to achieve notable success with higher-level problem solving involving real-world perceptual data. AI systems will never be able to engage in deep learning and decision making in a way that is equivalent to human nerve cells, by the continuous adjustment of their synapses to produce the desired outputs from their input patterns. And this feat is accomplished in mere milliseconds, I might add. No, there is nothing artificial about this extraordinary project. We will capitalize on the enormous potential of the human genome, which controls every aspect of every human capability."

"Where will you carry out this intriguing plan?" inquired Cristof, skeptically. "Are you daring enough to do it at NINDS, right under the U.S. government's noses?"

"No, that would be much too risky. It will be conducted at a remote facility on the east coast, where there is no chance we will be detected. Then, when we are ready for mass production, we will move our operation to Mexico, where you will be able to provide the highest level of security. I assure you, my plan is foolproof."

"If this works as you say, Dr. Lux, it will be very profitable for both of us. I pride myself on being an entrepreneur and am willing to bankroll your project, provided I am assured of a significant ROI. I am ready to venture out, to try something new. Drug trafficking and gun-running are getting boring. Besides, as I mentioned, this project is especially appealing due to my personal interest in Biology. It intrigues me."

Cristof smiled slightly as he continued, "We will be symbiotes, eh? Is that the proper term?"

"It is indeed."

"Then, we will seal *el acuerdo*, our deal, with my finest tequila." He signaled to his associate. "Luis, please pour some for us."

"*Salud*!" Cristof said, as they clanged glasses and gulped down the potent liquor.

He shook Lux's hand as he bid him farewell. "We will be in touch."

Once Lux had left, Vicente Cristof turned to his associate. "We will have to watch the good doctor carefully. At some point, when he is no longer valuable to us, we will need to take things into our own hands."

"*Entiendo*," replied Luis.

CHAPTER 21

Cayo Vizcaíno

"This trip would have been quick and easy, if it weren't for the throngs of all those spring breakers clogging the airport. Thank God we got through that long line in time. I really thought we might miss our flight," grumbled Aliya, as she took her seat on the plane.

"Those damn spring breakers! Glad we're not like them," replied Aaron sarcastically. "Don't worry. I guarantee it will be worth it."

As they waited for their Lyft at the Miami airport, Aliya and Aaron began to relax, delighting in the intense sunshine and penetrating heat. It was a welcomed change from the chilly, bleak days in the city. They spent a wonderful week lounging at the pool, swimming in the Atlantic, and basking in the sun all amongst the backdrop of tall palms and a vibrant green landscape. Aliya had gotten to know Aaron's parents when they had visited New York, and she truly enjoyed spending time with them. They were every bit as wonderful as he.

"What would you say if we do something different today and drive down to Key Biscayne? The drive over the causeway is really scenic, and we can check out the parks," suggested Aaron.

"Sounds good. Should we pack a picnic?"

"Actually, I was thinking we could grab a bite there. There are a couple of places I think you'll like."

"That sounds even better!" Aliya replied, excited for the day ahead.

Their first stop was Crandon Park, where they walked hand in hand along the sand dunes, searching for sea turtle nests, then relaxed on the wide beach, noticing how its smooth, windswept sand perfectly abutted the deep blue waters. They admired the skillful kayakers paddling along the wavy sea, and the pelicans that circled above, diving into the water when they spotted their prey.

Next, they headed to Bill Baggs Cape Florida State Park, where they rented bikes and rode along a winding path, taking in the breathtaking views of Biscayne Bay. As the path entered a treed area, Aliya rounded a corner and stopped dead in her tracks.

"Oh my God! What is that thing?"

As Aaron approached, he saw the small gray animal scamper into the trees. "It's just an armadillo," Aaron said, nonchalantly.

"Wow. I've never seen one before."

They pulled their bikes up to the beach and took off their shoes, strolling along the water's edge, feeling the gentle waves lap against their ankles. Aaron peered out at the sea. "Keep an eye out for manatees. They love this bay."

After their long ride, they returned their rentals and lunched at The Key Café.

"I'm definitely going for the agave sunset margarita and the sea bass with risotto," said Aliya, as she set her menu down.

"Sounds delicious. I think I'll try the New York strip steak with the sweet plantain mash, and a good old IPA."

Aliya studied the colorful sailboats that dotted the boundless ocean. "The views of the Atlantic from this upper-level balcony are absolutely stunning. And what an awesome morning. This place is beautiful. I could definitely live in a place like this, with the warm climate all year round, surrounded by the sea," Aliya said, gazing at Aaron adoringly.

"I could too. As long as I'm with you." Aaron smiled and rested his elbows on the table with his arms comfortably folded. "When I was a kid and we would take vacations to Miami Beach, my dad would bring us here to camp and fish. I remember sitting around the campfire and his telling us about how hundreds of slaves and black Seminole Indians would escape from this cape to the Bahamas on seagoing canoes. He told us a story of an abolitionist, Jonathan Walker, who got caught with runaway slaves on his boat while trying to get them safely to the British West Indies, where slavery had been abolished. He was convicted and labeled a 'Slave Stealer.' His punishment was to be tied to a pillory in the public square, where they branded 'SS' on his right hand. But he ended up being a hero to many, who said the 'SS' stood for 'Slave Saver.'" Aaron paused, cocking his head. "They say his ghost still walks these beaches."

Aliya gave Aaron a sweet kiss. "I love that you just told me that. And I love you."

They spent the afternoon hiking along the nature trails through the mangrove wetlands then went swimming and lounged on the beach, watching the local fisherman catch their limit. After a full day, they drove to the elegant Biscayne Bay Hotel to enjoy a romantic evening at their quaint outdoor restaurant, dining on peel and eat shrimp and gourmet burgers and watching the waves roll to the shore.

After dinner, they decided to take a walk on the beach. As the sun moved closer to the horizon, the beach became more and more deserted, until there was not a soul around.

"What are you looking at?" asked Aaron, noticing that Aliya was staring at the land adjoining the beach, which was overgrown with palm trees and tangled vegetation.

Aliya squinted and walked closer to the trees. "What are those things? Oh my God. They're iguanas. They're all over the place. And they're huge!"

"Yep. With all the trees and tasty plants, this is definitely iguana habitat. We used to see them all the time when we camped. In fact, we used to call Key Biscayne 'The Land of Lizards' when we were kids. Don't worry, they're harmless."

"That's a perfect name for this place."

Aaron pointed to a small, weathered sign next to a sandy path dividing the trees. "Look. They even call this motel the 'Iguana Inn.'"

"The Iguana Inn. Oh my God. Remember when we went to my parents to pick up Cas on our way back from Seaside? Mom mentioned that our old neighbor lived in the Florida Keys, and his Christmas card said he ran the Iguana Inn. Oh Aaron, we've got to go check it out," Aliya said, grabbing hold of his hand and running up the path.

They came to a long, white stucco, single-story building with narrow sliding windows at about shoulder level. The flat roof had an aqua green border, perfectly matching the color of each motel room door. Every now and then, a couple of fraying lawn chairs could be found perched near a door on the cement walkway.

"Whoa! This is like something out of the 1960s," said Aliya.

"Yeah, it's way cool. Totally iconic," Aaron replied, running his fingers along the stucco wall.

Aliya entered the door for the tiny reception area. "We've just got to see if Ralph is around."

A willowy older man with an unshaven angular jaw and square chin appeared from the back room. He had wiry salt and pepper colored hair that fell almost to his shoulders and was wearing well-worn jeans and a tattered Rolling Stones concert t-shirt displaying bright red lips on the front.

"May I help you?"

"Ralph?" Aliya asked, hesitantly.

"Yes," he replied, showing no hint of recognizing either of them.

"I'm Aliya McKenna, your neighbor from Ohio."

Ralph's eyes lit up as his mouth formed a smile. "Well H-O-L-L-Y shit! LeeLee? I should have recognized you from your long legs! My God, you're all grown up." After a moment to take it all in, he said, "How about we all have a beer and catch up?"

He invited them to join him in a room behind the reception area that had a few ratty chairs and an old refrigerator, and handed out ice-cold cans of Natural Light. Aliya introduced Aaron, and the two hit it off immediately, discussing their mutual fondness for the unspoiled natural environment of Key Biscayne. Ralph asked about Matthew, already aware of his Alzheimer's.

As Aliya spoke, he shook his head and looked away, genuinely saddened by the thought of his old friend losing himself. He asked about Ellie and how she was coping, saying he knew it must be difficult for her to watch Matt decline and also knowing how challenging it can be to be a full-time caregiver. And he wanted the full update on Aliya's and Sara's lives, which Aliya gladly provided. They conversed effortlessly, as if they had known each other forever.

The beer went down easily on the warm, humid night. One beer became two, then three, then four until they lost count. Ralph spoke a lot about the good old days. He retrieved an old photo album showing many pictures of Aliya's parents when they had first moved into their house. They were so young.

Aliya couldn't help but smile. "What a great neighborhood. It looks like you guys were always having picnics and parties. I can see where that tradition began. Ralph, do you mind if I take some pictures of these photos with my cell phone? I'd love for Mom, Dad, and Sara to see them."

Ralph nodded and smiled. "Of course. Take as many as you like."

A picture of Matthew in army fatigues surprised Aaron. "I didn't know your dad was in the military."

"Yes. He was. For just a short time, before we were born. He never talked about it, so I pretty much forgot all about it."

Ralph frowned deeply, but neither Aliya nor Aaron noticed. "He was in Desert Storm." Ralph thought for a moment then decided not to say any more about this and continued to flip through the photo album. He paused at a picture of himself standing with his arm around a beautiful young Black woman. His voice softened and his eyes moistened. "This was my wife, Breyona."

It was obvious from the picture that he adored her. He told Aliya and Aaron how much Aliya's parents had supported them both during his young wife's painful battle with sickle cell anemia and, eventually, her agonizing death. He never remarried.

There were many more pictures of all four of them having fun together—at cookouts, at the beach. Ralph smiled as he told them what good friends Ellie and Breyona were, and about the great times they all shared.

When it was time to go, Aliya and Aaron expressed their heartfelt thanks for the wonderful visit. They walked back down the beach, hand in hand.

"It was really good to get to know Ralph better tonight, now as an adult," Aliya said as the warm breeze gently blew back her hair. "Sara and I were just kids back then. I hardly remember his wife or that they were such good friends with my parents."

"Yeah. Nice guy. I enjoyed getting to know him too."

The sky turned magnificent shades of yellow, orange, and red, eventually becoming a dark background enlightened by only the moon and stars. There were so many stars that at first, it wasn't easy to discern their favorite constellation, but after some effort, Aaron was able to pinpoint Cassiopeia in the northern sky. Aaron pulled Aliya close to him.

"Liya, we've both had a lot to drink. I really don't want to drive all the way back to Miami Beach tonight. Let's get a room at the Biscayne Bay."

"Awesome idea," Aliya slurred. She playfully moved into him, and they both tumbled together onto the soft sand with Aliya landing on top."We can practice for our honeymoon," Aliya said, with a whimsical smile, straddling and kissing him.

CHAPTER 22

The Summons

Aliya and Aaron returned to NYC tanned and rested, happily reuniting with Cassie. Aliya headed to the lab right away to check in with Dr. G and start some experiments.

After exchanging pleasantries, Dr. G said, "So I assume you have not yet seen the email from Dr. Lux?"

"Uh, no," said Aliya. "I didn't check my email too regularly over break."

"You'd better take a look at it."

The subject line read: Exciting News

Dear Charles and Aliya,

I hope this email finds you both well. I have exciting news to share. I have just accepted a position at the prestigious Arthur R. Chester Laboratory in Bar Harbor, Maine. As you know, ARC Laboratory is a state-of-the-art research institution that is preeminent in the field of murine genetics. As such, it will enable us to catapult to the forefront of the vital research we are engaged in.

> I am beginning the process of moving my research laboratory from here at NINDS to Bar Harbor, and plan to have the new lab up and running by next month. Per our collaboration agreement, I expect you both to join me at the beginning of the summer and am making the necessary arrangements. Aliya, as you have only worked with bacterial systems, before the move you'll need to come to my lab at NINDS for a full-day training session on specific laboratory techniques we perform on mice, such as brain dissection, etc. We can discuss the particulars at our upcoming Zoom meeting, when I also look forward to hearing more about the phenomenal progress you are making with your research.
>
> Kind Regards,
>
> Drew

Aliya's heart sunk. Her shoulders dropped as she nodded in disbelief."He wants us to move to ARC Labs? I thought I could still live here with Aaron and split my time between our lab and Lux's lab in Bethesda, which is only about a three-hour drive."

"I guess we have no choice," said Dr. G, feeling defeated. "He has the resources and expertise that we need right now."

Dr. G's disappointment was palpable. He felt deflated. He was ashamed that he hadn't been able to secure ample funding for the past several years and was no longer independent. Now he would have to be subordinate to a person he had little respect for. JFU would be happy to see him go, he thought. As he was tenured, the university had been burdened with providing his financial support when his grant money dried up. When he was gone, they would give his lab space to a young, energetic scientist who could bring substantial research dollars to the university.

Aliya decided to wait to tell Aaron about all of this until she could do it in person. She pulled her hair into a ponytail, put on her latex gloves, and got to work. Later, when she arrived at Aaron's apartment, she found him perched on the couch with Cassie stretched over his lap, reading his Immunology textbook. He looked up at her and his smile turned to a frown as he immediately noticed Aliya's crestfallen expression.

"What is it, Liya? Is your dad okay?"

Aliya moved next to him, resting her head on his shoulder as he wrapped his arm around her. "I have to move … to Bar Harbor."

"What?"

Aliya recounted Lux's email and her conversation with Dr. G. "Dr. G said once the molecular analysis is completed, which we think shouldn't take any longer than a year, I can come back to New York while the mice are mated and the lines are established. Mice have a twenty-one-day gestation period and don't reach sexual maturity until they are six to eight weeks old, so there will be some downtime while they are breeding, when I can come back to New York and work on our initial manuscript. Then I would return to ARC Labs to do the final testing but could come back to NYC to write my thesis. So, it would be temporary. And we can visit each other on the weekends," Aliya said, trying desperately to convince herself that what she had just said was in fact as reasonable as she made it sound. "I don't want to be away from you. It's just … this is important."

Aaron took a deep breath and rubbed his hand on the back of his neck, trying not to look too shocked at the unexpected news. He and Aliya were so happy together. He was overjoyed when he thought about their marriage and moving in together, being with Aliya each and every day. He knew that in truth, visiting regularly on weekends would be unlikely, due to his heavy med school schedule and the distance to Maine.

"Well," Aaron said, as he changed his expression from that of a deer in the headlights to one of optimism. "Let's check out Bar Harbor. I bet they've got some awesome lobster!" He grabbed his laptop and googled Bar Harbor, Maine. The webpage that appeared was replete with scenic photos of tree-covered mountains, rugged coastline, and calm bays speckled with boats. The pristine natural landscape was beautiful and appealing, making the future seem a little more palatable.

CHAPTER 23

Drew

"We don't kill. We sacrifice."

He stepped behind her and reached his arms around her, placing his strong hands on top of each of hers. She breathed a deep breath. The scent of his aftershave lofted through her nose. It was alluring. She tried not to acknowledge the stirring sensation she felt, but rather brought her thoughts back to the gruesome task at hand.

She flinched as she watched the quick jerk of his hands and the body beneath them go limp.

"Now you try it on your own."

"I … I can't do this."

He wouldn't take no for an answer. "Place your right hand on the small of the neck. Apply pressure with your thumb and forefinger, firmly, like this. Place your left hand here, at its hind quarters. He looked into her eyes and smiled. "Yes, like that." He took a step back. "Now, a very quick motion. At the same time, press down and forward with your right hand as you pull back with your left."

She felt the bones separate under her fingers as life left the warm body.

"That wasn't so bad, was it? Quick and easy."

It should have bothered her, she thought. But it didn't.

"You see, in cervical dislocation, the first neck vertebra is dislodged from the skull causing severe damage to the brainstem and the spinal cord, which leads to immediate loss of consciousness and a quick death. It only takes a second. You'll be doing this a lot, both on your engineered mice, as well as age-matched control mice." He paused and picked up a razor-sharp stainless-steel scalpel.

"Now I'll show you how to dissect out the brain. We need to be sure we don't damage the tissue. That's why we don't use CO_2 gas to euthanize it. We don't want hypoxia to negatively affect the brain tissue. If we are to cure Alzheimer's, our specimens must be in pristine condition so as not to tarnish our studies."

Her eyes widened. "Really? You think we can actually cure Alzheimer's?"

"I know we can. And if your technology works the way we hypothesize, it will also have many, many other profound applications."

He made two horizontal cuts at the anterior and posterior borders of the head, then a longitudinal slice connecting them. Using his forceps, he carefully peeled back the skin to uncover the skull. He made similar cuts to the skull, releasing the brain. Using fine-tipped tweezers, he skillfully removed the meninges that covered the outer surface.

"We want to be sure to remove the dura, arachnoid, and pia mater so that the formaldehyde can fully penetrate and the tissue is adequately fixed for sectioning and immunohistochemistry."

When he was done, he plopped the yellowish mouse brain into a small glass specimen bottle filled with four percent formaldehyde. He took a black sharpie from his lab coat pocket and labeled the bottle, then placed it on the shelf in the large refrigeration unit.

"That went well. You are an excellent student. Come, let me buy you dinner to celebrate your success and engage in my most favorite pastime—talking science with a colleague."

He was so brilliant, she thought. His skill, intellect, and charisma were captivating. What a great opportunity, not only to learn highly technical laboratory procedures first-hand from such a proficient researcher, but also to be invited to have a personal audience with him, one of the world's most esteemed scientists.

Her pocket vibrated "Hey. Headed home yet? Miss u," read the text that popped up on her cell. Her shoulders slumped slightly. "Actually, I'll need to take a raincheck," she said. "I'm driving back to Manhattan tonight. But I really do appreciate the offer."

"Of course. Another time, for sure," he said, without showing his disappointment. "We have our work cut out for us. We will have ample opportunity in the very near future to discuss our shared scientific quest."

"Thank you so much for everything, Dr. Lux. I really appreciate it."

"Please, call me Drew. Dr. Lux is so formal."

She glanced around the lab before she left. It was immaculate, just like Dr. Andrew Lux. Every flask, bottle, and reagent was meticulously labeled and ordered on the shelves that divided the spotless laboratory benches. Each bench consisted of black epoxy resin countertops perched on top of crisp white metal drawers that were also neatly labeled to easily identify their contents. Long rows of cylindrical fluorescent bulbs furnished bright light within the expansive laboratory. It was eerily quiet, save for the sound of scampering mice in the few cages that sat in the fume hood, awaiting their demise.

He watched her as she turned and left, looking her up and down as he nodded his head slightly, liking what he saw.

She climbed into her Honda and replied to the text: "Leaving now. Be home around 9. Miss u 2."

As she pulled away, she glanced back at the prestigious campus of the National Institute of Neurological Disorders and Stroke. Like most research labs, the hierarchy of the laboratory setting was well established in the Lux lab—post docs taught grad students, grad students taught undergrads. It never occurred to her how unusual it was for Dr. Lux, the head of the lab, to be the one spending his valuable time teaching her, an undergraduate.

CHAPTER 24

A Heavenly Wedding

"Your parents actually own this whole place?" asked Aliya, engrossed in the website for the Sierra Alps Mountain Resort on her laptop.

"Well, my family owns it— my parents, uncles and aunts. My grandfather opened it in the 1950s," said Aaron, as they lounged in bed that morning.

"It looks amazing."

"Yeah, the Lake Tahoe region is one of the most beautiful places on earth. You're going to love it there."

"I bet. I'm sure everyone will. I just hope my dad is up to it," Aliya said, with a worried look.

The wedding planning had gone smoothly. With Aaron's connections, they were able to get the entire event organized in the short time between their engagement in March and their date in late May. They arrived in California several days early. On their first day, Aaron took Aliya on a tour of the South Lake Tahoe region. As they stood at his favorite overlook, he put his arm around her and held her close.

"I don't think I have ever seen water or the sky this blue or this clear," said Aliya. "It is absolutely gorgeous here."

"Isn't it though? No matter how often I come here, it never loses its luster. This lake is the largest alpine lake in North America."

"What does it mean to be an 'alpine' lake?"

"It means it's at a high altitude. We're above six thousand feet right now. The Great Lakes are larger in volume, but they are not considered alpine lakes. There are a few other alpine lakes in the U.S., like Crater Lake in Oregon and Yellowstone Lake in Wyoming. Someday, I'll take you to see those too."

"What makes the water so clear? Lake Erie never looks like this."

"It's because the water is colder, so stuff like moss and algae don't grow well in it."

Aliya marveled at the splendid panoramic view. "The mountains are incredible too. So majestic."

"Yep. Those are the Sierra Nevadas, home to the California gold rush. Back in the 1850s miners came from all over to Mother Lode Country in the western Sierras to seek their fortunes."

Aliya nestled even closer to him. "You sure know a lot about the West."

Aaron beamed, proud to have impressed his fiancée. He breathed in deeply, absorbing the fresh aroma of pine-scented air, taking another long look at the massive snowcapped mountains surrounding the reflective water of the calm lake.

"If you think this view is awesome, just wait. You're in for a real treat next."

"Where are we going next?"

“It’s a surprise.”

They returned from their tour and parked at the lodge. Aaron wrapped his arm around Aliya’s.

“Come on. It’s just a few minutes’ walk this way.”

As they approached the downtown area, Aliya spotted the large square cars encased in glass, hanging from a thick cable.

“A gondola!”

“Ready for an awesome ride?”

“Oh yeah!”

They climbed aboard and began the almost three-mile ride to the top of the mountain.

“You were right. I didn’t think it was possible, but the views are even better because we are so high up and can see so far in all directions. The wildflowers are so colorful, the pines so green, the lake so blue. The whole region is so incredibly expansive. I can see why you love it here.”

When they reached the top, they met up with Aaron’s family for drinks on the outdoor deck of a charming café, which provided even more stunning views of the exquisite landscape. The conversation was light and comfortable as they discussed the logistics of the wedding weekend that would hopefully ensure that everything went off without a hitch. Aaron and Aliya had made most of the arrangements from New York, choosing invitations, menu items, flowers, and the cake online. But Aaron’s mom had also been a tremendous help. She suggested a local favorite for the band for the reception and thought of details that Aliya had not thought of, such as arranging for a private service to shuttle guests between the airport and the resort.

Their wedding would be an all-day celebration. They had decided to have an outdoor morning ceremony at the peak time that the sun would crest the mountains, followed by a brunch on the deck. Their guests would have a few hours to relax before the cocktail hour, which preceded the formal reception in the rustic lodge that would be transformed into an elegant venue with shimmering white lights, linen-covered tables, and an abundance of white floral arrangements.

Aliya's family arrived the following day. Sara and Mark traveled with Ellie and Matthew just in case Matthew needed extra assistance. They were not too concerned. Although Matthew was declining, he had become somewhat docile and usually seemed pretty content. Aliya and Aaron had rented a large SUV and met them all at the airport.

Aliya was beyond excited for the wedding and incredibly eager for their arrival. But her enthusiasm waned as she learned how difficult the trip was for her dad. Leaving his normal routine at home disoriented him, which in turn, led to confusion, frustration, and agitation. Ellie finally resorted to giving him a sleeping pill on the plane, which knocked him out, but also made it very difficult to awaken him when they landed. He was so sleepy and listless that they had to get a wheelchair to transport him through the airport. The stress was written all over Ellie's, Sara's, and Mark's faces. But they downplayed the experience, saying that they were certain Matthew would adjust after a day or two in his new surroundings and would be just fine for the wedding.

When they arrived at the resort, Ellie took Matthew to their room for some downtime, agreeing to meet later for dinner. The rest of them headed to an outdoor bar, where they met up with Julie for cocktails.

"Dad looks a lot thinner and frailer than when I saw him last," said Aliya dolefully. "What if he's too confused and upset? He won't be able to walk me down the aisle."

"When we landed in Reno, Mom called his neurologist's office and told the nurse what had happened. The nurse said she would tell the doctor as soon as he was available, and that he would likely call in a prescription to a local pharmacy for an anti-anxiety med. So that should help," offered Sara.

"Has your dad been on anti-anxiety medications before?" asked Aaron, who knew that it could take time to get the proper dosing.

"No. He hasn't," said Sara. "We hadn't felt the need before this weekend. The nurse also said we should watch for altitude sickness. In his weakened condition, it may hit him harder than the rest of us, and since he is not so verbal these days, he may not be able to tell us what's bothering him."

"Well, I'm sure the medications will help. And we'll just have to take good care of him and make sure he drinks plenty of fluids," said Aaron.

Aliya sat quietly. Her crestfallen expression spoke volumes.

"Liya, you got this!" Julie said, with her natural capability of putting a positive spin on things. "You can walk down the aisle on your own if it turns out that way. Just remember how you walked a runway when you modeled. Did you ever trip back then?"

"Nope, never tripped," said Aliya with a slight smile. "You're right. This isn't about me. I was just really hoping Dad would be well enough to enjoy everything. It's so hard to see him like this. He was always so strong and full of life." Aliya was disheartened. Her dad's decline was precipitous. The sooner she got to ARC Labs, the better.

The rehearsal dinner was held on the following evening. Ellie watched as Matt paced nonstop about their hotel suite, a classic symptom of sundowning. Ellie knew she could ask another family member to stay with him and attend the dinner but felt it best that she be the one to stay with him. Even though he didn't necessarily know who she was, especially in this foreign environment, her comely face, her soothing voice, and her benevolent demeanor were familiar to him. She could bring him some sense of normalcy and calm amid his confusion. Plus, she wanted to judge how his anti-anxiety medicine was working. She hoped and prayed that he would sleep soundly and be able to partake in the wedding celebration, at least to some extent. But she worried. They had been there a few days now, and Matthew still seemed much more disoriented and agitated than usual.

The rest of the family and the wedding party met at the eloquent private dining room in the lodge. Extensive windows, encased in warm cherry-stained crown molding, stretched from the floor to the two-story ceiling, provided an amazing view of Lake Tahoe and the surrounding mountains. An enormous chandelier hung from the coffered ceiling above a talented pianist, who played soft melodies. The mood was light, and many laughs were exchanged.

Aliya's spirits were lifted as she glanced around the table, surrounded by her dear friends and close family. But her blissful moment was interrupted when Julie insisted on giving a toast. Aliya and Aaron both winced, quite unsure of what their free-spirited, unencumbered friend might say, especially since she already had many, many drinks that night.

Julie wobbled as she stood and loudly clinked her glass with a spoon to garner everyone's attention. "I'd like to propose a toast," she said loudly, with crinkled eyes and a huge grin on her face. Then she paused and took a deep breath. Gathering her composure, she said in a soft and genuine voice: "Even before this day, I have seen Aliya and Aaron fall in love over and over many times. That is the formula for a successful and happy marriage." Looking directly at her dear friends, she continued: "Liya, Aaron, may you always have a place to call home, and may you always be surrounded by those you love. May you have a long, healthy, and happy life together." Then, she loudly exclaimed, "Nostrovia!" as she flung her arm upward, casting the contents of her full glass of champagne all over the people around her.

After dinner, Aliya and Aaron went for a stroll, gazing at the starry sky on the eve of their wedding day. Cassiopeia shinned brightly. Aliya's whole body, her entire being, felt a warmth and calmness. They exchanged a long, impassioned kiss at Aliya's doorstep as they said goodnight. Aliya slept more soundly that night than ever before.

There was an air of excitement and anticipation as the guests gathered at the beautiful outdoor patio, chatting unobtrusively as the bridal party primped in the lodge. It was no surprise where Aliya inherited her good looks. Ellie and Matthew were an extremely attractive couple. Ellie was striking in her tea-length ivory and pink gown, a perfect complement to the alpine spring environment, which was bursting with wildflowers. She was tall and slender, with wavy chestnut brown hair that rested on her shoulders. Her natural smile lit up the room. Matthew, lean and fit, looked dashing in his full black tux. The casual observer would never detect the confusion in Matt's mind or the worry in Ellie's that morning.

Matthew had been disconcerted by all the hubbub, pacing around their suite at the lodge. Even though Ellie gave him his anti-anxiety medicine, he still had a very restless night. Ellie made the call, saying she thought it best if they sit at the start of the last row where they could watch the ceremony, but also make a quick exit if things became too much for Matthew and he became disruptive. As much as she wanted Matthew to be a part of this day, she wanted more for it not to be upset by him. He wouldn't want that either. They both would want Aliya's lasting memory of her wedding day to be a joyous one.

After Aaron's parents were seated, all eyes were on Aaron and his groomsmen as they entered the front of the gathering. Aaron's handsomeness was exceeded only by his tender and genuine expression of anticipation. The violinist began Vivaldi's "Four Seasons" as the processional of the bridesmaids commenced. After Sara, the matron of honor, joined with Mark and they stepped aside, there was a pause. The guests rose and turned to view the back of the venue as the guitarist and cellist began an ethereal rendition of Pachelbel's "Canon in D."

As Aliya stepped into view, the crowd was awed by her sublime beauty. Aaron's breath was taken away. Before Aliya took her first step forward, Matthew stepped out of his row and, with a warm smile, so naturally offered his arm to Aliya. It was as if it had been planned all along. Matthew had no confusion about this moment. This was what a father did. It was as profound of a moment in his lifetime as his beautiful daughter's birth. It was a moment of the purest clarity. Aliya joined her arm with his, and the two gracefully proceeded down the aisle.

CHAPTER 25

First Light

Aliya and Aaron had decided that their honeymoon would be in Maine. They would have a week or so together there to get Aliya settled before she had to report to the lab and before the start of Aaron's classes at Columbia Medical School. It was close to a nine-hour drive from Manhattan to Mount Desert Island, home to Bar Harbor, The Arthur R. Chester Laboratory, and Acadia National Park. In lieu of taking major highways, they had decided to take the more scenic drive along Route 1, which would bring them up the iconic coast of Maine, dotted with lighthouses nestled amid rugged granite cliffs battered by the rough sea, and enable them to visit some of the quaint fishing towns found along the eastern seaboard.

"How much longer?" asked Aaron, after they had been driving for a while.

Aliya checked her phone. "ETA is three hours and thirty-seven minutes."

"Let's stop for some food. I'm starving."

"We're not far from this cool-looking lobster place," replied Aliya, browsing trip advisor sites on her phone.

A short time later, they pulled into Whalen's Lobsta Shack, a small, brightly painted, red wooden building situated alongside a wharf. A white-framed chalkboard that listed menu options was displayed next to a walk-up window for ordering. A stone patio housed picnic tables with bright red and white canopies surrounded by large planters with equally bright red and white petunias in full bloom. They were greeted warmly by a friendly young woman whose wavy long hair was as red as a cooked lobster. Aaron's eyes grew wide as he read the menu board.

"I'll have the Rolls Royce lobster roll, please," said Aaron with no attempt at hiding his delight.

"Hmm, I don't think I need the jumbo size. I'll just have the regular-sized lobster roll," said Aliya.

"Great choices. Best things on the menu," replied the proprietor. "They both come with coleslaw, chips, and a pickle. Would you like something to drink?"

"How about a couple of Maine root sodas, blueberry, please. It's our first time to Maine so we want to really experience it," Aliya answered, with her infectious smile.

"Well, you picked the right place," replied the young women sincerely. "You can't get any fresher lobster than this. The lobstermen bring their daily catch right here to Whalen's wharf—the area's oldest working lobster wharf," she said, pointing to a building directly across from them. "We are family-owned and run. Our lobster roll has just four ingredients: a fresh New England roll cut on the top, not the center," she emphasized, "that is buttered and toasted on each side, with four ounces of perfectly steamed fresh lobster. And we use all the lobster: the tail, the knuckles, and the claws. Most places just use the parts and sell the tail separately. And there's no mixing in all that extra mayo with the lobster like at other places, which totally overwhelms the sweet flavor of the lobster. We just add some mayo directly to the roll," she added, with genuine pride.

Aaron could feel his mouth-watering as they carried their meals on paper plates to a picnic table near the calm water of the inlet. The woman was right. The lobster was sweeter and more succulent than any they had ever tasted before.

With full bellies, they were happy and content as they continued on to the final leg of their road trip. At their previous stop, Aliya had picked up a copy of the magazine: "NorEast." She read aloud an article about Mount Desert Island and Acadia National Park, as their favorite songs played on their playlist in the background. So far, she was loving their honeymoon.

"Wow, there are so many great things we can do. We are going to have such a good time," she said, as she turned up the music.

They pulled into town and stopped on Bridge Street to get their first look at the "Bar," a sandbar that materialized at low tide and provided a temporary land bridge to Bar Island. They casually strolled along the wet, gravely ground with the other tourists, taking in the stunning views of Frenchman Bay. Next, they drove up Main Street, which was lined with galleries, shops, and eateries. They turned onto Mount Desert Street and parked at the Peregrine Inn, a beautifully restored and immaculately kept building that was constructed in 1884 as a private home. It was painted a greenish-gray, with its many windows trimmed in white and accentuated by black shutters. Its inviting porch wrapped around the front and sides of the house and was lined with a crisp white banister and spindles. The large porch housed white wicker furniture and two porch swings, with numerous hanging baskets overflowing with colorful blossoms.

It was located in the heart of town, across from a local park that regularly hosted outdoor band concerts and art festivals. Importantly, it was only about one and a half miles from ARC Labs.

Aliya had leased a small apartment in the back of the inn that had a private entrance. She had the option of staying at a residence hall for the student researchers at ARC Labs, but there she would have had roommates. Now that she was officially married, she and Aaron wanted a place of their own.

The apartment at the Peregrine Inn was well appointed and tastefully furnished. It was warm and cozy, and Aliya felt at home right away. The landlords, a retired couple from Boston, had left a huge bouquet of fresh flowers on the dining table to welcome her. Aaron unloaded her things, carefully lifting Aliya's bike, which she planned to ride to the lab each day, out of their SUV. To *her* lab, Aliya thought. Soon she would be working at the prestigious Arthur R. Chester Laboratory. Finally, she would be able to move her research to the next level. She pulled out her lab notebook from her backpack and began to page through it. As much as she looked forward to spending the week with Aaron, she was also anxious to get back to her quest.

After going to the nearby grocery store, they walked into town and enjoyed trying new beers from local breweries while dining on lobster linguine, Frenchman Bay stew, and homemade blueberry pie at Murphy's, a hometown favorite. On their walk home, they leisurely explored the shops and galleries.

"Let's go into this one: *The Wild Blue Yonder*," Aliya suggested, peeking in the doorway.

Aaron followed her in. "They sure do love their blueberries here in 'Bah Hah Ba.'"

"Looks delicious. Let's get some of this stuff," replied Aliya, picking up blueberry syrup, blueberry jam, and blueberry muffin mix.

They returned to their front porch as darkness fell. As it was still early in June and the tourist season usually didn't get into full swing until July, they had the porch to themselves that warm evening. Together they relaxed on the swing as Aliya sipped wine and Aaron drank craft beers.

"In that magazine that I was reading on the drive here, it said that Acadia has an awesome ranger-led stargazing program at Sand Beach. Apparently, the expansive National Parks are considered the last havens for skies without artificial light pollution. When you think of it," Aliya continued, lost in thought as she gazed at the night sky, "all of us are made from the stuff of stars. Every atom that's in everyone and every thing originated from the expansion of the universe. Every being is connected to this same origin."

Aaron was always amazed by Aliya's deep thoughts. "I love you," he said, as he pulled her closer and kissed her.

The following morning, they arose early to begin their week of new adventures. They booked a morning whale watching and nature cruise that explored the Gulf of Maine. As the well-equipped vessel pulled away from the dock, Aliya and Aaron stood at the rail of the bow, looking out over the choppy waves, noticing a group of double-crested cormorants riding them like a rollercoaster.

"When we were kids and would go on family trips, we used to play this game where whoever was the first to spot some cool animal would get a prize," reminisced Aliya. "We would decide on the prize level before the game started. If it was a relatively common animal, the prize was small. So, like, pointing out an elk might be worth five dollars. But spotting a moose would get you twenty dollars. If you spotted the elusive grizzly bear with cubs, you really cashed in."

"Sounds fun, I'm down," said Aaron. "But I think we can be more creative with the prizes. This is our honeymoon."

"Oh, I like that idea. So, like, a bald eagle would be worth a kiss. A puffin, two kisses. Then we'd just go from there ... seals, porpoises."

"Exactly. And the biggest prizes would be for the whales. The brochure said minke and finback are usually spotted this time of year, but it's a little early for humpbacks. So, they would get the biggest prize."

Aliya practically jumped out of her skin. "Like that one," she shouted, pointing to a humpback breaching off the starboard side. Hearing Aliya's excitement, Aaron, as well as the entire tour group, cheered as they witnessed the magnificent creature catapult from the sea, creating an enormous splash upon its reentry.

When they returned from their exhilarating trip, they dined on a hearty lunch of chowder and Bar Island burgers then rode bikes along the carriage roads of Acadia National Park, visiting Jordan Pond and enjoying popovers and prosecco, as well as the magnificent view of the North and South Bubble Mountains from the Jordan Pond House Restaurant.

In the evenings, they would sit on their porch swing, sipping cocktails and planning the following day's adventure: kayaking at Long Pond, where the call of the loon could not be mistaken; hiking along the rugged, granite Otter cliffs, one of the highest headlands in the world; and visiting Thunder Hole, where they witnessed the eruption of an enormous spout of water due to violent waves colliding with the air trapped in a cavern just below the surface of the sea. They swam in chilly Echo Lake and explored several nearby trails.

They hiked along the sloped granite of The Great Head Trail and traversed the face of the exposed cliffs on the strenuous Beehive Trail. But by far, their favorite hike was Precipice Trail on the east face of Champlain Mountain, the most challenging hike in the park. Luckily for them, peregrine falcons had not chosen to nest there this season, in which case, the park rangers would have closed the trail to protect this endangered species. Precipice Trail was not for the faint of heart.

"Have you ever done any rock scrambling?" Aaron asked as he squinted through the bright sunshine and looked up at the prodigious cliff.

"Hmm, I don't think so. But then again, I'm not quite sure what rock scrambling is," Aliya said with a shrug.

"Scrambling is … uh, it's like between hiking and technical rock climbing, which uses ropes and tools. When you scramble, you use your hands for balance and to pull yourself up as you climb across a rock face or a boulder slide."

"That sounds doable."

"And I know you're usually not afraid of heights. But how do you feel about climbing up iron rungs on exposed cliffs? To get to the summit, we'll have to climb vertically for about one thousand feet. It's a steep ascent. There are some tight squeezes too—narrow granite tunnels that we'll have to crawl through. I sure hope you're not claustrophobic."

"Bring it on!" Aliya said as she playfully pushed by him, running ahead on the trail.

It didn't take long before they were both out of breath. They had been so focused on their footing as they climbed, knowing full well a slight slip or trip could be disastrous, that they had seldom paused to look out at the magnificent scenery. They stopped on a ledge that was only a few feet wide. Previous ledges had iron railings to hold onto that were drilled securely into the solid rock. This ledge did not.

Suddenly Aliya was overcome by the realization of the immense danger of it all. She plastered herself against the jagged cliff wall, moving as far as she possibly could from the edge. Her breathing became rapid and shallow, and the color drained from her face. Her heart felt like it was pounding out of her body. She was frozen in a state of profound fear.

Aaron was initially oblivious to this. He was standing a few steps in front of her, completely mesmerized by the breathtaking view. When he glanced back at her, the pleasant look on his face rapidly changed to one of surprise and urgent concern.

"Liya, you okay?"

She did not respond. She could not.

"Liya, we need to keep moving. You'll feel better once we are off this ledge. Once we get to the top, it's flat and then we'll go down another route, a much easier trail through the woods. But we have to keep moving now."

He was getting nowhere with her. She was practically catatonic. He brought his hand to his forehead, looked down and let out a deep, desperate breath.

"Jesus. What am I going to do?" he whispered. He glanced out at the scenery. It truly was a magnificent view. There was not a single cloud in the crisp blue sky. They were so high up. They could see for miles, all the way to Frenchman Bay. He pointed and gently spoke.

"Aliya, look at those islands. The bigger one is Bar Island, where we went the first day we got here. What do the other ones look like to you?"

She looked to where he was pointing. He breathed a sigh of relief when he realized he had successfully gotten her attention. She was now focused on the islands off in the distance, not the ledge. "Porcupines."

"Yes! Yes, that's right. They do look like porcupines. The one closest to Bar Island is Sheep Porcupine Island. The next one is Burnt Porcupine Island, then Long Porcupine Island. Can you guess the name of the last one? The one closest to the shore."

"It looks bald."

"Yes, it does! That's why they call it Bald Porcupine Island."

Aliya was completely distracted now. Her fear was temporarily forgotten. This was Aaron's opportunity to get her moving again.

"Come on. Let's keep going. We're almost there. It will be worth it," Aaron said with a warm smile as he took her hand and led her off the ledge. "Thank you, God," he whispered under his breath.

They arrived at the summit shortly thereafter. It was expansive, flat, and safe, just as Aaron had said it would be. Several other hikers were relaxing there after their own arduous climbs. Aliya put her arm around Aaron's waist, holding him close as a light wind blew through their hair, taking in the grand panoramic view. The grayish brown granite tops of the mountains gave way to rich vegetation that looked like a dense green carpet, abruptly ending where the dark blue Atlantic began. Looking closer, they could see parts of the trail, ever so steep, that they had just traversed. It appeared tiny, as if left by ants. They felt exhilarated. They had made it.

Aliya shook her head slightly. "That was a close call back there. It was like I was paralyzed with fear," she mumbled, as she tried to make sense out of what had happened.

Aaron shrugged. "It happens."

"Well, thank you. Thank you for helping me." Aaron didn't respond, just squeezed her tighter.

The night before Aaron was to leave, they attended the ranger-led "Stars over Sand" beach talk at Newport Cove. As they reclined on their blanket and gazed at the night sky, the ranger used a green laser to point out constellations such as Hercules, Cygnus, and Cassiopeia.

"I miss Cas," Aliya said. "And I'm really going to miss you." Her eyes welled with tears. Tears filled Aaron's eyes too.

"I know. But remember, we can fly non-stop between LaGuardia and Bangor in under an hour and a half. So, I can come see you, and you can come home to Cassie and me as often as we want," Aaron said, trying to sound optimistic.

"But it's just not the same."

"Well, we'll give it a try. And if it isn't working, we'll figure something else out. I promise."

"Right. We'll give it a try," Aliya repeated, still not feeling any better.

Early the next morning, before Aaron had to catch his flight back to New York, Aliya and Aaron drove the winding road to the top of Cadillac Mountain. They huddled together on a piece of flat, grayish brown granite on top of the dark mountain, wrapping themselves in a blanket to stave off the chilly predawn air. Cadillac Mountain was famous, not just for its spectacular views of Mount Desert Island

and The Gulf of Maine, but as the highest point along the North Atlantic seaboard, the summit of Cadillac Mountain held the title of being the first place to view the sunrise in the United States.

"When you think of it," Aliya pondered, as they nestled close together, "there really isn't just one sunrise. There are countless sunrises. People all over the world experience their own unique sunrises at their own dawns, which occur at different times during our day. But here, we get to see the very first sunrise out of every sunrise that will happen today in the nation. We are the first to experience the light of a new day in the entire United States."

Aliya paused and let out a deep, sorrowful sigh, knowing each moment that passed was one moment closer to when Aaron would leave.

They watched as the first light gradually invaded the darkness, giving rise to a splendid sunrise. Indeed, a new day was dawning for them.

CHAPTER 26

ARC Labs

A lump in her throat swelled. Tears streamed down her cheeks. Her soul was filled with sadness. Aliya cried as they parted, as she watched Aaron's plane take flight, and in her bed well into that night. Her pain was profound. Finally, sleep descended upon her.

The next morning, she came to the realization that it was time to move forward and make a plan. She wanted desperately to be with Aaron again, so she needed to complete her project and discover a way to help clear the fog in her dad's mind. She would eat healthily, exercise regularly, get adequate sleep, and work her ass off in the lab.

Aliya had done her homework, thoroughly researching her new workplace. She read that The Arthur R. Chester Laboratory was a state of the art, multi-building facility situated on forty-seven acres that were secluded between the North Atlantic and the mountains of Mount Desert Island. Its mission statement read: "To develop novel therapies to eradicate human disease by elucidating the precise functioning of the human and murine genomes, and to provide valuable resources to the worldwide scientific community for the benefit of all." In addition to serving as a world-renowned, international center for biomedical research, it employed over three thousand workers who maintained roughly fifteen thousand strains of genetically characterized mice. It also served as a resource for scientists across the globe, enabling them to order a particular mouse strain for their research without delay. In one year alone, ARC labs could distribute more than two million mice to over twenty-five thousand researchers.

ARC Labs was also an international center for scientific conferences and education, and adeptly managed the Mouse Genome Informatics database, which was an online bioinformatics resource used globally. The more she read, the more she realized she was entering "The Big Time."

Aliya had planned to meet Dr. Gustaffason at eight a.m. that Monday morning. He had moved to Bar Harbor a few weeks earlier and had begun working right away, overseeing the transport of their genetically modified bacterial strains and other lab materials from Franklin University to Lux's new laboratory facilities at ARC Labs. Aliya signed in at the security desk and asked for directions to the cafeteria. She found Dr. G sitting at a corner table in the large, sunny atrium that was teeming with ferns and evergreens.

"Aliya," Dr. Gustaffason said with a genuine smile, giving her a warm embrace.

"It's so good to see you, Dr. G."

They spent the hour catching up. Dr. Gustaffason told Aliya how much he thoroughly enjoyed her wedding and inquired about Aaron. He asked how she was doing as she settled in her new home here in Bar Harbor and told her to let him know if she needed anything. Aliya told him about the wonderful time she and Aaron had the past week. Dr. Gustaffason said that it was daring of them to hike Precipice Trail and warned her to be careful at Thunder Hole, as it wasn't too long ago that a sightseer died there. A woman was swept out into the turbulent sea from the shore by the raging water. Because of this, he said he stayed away from Thunder Hole.

Aliya asked how the process of setting up the lab was going and told him she wouldn't be able to assist him until she completed her official orientation and onboarding sessions. Dr. G remarked that, here, Lux must not have been such a bigshot after all, as his lab space and mouse room were located in the bowels of the farthest research building, at the farthest point away from the rest of "civilization."

Then Dr. G asked Aliya to give him a thorough update on the status of her research. He told her to explain her research as if she was giving a seminar, which was something she would be doing a lot of in graduate school, and start with the basics so that an audience from varied backgrounds could understand her. This would be good practice, he said, for when they attended the World Conference on Murine Genome Science and Therapeutics, which was to be held in London at the end of the summer. It would be a great opportunity for them both to learn about the newest, cutting-edge technologies in genetic engineering and to introduce their own findings to the scientific community.

Aliya started by saying that her focus was on isolating a protein that could be directed to a specific sequence of DNA. DNA was made of four molecules—or deoxyribonucleotides, represented as A, G, C, and T—linked together in a unique series. For example, AGTTCA represented the sequence for a specific region of DNA. A sequence of DNA could encode genes, just like the letters in the alphabet make words.

RNA was also made up of four molecules, but instead of a T, it had a U—RNA's ribonucleotides were denoted by A, G, C, and U.

RNA was made by using DNA as a kind of template. A particular deoxyribonucleotide in a DNA sequence matched with a particular ribonucleotide in the RNA sequence. A paired with U, and G paired with C. To make an RNA, the ribonucleotides were linked together in a series based on how they matched with their corresponding DNA sequence. If the DNA sequence was AGTTCA, the matching—or complementary—RNA sequence was UCAAGU. Specific sequences of RNA that were derived from the DNA that encoded for genes could then be used to make protein molecules.

"But RNA sequences are not always used just to make proteins," Dr. G added. "They can hang out in the cell and form complexes with other proteins too."

"Right. That is a very important piece of information that is especially relevant to my research," Aliya agreed.

Before she left New York, Aliya had completed the final purification steps of the protein that could be directed to a specific DNA sequence. Once there, this protein cut the DNA (thus functioning as an enzyme). She found that this unique protein was associated with two specific RNAs, which she referred to as RNA1 and RNA2.

RNA1 was the RNA that was complementary to the DNA sequences that Dr. G had previously identified in bacteria. These DNA sequences were clustered at many locations in the bacterial genome, which made him suspect that they must be important since they were so prevalent. These DNA sequences were unique in that they contained palindromic repeat sequences, which were sequences whose complement is the same when read backward (like the word "kayak" or GGATCC/CCTAGG) and spacers, which were sequences of non-coding DNA (DNA that did not comprise a gene) that were located in between the repeats.

RNA2 was what Aliya called "trans-activating RNA," because it was necessary to activate the enzymatic function of her newly discovered protein, thereby enabling it to cleave DNA. Aliya determined that RNA1 and RNA2 bound to each other and then associated with her newly discovered protein, forming a complex. Aliya referred to the RNA1 and RNA2 grouping as "guide" RNA, because the sequence in RNA 1 was complementary to, and could pair with, the specific stretch of DNA that had spacers and repeats in the bacteria's genome. It functioned to "guide" the protein to that specific piece of DNA. Once there, the protein's enzymatic function was activated, with the help of RNA2, creating a break in the DNA.

When the DNA was cut, the cell automatically activated a repair mechanism to glue the broken DNA ends back together. But this mechanism was prone to error and frequently resulted in improper repair, which led to deletions and insertions in the DNA. If the particular sequence of the DNA that was cut encoded for a gene, and it was repaired improperly, then that gene would be mutated and would likely be non-functional.

There was just one more component that was needed for her system to work. Aliya discovered that the DNA sequence that she wanted to target had to have a small, unique sequence of deoxynucleotides near its end. She called this the proto-spacer adjacent motif, which was a very short DNA sequence consisting of about three deoxynucleotides—for example, any of the four nucleotides followed by GG, such as AGG, CGG, TGG, GGG. This motif helped the protein to bind to the DNA that it would cut. She could quickly find the locations of these particular motifs by searching databases that contained the complete sequence of A's, G's, T's, and C's that made up the entire DNA sequence in an organism.

Once she discovered all the components in her system, she needed to try it out. She linked the two RNAs (RNA1 and RNA2) together to make a single guide RNA. Then she associated this single guide RNA to her newly discovered protein, thereby making an RNA/protein complex. She transferred this special RNA/protein complex into bacterial cells. If she had in fact, identified the correct protein, the bacterial DNA would be cut only at the specific DNA sequence she targeted, which was complementary to her RNA1.

After she introduced her RNA/protein complex into the bacteria, she cultured the cells by allowing them to grow and replicate in a rich nutrient broth at a warm temperature. She collected the bacterial cells and extracted their DNA for analysis. She found that her protein had indeed cut the bacterial DNA exactly where she wanted it to and nowhere else in the bacteria's genome. She repeated this experiment over and over again, obtaining the same result, which verified its validity.

"But now, the true test would begin here at ARC Labs," Dr. G said, after Aliya had completed her thorough explanation. "Could this extraordinary system in bacteria be adapted for use in mammals? Could it be used to precisely target mammalian genes? And if so, could it be used not only to cut DNA at specific locations but also insert DNA at specific locations? Since genes are comprised of DNA, could she disrupt specific genes by cleaving them, or insert specific genes into regions where the DNA had been cut? Could she effectively 'edit' the genome by mutating bad genes and inserting good genes?"

"Time will tell," replied Aliya. "All I will need to do is to replace one component, RNA1. Instead of using RNA that is complementary to sequences found in bacterial DNA, I will synthesize an RNA that is complementary to the DNA sequence of the gene I want to target in mouse DNA. This will guide my RNA/protein complex directly to the targeted gene."

"The first genes I want to target are those that are thought to be abnormal in people who develop Alzheimer's Disease and thus are likely to be responsible for the disease," she said resolutely. "I have already identified DNA sequences from these so-called 'Alzheimer's genes' that are located near a proto-spacer adjacent motif that must be present for my RNA/protein complex to bind to the DNA. I was able to find the locations of these motifs by searching a database that contains the complete sequence of A's, G's, T's, and C's in mouse DNA. All I have to do now is to link an RNA sequence, my 'RNA1' that is complementary to a DNA sequence found in an Alzheimer's gene, to the trans-activating RNA, RNA2, to make a single guide RNA. I'll associate this single guide RNA with my protein and transfer the whole complex into mouse cells."

"Inside the cell, my RNA/protein complex will be guided directly to the target sequence in the mouse DNA and will bind to this DNA, with the aid of the nearby proto-spacer adjacent motif. If the system works, I'll be able to target the specific DNA sequences found in the abnormal genes that are thought to contribute to Alzheimer's in the mouse's DNA. Once there, my protein, which functions as an enzyme, will cut the DNA sequence of the gene, thereby disrupting the gene so that it will no longer be able to make its corresponding abnormal protein. In this way, I can precisely target and inactivate the abnormal genes that are thought to cause Alzheimer's Disease."

"If that works, my next step will be to use my system to insert DNA sequences into the mouse's DNA."

"Also known as a 'gene knock-in,'" added Dr. G.

"Right," continued Aliya. "We know that in a cell, when DNA is cut, it may be glued back together improperly to create a mutation. Or I can use my system to deliver sequences that correspond to the correct DNA in order to repair a mutant gene, or even to add an extra gene. The cut, or opening in the DNA, can be used to insert a correct sequence. This is called HDR, homology-directed repair. To do this, when I add my RNA/protein complex to cells, I also add a DNA sequence for the normal version of the gene. On either side of my normal gene sequence, I'll add sequences that match the DNA on either side of the breakpoint in the target sequence. The cell will repair the cut in the targeted sequence by recombining the DNA, incorporating the sequence I added in the process. So instead of 'knocking-out,' or rendering non-functional, a bad gene, I will 'knock-in' a good gene."

"But there are also other useful applications for this technology. For example, I can scan the databases to see if there are genes that are believed to be protective against Alzheimer's Disease and knock-in more of those genes, which could help prevent the disease. I can also knock-in genes that make proteins whose job it is to increase or decrease the expression of other genes, turning them on and off where and when I want," explained Aliya.

"Right. Like the genes for the master regulatory proteins," interjected Dr. G. "These proteins upregulate or down-regulate the expression of other genes, just like the conductor of an orchestra precisely signals the different components of the orchestra, like the violins or wind instruments, to start or stop playing at certain times."

"Or even directs them to play louder or softer at certain times," added Aliya.

"Exactly!" said Dr. G. "Resulting in a flawless symphony."

"These experiments are quick and easy and will provide a wealth of information about the causes of Alzheimer's. Once this information is known, targeted therapies and medications can be developed for humans to prevent, treat, and hopefully cure this awful disease," Aliya concluded.

"As well as many other awful diseases," Dr. G said, with a grand smile. "Well, one of these days, you're going to have to think of a clever name for your new system, and shorter names for the components in it. You can't just call it 'The RNA-protein system that is guided by complementary RNA sequences to specific DNA and then bound to the specific DNA with the help of proto-spacer adjacent motifs and then activated to cut the DNA by trans-activating RNA.' It's much too cumbersome!"

"Yes," agreed Aliya. "That does sound really complicated, when in fact, this is a really simple system. It only involves three components: unique RNAs, a specific protein that functions as an enzyme, and a DNA motif. Well, I'll think on it. But now, I've got to get to my orientation session that begins at nine. I'll see you later this week, once I've been successfully 'on-boarded.'"

Aliya's orientation lasted three full days. She had to complete many modules and courses on such topics as laboratory safety, hazardous waste disposal, infectious disease, animal handling and safety, compliance, conflict of interest, and proprietary rights. She attended information sessions on benefits, health insurance, and wellness, where she was happy to hear that ARC Labs had an on-site fitness center. She had a TB test, underwent a background check, and obtained her photo ID for security clearance. She also received a tour of the facility and learned about the history of The Arthur R.

Chester Laboratory and the research currently conducted there. This all made for long days.

In the evenings, Aliya returned to her apartment and worked on her laptop. Dr. G was right. She did need a better way to refer to her system. Scientists were notorious for coming up with quirky names and clever acronyms for their discoveries. She recalled learning about the *Hedgehog* genes, so-called because fruit fly larva with a mutation in one of these genes appear short and spiny, resembling a hedgehog. As more members of this gene family were discovered, they received names from the hedgehog family, such as *desert hedgehog* and *Indian hedgehog*. The most studied *hedgehog* gene in the family was named "*sonic hedgehog*." The scientist who discovered this important gene named it *sonic hedgehog* after a character in a video game that his kids played.

Aliya began randomly jotting down a list of terms in her notebook:

proto-spacer adjacent motif

trans-activating RNA

single guide RNA

regulatory

clustered

short palindromic repeats

protein

interspaced

She found it difficult to find cohesive names to synthesize the components of her new system in a simple way. She was only able to come up with an acronym for the first term: proto-spacer adjacent motif, which she termed: PAM. Maybe her mind was just too tired. It had been a full day. She would work on it again tomorrow.

It was very late when she finally climbed into bed. The bed felt empty without Aaron next to her and Cassie curled up at their feet. She longed for them both.

Elsewhere that night, a nondescript vessel pulled up to the concealed dock on the secluded inlet. It could have easily passed for a lobster boat, which was what was intended. The sky was shrouded in clouds that blocked any light from the stars or moon, cloaking the dock in darkness. The only illumination came from a few small lights on the boat and the headlights of the truck parked on the shore. A short, stocky man disembarked and greeted the woman who stepped from the truck, accompanied by two sturdy males.

"*Hola, señora,*" the captain said in greeting.

"Hello," replied Meredith tersely.

"I have all the material you've requested."

"Bring it out."

Two crewmen rolled out a dolly that carried a padded wooden crate that housed a large, shiny stainless-steel container. Meredith recognized the words stenciled on the wooden crate.

She cocked her head with a look of surprise. "This is from Russia?"

"*Sí.* The Russians are our supplier. Most of my countrymen are either too poor or too religious to partake in such a thing."

The captain gestured to one of the men, who used a crowbar to open the top of the crate. Meredith put on thick blue gloves. She turned and lifted the heavy lid off of the container, allowing a blast of cold, smoke-like liquid nitrogen vapor to escape. She reached in and lifted out one of the stainless-steel racks that were lined with boxes shelved on top of each other. She opened a box and examined the contents before returning it to the rack and placing the rack back inside the container, screwing the lid on tightly.

"All looks to be in order," she said, as she signaled to her men to load the crate onto their truck. She handed the captain a thick envelope, which he immediately opened to inspect the contents.

"It's all there," Meredith said as she turned and climbed into the truck.

The truck traversed the hilly, winding road through the deserted Acadia National Park to reach ARC Labs. The guard at the security station glanced at his watch as he saw the headlights approaching. It was 3:27 a.m. No one else was around. He adjusted a knob on the security camera system, extending the rotational trajectory of the camera farther than normal so that the entrance would be briefly out of view.

The truck pulled up, and Meredith handed the guard an envelope, which the guard opened and examined, before promptly raising the gate. They proceeded to the vacant loading dock at the farthest building on the campus. One of the men keyed in a code to unlock the door, enabling the other to push the dolly with the crate inside. Meredith walked ahead, down the empty hallway, and swiped her badge to unlock the laboratory door. The men removed the shiny tank from its crate and placed it behind the others.

Andrew Lux glanced at his phone that was charging on his nightstand. It was 4:02 a.m. when it vibrated. The text message had a single emoji of a golden eagle, a symbol of the Mexican Federation. Lux drifted back to sleep, relieved to know the delivery went smoothly.

CHAPTER 27

Edwin

The next morning, Aliya woke early. She was greeted by the bright sunshine and crisp, clear blue sky that is customary for a Bar Harbor summer day. She rode her bike to the lab, negotiating the steep inclines and winding road, arriving in time for an early morning yoga class. Afterward, she went to the cafeteria to get her signature morning drink, a white chocolate mocha latte. She then placed a bowl of granola topped with fresh berries and an orange on her tray, which promptly rolled off. The portly man next to her picked it up.

"Here you go," he said timidly, with a slight smile. He was tall and large and was dressed completely in light blue scrubs. He wore a paper hat, the kind a surgeon would wear, that looked to be covering a short, balding head of hair. Aliya could tell immediately that he wasn't a researcher. He had to be one of the mouse handlers, whose job it was to clean mouse cages daily and supply the mice with fresh food and water. It was a menial job with low pay and little status.

"Thank you very much," she said as she extended her hand to shake his. "I'm Aliya. I'm new here."

"Ayuh," he replied with a nod, feeling uncomfortable and somewhat surprised that a prestigious ARC scientist would bother to be so cordial to a lowly worker like him.

Aliya smiled her gorgeous smile and said, "Well, I know you must be a true Mainer because they are the only people I've met here that say 'Ayuh.' What's your name?" she pleasantly asked.

"Ed-win," he replied, saying it slowly, in such a way that suggested he likely had a learning disability.

Aliya smiled with genuine warmth. "It's very nice to meet you, Edwin."

Andrew Lux, who was seated at a nearby table, approached them. He did not hide his distaste for Edwin, glaring at him most condescendingly. As if Edwin weren't present, he spoke directly to Aliya.

"Aliya, I'm so glad to see you," he said, looking at her a bit too lustfully as he touched her bare arm. "Do join me so we can catch up."

Aliya turned to Edwin, "Bye, Edwin. Hope to see you again soon." Once Aliya and Dr. Lux were seated, he immediately expressed his disapproval.

"Aliya, I know you're new here, but, well the locals who work here as cage cleaners are, uh, to put it nicely, are, shall I say, simpletons. You'll want to steer clear of them and spend your valuable time associating with the research staff."

Dr. G's impression of Lux was right, thought Aliya. He could be a real jerk.

Lux droned on and on for a very long time about his favorite subject, himself, before asking Aliya about her work. "Charles tells me you are right on schedule, that you purified the protein and it works in bacteria. Congratulations. So now we hope your system will work the same way in mammals. I will need you to email me your protein isolation and purification protocol. Please do this today. I will have my lab technician purify large quantities of it so you won't have to bother with that step, and you can get right to complexing it with guide RNA that is complementary to Alzheimer's genes. My lab staff has been synthesizing guide RNAs for the genes that I would like to focus on, so we will also use your protein."

"Which genes do you plan to focus on?"

"Oh, there are so many genes!" replied Lux, as he avoided directly answering her question. "Join me for a drink tonight, and I'll tell you all about it," he said in a very suggestive tone. Aliya was caught off guard. She wasn't quite sure how to respond. "Sorry. Uh, can't tonight," she muttered as she stood to leave.

"Of course. Perhaps another time," said Lux, certain that sooner or later, he always ended up getting what he wanted. She would be his next conquest, he thought brazenly, as he watched her walk away.

As Aliya headed to her lab, she began to realize that Lux was not only a conceited jerk; he was a total asshole. She was married. And he knew it.

Aliya worked diligently late into the evening. She wanted to get back before it got dark since she was riding her bike home. She planned to get some dinner and then do more work on her laptop. As she was leaving, she spotted Edwin sitting on a bench on the grassy quad in between the buildings.

"May I join you?" asked Aliya.

"Ayuh," replied Edwin, shooting her a kindly glance but averting direct eye contact.

"I'm sorry Dr. Lux was so rude to you today in the cafeteria. There was no reason for him to act that way."

"What were you listening to?" asked Edwin, noticing Aliya's AirPods.

"Oh, it's a song I like. It's by a singer named Christina Carlton. Would you like to listen to it?" she said as she handed him her AirPods.

"It's a very nice song. The lady has a very pretty voice."

"Yeah, it reminds me of my mom. When I was a teenager, she took me and my sister to see Christina Carlton perform a concert at a small music hall. The stage was dark except for little twinkling lights that looked just like stars, and Christina opened with this beautiful song that you are listening to now."

Edwin smiled peacefully as he listened to the entire song before giving Aliya her AirPods back. "Christina is a pretty name," he said. "What is your mom's name?"

"It's Ellie."

"Is she pretty like you?"

Aliya showed him a picture of Ellie from her wedding on her phone. "Oh, she is very pretty."

"She is very pretty," agreed Edwin, looking at the photo. "You are just like mice."

"What do you mean?"

"Traits get passed down. She is pretty, and you are pretty. Although she is much prettier than you," Edwin said with brutal honesty, but with no intention to insult Aliya.

"Thanks, I think?" Aliya laughed. She swiped to another photo and smiled gently. "This is my dad. His name is Matthew." The next photo was a recent one of her and Aaron at the top of Precipice Trail, overlooking the breathtaking view of the Atlantic Ocean. "And this is my husband, Aaron." Her heart grew heavy, both with happiness and longing as she continued to swipe through her pictures, getting lost in her emotion. She showed Edwin pictures of Sara and Mark, Julie and Cas, then came across a picture she had taken from Ralph's photo album of him and his wife.

"She is like a C57 black 6, and he is like a BALBc, so their offspring could be like a B6 agouti," Edwin said, pensively.

"Okay. You've totally lost me now," Aliya said, completely baffled.

Edwin's confusion was surpassed only by his sheer surprise. "You are an ARC researcher, and you don't know what the color of a mouse's fur is called?"

"Oh. Uh, I'm actually new to using mice for research. I've only worked with bacteria. But I think I can figure it out. A C57 black 6 mouse is black, and a BALBc mouse is white, so an agouti mouse must be light brown?"

"Ayuh. Like the color of your coffee this morning."

Aliya smiled. She was already growing very fond of Edwin. "Do you like working here, Edwin?"

"Oh, yes. I like it very much. I like to take care of the mice. They are very nice. Well, most of them are. Some can be mean and bite," Edwin said, as his eyes grew wide. "But most are gentle, like the sheep."

"Oh, do you own sheep?"

"Ayuh, I help out with them on the farm. I sheered them in the spring."

"Well," Aliya said. "It will be dark soon. I need to get going."

"Aliya. That's a funny name."

"Hmm. You're right. It is kind of unusual. My dad calls me 'LeeLee.' Would you rather call me that?"

"LeeLee," repeated Edwin, as he smiled and nodded his head.

The following day, Aliya saw Edwin again, sitting at the same bench.

"May I hear that nice song again, LeeLee?" he asked eagerly.

Aliya gave him a confused look. She had forgotten about the song.

"By Christina," he said.

"Oh, sure."

"She had twinkling lights, like stars?"

"Yes. That's what it was like when she played this song. It was really magical."

Edwin smiled as he envisioned Christina singing the beautiful melody on a star-lit stage.

"The stars light the way of the good walk," said Edwin.

Aliya cocked her head. "What?"

"The people who lived on Mt. Desert Island a long time ago were the Wabanakis. Their name means: "People of the Dawn." They said that the stars light the path for a person's journey after they die. If you are good, you will walk the good walk, which is lit by the stars so you can find your way to peace and happiness. Bad people wander under a black sky, where the stars can't be seen because of all the thick clouds. They spend their whole time wandering around blindly, never finding peace and happiness. The stars save us," asserted Edwin, matter-of-factly.

"What a nice story, Edwin. Thank you for telling me that."

"Lux is bad," said Edwin, abruptly.

"Well, he certainly doesn't treat others with much kindness. He's kind of a conceited jerk," said Aliya.

"I do not like the way he looks at you," stated Edwin in a very serious tone.

Hmm, thought Aliya. Edwin had noticed this too?

In the days that followed, Aliya often met up with Edwin on the quad at the end of the workday. She told him more about Aaron and Cassie, and her mom and dad, and about how much she dearly missed them all. He told her about his job, about his tricks for not letting the mice escape when he changed their cages, about how he needed to read the notches in their ears to determine their identification number, and about how important it was to turn the knob on the timer for the room lights so the mice were kept on a twelve-hour day/night schedule in their windowless rooms.

Aliya was also starting to get to know the other graduate students who worked at ARC Labs. One Friday, her new acquaintances convinced her to join them at a bar in town to celebrate a birthday. Aliya never went out socially, as she was determined to finish her project and get back to Aaron as soon as possible. The only things she allowed herself to do outside of her lab work was to get regular exercise by going to yoga classes and on frequent runs on the carriage trails through Acadia National Park. But she reluctantly joined them that evening, telling herself that she would have to get a bite to eat at some point. She also had met the researcher whose birthday it was through Edwin. He was a friendly guy who always treated Edwin respectfully. Edwin considered him a good friend.

The Acadia Brew Pub was packed with sociable ARC researchers. Aliya began to relax and enjoy the festive atmosphere, mingling and fitting in well with the others as the time flew by. She did not see Dr. Lux sitting with other staff scientists at a table in the corner, nor did she know how much he had been drinking. He approached her and put his hands on her upper arms.

"Aliya, you look ravishing, as always," he said as he moved too close to her, blatantly staring at her breasts. Aliya was immediately taken aback by his salacious behavior. He pulled her closer and whispered in her ear. "You know, someone like me can be very helpful to you in the world of science. I can make or break careers. If you are good to me, I will be good to you. What goes around, comes around, Aliya," he said, arrogantly, as he slid his hands down her arms and grasped her wrists tightly, jerking her even closer to him.

For a moment, Aliya was in such shock, she didn't know what to say or do. Edwin came out of nowhere. "You shouldn't do that," he said, as he stepped his large body between Aliya and Lux, placing his face a couple of inches from Lux's. "You should NOT do that!" he repeated, as his face reddened and the veins on his neck began to bulge. Lux realized Edwin could, and would, rip him to pieces. He lifted his hands in concession.

"Okay," Lux said as he stepped away and exited the bar, seething with anger at both of them.

Aliya stood, trembling, not sure what to do next.

"Come on, LeeLee," Edwin said calmly. "I will walk you home."

Aliya had regained some of her composure by the time they arrived at her apartment. Edwin did not enter. "Thank you, Edwin," she said, giving him a hug.

"Don't worry, LeeLee. I am very good at looking after the sheep and the mice. I will look after you too," he said solemnly.

Aliya closed and locked the door before she collapsed on the couch. She put her head in her hands and began to sob. After several minutes, she collected herself. She picked up her phone and texted. "Hey, got time to talk?"

Julie happened to see the text immediately "Sure. Want to FaceTime, as usual?"

"No," texted Aliya, whose eyes were red and puffy. "Call when ur ready."

When Julie called, she could immediately detect the strain in her friend's voice. "Liya, what is it?"

"I just really miss everyone. I want to come home."

"Well. Why don't you? Can you grab a flight tonight or tomorrow? Or just jump in the car first thing in the morning. You've always been an early riser. You could be in NYC by early afternoon."

"I mean I want to come home for good," said Aliya, dejectedly.

"Oh. I see." Julie paused. "Well, why don't you just start by getting out of there this weekend?"

Aliya sighed. "I can't. Aaron's got his first set of major exams this week. He is totally stressed. If I come home, I know I'll just distract him."

"I'm sure you would," quipped Julie. "Oh, I'm sorry, Liya. That just slipped out. Then just come see me." Julie was staying in New York the summer after graduation to study for the CPA exam before starting her job as a financial advisor in Chicago in the fall.

"I actually can't do that either. I'm on call this weekend."

"What do you mean 'on call'?"

"Each weekend, someone has to stay close to the lab in case something causes our minus eighty degree freezers to go down. This is where all our specimens are preserved. An alarm will go off that alerts the security guards. The freezers are connected to a battery backup, but that only lasts twelve hours, so one of the lab personnel is responsible for moving the samples to another cryopreservation system so that they are not lost forever."

"Hmm. Bummer. You sure you're just homesick, Liya? My Spidey-sense is telling me there is more to this."

Aliya let out a deep sigh. "Well…" she said, as she began to relate what had happened at the brewpub.

"Jesus, Aliya! Why didn't you tell him off?"

"I was so flabbergasted; I didn't know what to say."

"Okay, I'll tell you exactly what to say. Say: 'Get your grubby hands off me, you motherfucker!'"

"I can't say that to him! We were right there in the bar, and there were other people from ARC Labs all around. He's one of ARC's top scientists. Hell, he's one of the world's top scientists! This isn't New York, Jules."

"I'm on the next flight. You need a dose of 'Julie therapy,' my friend. Oh, and by the way, do you still have that voodoo doll you picked up in NOLA?"

Aliya glanced at the bookshelf above her desk. "Yeah."

"Good. Because I'm gonna stab the hell out of good ol' 'Drew Voo-Doo' as soon as I get there!"

CHAPTER 28

Naming

Julie caught an early flight out of LaGuardia and arrived in Bar Harbor late Saturday morning. Aliya felt better after a night of sleep and was a little embarrassed that Julie had felt the need to drop everything to come to visit her. Still, she was really happy to see the familiar face of her good friend. She knew the more "Julie" she had in her life, the better it got.

"Wow, it's really cool here," said Julie, as the two friends sipped coffee and enjoyed their fresh blueberry muffins at the quaint café overlooking Frenchman Bay.

"Yeah, it is a beautiful part of the country. I do love the natural surroundings." Aliya let out a long sigh. "What am I going to do, Jules?"

"What do you want to do? I mean, really want to do?"

"I really want to finish this project as soon as possible and get back to New York so I can be with Aaron every day."

"That's what I thought you would say. How is your work going? Is it progressing?"

"Yes. It is. It's amazing how quickly you can get things done when you have everything you need at your fingertips. I don't even have to make or autoclave my own solutions, or pour my own plates, or, God, do just about anything that a technician can do. To get supplies, I just submit a request online, and an ARC worker delivers them to our lab from their central processing center, literally in minutes."

"Sounds like you've made it to 'The Big Time.'"

"Yup."

"Then you should stay," Julie asserted. "You're an expert at handling creepy guys. What number were we up to in New York?"

"Oh God, like thirty, I think. The most recent was that A-hole we met at the concert at Barclays in Brooklyn."

"Oh yeah, that guy! How could I ever forget him? You sure know how to attract the psychopaths, Aliya," Julie said, rolling her eyes. "One more thing … while I'm here, you need to take the weekend off. I know you, Liya, and I can tell you need a little R & R or else you'll lose it entirely." Then she promptly summoned the waitress and ordered two extra-large mimosas.

"I think I've got a little buzz going," said Aliya as they walked up Main Street toward her apartment.

"Me too. Might need a little power nap before we venture out again," replied Julie, peeking at the store windows as they passed the many gift shops. "Looks like they are really stoked about their moose, puffins, and whales around here."

"That they are. And lobsters too."

"Mmm. Lobsta. That's what we need."

"I know just the place."

Later that afternoon, they stopped at a local store, picked up a twelve-pack, then drove through Acadia National Park, loudly playing and singing along to their favorite music, stopping here and there to see the sites.

"We do need to be a little careful. You can't have open containers of alcohol in public areas here," Aliya said smiling, as her words made her think of Aaron. They stopped at a makeshift wooden stand where fresh corn on the cob, potatoes, tomatoes, and other garden vegetables were being sold, as well as lobsters fresh off the boat.

"This is just like the produce stands on the corners in New York City during the summertime. Sans the fresh lobster, of course," said Julie.

They purchased a couple of large lobsters and a bag full of vegetables and headed back to Aliya's apartment. When they arrived, Julie decided they needed better drinks than just beer.

"Is there a store nearby?" Julie asked.

"Yep, only two blocks away on your right. I usually just walk there. It has everything."

"Such as tequila and limes?" asked Julie.

"Absolutely."

"I'll go get what we need and be right back."

"Sounds good," said Aliya. "I'll start cooking."

Aliya went outside to the backyard to tend to the lobsters, corn, and vegetables that she had put on the grill, brushing the veggies with olive oil, then sprinkling them with freshly grated parmesan. When Julie returned, Aliya went back to the apartment and found Julie with a goofy smile on her face, holding both hands behind her back.

"Aliya," she sang, as her smile grew even wider. "I have a surprise for you."

Julie held out an adorable kitten that was not much bigger than the palm of her hand.

"Oh my God! Where did you get that little baby?"

"Isn't he precious?" said Julie. "On my way to the store, there was a sign that read 'Free kittens to a good home.' I just walked right by it. But on my way back, they actually had them out. And this little guy is so cute, I couldn't pass him up. He will be perfect for you, Aliya. Cats are really easy to take care of. And you're so lonely here. He'll make a great companion for you. Besides, he needs you."

Julie had made a convincing case, and the kitty was incredibly sweet and lovable. He was mostly black with gray stripes and had a fluffy white chin and belly, with a white "sock" on each foot. His eyes were a brilliant blue.

"He sure loves to purr," said Aliya, as she held him on her chest, gently stroking his fur.

"It means he loves you. Will you keep him?" Julie asked.

"Of course I'll keep him. Thank you," Aliya said with heartfelt sincerity.

"Just some of my 'Julie' therapy," said Julie, as she made a pitcher of very strong margaritas. "What are you going to name him?"

"Um. I don't know."

"I think we should keep drinking. I'm sure that will help us come up with a good name," Julie reasoned.

"Good plan."

As they drank another of Julie's potent margaritas, their suggestions for names became more and more absurd.

"How about 'Kit-cat'?" asked Aliya.

"No. That makes me think of candy you get at Halloween," replied Julie. "How about 'Nard cat,' you know, like 'Nard dog' from *The Office*?"

Aliya and Julie burst into laughter, clearly feeling the effects of their day-long drink fest.

Julie grimaced, "What's that smell?"

"Oh shit! I forgot about all the food on the grill."

The food was burnt to a crisp. Instead of the lobsters turning a bright red, they were so badly charred that they were now completely blackened with stripes of gray ash.

"Wow. Those lobstas sure look crispy," said Julie. "They are actually the same color as the kitty."

"Maybe we should name the kitty 'Crispy,'" Aliya offered.

"No, that's not 'bougie' enough."

"Hmm," said Aliya, giving it some more thought. "How about 'Cris-purr,' since he purrs so much? And to make it extra bougie, I'll spell it: K-r-i-s-p-r."

"I love it! And it goes well with your other child's name, Cassie."

"Yes. Krispr and Cas. It has a nice ring to it," agreed Aliya.

Julie passed out on the couch with Krispr curled up next to her. Aliya stumbled into her bedroom and slept soundly for a few hours, but awoke in the middle of the night, parched. Thankfully, at some point, Julie had strategically placed water bottles next to where they each would sleep. Aliya chugged hers down, but then had trouble falling back to sleep. She decided to read for a while, hoping that would help her get back to sleep. Her notebook was lying on her desk, so she picked that up instead. It was open to the page of terms she had jotted down when she was trying to figure out what to call the new system she and Dr. G had discovered. She had already decided that "proto-spacer adjacent motif" could be abbreviated as: PAM. But what about the other terms? She started to list her ideas next to each term.

trans-activating RNA: tracrRNA

single guide RNA: sgRNA

regulatory: reg or just R

clustered: cl or just C

short palindromic repeats: S-P-R

protein?

interspaced: I

It practically jumped off the page at her: Clustered Regulatory Interspaced Short Palindromic Repeats or CRISPR! And who was Krispr's big sister? Cas, for CRISPR-associated, which was exactly what her protein did: it associated with the CRISPR sequences in bacteria. Perhaps she should make it more 'bougie,' thought Aliya. She titled her page: "KRISPR Cassiopeia: A Novel System for Precise Gene Editing."

CHAPTER 29

PAM

Time passed quickly that summer. Aliya and Aaron spoke each day, but Aliya decided not to tell Aaron what had happened with Lux at the Acadia Brew Pub. She would tell him, someday, just not while they were still living apart. It would upset and worry him too much. Every two to three weeks, either Aliya or Aaron would travel so that they could spend the weekend together. It was never enough. They missed each other tremendously. Their reunions were as rapturous as their goodbyes were heart-wrenching.

Aliya also dearly missed her family. Although she knew her parents would be overjoyed to see her and would love to experience the natural beauty of Maine, her dad would not be able to handle the travel and the unfamiliarity of a new setting, and her mom would not leave him under the care of someone else. She and Aaron had planned to visit them at the end of the summer for her dad's birthday. She could hardly wait to see them.

Aliya did her best to avoid Lux as much as possible. It was clear that he was bitter about her refusal of his advances, even more so because she dissed him in the presence of his colleagues, and was infuriated by Edwin's defense of her and his watchful eye, particularly because now Lux was held accountable by the type of person he abhorred the most in this world—in his view, a fat, ignorant retard. Aliya noticed that Lux seemed to be growing even more irritable and abrasive each time she saw him.

"How times have changed. It used to be that the female researchers were all … um … well, rather dowdy," remarked Lux's companion, a much older staff scientist, as they sat drinking coffee in the atrium. Aliya was walking in their direction, not quite close enough to hear their conversation.

"Yes. She is quite attractive." Lux replied. His glare was piercing as he salaciously looked her up and down.

"Aliya, do join us. I'd like you to meet my colleague," Lux said as she approached.

Aliya could see right through Lux's façade. He knew there was no chance in hell she would join them.

"Oh, I wish I could. But I've got to get to my restriction digest before the DNA degrades. Maybe another time?"

Lux continued to glare at her, nodding slightly.

She kept walking, as if the exchange didn't bother her. But it did. Fortunately, her ongoing friendship with Edwin, and the fact that her experiments were proceeding beautifully, were her saving graces at ARC Labs, giving her the will to continue, regardless of her prickly relationship with Dr. Lux.

Aliya joined Dr. G at a corner table and began to update him on her progress.

"I've been able to effectively edit the genes we chose, the ones we believe are involved with Alzheimer's Disease, in the cultured embryos."

"That's great, Aliya. And you used the embryos from the offspring of the mice that are models for Alzheimer's Disease, right?"

"Yes. The strains I used are from mice that have abnormal brain pathology—plaques and tangles, and from mice that exhibit the classic symptoms of Alzheimer's, such as memory impairment and confusion. Now I need to implant these genetically engineered embryos into the uterus of the surrogate mothers. If I have corrected the genes that cause Alzheimer's, the mouse pups that are born should not exhibit symptoms of the disease."

"Exactly. This will enable you to precisely determine the effect of the specific genes you targeted on Alzheimer's Disease. We'll then be able to use this knowledge to advance the treatments for it."

"That's the plan," Aliya said with a smile. "I've got to get back to the lab now. I'll see you later."

Before going to her lab, she decided to stop in the room where her mice were housed. One would never guess there were hundreds of rodents in this room by the aseptic smell of it. Edwin always kept everything so clean and organized, she thought. She walked up and down the rows of cages, shelved on tall, shiny stainless steel movable carts. Everything was in order. She stopped at the cages that had "Arc" written on their cage card. Per Dr. Gustaffason's suggestion, the first gene she decided to edit encoded for the activity-regulated cytoskeleton-associated protein (Arc). What a coincidence, she thought. This gene had the same acronym as this research facility.

From the journal articles Dr. G had suggested she read, she learned that the Arc protein played key roles in synaptic plasticity, memory formation, and learning and is also associated with the generation of beta-amyloid, a protein that forms plaques in the brains of individuals with Alzheimer's Disease. She decided she would edit this gene in mouse embryos not only by knocking it out in mice that had a mutation in it but also by knocking-in the correct version and over-expressing it, potentially producing mice with better memory. Once these engineered mice were old enough, she would subject them to a number of tests, such as the Morris water maze.

She reviewed the experimental methodology in her mind: mice swam in a tub of water until they found a platform that resided under the surface of the water. Because a mouse's eyes were on top of their heads, they couldn't see the platform but would find it eventually. By remembering its location, control mice with normal memory function would swim to the platform readily the next time they were tested. Mice that had impaired memory would not.

She peered into the cage. The mice looked well. They would be old enough for testing soon. She went to her lab and gathered the reagents and instruments she needed for her next experiment. When she was ready, she sat straight and tall as she looked through the eyepieces of the state-of-the-art Zeiss inverted microscope, skillfully injecting her KRISPR Cas constructs into the minuscule embryos. Many hours had passed before Dr. G entered and asked if she could take a break from her work.

"Lux is really agitated. He wants to meet with us right away in the conference room."

Dr. Lux was sitting with three of his top research associates, who looked quite nervous. The mood was tense. Lux didn't greet them, just proceeded with his rant.

"Your supposedly 'revolutionary' system fails the foremost test of science. It is not reproducible!" Lux said angrily. Then, glaring directly at Aliya, he said with the utmost vitriol, "You have failed enormously, Aliya."

Aliya felt her blood boil. She was exasperated. "Hey! My experiments work," she said vehemently. "Perhaps your fine technicians here don't know how to follow a protocol." Aliya immediately felt bad about taking out her abhorrence for Lux on his research associates. They were all highly skilled PhDs who probably hated working for him. She would apologize to them later.

Before tempers flared any further, Dr. G spoke up. "There's probably just something trivial that has been overlooked. Let's go through the protocol and troubleshoot. I'm sure we'll have this issue resolved in no time," Dr. G said, in an attempt to placate the others.

Aliya shook her head. Her face was warm and reddened. She felt absolutely no desire to help them. Dr. G gave her a pleading look. She rolled her eyes, let out a big sigh, and then painstakingly began to examine each and every step in the process of using her system to edit a gene, asking the research associates to explain every detail of what they did.

"Did you use sterilized, distilled water in your solutions?" asked Aliya.

"Of course they did!" replied Lux indignantly, as he continued to glare at Aliya.

Dr. Gustaffason's many years as a scientist made him a skilled observer. He sat back and carefully watched the exchange unfold. Something was not right. He had witnessed Lux losing his composure too often over the past few weeks. Lux was a prominent scientist with many ongoing successful research projects. While this one project did hold a lot of promise, it would not be the end of the world if it didn't work. It would in no way derail the massive success Lux had already achieved. Could it be that he was just angry at the thought of a lowly graduate student getting something to work that he could not? No, it was more than that.

As the others conversed, Dr. G took a scrap of paper out of his pocket and typed the words that were on it into the google search app on his phone. Aliya was mere moments away from saying: "Oh my God … I know what it is" when Dr. G abruptly sat up straight in his chair and closed out of the page he had opened on his phone.

"Aliya!" he exclaimed, looking directly at her. "We've got to go. You'll have to continue this conversation later. I just got a text from Aaron. He's been trying to reach you. It's an emergency."

Aliya's face dropped. "I hope it's not my dad."

Dr. G took Aliya's arm and quickly escorted her down the hall. When they were out of earshot of Lux, Dr. G said, "I'm so sorry, Aliya, but I had to do that. There was no text. There is no emergency. Come on, let's go for a walk on campus. Be sure to look upset."

Aliya was totally confused. But she trusted Dr. G, so she played along.

"I just needed to get you out of there quickly. You were just about to tell them about the proto-spacer adjacent motif, weren't you?"

"Yes. That's exactly right. I must not have included the information about how the genes they choose to target need to have a PAM sequence nearby. Since it's bioinformatics, it's not really a part of the main protocol, which describes the actual work that is done in the laboratory, such as the steps to purify the protein." She paused, still fully confused.

"But why on earth did you do that?"

"Because, as I watched everything unfolding in the meeting, how upset Lux was, how nervous his research assistants were, something just didn't seem right. Then I remembered seeing these words stenciled on a broken-up crate in the back corner of Lux's lab earlier today. Dr. G handed Aliya a scrap of paper from his pocket with the words he had jotted down earlier: *Khrupkoye*; *Obrashchat'sya ostorozhno*; *Embrion cheloveka*.

"No clue," she said. "Maybe it's some Eastern European language?"

"That's what I thought too, so I googled it." He handed her his phone.

"Human embryos?" Aliya questioned.

"Yes. It's Russian. And the other words mean 'Fragile. Handle with care.'

"He wants to use KRISPR Cas on human embryos? That's totally unethical. He'll never get approval for that."

Dr. G pursed his lips. "I don't think he plans to seek approval."

When they returned, Lux was waiting for them at the building entrance.

"Is everything okay, Aliya?" he said in a genuine tone, sounding as if his concern was sincere. "What was the emergency?"

Aliya was caught off guard at first but then said convincingly, "Well, you know my dad has Alzheimer's, but he seemed to be experiencing chest pain. So, my mom rushed him to the hospital. Once they got him all checked out, it turned out just to be indigestion. So, he's okay now."

"I'm glad to hear that," said Lux, keeping up his facade. "It's getting late in the day, and I have an important meeting to attend, but I would like to continue troubleshooting with you and my research associates first thing tomorrow morning. We'll meet in the conference room at 8 a.m. sharp," he said, as he left them.

"Good work. Way to think on your feet," Dr. G said to Aliya, quite impressed.

"He sure can be a Dr. Jekyll, Mr. Hyde. He was nicer than ever just now."

"That's because we are the only ones who know what he desperately wants to know. That is why we must never tell him."

Aliya shook her head in agreement and smiled. "I'm going to have a lot of fun 'troubleshooting' with them tomorrow," she said sarcastically, planning to take them on a wild goose chase.

Lux returned to his office and put his "Do not disturb" sign on his door, which was usually reserved for when he was writing a grant when a deadline was looming. But this time, he made a long-distance phone call.

"It's the girl, señor. She's incompetent. Her work is not reproducible," Lux said into his cell phone. "I know we are behind schedule. The girl had a family emergency today, so we had to postpone the rest of our meeting until tomorrow. But don't worry. I will get to the bottom of this."

"I see" was all Vicente Cristof said before turning off the speaker and disconnecting the call. He sat back in his chair and folded his arms. "What does Alejandro say about all of this?" he asked, turning to his assistant, Luis.

"Al, as he is called in the laboratory, insists that he and the other 'research associates' are meticulous in their technique. And I have no reason to doubt him. He is one of Mexico's finest scientists. He believes there is something that the old man and the girl are not telling them."

"Well, perhaps we will need to find a way to make them share their little secret with us," said Cristof. "Tell me about the old American scientist. Does he have a family?"

"No, he is a childless widower. He devoted his life to science. We can try to get him to talk, but he is old with no family. He doesn't have much to lose if he if chooses not to acquiesce."

"He is expendable, then," said Cristof, shaking his head slightly. "But the girl. She has more at stake. Tell me, Luis, what was her family emergency today?"

Luis thought for a moment, a bit perplexed. "We are watching her family closely, and my men report to me every day. They would have told me if anything unusual had happened with the girl's husband in New York, parents in Ohio, or sister and brother-in-law in Chicago. But I will check with them again, to be sure."

"Hmm," said Señor Cristof as he stroked his chin. "I see."

CHAPTER 30

Edwin's Elephant

As Aliya headed out for the day, she was happy to see Edwin sitting on the bench in the quad, swaying to the music coming from his earphones. He had told her he had a special surprise for her and asked her to meet him there. He took his earphones out when he saw her.

Before she had a chance to even say hello, he said, "Surprise!" and handed her a large box with a red bow.

"Oh, thank you. But what's the occasion? It's not my birthday."

"I know," replied Edwin. "It makes me happy, so I thought it would make you happy too. I can see how sad you are some days because you miss Aaron and Cassie and Ellie and Matthew and Sara and Mark and Julie. Open it!" said Edwin, hardly able to contain his excitement.

Aliya pulled a beautiful white sheepskin from the box. "Oh my goodness. It's lovely. Absolutely lovely," she said genuinely, with her radiant smile.

"It's from my very best sire of all time," Edwin said of his prized possession.

"Oh, but Edwin. I can't accept this. It's too special to you. I don't feel right about it."

Edwin's large smile turned into a large frown, and Aliya knew immediately that she had said the wrong thing.

"Actually, I do really love it and would like to keep it. It will bring me so much happiness while I am here in Maine. But maybe when I am done with my work here, I can give it back to you, since it means so much to you."

"Okay," said Edwin, thinking that was a very reasonable plan.

"And I have good news for you too! I was looking on the internet, and Christina has announced her next tour."

Edwin looked confused.

"That means she will be traveling around the country playing her music at concerts for people. She is coming to Bar Harbor this fall."

"When all the leaf peepers come?" asked Edwin.

"Yes, that's right. Hmm, it will be crowded here. Plus, she's at a small outdoor venue, the Acadia Amphitheater. Her concert will probably sell out quickly. I'll have to be sure to get us tickets the moment they go on sale." She glanced at the soft sheepskin on her lap, running her fingers through it. "And this sheepskin is so comfy. It will be perfect to put on the grass to sit on at the concert."

Edwin grinned in delight. Aliya had loved his gift, and he loved that he would get to hear Christina sing in person. It was his best day ever.

"Edwin, you take care of Dr. Lux's mice, right?"

"Ayuh."

"Do you know what projects he's working on?"

Edwin cocked his head, in need of some further clarification.

"Like, you know how I work specifically on genes for Alzheimer's Disease. I'm trying to figure out what types of genes Lux's lab works on? What are they related to?"

In addition to Edwin's responsibilities of cleaning the room and cages, and making sure the mice had fresh food and water, he also knew how to read the cage cards, which were color-coded and attached to every cage, providing such information as birthdates, the genetic strain of the mice in the cage, when the male and female were mated, and when new litters were born. In the labs he was responsible for, he had enough know-how as a sheep breeder to properly mate mice to yield the specific crosses the researchers wanted. He did not always know what the nomenclature of each strain meant in scientific terms, but he did know that Lux had a lot of different strains, representing all kinds of genetic permutations. Oftentimes, he would overhear lab conversations. He had a sense of what Lux was up to but didn't quite know how to articulate it.

"It's like the blind men in India that are trying to figure out an elephant," Edwin said.

"Okay…" Aliya replied, intrigued to see where this was going.

"You and Dr. Lux and his researchers are all trying to figure out what exactly an elephant is. Once you know, you can fix it … make it perfect. But you all have blindfolds on. You only feel one thing—the top of the elephant's head—and say that elephants are dry and wrinkly, but Dr. Lux and each member of his team feel a different part of the entire elephant. The person who feels the elephant's tusks says an elephant is smooth and pointy. The one who feels the ears says an elephant is thin, like paper. The one who feels the elephant's tail says an elephant is long and skinny. Get it?"

"Uh, no, I'm still not quite getting it."

Edwin just shrugged. That was the best he could do.

Later that night, as Aliya was lying in bed, she thought about how fond she was of Edwin and his child-like demeanor. She gave more thought to the silly parable that Edwin had told her earlier. It had absolutely nothing to do with anything. Or did it? She thought. Edwin may come across as slow, but he was not stupid. He was always very deliberate about what he said. He said what he meant and meant what he said. And he was very observant. So, she thought, I just feel one part of the elephant and am focused on that, but Lux and his research team are feeling every part of the elephant, so they know about the entire elephant. But why? Why is that important? she pondered, as she drifted off to sleep.

CHAPTER 31

Heartbroken

The Bar Harbor summer was winding down. Aliya was preparing to go to London with Dr. Gustaffason to attend the prestigious research conference he had registered them for months earlier. She had given Edwin a key to her apartment so he could stop in and take care of Krispr while she was away.

When Aliya finally made it to their departing gate, Dr. G had not yet arrived. She called Aaron, just to hear his voice one more time before her trip, telling him she would text him when they landed in London. As their boarding time was nearing, she texted Dr. G to see where he was. He did not respond. She called his cell, his home phone, and the lab. No answer. It was so unlike him to be this late. If he didn't arrive soon, he would miss the flight. She called the ARC Labs security number and explained who she was and the situation. A security officer checked their lab and Dr. G's office, but Dr. G wasn't there. She asked the officer if he could check to see if Dr. G had swiped into ARC Labs that day. He had, earlier in the day. Then she asked the officer if he could please examine the tapes from the security cameras that were positioned at all the entrances and exits to the building, to see what time Dr. G had left. This was a lot to ask, but Aliya knew this security guard, as well as all the other guards. She never hesitated to flash them her gorgeous smile when she entered the building or saw them in the hallways. She still had a touch of her New York modeling vibe, and she knew it. When working in her lab, she wore the typical white lab coat per ARC rules. But most other times that summer, she wore fitted, sleeveless tank tops (often cropped to reveal her belly button and a bit of her flat waistline) with her stonewashed, cut-off jean shorts that were frayed at the ends. Her outfits accentuated her fit young body, revealing her lean arms and long, smooth legs, showing a tiny bit of cleavage (not enough, of course, to be deemed inappropriate, but enough to draw attention).

All the security guards knew exactly who Aliya was and always enjoyed seeing their "eye candy." So, the guard agreed to do it for her. He started with the tapes from the main exit recorded just a few hours prior to their departure time, and lo and behold, the tape showed Dr. G leaving ARC Labs.

"I'll check the lot for his car, but I bet he's just late," offered the security officer. "Maybe he hit some bad traffic on his way to the Bangor Airport. As it's the end of the weekend, there are a lot of people leaving the island today, plus a lot of ARC researchers are headed to the same airport to travel to the conference. Don't worry. We'll be sure to follow up. I know Dr. Gustaffason is elderly, so we'll want to make sure he is okay."

Aliya was reassured to know that Dr. G had been fine a few hours earlier. The security guard was right. Dr. G was up in years and had been slowing down quite a bit.

Next time, I'll be sure to go to the airport with him, she thought.

She boarded the plane, assuming that Dr. G would have to catch the next flight out. She knew of other ARC scientists taking the later flight, so he would have companions during his travel. She would not have access to Wi-Fi until the plane reached cruising altitude but was sure he would respond to let her know why he was delayed. She put her phone on airplane mode and made herself comfortable, enjoying the extra space provided by the empty seat next to her.

Their landing at Logan Airport in Boston was delayed, resulting in her having a very tight connection for her next flight to London. She did have time to briefly check her phone, but there were still no messages from Dr. G. She texted him again and also texted Edwin, to ask if he had seen Dr. G. Edwin had not, but told her he was happily on his way to feed Krispr.

She worried about Dr. G but concluded he was probably just fine, likely occupied with the new travel arrangements he had to make. This was an important conference. She knew he wouldn't miss it.

Aliya boarded her flight to London. The airplane was larger and more spacious than the one she was on for the flight from Bangor to Boston. The overnight flight across the Atlantic wouldn't be so bad after all, she thought. She ordered a glass of wine with her meal, knowing it would make her drowsy. It wasn't long before the cabin lights were turned off, and she was fast asleep.

She was awakened hours later by an announcement over the sound system indicating they were on their final descent into Heathrow and directing the passengers to turn off all electronics and properly stow their items. Aliya inhaled deeply and stretched in her seat. She was delighted that she had slept so soundly during the entire flight and felt so rested. She pressed her face to the window and studied the towering buildings passing below, excited to be traveling abroad, as she had never done so before. With the five-hour time change, it was now early in the morning in London. She was ready for the day that greeted her.

When the plane arrived at the gate, she pulled out her phone. It had blown up with messages. The first was from Aaron. "Liya, call me ASAP. Terrible accident." The next several were from Edwin.

"LeeLee! Krispr is very sick."

"I found him lying by his food."

"He looked dead."

"I took him to my sheep vet. She is very worried about him. She thinks he ate poison. I told her you don't have any poison. It is awful. I am very sorry, LeeLee. I know this will make you very sad."

His next text read: "And your apartment was so messy. This is all so bad."

Aliya slumped and brought her hand to her forehead, covering her eyes as the other passengers exited. She was bewildered. She could tell from Edwin's texts that he was beside himself. Who would do such a thing, she thought in disbelief. She pulled herself together and walked up the jet way, following the other passengers directly to customs, which she passed through without a problem. She found the first open seat in the terminal, dropped her backpack on it, and called Aaron.

He answered immediately. "I'm so happy to hear your voice, Liya. Are you in London?"

"Yes. We just landed. I'm at the airport. Edwin texted me about Krispr. I can't believe it."

"What happened to Krispr?"

"Isn't that what you texted me about?"

"No. I have some very sad news. Dr. G had a terrible accident. He must have slipped on the rocks by Thunder Hole and was swept out to sea. They found his body late last night. I'm so, so sorry, Liya."

Aliya gasped.

"Aliya, are you there?"

Aliya could only whimper.

"I know. It's crazy. But the water is so turbulent there. I figured you'd want to come home, so I looked into flights. There are direct flights from Heathrow to JFK, but none anymore today. There is one that leaves tomorrow evening, your time. I can pick you up from the airport. Oh God, Liya, I'm so sorry."

Aliya's mind started to race. "Aaron," she paused for a moment to process before continuing. "Someone broke into my apartment and poisoned Krispr. Edwin found him. And there is no way Dr. G's death was an accident. He knew Thunder Hole could be dangerous and told me he stayed away from it."

"What?" he said, at first incredulous. Then it sunk in. "Holy shit, Aliya!"

"This is huge, Aaron! They will stop at nothing. Lux must be planning to use KRISPR Cas in human embryos. God only knows what he is up to."

"But why kill Dr. G? What has he ever done to them?"

"Because Dr. G and I are the only ones who know about PAM," Aliya said, realizing the gravity of the situation.

"If they murdered Dr. G, they will come after you. You've got to get to safety, Liya."

"Right. I need to at least get away from this terminal. They probably know what flight I was on. I'll call you as soon as I get somewhere else that's safer."

"Okay. Oh my God …" mumbled Aaron.

"And Aaron … you need to go somewhere safe too. Now."

"Okay, I will. I love you, Liya."

"I love you too."

Aliya moved quickly through the vast airport to another terminal and entered a single, handicapped restroom where she could be alone with the door locked. She pulled out her phone and saw that there was a message from an unknown number that she had not opened earlier. It read: "Do not mention your secret to KRISPR Cas to anyone at the conference. You are only to tell us ... or else the rest of your family—your beloved husband and sister—will end up like your mentor and precious pet."

Aliya immediately called Sara. She quickly told her what was happening and read the text to her, saying she and Mark needed to get out of Chicago right away.

"What? That's crazy. This is crazy. Are you sure this isn't just some kind of a joke that someone is trying to play on you? This shit doesn't happen in real life, LeeLee."

"Jesus Christ, Sara. Listen to me. This is no fucking joke!"

Sara gasped at her sister's outburst. She paused and took a deep breath, shaking her head as she tried to process what she had just been told. "This is so crazy." Her voice tapered off as she began to think straight. "LeeLee … why does the text say, 'the rest of your family,' but only says 'your husband and sister'? What about Mom and Dad?"

"Oh God, Sara…"

"Maybe they're okay. We would have heard if something was wrong. I'll call Mom and call you right back."

"Sara, call her from your car. You and Mark need to leave."

Minutes felt like hours as Aliya sat trembling in the cramped loo, filled with dread. Every drip from the leaky faucet loudly pierced the muted background noise that originated from the other side of the door. She glanced around the tiny room. Everything was mundane … white and silver: white walls, floor, toilet, paper towel dispenser; a silver mirror, faucet, and fixtures—almost paralyzing in its blandness, not unlike the profound fear that was paralyzing her.

Ellie did not answer the call from Sara. Sara looked at her watch. She knew Dad's home health aide had a key to her parent's house and should be arriving for his shift soon, but she didn't know his direct number. Mark was just about to suggest that they call the local police to check on Ellie and Matthew when Sara received a call from the police detective.

"I'm very sorry to have to tell you this, ma'am. The home health care employee found your mother in her bed this morning. She had passed away in her sleep. The fire department is there now and suspects that their heating and cooling system malfunctioned, filling the house with carbon monoxide. They determined that the battery in your parents' CO detector had not been replaced in a very long time, rendering it non-functional. We searched the house and are searching the neighborhood, but we haven't found your dad yet. The health care aide mentioned that he would occasionally try to wander, but said your mom usually kept a very close eye on him and he never got very far. Do have any idea where he might go?"

In her anguish, Sara could barely get the words to leave her mouth when she tried to tell Aliya the devastating news. Her sobs were uncontrollable. Mark gently took her cell and spoke to Aliya. Aliya strained to take a breath. The news was such a shock. It was unimaginable … her mom was dead? As it sunk in, she fell into a state of hopeless despair.

Mark looked Sara in the eyes as he spoke softly, but firmly. "Sara, we've got to keep moving." He handed Sara back her phone.

"LeeLee. Oh God."

Aliya slumped and ran her hand through her hair as her tears streamed down her cheeks. "I know. I know." She brought her hand to her forehead, trying to think … to make sense of it all. After a few moments, she said, "Fuck it. I'll just tell Lux and his goons about PAM. They can do whatever the hell they want as long as they leave us the hell alone!"

"LeeLee," Sara said, as she pulled herself together and tried to be as rational as possible. "Once you tell them, not only will they have no need for you anymore, but you will be a liability to them as long as you are alive. We all will be. They do not want any of us to go to the authorities and have there be an investigation. If we are going to live, we need to run."

Aliya's phone chimed. She had received another text from the unknown number. It read: "If you simply introduce us to your friend, Pam, we trust that you will not say another word about this (or you will regret it) and we will agree to leave you and your remaining loved ones alone."

Jesus, thought Aliya. They must be tapping her phone. How else would they have heard the word, PAM? After the meeting with Lux and his research assistants, when Dr. G realized they were up to no good, Dr. G had destroyed all the files he had on KRISPR Cas. The only information about it was kept on Aliya's laptop and in her notebook, which she carried in her backpack and kept with her at all times.

"Get to safety, Sara. I love you," Aliya said softly, as if in a trance. Then, in a fit of rage, she smashed her phone against the concrete floor. She picked it up and removed the SIM card, flushing it down the toilet, and threw her broken phone in the garbage can. She changed into the fresh outfit she had carried in her backpack in case her luggage got lost, pulled her hair up under her black New York Yankees baseball cap, and joined the throngs of people in the terminal of the busy international airport.

The two men initially had been waiting at the baggage claim for Aliya, as it would be much easier to get her to their car from there than to traipse her through the airport, even if they discreetly held a gun to her. But they had unknowingly just walked past her. Their focus was on the restroom and heading directly to it. Hacking into Aliya's phone had also provided them with her location. She had barely missed them.

CHAPTER 32

Taking Chances

"Mind the gap," said the soft British female voice over the sound system as Aliya boarded the Piccadilly line of the London Metro from the terminal at Heathrow. She had replaced her black New York Yankees cap with a navy Manchester United cap that she had purchased at a shop in the airport. She kept her head low and buried in a magazine as she rode the Tube, looking up every now and then to watch the scenery pass by and glancing at the lighted sign that rolled words which matched the gentle British voice announcing stops along the way: Hammersmith, South Kensington, Piccadilly Circus, Holborn, and finally, Kings Cross/St. Pancras. She purchased her Eurostar ticket and went to the Le Pain Quotidien in St. Pancras station as she awaited her train, glancing around intermittently and scanning the crowds to make sure no one had followed her. She ordered chai tea and an avocado tartine but could only pick at her food. Her appetite was non-existent. She boarded the high-speed train and discreetly took her seat, putting in her AirPods and burying her head in her magazine to avoid any potential small talk with the passenger seated next to her.

At speeds of up to 186 mph, the train passed through the channel tunnel in only twenty minutes but still had to traverse the scenic French countryside on its way to Paris. Aliya stared out the window as the train passed through the Thames Marshes and rolling farmland dotted with church towers and hilltop villages. She thought about all that had happened since she left Bar Harbor. It was surreal. Her heart ached. She needed Aaron.

She swore that she would find him and be with him again. That hope was all she had left. She prayed that he had gotten to safety and was still alive. But where would he go? Where would Sara and Mark go? Where could they go? And for that matter, where would she go?

She knew she had to get out of London and thought of France first because she had graduated with a French minor and knew the language. She thought it would be safer and less conspicuous to take a train than to try to fly out of Heathrow. She planned to stay in Paris and try to figure out how to contact Aaron and Sara, perhaps by way of Julie, then fly back to the States from France. She prayed Lux's gang was not watching Julie too, as Julie was her only hope of connecting with her family. But the last thing she wanted to do was to put her dear friend in harm's way.

She tried to focus. How would she ever pull this off? She squeezed her eyes shut, bent over in her seat, and clutched her arms at her belly. She was terrified.

The train pulled into the *Gare du Nard* station in central Paris, and Aliya followed the signs that read "*Sortie.*" She had decided to take a taxi to the city, where she would be less conspicuous in the midst of the myriads of locals and tourists. Being a New Yorker, she felt at home in the hustle and bustle of a big city. She decided she needed all the comfort she could get to help calm her frazzled nerves. Plus, she needed different clothing. She never retrieved her luggage at Heathrow Airport. All she had with her was her backpack, which carried only the one extra set of clothes that she was now wearing, her chargers, notebook, and her laptop. She exited the taxi in the shopping district and walked along the narrow street, unable to enjoy the charm of Paris, focused on her task of finding clothes and a hotel.

She worried that if Lux and his accomplices were able to hack into her cell phone, they could also track her credit card transactions. If so, they would know she purchased a Eurostar ticket and could catch up with her. She had some cash on her, which she exchanged for Euros, but it wasn't enough to pay for everything she needed. She would have to take a chance and use her credit card. She decided she would save her Euros to pay for the hotel, so that it couldn't be traced, but use her credit card to purchase food and a change of clothes, figuring that she would be gone from the stores by the time the transactions were posted, although they would know she was in the vicinity. It was a chance she had to take. She had no other choice.

CHAPTER 33

Sheep Meadow

Her eyes frequently darted from the page of her book to scan the landscape as she tried to look natural, like any other New Yorker relaxing at Sheep Meadow that warm afternoon. Her thoughts were fixated on her best friend. Aliya was always so passionate, so driven … even more so when it came to her loved ones. It was heartbreaking for her to witness her dad's decline, especially at such a young age. She knew Aliya felt compelled to use her knowledge and skill to help him. But what had she gotten herself into? This shit was real. Aliya and her family were in serious danger.

The waiting felt like an eternity. She fidgeted. She tapped her heel, then set her book down while she stretched and glanced around, only to pick it back up again and pretend like she was reading. A few moments later, she spotted them in the distance. She let out a deep sigh of relief. As they approached, the worry in his eyes and the paleness of his face revealed his overwhelming distress. She gave him a confident look and a nod, as if to say "We got this."

Cassie recognized Julie immediately. She wagged her tail and pulled Aaron toward her. They had not anticipated this. So much for being inconspicuous, thought Julie. As Aaron pulled Cassie away, his sunglasses fell to the grass. He picked them up, along with the car keys that had been left on the ground there. As Aaron and Cassie continued on, Julie couldn't help but wonder if they would ever see each other again.

CHAPTER 34

Paris

Aliya sat awake and alone in her dimly lit, musty hotel room. She was in the depths of despair. She grieved for the loss of her loving parents, for the loss of her beloved mentor. Her pain was practically unbearable. She tried desperately to change her thoughts to her present situation but could barely do it. She needed to find Aaron. She would do everything humanly possible to be with him again. But what about Lux? He had her mother killed. He had Dr. G killed. And where was her dad? Did they take him? Was he dead now too? She could hardly imagine how Edwin felt when he found Krispr in her apartment.

She wanted revenge so badly she could taste it. She turned the light on and began pacing like a caged animal in the small room. After a while, she plopped herself down on the bed, slumped over in silence in near exhaustion. She had never been very religious, but she was spiritual, in a yoga sort of way. She prayed for strength, for a solution. She glanced at the desk that was near the bed. There was a flashy tourist brochure with articles describing local attractions in Paris that month. One of the sub-headings on the cover read: "*Défilé de mode par Hai Pei.*" She let out a whimper and brought her hand to her mouth. All at once, the tension left her body as she whispered "Hai Pei." She took a deep breath and searched the depths of her mind.

"*Défilé. Défilé.* What does that word mean?" She rubbed her forehead as she struggled to remember. Then her smile grew wide, and she let out a small giggle as she brought her hand back to her mouth.

A parade. Hai Pei's parade.

CHAPTER 35

Hai Pei

The next morning, Aliya walked quickly down the cobblestone sidewalk, eyeing every shadow she passed. Paris was overflowing with culture, art, and beauty manifested by its exquisite gardens, grand fountains, wrought-iron lampposts, and centuries-old Parisian architecture. She noticed none of it. After several short blocks, she came to MONOPRIX, a department store on the *Av. des Champs-Élysées*. As she stood in line to purchase the items she had chosen, she saw a magazine with a drawing of a bizarre-looking Frenchman on the cover, along with the word: "*Tarrare.*"Something about it was familiar. She couldn't resist buying it. She went directly back to her hotel room, thinking it was safer there than being out on the streets where she could be detected.

Once back in her room, she pulled out the magazine. *Tarrare*—yes, she thought.It was the name of a man who lived in France in the late 1700s. She had learned about his freakish life story in a French history class. *Tarrare* was a showman in a traveling circus. It was said he had an insatiable appetite and could eat a meal intended for a dozen people in one sitting. He would eat anything and everything he could: garbage, stones, even live animals like puppies, cats, and snakes. He agreed to be treated by doctors and was hospitalized, but his ravenous appetite was uncontrollable. He was caught attempting to eat the corpses from the hospital morgue, and later expelled from the hospital when he was suspected of eating a baby. He died soon after.

Aliya looked away, deep in thought, and repeated the words: "His ravenous appetite was uncontrollable."

She powered on her laptop and began researching The Arthur R. Chester Laboratory website, scanning the numerous genotypes and phenotypes of the abundant variety of mouse strains that were housed there. She found many of interest, such as the *ob/ob* and *db/db* genotypes. *ob/ob* mice have a mutation in the obese gene, which encodes the protein hormone: leptin. *db/db* mice have a mutation in the leptin receptor. Both mouse strains have a similar phenotype: profound hyperphagia. She continued her research well into the afternoon, listing in her notebook several mouse strains with genotypes she was interested in. Next, she googled the extended weather forecast for Mount Desert Island. She gently nodded, whispering "perfect" to herself.

She emptied the contents of her shopping bag on her bed. Along with clothing, cosmetics, and a styling wand for her hair, she had purchased a fashionable black leather Goyard tote to replace her weathered backpack. She spent the next two hours transforming herself. When she left, she was donned impeccably in black leggings, a black crop top, and four-inch black heels, with perfect hair and makeup.

As she made her way down *Avenue George V*, she tried to look natural, to fit in. But her body betrayed her. Every muscle fiber was tense. She had an uneasy feeling. She sensed something was off.

She shot a quick glance over her shoulder. Two men walked briskly behind her, abruptly cutting through the throngs of people bustling about the city that busy Saturday afternoon. Her bloodstream flooded with adrenaline. They had found her. She turned onto *Av. des Champs-Élysées* and approached the magnificent, towering corner building flying the French flag from its golden dome. She entered the twenty-meter-high atrium with its hundreds of linear stems of polished steel descending along the circular walls, refracting the light from the magnificent chandelier. A debonair male attendant greeted her. "*Bonjour. De cette façon s'il vous plait*. This way please." As he escorted her to the top floor of Louis Vuitton *Maison Champs-Élysées*, she couldn't help but notice his polished golden Rolex and how perfectly it complemented the gold in his cufflinks and pocket-handkerchief. It had only taken one look for the attendant to presume that she was another one of the high fashion models who would be walking in the fashion show that evening.

She spotted him across the room. He had his back to her and was holding a pair of Louis Vuitton stilettos, comparing them to one of his glamorous gowns. The bright red on the underside of the shoes perfectly matched the red adornments on the traditional gold and black Chinese garment he was dressed in. She approached him and gently touched his shoulder.

"Aliya!" he exclaimed in surprise, recognizing her right away.

He tapped a kiss on each of her cheeks, saying: "*Bonjour*, what brings you to *La Ville Lumière*, my friend?"

"I'm in trouble. I need your help."

He immediately recognized the desperation in her eyes. Her once confident young voice was now weak and quivering. "Come, let us catch up in the office," he said, wrapping his arm around hers as he led her to a nearby room.

She tried in earnest to maintain her composure as she related her story. He listened intently, then frowned as he shook his head with revulsion. His face reddened as he scowled. "*Húndàns*!" He told her to wait in his office and took the elevator to the main level. He glanced around at the multitude of shoppers and when he returned, his frown had grown even more. "They are here. Many of them. They are very conspicuous. Their overwhelming lack of fashion sense gives them away," he declared in disgust. "I will help you, my friend," he said gently, with a reassuring smile. "I have a private jet at *Aéroport de Paris-Charles-de-Gaulle* and will take you anywhere. But we must first get you to the airport safely. It would be too suspicious if I send you on it without me, or if we leave now before the show. Come with me. I have an idea."

She followed him into a large room teeming with beautiful models, makeup artists, and hairstylists. He spoke briefly to the fashion manager, giving him explicit directions, then nodded to her affectionately as if to say "It will be all right." He turned to the group, cast his left hand into the air, and shouted, "Let the magic begin!"

After a few hours, he returned. He scanned the room, assessing all of his models. They were in various stages of dressing, some only clothed in their undergarments. Their hair and makeup were meticulous, crafted impeccably. Along with several others, Aliya wore a gorgeous wig that looked perfectly natural. These girls will look striking in my magnificent gowns and matching Louis Vuitton stilettos, he thought, well pleased.

"Hai Pei," implored the nervous store manager in a heavy French accent as he entered. "These men say they are from INTERPOL. They are here on special business, looking for an American woman who is very dangerous. I told them you could not be disturbed, but—"

Cristof's henchmen immediately began to inspect the room, scrutinizing every woman as the headman approached Hai Pei. Before he could address the eccentric fashion designer, Hai Pei screamed loudly in exasperation, tossing both of his hands into the air."Oh, and who has given you permission to be here? Can't you see these women are half-naked! Get out of my dressing room. Now!" Hai Pei commanded ostentatiously. "Or I shall have my bodyguards forcibly remove you!"

The leader glanced at his men, and they shook their heads in reply, concluding that their fugitive was not in this room. He motioned to them to leave, and with a furrowed brow, took one last glance at the women before they continued their search in other parts of the building.

Aliya sat perfectly still at the dressing table with her back to the rest of them as the intimidating men left the room. The makeup artist added more rouge to her cheeks, as the blood had drained from her face, leaving it white with fear.

"Show's over. Carry on," directed Hai Pei. "We have a performance to do tonight, and it must be extraordinary!"

Cristof's men had followed Aliya into this building and were certain she had not left it. They positioned themselves at the store exits and seated themselves in the audience along the runway, patiently awaiting the start of the fashion show held in the spacious private room on the second floor.

The beat began, and the strobe lights flickered. The audience was awestruck as the first gorgeous model stepped onto the runway and strutted down it. Thank God it all came back to her: the form, the walk, the stop and pause at the end of the runway, then the drop of the shoulder, a tilt of the head, a small step right, a small step left, a turn, and the strut back. Her gait was smooth and just the right speed. She was completely poised, graceful, and elegant—a true professional. It felt good to her, natural. Muscle memory at its finest, thought Aliya.

Cristof's men examined each model intently. Hai Pei's team had, indeed, worked magic. Aliya had been transformed. She strode right past them, incognito. She was the third model to walk the runway. There were still many more to come for the men to examine, giving her time to escape. Once backstage, she knew she needed to get out of there—fast. As she turned to rush down the back hall, an impeccably dressed, extremely attractive man came out of nowhere, stepping right in front of her and stopping her cold in her tracks. She gasped and froze, terrified that she had been caught, that this was the end.

"*Bonjour, Mademoiselle.* My name is Étienne …eh—Stephen," he said with a warm smile and in the most alluring French, as he extended his hand in greeting.

Unsure if he was one of Lux's accomplices, Aliya did her best to conceal her nervousness as she gently shook his hand and replied with her trademark gorgeous smile. "*Bonjour. Je m'appelle…* Christina."

"*Enchanté.* Please allow me to introduce myself. I am the personal associate of Werner Gerhard, creative director for CHANEL and Fendi. Werner is, in his words, '*amoureux*' … eh … enamored, by your beauty. He would be delighted for you to join him for a drink to discuss, eh, potential opportunities?"

Aliya knew exactly who Werner Gerhard was. Everybody did! How ironic, she thought. Where the hell was he five years ago? She smiled coyly, and using her best French, replied, "*Je serais ravi. Mais* *d'abord, permettez-moi de me rafra*îchir," which meant, "I would be delighted. But first, please allow me to freshen up."

"*Bien sûr*. Of course," Étienne said, again smiling warmly, clearly impressed by her flawless French. He bowed slightly as he stepped aside to let her pass. She quickly made her way down the back stairs, where Hai Pei was waiting. He took one look at her and said, "Breathe." It was then that Aliya realized she hadn't taken a breath in quite a while. They exited into a back alley where Hai Pei's driver was waiting.

"Fun fact," quipped Hai Pei. "Louis Vuitton always made sure his buildings had a hidden exit." As they pulled onto *Av. des Champs-Élysées*, it was not long before a car filled with Cristof's men sped behind them. Hai Pei's tone became serious. "They are onto us. We must lose them," he said to the driver.

"*Considère que c'est fait*. Consider it done," replied the driver, exhilarated to take on the challenge. He drove directly to the traffic circle around *The Arc de Triomphe*, where numerous boulevards converged. The traffic was insane, but Hai Pei's driver was even more insane, weaving in and out of the lanes like a Formula One racer. Aliya hung on for dear life, shifting in her seat at every swerve, holding onto the armrest so tightly that her knuckles were white. Cristof's men were no match to the skillful driver, who knew these streets by heart. He sped off without them.

Hai Pei's private jet was ready and waiting on the runway as they boarded it and quickly took flight. "You are safe now, Aliya. They have no way of knowing where we are headed. We can go anywhere," assured Hai Pei.

"It's not over yet," Aliya replied, as she took out her notebook. "May I borrow your phone?"

CHAPTER 36

Étienne

Richard Delaney turned his attention from his computer screen to the phone resting on his mahogany desk in his impressive corner office at the George Bush Center for Intelligence. "Yes?" he answered into the receiver.

"Special Agent Michael Conrad—Operation Golden Eagle is on the line, reporting from France, sir," responded his administrative assistant.

"I'll take the call."

"I followed the protocol to pose as a fashion representative so as not to alert the men from the Sonora Cartel. If they recognized the CIA there, they would have realized that we are aware of the increased chatter in their communications. She agreed to meet with me after the fashion show. She said she had to freshen up. I took that to mean change out of her gown. But then somehow, she got out of the building. There must have been a concealed passage because all the known exits were under intense surveillance by both our agents and the men from the cartel. We knew she could not have gotten far. The agents we had stationed on the periphery located her with a driver. They were being followed by the cartel. They went directly to the traffic circle at *The Arc de Triomphe.* Traffic was an absolute nightmare, sir," he said with frustration into his cell. "Our agents were gridlocked. They lost her. The good news is the cartel operatives lost her too. Their car was found at a local transit station. But there is no indication that she boarded any train. It's like she disappeared into thin air. We are continuing to monitor the cartel's communications. Will you have the French authorities close the borders?"

"No," Delaney replied. "That would draw too much attention. Especially if the press were to find out. They would certainly question why the French would do such a thing. We must be more discrete. Do you think the Sonora Cartel operatives identified you as an agent?"

"No, sir. They didn't recognize her when she walked the runway. When I spoke with her afterward, they were not present."

"The marked increase in chatter in the communications we've intercepted from within the cartel certainly sounds an alarm. We need to find out why she is so valuable to them. What secret does she keep?" Richard Delaney replied, as he stroked his chin and mentally began to formulate his next course of action.

CHAPTER 37

Adieu

Once safely in flight, Aliya used Hai Pei's phone to call Edwin. When she finished speaking with him, she walked up the aisle to return his phone. Hai Pei's seat had been converted to a comfy bed, and he was fast asleep. Aliya set his phone next to him and returned to her seat, exhausted. She unfolded it to a bed and entered into a peaceful slumber, feeling somewhat safe for the first time in days.

Hours later, she was awakened by Hai Pei. The pilot had told him that there were gale force winds along the Atlantic seaboard. It would be a rough ride into the Bar Harbor airport that evening. Did she still want to go?

Aliya nodded without hesitation. As Dr. Gustaffason would say, "The die was cast."

The Bar Harbor Airport was a small county airport with only two runways and no control tower. The highly skilled pilot made a masterful landing amid the powerful winds. While they waited on the plane, Hai Pei's personal assistant exited and went to pick up the rental car she ordered, using her own credit card. She was a former French model and was now Hai Pei's inamorata. She was tall, slender with auburn hair, and bore some resemblance to Aliya.

"*Merci, mon amour*," Hai Pei said to her when she returned. She handed Aliya the keys to the rental car, her credit card, and her driver's license. "For your journey," she said, giving Aliya a brief kiss on each cheek as she bid her adieu. Hai Pei and Aliya shared a long embrace. He stepped back, looked into her eyes, and smiled. "*Bon courage*, my friend. Until we meet again."

CHAPTER 38

Karma

Aliya drove to the Walmart in nearby Ellsworth to purchase the clothing and supplies she needed using Hai Pei's girlfriend's credit card. Before leaving, she stopped in the ladies' room and slipped her new blue scrubs on over her clothing, stuffing a pillow under her shirt. She put on the large black parka and pulled up the hood. The blustery island was enshrouded in darkness as she headed east on Route 3, arriving at ARC Labs shortly after midnight. She grabbed her bag and walked to the bench on the quad. She sat down and slid her hand along the underside, finding Edwin's ID taped to it, which she used to enter the door on the backside of the building. It wouldn't be unusual for the security guards to see Edwin on camera coming in late at night. As a lowly lab worker, he typically would be the one to do the grunt work that needed to be done at times that were undesirable to the research staff … weekends, holidays, nights.

ARC Labs was eerily quiet. There was not a soul around. Aliya went directly to her lab's mouse room and turned the knob for the timer that was located on the wall outside the room entrance. It controlled the lighting system in the windowless basement room, which had been on the dark part of the twelve-hour cycle prior to Aliya turning the knob halfway to illuminate it. She entered through the heavy stainless-steel door and immediately recognized the familiar smell of the mouse room as she set her bag of supplies on a nearby chair. It was a level two animal holding room with five large stainless steel shelving units on each side of the room. Each wheeled, movable unit had ten shelves on its front side and ten shelves on its back side. Each shelf fit eight cages. Edwin had diligently filled every open space, delivering one thousand, six hundred cages to the room, each with one restless and noisy mouse in it.

Aliya walked up and down each aisle, inspecting the cage cards attached to the cages. Racks were filled with cages of *ob/ob* and *db/db* mice strains, as well as mice with mutations in the genes: *MAOA*, *COMT*, and *5HTR2A*. Edwin had done a stellar job. Now it was her turn to get to work. If, as Edwin thought, that Ellie had passed down to Aliya her trait for beauty, Matthew had certainly passed his traits for ingenuity and resourcefulness.

She took the pulleys, hooks, and clothesline from her bag, grabbed the step ladder in the corner, and began to work *her* magic, starting by using the battery-powered screwdriver to secure the brackets into the ceiling and walls.

Once she completed her task, Aliya went to Lux's primary laboratory, swiping Edwin's ID badge in the card reader to gain entrance. She moved through the lab to where the liquid nitrogen cryopreservation storage tanks were kept and saw that they all were labeled except for one in the back. That must be the one with the human embryos, she thought. The tank was on wheels, so it was relatively easy for her to move it to the unused storage closet that Edwin had told her about in ARC Labs Building #1.

She returned to Lux's laboratory and entered the adjoining office. Edwin had a master key and had left Lux's office door unlocked for her. As a result of his skillful snooping, he also had learned Lux's computer password and had given it to Aliya. She sat down at Lux's desktop computer and typed in his password "LuxJason17!" and began perusing the files on his desktop.

When she opened the file named "*El Acuerdo,*" she discovered spreadsheet after spreadsheet entitled: "Data from GWA-Genome Wide Association Studies." The spreadsheets were lined with columns, accompanied by a brief description. The first page read:

Gene	Protein	Function	Potential Uses
ACTN3	Actinin	Fast muscle twitch: strength, speed	Athletes (Olympics), Mercenaries
ADAM-12	Disintegrin metalloproteinase	Neurogenesis (cell interaction)	Intellectuals, Academics
ARC	Activity-regulated cytoskeleton	Synaptic plasticity, learning, memory	Intellectuals, Academics
COMT	Catechol-O-methyltransferase	Hostility, physical agression	Mercenaries
CCNA2	Cyclin A2	Cell cycle regulation/mitotic rate	Accelerate development:embryo to adult
DRD4	Dopamine D4 receptor	Heightened sexual apepitite	Prostitution, Sex trade
FAAH	Fatty acid amide hydrolase	Insensitivity to pain	Mercenaries, Athletes (Olympics)
5HTR2A	Serotonin receptor 2A	Agression and criminality	Mercenaries
HMGA2	High mobility group A2	Tallness	Universally desirable
MAO-A	Monoamine oxidase	Violence and impulsivity	Mercenaries
MYRF	Myelin regulatory factor	Fast traveling nerve impulses	Intellectuals, Mercenaries, Athletes
NCoR1	Nuclear receptor corepressor	Increase muscle mass, performance	Mercenaries, Athletes (Olympics)

Notes:
Criteria for aggression:
-Easily provoked, abrupt attack;
-Disregard of surrender or appeasement signals;
-Frequent and high intensity assault, leading to significant bodily damage;
-Lack of normative behaviors; little consideration or misjudgment of opponent (age, strength)
-Significantly long bursts of violence

Aliya gasped when she was struck by the realization of what Lux was doing. Edwin's parable made sense to her now. I just want to know about one aspect, but Lux wants to know about the entire elephant. As Edwin said: "Once you know, you can fix it—make it perfect." Lux planned to use her KRISPR Cas technology in human embryos to edit the genome and increase the expression of genes that resulted in sought-after traits.

The embryos would then be implanted into the uterus of a surrogate mother, in the same manner that embryos resulting from in-vitro fertilization come to term. And by upregulating the cyclin gene, he would make the body cells race through mitosis and divide more rapidly, profoundly speeding development, essentially enabling a genetically modified baby to grow to an adult in a much shorter time period. Aliya felt her body tense up as the realization hit her. He was planning to use KRISPR Cas to create engineered embryos—engineered humans, to be sold on the black market!

She recollected a college course she had taken on World War II, where she learned about horrific eugenic experiments performed in Nazi Germany. White supremacy was on the rise these days, she thought. With KRISPR Cas technology, affluent parents would be able to make "enhancements" in germline cells that could be passed to future generations, thereby "designing" their own children … blond hair, blue eyes, high IQ, outstanding athlete. Looking at the spreadsheets, it was obvious that Lux was up to something even more sinister, with genes listed that, when mutated, were known to contribute to violent behavior. A shiver ran through her when she realized an intended use for her technology was to engineer genes in girls for heightened sexual appetite and then use them for sex trade and prostitution.

And where would it end? What would be the consequences? The rich and powerful would be the only ones who had access to this technology. Her mind replayed disconcerting images from a book she had once read, *Brave New World*, which portrayed a frightening dystopian world where people lose their individual identity and are under the total control of the dominant class. Deep in her heart, she knew this technology held so much promise for the treatment of human disease. It held the potential to alleviate so much human suffering, the kind of suffering her own father had endured: losing his memory, losing his sense of "self." But she realized that in Lux's hands, it was a curse.

He and his accomplices did not hesitate to murder kind, gentle … innocent people—Dr. G and her own mother. And what have they done with her father? Her technology was very much like the fire that Prometheus had given to mortals. It was a means to mighty ends, but at the risk of overreaching or unintended consequences. If she had held any doubts about what she was about to do, they were completely eradicated now.

Aliya, still dressed as Edwin, exited ARC Labs by the back door, ensuring that the security camera would show him leaving at that time. She returned Edwin's ID badge to the underside of the bench. Then she removed her scrubs and pillow and discarded them in a nearby garbage receptacle. She walked to her building and entered the main entrance, using her ID to swipe in. She went directly to her lab's mouse room and tried to summon her courage.

She remembered how her dad always had some saying or quote for just about any situation, especially when she needed encouragement. What would he say to her now? She smiled a gentle smile as the quote by Gandhi came to her: "Bravery is not a quality of the body. It is of the soul."

Lux was awakened by the chiming of his cell phone. "Yes?" he said, quickly becoming alert when he saw who the call was from.

"She has returned as expected," replied the gruff voice.

"Please, allow me the honor." He had waited a long time for this, he thought, lustfully. He was greatly looking forward to having his way with Aliya before arranging for her to have a most unfortunate accident, like the others.

Aliya was standing by a shelving unit in the middle of the mouse room, about halfway between the desk and the entry door, when Lux arrived. He relished how genuinely horrified she appeared when she saw him.

"Ah, I take it you weren't expecting me. Well, our little game of chase is over," he said, as he drew a gun from his belt and pointed it at her. "You have proven to be a formidable opponent. But alas, you have lost. You are not only beautiful ... and sexy," Lux said, as he moved closer to her. "You are smart, too. But you have one flaw, your unwavering loyalty. I knew you would return to save your precious friend, Pam, who holds the secret to KRISPR Cas. And now, you must tell me who she is."

Aliya looked directly at him, steadfast in her resolve not to divulge her secret.

"Have I mentioned to you that my accomplices took your dad and have found Aaron, Sara, and Mark? They are ruthless, those men. They are not opposed to torture. In fact, they rather enjoy it. You wouldn't want that, Aliya, would you? Spare your beloved family, and tell me about Pam." Lux paused before continuing. For a moment, Aliya considered, once again, giving up the secret to her KRISPR Cas technology. Then she remembered what Sara said, "These people are ruthless. Once they get what they want, they will not only have no need for us. We will all be a liability to them." Besides, Aliya thought, Lux hates me. He'll ensure that they are killed regardless, just to spite me. I have no way of helping them now. It's over. I am at the point of no return. She glared at him in the deafening silence, feeling both angry and broken at the same time.

"You think you are so righteous, don't you?" He snarled. "You will only use this technology for what you decide is good—understanding disease and developing therapies. But you can't be that naive. You must know it has so many other uses. With it, we can fulfill people's burning desires. We can have the *ideal*. We can have perfection. There would be no more deformities. No more suffering. No more ridiculing."

Lux looked vacantly off into the distance, seemingly no longer speaking to Aliya, but rather to himself. "My childhood would have been so different. So incredibly better. Jason, my brother. Born with such severe deformities. He was a … mutant. And the world is cruel to mutants. But if we had this technology, there would have been screens for embryos. He could have been helped. He would not have gotten so sick. He would not have suffered so much. He would not have been the object of constant ridicule. Every day was more heart-wrenching than the next. His medical bills bankrupted our family. I was young. I loved him but I didn't know what to do. I grew depressed … numb. I placated myself by indulging. I had no self-control. We lived in a poor neighborhood. It was a food desert. There was nothing of nutritional value to eat in our home. I became obese and was the object of endless bullying. I was miserable. But there was no way out."

Lux's eyes met Aliya's, his face awash with pain. "Jason died when he was seventeen. That was the turning point. That's when I changed my life. When I decided to become the man I am today. My brother had no choice. His destiny was fated by his genes. But I did have a choice. I would no longer be the outlier. I would be one of the beautiful people. Because the beautiful people go further in life than the others. They get what they want. I worked extra jobs so I could eat healthily. I exercised and became lean and fit. I studied hard and got into college with a scholarship. Even though I felt like an imposter, I became revered by others." Lux paused and gave Aliya a pleading look. "Don't you see, Aliya? With KRISPR Cas, no one will ever have to be imprisoned by their genetic make-up. No one will have to experience such suffering, such misery. We can free humanity with this." He looked at her intently. Then his usual demeanor returned, and his tone became arrogant and lustful. "We are both beautiful people, Aliya. It is only natural that you and I, together, should do this great thing."

Aliya shot a quick, nervous glance to the desk where her laptop and open notebook sat.

"Ah!" said Lux, turning his attention to the desk. He walked toward it, briefly turning his back to Aliya. She took a few steps toward the door. Printed in small letters on the notebook page was "PAM: Protospacer Adjacent Motif." Lux picked up the notebook with his left hand to look at it closer and abruptly dropped it back on the table.

"What is this shit? Isn't that dullard, Edwin, even capable of wiping off a table?" He wiped the syrupy substance from his hand on his pant leg and turned to Aliya.

Aliya harnessed all the vitriol that had been brewing in each and every cell of her body. "There was a time when I admired you, Dr. Lux. But then I realized what a sick, twisted bastard you are. You killed Dr. Gustaffason. You killed my mom. You've taken everyone I love from me. What goes around, comes around. YOU … MOTHER … FUCKER!"

She yanked on the clothesline cord that was wrapped around a bracket on the wall. It rose through a pulley on the ceiling and was attached to a mouse cage that hung from the ceiling directly above the desk. Pulling the cord caused the cage to tip, delivering a horde of mice to Lux's head and face. As Lux flailed around to throw the mice off, Aliya grabbed hold of another cord. This cord was connected to a pulley system likewise hidden on the ceiling that hung above each of the stainless-steel racks where the mouse cages were shelved. It was threaded through the lightweight, metal framework of bars that comprised the mouse cage lids. Using all her strength, Aliya pulled the cord to the floor, raising the lids on the one thousand, six hundred cages, enabling one thousand, six hundred voraciously hungry, vicious mutant mice to escape.

The mice used their keen sense of smell to quickly direct them to the sticky molasses-like, glucose/glycerol suspension on Lux's hand and pant leg, as well as the warm tasty flesh of his body, first finding the soft tissue of his eyes most accessible. They engulfed him like a swarm of bees.

Aliya quickly stepped out of the room, pulling the door closed. She punched in the code on the keypad next to the light dial, which, according to Edwin, was the standard operating procedure for locking down a room in the event of an emergency. Then she turned the dial that controlled the room lights clockwise, setting it to twelve hours of darkness. For a few minutes, she stood outside the door, emotionless, listening to Lux's screams as he was brutally attacked and eaten alive.

Aliya quickly walked down the hall and completed her last task before exiting the building from a nearby back door. Wind gusts ripped through the cool night air as she ran to her rental car.

She drove to the top of Cadillac Mountain. As it was the middle of the night, no one else was there. She sat on the same flat piece of granite that she and Aaron had sat on months before. As she looked out from the mountaintop, off in the distance she saw the flickering light of the lighthouse that resided on the coastal piece of land where Edwin's farm was located and felt relief. She revisited the past forty-eight hours in her mind. Aliya's plan came to her in her hotel room in Paris. She had learned about the *ob/ob* and *db/db* mutant mice in her college physiology course. These mice had insatiable appetites and served as mouse models for obesity. They were being used for diabetes research. When she typed "mouse models for aggression" into the ARC Labs search engine, a page appeared that described the criteria for aggression and listed the affected genes in the related mouse strain, indicating which laboratory used each strain. She was a bit surprised that Lux's lab housed most of these strains. Perhaps he was also studying mental illnesses that involved aggressive behavior, she surmised, not yet realizing what his true intentions were.

Her thoughts then turned to Edwin. When Aliya called him from Hai Pei's plane, Edwin had listened intently to Aliya's every word. She told him how sorry she was that he had to find her kitty, Krispr that way. Some bad people must be playing a terribly mean prank on her. She was also sorry about Dr. G, but said that he was now in heaven, reunited with his wife, who he had not seen for a long time. Aliya's words soothed Edwin. He decided if she was not sad, he should not be sad. He also offered to help her clean up her apartment, as it was so messy. Drawers were left open with their contents spilled out on the floor; her things were pulled out of her closet, and her books were scattered all over. She thanked him for his kind offer and told him that would be very helpful. But she did have another favor to ask of him. He was happy to oblige and said he would do everything she asked with great care.

Aliya told him she was about to begin a big experiment, in collaboration with other ARC researchers, and she needed his help. He wrote down her explicit directions so he would not make a mistake. He went to the mouse room used by her laboratory and removed all her mouse cages, placing them in an available room nearby. He replaced her cages with the ones he had gathered from various research laboratories at ARC Labs. Most came from Lux's lab. He made sure there was only one mouse in each cage and provided them with only water, just as Aliya had told him, so that she could begin a study on the effects of a fasting diet on Alzheimer's Disease. Edwin understood why she had only wanted one mouse per cage—starving rodents will eat anything, even each other. Edwin reminded Aliya that mice, unlike humans, can only go about two days without food, and so she would need to be sure to complete her study and feed them by then. Aliya assured Edwin that she would take good care of the mice and that they would be back in their own rooms before the researchers that studied them returned from the conference in London.

She also told him that he should not tell anyone about this experiment, as she wanted to get the results first. Then she told him she had an even more important secret for him to keep. She told him that she was leaving Bar Harbor and that no matter what anyone said, assured him that she would be safe. He should not worry about her. She would contact him sometime later. He said he was very, very good at keeping secrets and promised to do so.

She would not have time to properly say goodbye, so she asked him if he would set the light in his lighthouse to flicker rather than to remain lit continuously. This would be his way of waving goodbye to her. He happily agreed. This would also let her know that Lux's men had not gotten to Edwin too, and at least provide her with some solace. That was all she told Edwin. There was no need to tell him any more about what would transpire that night.

Aliya turned her attention from the flickering lighthouse and looked off into the distance in the direction of ARC Labs, able to recognize it by the glow of its faint lights. She recalled her orientation session where she learned about the history of the facility. It was founded in 1928 and named after Arthur R. Chester, a successful businessman and philanthropist. 1947 was known as "The Year Maine Burned." That summer and fall, Mount Desert Island received only 50% of its annual rainfall. It was the driest summer and fall on record, creating a virtually parched environment. On Friday, Oct. 17, Mount Desert Island was experiencing hurricane-force winds. The conditions were ripe for a catastrophic firestorm. To this day, no one knows the cause of the fire, but when it was finally extinguished, 17,188 acres had burned. The Arthur R. Chester Laboratory, with all of its straw-like mouse bedding, was perfect kindling for the fire. It burned to the ground in its entirety.

Aliya was still looking toward ARC Labs when she heard the first explosion, followed by another and another. Flames and smoke arose in the distance. The Arthur R. Chester Laboratory was once again succumbing to a disastrous blaze. But this time, the cause would be known: a very unfortunate gas leak. Before Aliya left the building that night, she lit a long piece of twine that she had soaked in kerosene, using it as a fuse. The end of the twine was attached to a Bunsen burner that sat on a lab bench, which was attached to an open gas line that was spewing gas, just like all the other gas lines that she had opened in her laboratory, as well as in Lux's lab, and all the surrounding labs in that wing of the ARC Labs building.

Tears flooded Aliya's eyes as she watched the inferno. It was over. Her plan had worked. Lux would die and along with him, KRISPR Cas. This revolutionary technology would never be known to a world filled with those incapable of restraining themselves from the insatiable need to gain wealth and power, no matter what the cost. It was a sacrifice she had to make.

Now what, she thought, as tears streamed down her cheeks. Her mom and Dr. G were dead, and she was certain that her dad, Aaron, Sara, and Mark would be dead too, just as Lux had said. She had no way of saving them. She couldn't bear to think of it. She was dying inside. Her thoughts turned to a class she had taken in college, called "On Death and Dying." She recalled the five stages of dying: denial, anger, bargaining, depression, and acceptance.

Somehow, she knew she needed to find the strength to endure the unendurable. She looked at the night sky one last time. There were no stars out that night. Not a single one could be seen.

Soon dawn would come. It was time for her to leave.

CHAPTER 39

This Cup

Aliya passed several fire engines with blaring sirens as she drove west on the narrow two-lane highway toward the mainland. She didn't know where to go, so she just drove and cried, until she had no more tears left to cry. She turned south onto Route 1, driving the same way, albeit in the opposite direction, that she and Aaron had months before when she first moved to Bar Harbor.

"Why me?" she questioned. "Why did I have to drink from this cup?" She felt a numbness like she had never felt before. Everything seemed so surreal. A song came on the radio. It was entitled: "Just Exist." She felt as if the lyrics were speaking directly to her at that moment. From now on, her life would be nothing more than a mere existence.

Aliya's breathing grew fast and deep. She clenched her fists on the steering wheel and banged her head against the headrest. The pain of her emotion was profound, agonizing. She swerved to the side of the road, threw the car in park, and ran aimlessly into the tall, wheat-like field that abutted the highway, eventually falling face forward onto the ground, disappearing into the high, golden grass. The dark night enshrouded her as she curled into the fetal position. She drifted into a trance-like state. Her memory replayed scenes from her life: her mother's comforting smile and warm embrace, she and Sara playing in the fort, slow dancing with Aaron the night they met, placing the plastic baby Jesus in her dad's strong hand…

How long she lay there, she would never know. She was aroused by gentle raindrops from the clouds that opened above her as the first-morning sun rays pierced the sky. A melody played loudly over and over in her mind, as if it were stuck there. It was familiar to her, but she just couldn't place it. She could not put a name to it. Then, all at once, an enormous calm set in. She felt comfort … tranquility. And that's when she realized what the melody was. It was the song she had chosen to play at her wedding when her dad walked her down the aisle. It was a song that belonged only to them. She got up, walked back to her car, and drove on.

A few hours passed, and Aliya's head began to nod. She was falling asleep at the wheel. In addition to her jet lag, she had been up all night. She was exhausted, both physically and mentally. She knew she needed to either pull over somewhere so she could sleep or to get some strong coffee. She saw a sign for South Westin. The name was familiar, but she could not remember why. She turned toward it. In a few miles, the brightly painted, red with white trim Whalen's Lobsta Shack greeted her.

"Sorry, honey, we don't serve lobsta rolls this early in the morning, but I've got some freshly baked blueberry muffins and delicious coffee. And you sure look like you can use some." She frowned in sympathy, noticing Aliya's bloodshot eyes and drawn face. "It's the best kind of coffee, grown in the Jamaican shade," she continued, trying to sound cheerful.

Aliya sat quietly at a corner table, sipping her coffee, lacking an appetite. The owner had the radio on, listening to the newscast.

"Did you hear about the horrible fire at that fancy laboratory in Bar Harbor?" said the nice lady to Aliya, who was her only customer. "I guess they were able to keep it contained to just a part of one building. Thank goodness. With the terrible winds last night, that fire could have taken out the whole island, just like the fire of '47." She turned up the volume as the fire chief was about to give a press conference.

"I am pleased to report that the fire is completely extinguished, thanks to the hard work of our many brave first responders. We have determined that the fire began in the basement of the east wing of Laboratory Building #5, and fortunately, we were able to keep it contained to that area. Overall, only two laboratories and their associated mouse housing facilities were destroyed. We suspect that there was a major leak in the gas lines that were connected to each laboratory, and that the fire was accidentally ignited by the flame of a Bunsen burner that was inadvertently left on. The blaze burned so hotly that nothing was salvageable. I regret to say that we believe that a male and a female researcher perished in the fire, based on the Chester Laboratory's records of the personnel who swiped into the building that night and their security camera footage, and who have sadly, not been accounted for. We are withholding their names until their next of kin can be notified. Due to the extreme temperature of the blaze, we feel it will be highly unlikely to recover their remains."

"Well, that's really too bad. And those poor little mice," said the lady as her voice trailed off. "I'll put some nice relaxing music on now." She changed the station to Sirius Internet Radio. "This is my favorite, the Acoustic Sunrise Program."

Aliya slumped in her seat, with a pained expression.

"Ah, honey. I didn't mean to make you sad."

"My husband and I always used to listen to this," Aliya said, as the tears welled in her eyes and her thoughts took her back to the leisurely weekend mornings spent in Aaron's apartment.

"Now this next dedication is really interesting," said the DJ. "It's for one of my new favorites by a young band out of Cleveland, Ohio called 'As Well.' This song is from their debut album: 'Awake/ Asleep.'Check out this awesome tune. It's called 'Cassiopeia.'"

The sweet-sounding melody began as the DJ continued, "It's dedicated to 'the beautiful lady from The Mountaintop of the First Light, from the boy who awaits her in The Land of the Lizards.'"

Aliya's eyes grew wide, and her mouth dropped open. The tears followed in droves, but this time, they were tears of pure joy. Although all she wanted to do was to drive, she knew she needed sleep. She stopped at a hotel and used Hai Pei's girlfriend's credit card to pay for a room. She slept soundly. When she awoke, she took a wonderful shower, ate heartily, purchased snacks, and filled her tank with gas. The direct route would be a twenty-seven-hour drive on I-95 South. But she decided to take a little detour on her way. She needed to send her friend a Thank You.

CHAPTER 40

Healing

Aliya held her hand to her forehead to block the bright sun as she walked barefoot down the beach, holding her sandals in her other hand, feeling the warm sand push up between her toes. It was vacant except for one solitary figure holding a fishing rod and a playful dog frolicking at the water's edge. The golden retriever abruptly stopped and stared intently at the speck walking toward them, before making a beeline for her. Aliya dropped to her knees as Cassie leaped, yelped, and licked her face.

Aaron's heart fluttered when he saw her. This wasn't a dream. It was really her. She was really here. He ran toward her, and the two soulmates embraced and kissed, flooded with emotion.

Aliya looked into Aaron's eyes and said, "You knew I would come." They held each other for a very long time before Aliya spoke again. "I thought Lux's people had you. How did you get away? And what about Dad, Sara, and Mark?"

"Sara and Mark are safe. Julie's been helping them."

"Oh, thank God," Aliya said, as her body filled with relief.

"But … they haven't found your dad."

Aliya's shoulders slumped and her eyes teared. She couldn't bear to think what had happened to him. He already was in such a fragile state.

"Liya, you look exhausted. You need rest. Then we'll talk more. Come on. I want to show you something."

Aliya melted into Aaron as they walked together down the beach to a path through the tall grasses that gave way to a wooded area shaded by palm trees. Aaron moved several large branches covered in palm leaves to unveil a perfect replica of her childhood fort.

"Ralph helped me make it," Aaron said proudly.

"It's … incredible!"

"Well, we added a few upgrades, like screens on the windows to keep the iguanas and mosquitoes out, and we put a lock on the door. Otherwise, it's pretty much the same. I learned a lot about carpentry. Ralph told me your dad always used to say, 'Measure twice, cut once.'"

"Yes, he did say that," Aliya said with a smile. "I love it." She gave him an impassioned kiss as they gently moved onto the thick sleeping bag that was strewn on the floor, making the most heartfelt love to one another before drifting off to sleep in each other's arms to the soothing sounds of the ocean waves.

Aaron awoke first and spent a long time gazing at Aliya's angelic face, relishing every contour of her natural beauty as she slumbered peacefully. Tears formed in his eyes. She had been through so much, he thought. More than enough pain for one lifetime. She would need time to heal. He vowed then to do whatever he could to bring her happiness for the rest of their lives.

Aliya awakened and noticed his tears. “Hey,” she said softly. “You okay?”

“I’m just so sorry, Liya … for everything you’ve been through.”

“I know,” she said, taking a deep breath. “Sometimes I think I’ll just wake up and this will all have been a bad dream. I thought you were dead, Aaron. It was the worst … I didn’t think I could go on.”

“I know, Liya, but I’m here now, and we are together. We will be together for the rest of our lives. I promise.”

Aliya found great comfort in what he said, knowing with all of her heart it was true. Moments passed in silence. Sadness engulfed her. “Mom and Dad are gone. I’ll never see them again. And I didn’t even get to say good-bye,” she murmured from the depths of her grief. Aaron held her tightly against him as she wept into his chest. Then she sighed and dried her eyes. “Where are Sara and Mark?”

“After Sara spoke with you, they left Chicago and drove toward New York. Julie met them at a truck stop along the way, and they switched into a car she rented, to throw off whoever Lux is working with, who they knew were trying to catch up with them.”

“Dr. G thinks … thought,” Aliya corrected, “that Lux is colluding with Russian criminals, since the words on the crate that carried the tank with the frozen embryos were in Russian. I think he’s right. Lux would have to be working with some pretty formidable thugs in order to be able to hack into phones and have people killed.”

“Makes sense,” agreed Aaron. “So, Julie took Sara and Mark to Seaside and laid low for a few days to make sure they hadn’t been followed. Then she booked them on cruise, and Sara came up with a plan to get off at one of the ports and tell the cruise director that there was a death in the family and they needed to fly to Seattle for the funeral, asking that their luggage be sent to an address there.”

"Why Seattle?" asked Aliya.

"She just picked Seattle. I guess thinking it's far away. She didn't want to underestimate Lux and his accomplices. They could have been bribing anyone for information or hacking into computer systems—who knows what they're capable of."

Aliya smiled and shook her head. "Sara's so god damn smart."

It was almost evening when Aaron and Aliya finally emerged from the fort. They headed to the ocean for a quick, refreshing swim, then Aaron started a bonfire, cooking up some of the fresh fish he had caught, and grabbing beers from the cooler he had placed in the shade.Aliya saw a figure walking up the beach toward them and gasped, trembling with fear.

"It's okay," Aaron said, putting his arm around her to calm her. "It's just Ralph." He comes by to eat with me and bring me supplies. He will be so stoked to see you."

The three relaxed on the quiet beach, eating and drinking by their bonfire as the sun descended toward the tranquil water. Aliya told them all that happened from the moment she had boarded the plane to London. They were both incredibly impressed by her resourcefulness—how she was able to successfully get to Paris and evade her formidable adversaries. Admittedly, Aaron was a bit shocked by the way in which she dealt with Lux. He didn't know she had it in her.

Ralph, who was naturally a bit rough around the edges, smiled as he thought, "She reminds me of myself. Don't fuck with me or my loved ones, or else..."

Aaron and Ralph related what they had been doing. When Aaron showed up at Ralph's doorstep and told him what had happened, Ralph did not hesitate to take him in. They decided it was best for Aaron to stay out of sight while they figured out how they would find Aliya, thinking she was still abroad. When the girls were young, Matthew and Ellie had named Ralph the executor of their will and never got around to changing it to Sara and Aliya when they became adults. Ralph went back to Ohio for a couple of days to look for Matthew, hopeful that he had in fact wandered the night Ellie died, and to arrange for Ellie's cremation. He closed up their house and put the McKennas' belongings in storage, knowing that someday Aliya and Sara would want to keep what was special to them.

Aliya's eyes moistened as she spoke with heartfelt sincerity. "Thank you so much, Ralph. I can't tell you how much I appreciate your taking care of everything at home." Then she smiled. "And also for building the fort here too. It's amazing."

"Building the fort provided a much-needed distraction, LeeLee. I was so worried about you."

"What will happen to our house now?"

"Well, legally, it belongs to me because your parents never changed their will when you and Sara became adults. I'm sure they intended to, but once your dad got Alzheimer's, that became their primary focus. I can't leave it to you now since you died in that awful fire," Ralph said with a wink and a smile. "I'll hold on to it and take care of it for you. But I'm not getting any younger. Do you know of anyone I can leave it to in my will?"

"We can leave it to Julie. She's my dearest friend. She's helped us so much. I don't know what we would have done without her. Plus, she's great at business and would be good at selling it. I trust her. She'll give us the proceeds when the time comes."

"I'd be happy to leave it to your friend. I'd like to leave my land with it. It goes well with your house. But there's only one condition.

I don't want my land to ever be sold to the developer, or any of his descendants who might take over his business someday."

"Oh yeah. I remember hearing that you didn't like the developer. Do you mind me asking why?" inquired Aaron.

Ralph took a deep breath, taking a moment to choose his words. "Because he's a real prick." Then looking at Aliya, he continued, "When I was first married, Breyona and I lived in South Carolina. When my parents passed, as an only child, I inherited the land in Ohio that belonged to my family for many years. At this time, the western suburbs were really building up as more and more people moved to what was once farmland. A developer bought up the land around my property and built these beautiful homes, making a really nice neighborhood that was a great place to raise a family. He wanted to buy my land too. My property was very valuable to him. He agreed to build a home for me at a much-reduced price if I would consider selling him some of my property. I told him 'Go ahead. I'll consider it.' So, he built a 'spec' home. This is when a developer builds a house but leaves it unfinished so that the new owners can customize it to their tastes—like choose all the cabinetry, floor coverings, paint colors, etc. This takes much less time than building a home from scratch. Breyona wasn't feeling well—of course, back then, we didn't know how sick she really was—so I made the trip to Cleveland by myself to check it out. I loved it. It was nicer than anything we had ever owned. I thought it would be a great place for us to raise a family. I told Breyona all about it, and she agreed that I should close the deal because at that time, the homes were selling like hotcakes. In fact, your dad and mom had already moved into your house. I met them that weekend and knew right away they'd be great neighbors. So, we put our house on the market, and then Breyona came to

Cleveland with me to see our new house and to start picking out the finishing materials."

"I'll never forget that day. It was hot out. Your mom and dad stopped over with lemonade and beer. The developer stopped by too. He took one look at Breyona and began saying the most heinous things. I was so pissed, I grabbed him and was about to pummel him when your dad stopped me. That guy was the most hateful, prejudiced son of a bitch I have ever met in my life. He couldn't bear the thought of allowing an interracial couple to live in his pristine neighborhood. To him, an interracial marriage was disgusting."

"He also thought this was sure to ruin his reputation and bring down the value of his homes. He tried everything he could to renege on the deal. But the contract was signed. He had no choice. He had to sell it to us but was certain to make life hell for us. He treated us like crap, both to our faces and also by intentionally delaying the finishing work on our house. It was a nightmare for us because our home in South Carolina sold quickly, and we needed to get in. In the end, your dad did all the finishing work, and it was done much better anyway. The thing is, everyone else in the neighborhood was white, and they were wonderful to us. They welcomed us with open arms. Not an ounce of prejudice. We had such a fun neighborhood. We were always having block parties and getting together socially. And all the kids played so well together. There was never any racial tension."

"It's shitty that, after all these years, there are still so many prejudiced assholes out there," replied Aaron, shaking his head. Aliya stared off into the distance in silence, feeling both saddened that Ralph and his wife had to go through all this and angry that this was the kind of world they lived in.

As the evening wore on, their bonfire dwindled. Aaron went to collect more driftwood to fuel the fire. Ralph waited until he was out of earshot before he spoke. "I learned something about you tonight, LeeLee," Ralph said, looking down at his fresh can of beer as he pulled the tab to open it before taking a sip. Then he looked to Aliya and continued, "You and I have something in common."

Aliya looked up from the glowing embers, locked eyes with him, and cocked her head inquisitively.

"We both see the value in poetic justice," he said as he nodded his head slightly. "When Lux came to the lab that night, you could have just locked him in the room and let him burn. But instead, you went to great lengths to have him pay for what he did by having his own aggressive mice eat him alive." He paused, then shook his head and smiled. "That's what I call poetic justice."

Aliya returned her gaze to the dwindling fire, knowing he spoke the truth. She thought back to the day Lux taught her how to 'sacrifice' a mouse by cervical dislocation, and how doing such a gruesome act for the first time should have bothered her, but it didn't. Killing Lux that way didn't bother her either.

At the end of the night, Ralph and Aliya exchanged a long hug. Then Ralph headed for his motel, saying he would be back the following day. He would also call Julie to tell her the good news that Aliya was there safe with them, and to start making the arrangements they had discussed that evening regarding their next step.

Aliya and Aaron sat with Cassie on the deserted beach for a long time, enjoying the warm night, the rolling waves, the bright stars, and the soft moonlight. But what they relished most was just being together again.

CHAPTER 41

Matthew

The ocean glistened that warm afternoon as the bright rays of sun bounced off it. Aliya, Aaron, Cassie, and Ralph stood on the dock, watching the large sailboat approach. As it got closer, Aliya noticed its colorful flag fluttering in the wind. It was black and green with a yellow "X" in the middle. Somewhere, she had seen a flag like that before. My God, she thought, it was in the hippie's elevator that she and her mom took to her first photoshoot!

The gentle Reggae beat of Bob Marley's "One Love" could be heard from the sailboat as Julie, who was perched at the bow, loudly sang along.

"Jamaican Welcome, mon?" a grinning Julie offered, while holding up two red plastic solo cups filled with rum and punch as the boat pulled up to the dock. Upon hearing from Ralph, Julie had taken the first flight to Miami and hired the chartered sailboat.

Ralph shook Aaron's hand and wished him well, telling him he would be in touch.

"Thank you for everything," Aaron said sincerely.

Ralph and Aliya affectionately embraced. He took a step back and said with a smile, "You look so much like your mom, LeeLee."

Then he handed her two envelopes: one addressed to Sara and one to Aliya.

"When your dad learned he had Alzheimer's, he told me he wrote you and Sara letters. I made sure to find these when I went back to your house. Please give Sara hers when you see her."

Later that evening, Aliya found a quiet spot on the deck and took out the letter from her dad. Just seeing his handwriting filled her with deep emotion. It was so familiar. So unique to him. So intimate. A part of him was there with her now.

My Dearest LeeLee,

My heart is full of so much love as I think of you as I write this letter. I recall when you were younger and you were always taller than the other children, you often felt that your height was a curse. You even blamed Mom and me for naming you "Aliya" because it means: "tall and towering." But we may have never told you that it also means "excellent, highest social standing."

Even as a little child, you have always been such a wonderful person. So caring and thoughtful—so aware of others' conditions and always ready to reach out to them and make them feel accepted and loved. You are a great friend, wonderful sister, and terrific daughter. You bring joy to our family with your consistent positive outlook and happy disposition, and we all greatly admire your strong drive to succeed. When the going gets tough, you find ways to make things get better, whether it's with your relationships with others, your schoolwork, or your outside interests. You are pensive and think deeply about things—then make decisions. Sometimes, your decision is to choose another path. Even so, you always find your way. I am so very proud of you each and every day. I'm proud of the sincere kindness and generosity you show others, your deep spirituality, your reliability, and your resolute work ethic. You have been blessed with these gifts, and I know you will use these to the best of your ability. Never underestimate yourself. You are a very bright, articulate, and talented person. You will go far! Just always remember to enjoy the journey. Search for what you love to do, for what makes you truly happy; make a plan, set your goals, and strive!

It is inevitable that sometimes your journey may be rocky, or uphill, just like that off-trail hike that I took us all on to the beautiful, frigid mountain lake in Yellowstone. When I experience times like these, I remind myself of Einstein's quote: "In the middle of every difficulty lies opportunity."

As you continue on your journey, my wish for you is that you will be able to reflect on all that you have accomplished, all the wonderful people and things that you have experienced and hold dear to your heart, all that you have to give, and all that you have to look forward to. May you feel a sense of gratitude and hope each and every day.

My beautiful, compassionate daughter … I love you so very much!

Stay well.

Be careful.

Strive to be happy.

My Love Always,

Dad

A few days later, their sailboat pulled up to the dock at Montego Bay. Sara and Mark were there to greet them.

CHAPTER 42

Inquisition 1

After seeing Aliya, Aaron, and Cassie safely set sail, Ralph returned to his office at the Iguana Inn and began to look into flights to Cleveland. His search was interrupted by the sound of a car pulling into the parking lot. He glanced out of his window to see a uniformed police officer, accompanied by a middle-aged man in a dark black suit (unusual clothing for the sweltering heat this time of year, he thought), and a third man who was younger and well-dressed, wearing a light beige suit. When they entered the small reception area, Ralph was there to greet them.

"Mr. Simpson?"

"Yes. May I help you?"

"I'm Officer Rawlings. This is Detective Mulloy and Special Agent Conrad. We would like to ask you some questions."

Ralph had a puzzled look. "Uh, okay. You guys want to sit down? I can grab some chairs from the back."

"Yes. That would be fine," replied Officer Rawlings, as the detective and agent examined Ralph's demeanor closely.

Ralph returned with the chairs, and they took their seats. "So, what's up?"

The man in the dark suit reached to shake Ralph's hand. "Tom Mulloy. I'm a detective from Cleveland, Ohio, and am leading the investigation on the McKenna family. In what capacity did you know them?" he asked, already knowing the answer but wanting to hear it from Ralph.

"Uh, I was their neighbor, many years ago. We were very good friends. When my wife passed away, I moved here, and we kind of lost touch. We pretty much just exchanged Christmas cards each year, to keep each other updated. We reconnected when Matt called me out of the blue one day and told me he had early-onset Alzheimer's. We talked for a long time that day."

"And you are the executor of their will?"

"Yes. When I was contacted by the police about Ellie and they told me they couldn't locate Matt or the girls, I went to Cleveland to take care of things." Ralph shook his head, incredulously. "Then I heard about the fire at the lab where LeeLee worked."

Agent Conrad spoke next. "So, Mr. Simpson, do you find this all … a little peculiar?"

"Hell yeah! It's shocking. And awful. And bizarre. Ellie and LeeLee have died. Their other daughter, Sara, is nowhere to be found, and Matt wandered off somewhere and still hasn't been found. What the hell do you all think is going on?"

"That's what we are trying to determine," replied Detective Mulloy. "Do you know of anyone that might want to harm them?"

"God no. They are wonderful people."

Agent Conrad looked closely at Ralph. "When was the last time you saw Mr. and Mrs. McKenna, Mr. Simpson?"

"Oh, I haven't seen them in years. Since I moved away. I was invited to the girls' weddings, but I didn't feel up to going."

"So that was the last time you saw their daughters too … Sara and, what did you call Aliya?"

"Oh, LeeLee. That was her nickname. Right, that's the last time I saw all of them. The girls were in grade-school."

"So, you didn't see LeeLee this past March?" asked Agent Conrad, looking intently at Ralph in an attempt to gauge his body language.

"No," answered Ralph, without an ounce of hesitation. "Why?"

Detective Mulloy shot a glance at Agent Conrad before responding. "Aliya and her husband were in this area during their spring break. They even stayed a night at the Biscayne Bay Hotel, which isn't far from here." Ralph just shrugged. Agent Conrad continued with the questioning. "When you went to Cleveland, it must have been a big job to take everything from their house and put it in storage?"

"It wasn't as bad as I thought. Ellie was very organized. With the girls out of the house, she had already been getting rid of stuff. When I spoke with Matt when he was first diagnosed, he told me they were planning on moving to something smaller. I put everything in storage because I figured Sara couldn't have just disappeared into thin air. She would have to turn up at some point."

"So, you took everything out and put it in storage? You didn't leave anything in the house?"

Ralph didn't flinch, just responded naturally. "Yeah. Well, except for the food. Most of it I pitched. But anything non-perishable, I donated to St. Joe's shelter. I also gave them their cleaning products and stuff like that."

"We noticed you did a good job at clearing out the house. Everything was gone and it looked really clean," added Detective Mulloy.

"Well, that's Ellie's doing. The house was super clean when I got there. I just swept up a bit after the movers took everything out."

Agent Conrad rubbed his forehead. "And you're sure you completely locked their house up?"

"Yes. I mean, yeah … I'm pretty sure I did. Why? Did someone get into their house?"

"We're just trying to conduct a thorough investigation, Mr. Simpson," replied Detective Mulloy. "Do you know if someone else would have had a key?"

"Uh, no. Well, I don't know … maybe a neighbor. We used to have keys to each other's houses when we lived there. They had a really cute dog. My wife and I would take care of her, water their plants and stuff when they went on vacation. They did the same for us. So maybe a current neighbor had a key?" Ralph was pleased with his ability to plant the idea that he wasn't the only one who may have had access to their house and could potentially have left a door unlocked.

Detective Mulloy glanced at the other two men, stood, and let out a deep sigh."Okay. Well. That's about all for now. Thanks for your time."

Ralph stood and shook the detective's hand. "They were good people. If there's something fishy going on, I sure hope you get to the bottom of it."

Ralph watched the men leave then breathed a sigh of relief. He hadn't anticipated a visit from the authorities. In retrospect, maybe he should have. He knew it was best to keep Aliya's secret. She could be thrown in jail—at the very least—for setting ARC labs on fire and intentionally murdering Lux. It's best everyone thinks she is dead. He got a beer and returned to his computer, finding a flight from Miami to Cleveland the first thing in the morning. He grabbed his tool belt and walked to the fort, carefully dismantled it, and burned its pieces in a bonfire on the beach.

CHAPTER 43

Scrutiny

Detective Mulloy perused his notebook.

"His story checks out. His phone records show he didn't call the McKennas except for the one time he told us about. And there is no indication he has traveled to Cleveland for several years. I don't think he's involved. He really has no motive. He is the executor of the will and gets the house, but he's not a beneficiary for anything else. The daughters are the only beneficiaries. So, he has nothing that valuable to gain from any of their deaths."

Special Agent Conrad leaned back in his chair. "So, it's just a coincidence that Aliya and her husband stayed so close to his motel in March?"

"Yeah. I think it is. I don't think he knows anything more about this whole ordeal than we do."

Agent Conrad shook his head slightly and looked away. "I'm not so sure." He paused, lost in thought. "And you have already interviewed family, friends, and neighbors of the McKennas, as well as Sara and her husband Mark's family, friends, and co-workers, right?"

"Yes. They are all shocked by everything that has happened. They couldn't provide any leads. We still have to interview Aaron's family in California."

"I'd also like to learn more about Aliya. She's a recent graduate. She likely still kept in touch with college friends. And I'd like to interview her co-workers at The Arthur R. Chester Laboratory."

"Why the interest in Aliya?" asked the detective. "I mean … she's dead. Not sure how learning more about her will help figure out where her family members are at this point."Agent Conrad remembered that Detective Mulloy wasn't privy to the details of the CIA's investigation of Aliya, nor what had transpired in Paris.

"Let's divide and conquer. Why don't you interview Aliya's college friends and continue with the investigation in Cleveland, and I'll head to the coasts to interview Aaron's family and Aliya's co-workers."

CHAPTER 44

Hideout

The sisters leaned into each other with their arms intertwined, full of anticipation as they stared out the large window, scanning the sky. They could hardly contain themselves when the Cessna 172 came into view. Sara rubbed her little sister's arm affectionately as they watched it taxi to the gate at Norman Manley International Airport in Kingston, Jamaica. As the two men approached, Aliya began an all-out run until she was slowed by Sara's hand on her shoulder.

"Aliya. We've got to take it easy. He's been through a lot."

Aliya nodded and latched onto Sara's arm as they gingerly approached together. Matthew looked tired and thin. Aliya gently grasped Matthew's hand. "Hello, Daddy. It's LeeLee and Sara." When Matthew looked at Aliya, his face immediately softened. To him, she looked like a young version of Ellie, and this brought him great solace.

"He did really good on the plane ride. Looked out the window the whole time," said Ralph with a grin, as he patted Matt's arm. "I'm proud of you, man."

Aaron grabbed the luggage as Mark pulled their SUV up to the baggage claim area. Matt was content, sensing that things were okay now. When they arrived at the house they were renting, Cassie greeted him warmly. "I think he remembers her," said Aliya, with a gentle smile.

Sara immediately made one of Matt's favorite lunches: a turkey, salami, mayo, and cheese sandwich with some fresh strawberries, accompanied by a bottle of Ensure, making sure to include a straw. After his hearty lunch, he drifted off to sleep in the cozy chair they had purchased for him.

Aliya and Sara had been sitting with Matthew, while Aaron and Mark prepared lunch for the rest of them and Ralph enjoyed a cold beer in the screened-in sunroom. While Matthew napped peacefully, they gathered at the dining room table for lunch.

Sara was in awe. "It's like a dream come true—that's he's alive and well."

Aliya smiled and nodded her head in agreement, equally grateful.

Aaron handed Ralph a fresh beer. "Fill us in. Julie didn't have time to tell us the whole story because she needed to focus on making the arrangements to get you both here."

Ralph took a long sip of his beer and smiled. "Something just told me that Lux's goons didn't have him. That he was still with us. I was just hoping he wouldn't go too far … that I could find him. Believe me, that first trip to Cleveland I looked high and low for him. All over the neighborhood. All over the damn city. But he was nowhere, and I knew I had to get back to Aaron. Before I left, I made sure to leave the doors unlocked and plenty of non-perishable food, bottled water, and that Ensure stuff, as well as a couple of blankets, out in the kitchen. It's such a classy neighborhood, I didn't expect any vagrants to come in. And I planned to return to Cleveland to look for him some more once I got Aaron situated. When Aliya showed up, I needed to get them on their way here right away."

"Once they set sail, I returned to my office, and it wasn't long before the police paid me a visit. I could tell by the questions they were asking that they thought I purposely left the door open. I about shit my pants when the detective said I did a nice job cleaning the house—that there was nothing left out. That meant someone had to take the food I left in the kitchen. I was praying it was ol' Matt. But the police hadn't found him. So, where the hell could he be? Then it dawned on me. The fort. The freakin' fort. I hadn't even thought to look there. I called Julie and told her that there was a shot he'd be there."

"She started looking into chartering a flight from Cleveland to here in Jamaica because we figured the police might check in on me again and I needed to cover my tracks. Julie arranged to get me a private driver from the airport in Cleveland and I had him drop me off a few blocks from your house. She paid him a pretty penny to keep things quiet about us while he drove us around."

"Julie sure does think of everything," said Aaron.

Ralph drank more of his beer and sat up straight before proudly continuing with his epic story. "Then I ran through the woods to the fort. And there he was, looking pretty content sitting there in the fort, drinking a beer."

Sara threw her arms up. "What, you left him beer too?"

"Well, just a six-pack. With the warm weather, I figured he'd enjoy it. And you're right, Aaron, Julie does think of everything. She suggested I go to the storage facility and pack up some clothes for

Matt, as well as grab his medications, which I had left with their other stuff. I could never throw away good drugs. Just ain't my nature."

Aliya, Sara, and Mark sat back in their chairs, astonished. "That's one hell of a story," said Mark.Aaron was already thinking ahead. He would check to see how much medication was left and when they would need to get more. Julie was wiring them money from Aaron's parents, so they should have no problem with the cost, but they would need a prescription.

Sara brought her hand to her forehead and gave a perplexing look. "Wait. So, Dad was capable of taking care of himself and staying out of sight for what, like, over a week?"

"I wondered about that too, Sara. But I think I figured it out. I saw tracks on the dirt path leading to the fort. They looked like tracks made by bicycles." Ralph shook his head and let out a little laugh. "When I brought Matt through the woods to the car, I saw three boys on bikes … couldn't have been more than ten years old. I thought I heard the one kid say, 'Hey Mister, where you takin' our hobo?' The other kid told him to shut up and they all rode off lickety-split."

CHAPTER 45

Inquisition 2

Agent Michael Conrad sat motionless as he stared at the blueness from the small, oval window. He was deep in thought for quite a while before he began typing up his notes on his laptop during the flight from Sacramento to Bangor. Aaron's parents told him how concerned they were that their son was missing, but they didn't necessarily act that way. Clearly, they were very affluent. In the vast majority of cases when a loved one has gone missing, affluent relatives will offer their own monetary reward for leads and frequently will hire their own private investigator. Aaron's parents had not considered either of these options.

Agent Conrad went directly to Bar Harbor from the Bangor Airport. The quaint vacation town was buzzing with tourists milling in and out of the shops and eateries, pausing to pose for selfies with their phones. His first stop was the Peregrine Inn, where he spoke with Aliya's landlords. They were very fond of Aliya and saddened by her death. They mentioned that her friend from ARC Labs had come by to pack up her belongings and that they were now preparing to rent out her apartment.

His next stop was ARC Labs. As he pulled up to the security gate, he couldn't help but notice the well-designed entrance. A large sign ran across a wall of granite stones with the creative double helix-shaped company logo accompanying the sizeable white letters on a slate gray background. The campus was equally impressive with state of the art, modern buildings intertwined with imposing, older buildings, situated around a grassy quad. He was directed to a corner table in the atrium where he was scheduled to meet with some of Aliya's co-workers.

As he sipped his coffee, he observed the people around him in the bright, sunlit area. He couldn't understand most of the conversations he overheard as they were much too scientific, filled with highly technical jargon. There certainly are a lot of extremely intelligent people who work at this laboratory, he thought. All the researchers he spoke to directed him to the same person.

A large man, dressed in light blue scrubs approached."You must be Edwin," Agent Conrad said as he stood to greet him.

"Ayuh."

"Please sit down. Can I get you a coffee?"

"No, thank you."

"Well, it's a real pleasure to meet you. I understand you were very good friends with Aliya McKenna. I'm so very sorry for your loss."

Edwin automatically beamed when he heard Aliya's name. Then, he abruptly realized that he must act sad. He had promised LeeLee he would keep her secret. He slumped in his seat and looked down.

"The folks who run the Peregrine Inn told me you packed up Aliya's things from her apartment for her. I'll need to look through them."

"Okay. All her stuff is in my basement."

"Good," Agent Conrad said with a smile. Then he spoke slowly and deliberately, focusing on Edwin's reaction to his next question. "Now, can you tell me about her relationship with Dr. Andrew Lux?" Edwin shook his head "No."

"I mean, aside from collaborating on research projects, I heard Dr. Lux really liked her." Edwin did not respond. But his body language showed his anger.

"Did Dr. Lux want Aliya to be his girlfriend, Edwin?"

"Dr. Lux was bad. Aliya loves Aaron."

"You meant to say 'loved' Aaron, right?"

Edwin's face dropped. "Ayuh. That's what I meant."

Agent Conrad pulled out his badge and set it on the table. "Edwin, I want to show you something. This is my badge. It means that I am a Special Agent for the United States Government. I am conducting a very important police investigation. I'm afraid your dear friend Aliya had gotten herself into some very big trouble. I need you to answer my questions truthfully and tell me everything you know. Okay?"

Edwin looked nervously at Agent Conrad. He was petrified inside. It took everything he had not to show it. He told LeeLee he would always protect her, and he promised her he would not tell a soul that she was okay, no matter what anyone said. Because she explicitly told him she would be okay, he never once entertained the idea that she died in the fire.

Agent Conrad looked Edwin directly in the eyes. “Edwin, is Aliya alive? Has she been in contact with you? Edwin looked up, meeting Agent Conrad’s steady gaze. His eyes became teary.

“No, she is dead.”

CHAPTER 46

Inquisition 3

"So how do you like Chicago?" Detective Mulloy asked pleasantly.

Julie took a sip from her cup of green tea before answering. "It's a bit tamer than New York, but I still love it."

"Well, as you know, I'm here to ask you about your friend, Aliya McKenna. I'm very sorry for your loss."

Julie did her best to appear heartbroken. When Detective Mulloy had contacted her to schedule a meeting, she practiced looking sad in her mirror and had pretty much mastered it. Her years of being in her high school plays were paying off.

"How did you find out that she died?"

Julie had to think quickly. Aaron had told her that Aliya was on the run in London, so she did not suspect that Aliya was the female researcher who died in the fire when she learned about it on the news. The next thing she heard was that Aliya was safe in Key Biscayne. So how did she find out that Aliya had died?

"Aliya and I were good friends. We kept in touch by texting frequently. I knew she was headed to London for a big research conference, so when I heard about the fire on the news, I texted her to see what she thought of it all. You know, like if it affected her lab or people she knew. I never once thought she was in the fire. But she never responded, which was unusual. So, I tried to contact Aaron, her husband, but he didn't respond. After a while, I called her parents. There was no answer. Then I called ARC Labs, and they told me she died in the fire." Julie buried her face in her hands. Her voice cracked. "I … I couldn't believe it."

Detective Mulloy's expression was one of genuine sympathy. "Miss Harris, did you know that Aliya's mother passed away and that her husband, father, sister, and brother-in-law are all missing?"

"What? God. No," Julie said, appearing to try to take it all in. "I have been trying like crazy to get a hold of them. I knew they would want to have a funeral. I was planning on driving to Cleveland if I didn't hear from them soon." Julie paused. "Where is everybody?"

"That's what we are trying to find out."

CHAPTER 47

A Conundrum

Special Agent Michael Conrad sat across from Director Richard Delaney, separated by his large mahogany desk at the George Bush Center for Intelligence.

Agent Conrad frowned. "I'm afraid we're still not much closer to having our questions answered, sir. Why would the Sonora Cartel be so interested in Aliya McKenna? And why did so many people close to her die or go missing?"

Director Delaney tapped his pen on his desk then looked at Michael Conrad. "Whatever the reason, the Cartel must have had someone on the inside. Someone at ARC Labs that was connected to Aliya. Who could that be?"

Agent Conrad thought for a moment. "I don't believe it was Edwin. He is not mentally capable of such complex activities. Perhaps her PI, Dr. Charles Gustaffason. His death was suspicious."

"PI stands for principal investigator, the head of the lab, right?" asked the director.

"Yes, that's correct. Or maybe Dr. Andrew Lux, her collaborator, who also died in the fire."

"That is, if Aliya and Dr. Lux did, in fact, perish in the fire. Their remains have never been found. Is it possible they were romantically involved? Sometimes lovers will go to great lengths to be together. Perhaps they had something that the Cartel wanted, something the Cartel would pay mightily for, and had an agreement with the Cartel, but decided to renege on the deal, fake their deaths, and live happily ever after in each other's arms."

"Well, it was no secret at ARC Labs that Drew Lux had a thing for Aliya. And they were both very attractive people. They would go together well and make a nice-looking couple, with a shared interest in science. But then why would Aliya's relatives go missing?"

Director Delaney shrugged. "Maybe the Cartel went after them to get to her."

As he paused in thought, Agent Conrad glanced at the identically framed portraits of previous CIA directors hanging in alignment on the cream-colored office walls. "So many things about this case don't sit right with me. Things just seem a little bit off. I have a sense that the folks I interviewed were withholding information. Someone knows something. I guarantee it. I didn't interview Aliya's best friend from college myself, but I feel like she must know more. Girlfriends that close confide in one another. They tell each other everything." He paused and cocked his head. "And Aliya McKenna sure was resourceful. She managed to slip away from one of the most notorious cartels and the CIA!"

"Yes. Good point. And now that she is gone, the chatter we were picking up between the Cartel members has ceased abruptly, which makes me think they are done with her. Still, we need to get to the bottom of this. I trust your instinct, Michael. I will order 24/7 surveillance on Aaron's family and the people Aliya was close to, such as her co-worker, Edwin, and her college friend, Julie. I will keep you posted on any new developments."

CHAPTER 48

Connections

Months later, Aliya stood confidently at the blackboard that was adjacent to the screen. She tapped on her handheld remote to advance the PowerPoint slide as the room full of eager young faces stared back at her. Projected onto the screen was the photo of a delightful-looking older gentleman: warm and welcoming in his well-tailored suit jacket, black-rimmed round classes, signature bow tie, and magnanimous smile. The photo immediately invited reciprocating smiles from the students in their crisp uniforms, reverently seated in the high school AP Biology class.

"Dr. Eric Kandel, a researcher at Columbia University in the United States, won the Noble Prize in Physiology or Medicine for the elucidation of the molecular basis of memory," Aliya explained.

A hand shot up immediately. "Miss Aliya?" interjected the eager voice of the affable student in her unmistakable Jamaican accent.

"Yes, Miriam?"

"He looks really nice."

"He is," Aliya responded. "I've met him before."

The students' eyes grew wide as they smiled, quite impressed.

Aliya smiled as she reminisced. "You see, I used to live in New York City. That's where I met my husband."

The students giggled. Many knew her husband from the town clinic. He was kind, smart, and very handsome. He volunteered regularly with the local doctor as he attended medical school.

She flipped to the next slide, showing a large slimy sea creature that evoked exasperated faces and giggles.

"Dr. Kandel's simple, yet eloquent studies in the giant sea slug, Aplysia, described the phenomena of long term potentiation: the foundation for memory, and long term depression: the basis for forgetting. You see, it all has to do with the strength of the connections between the nerve cells in the brain ..."

The sun had set by the time Aliya left her school office. As she walked in the darkness to her car, she gazed at the night sky. Cassiopeia, the "W," was always so prevalent, she thought. It was then that she realized that there was something else that was endearing her to the starry sky that night. "Connections," she mused, with a warm smile. Today was October 7th. She recalled the detour to New Orleans that she had taken on her drive to join Aaron in Key Biscayne. This was where she went to purchase and ship her special friend a special gift —ensuring that others would not know it came from her.

He stretched out his prized sheepskin on the cool grass. It was October 7th, the day he could hardly wait to arrive. As night fell, the beautiful lady began to play the dreamy opening chords on the piano, accompanied by the cellist. As the guitarist joined in, her soulful voice began. He glanced down at the ticket stub and the note that he had carefully placed on the sheepskin next to the small plastic baby Jesus. These had been tucked inside the king cake he received from the anonymous sender. As he read the lovely handwritten message, he could hear her soft voice in his mind:

My dearest Edwin,

I hope you enjoy my gift to see Christina perform in person. When you look up at the stars, always remember that wherever life takes us, we will always be under the same bright stars; and they will always be there to guide us along the good walk.

Thank you for being my friend.

Yours,

LeeLee

CHAPTER 49

Discord

Aliya and Sara relaxed at the crowded café, sipping their sorrel teas.

"This Jamaican tea is really refreshing. What's it made of?" asked Sara.

Aliya read the description off the menu. "A tart, lemony tea chilled on ice and made with sorrel (dried hibiscus buds), fresh ginger, sugar, a squirt of lime, and a splash of soda water."

"Mmm. So good," Sara said. She glanced around at the locals in the café. It was a young crowd. Many looked like students working on their laptops or enjoying a good read. "It's so nice to get out for a while—have a change of scenery."

Aliya's expression softened. "I really appreciate your taking care of Dad all day. I know it can be difficult."

"I'm happy to. I really am. But it is hard at times. I can tell that even though he is confused, he misses Mom so much. I mean, we all do, for that matter." Sara paused before continuing. "It's just so different here."

"I know what you mean. There are things I love about Jamaica—the warm climate, the beautiful ocean," Aliya said, as she admired the crimson flowers in the glass vase at their table. "But there's also a lot of blighted areas and a high crime rate. Sometimes I'm not comfortable going out for a jog alone, even in daylight. And I'm always nervous walking to my car at night. Even in the shady parts of New York, I never felt quite like this."

Sara nodded in agreement. "Yeah, I know. And I wonder … will we ever really be safe here? Will we always have to stay in hiding?" She paused for a moment, stirring the ice in her tea. "And, even if everything does work out and we are safe here … I know this sounds trivial, but I'm just used to working. I liked my job in Chicago. I miss it. I think it's great you were able to land that teaching job. Your income certainly helps. We can't expect Aaron's parents to keep fully supporting all of us. I guess it's just taking me time to get used to this 'new normal.'"

"I know. I feel the same way. It is different here. And I do think you'd enjoy working and having an opportunity to put your skills to use. Once Aaron finishes medical school, I'll take over as Dad's full-time caregiver and then you can go back to work."

Sara sighed. "Well, if he makes it until then."

Aliya took a sip of her tea, deep in thought. "After not seeing Dad for a while when I was in Bar Harbor, and now that I'm with him on a daily basis, I can tell he's really deteriorated mentally. Even though he doesn't talk so much anymore, when he does, he is really forgetful. He struggles so hard to find the right words. He always seems confused. I honestly don't think he knows who any of us are most of the time. I figured it would be bad while he got used to our new situation here in Jamaica. But then I thought once he got accustomed to his new routine, things would get at least a little better. But he's getting worse. The more disoriented he gets, the more agitated he gets. It's just going to be harder and harder to take care of him. The thing is, he is still young, and he is in excellent physical health. Even though early-onset Alzheimer's sometimes progresses faster than late-onset, I think it's likely his body won't fail him the way his mind is. He may live another ten to fifteen years or more."

Sara's expression saddened. "What a horrible way to live. It breaks my heart to see him so lost, with no memory of his life, his loved ones … of himself. He must feel so empty. At times, he seems so depressed."

"It breaks my heart too," said Aliya, as she thought about KRISPR Cas and all the promise it could have had for helping their dad.

Sara took a deep breath and looked out the large window at the bright sunshine and vibrant green landscape of the tropical island they now called home. "Well, I guess there are some good things. The weather certainly is much better here than in cold, cloudy Cleveland. I bet Dad likes that."

Aliya smiled. "And he loves to fish with Aaron and Mark. I wonder if they're catching anything?"

"He does love to fish. I'm so glad that's something he can still do," said Sara, sipping her tea and continuing to contemplate all of their new lifestyles. "I will say, never in my wildest dreams would I have thought I'd see you, of all people, teaching in a private Catholic School."

Aliya laughed. "Oh my God, I know. Organized religion is so not my thing. But I'm, adapting."

When the sisters returned home, they found Matthew worn out from a busy day of fishing in the Jamaican heat. His confusion was greatly amplified by his tiredness. Aliya recognized this right away by the way he glanced around at them and the room with emptiness in his eyes.

"Dad, let me help you get ready for bed," Aliya said as she escorted him to the bathroom and handed him his toothbrush. He stared at it. She put toothpaste on it and handed it back to him. Again, he just stared at it. Aliya felt as if she were talking to a toddler.

"Okay. Open up," she said, as she motioned to him to brush his teeth. "Now spit. And now let's rinse." Her heart sunk. Is this what Mom had to do? She helped him to bed and ensured he was comfortable. "Good night, Dad. I love you."

Sara and Mark were nestled together on the couch watching a movie and would be available if Matthew were to get up, which was happening more frequently these days. Aliya took this opportunity to ask Aaron if he would join her for a walk on the nearby beach.

"Love to!" replied Aaron, excited to have some personal time with Aliya, which they hadn't had much of since their honeymoon. "I'll make us a few cocktails to enjoy while we watch the sunset."

They strolled along the white sand beach holding hands, delighting in the serenity of their surroundings—the warmth of the sun, the quiet waves, the soft breeze through the palm trees. Aliya spoke first."Aaron, I've been thinking…"

Aaron smiled, captivated with how beautiful she looked that night against the backdrop of the turquoise sea.

"Yeah? What have you been thinking about?"

"About my dad. He's really declined."

"I know. It's so hard to see him like this. Even just sitting in a chair, holding a fishing rod was confusing to him today. He kept looking at the rod, trying to figure out what to do with it."

"I want to try to help him."

"Well, I don't know how much more we can do than we are doing now. He's getting great care. You and Sara are doing an amazing job."

"Lately I've been reading a lot about the current research using stem cells to treat disease. Stem cell transplantation in humans to replace blood cells has been safe and effective for a long time."

"You mean bone marrow transplants, right? Yes. They are effective when done correctly. You have to make sure you have a suitable match if it's an allogeneic transplant, where the stem cells are harvested from a donor."

"I was thinking more along the lines of pluripotent stem cells, ones that can give rise to just about all cell types, not just blood cells."

Aaron thought a moment. "Like iPSCs, induced pluripotent stem cells, adult cells that have been reprogrammed genetically to an embryonic stem cell-like state?"

"Well, why not just embryonic stem cells. Some of the reprogramming factors used to return iPSCs to the embryonic state have been known to cause tumorigenesis and serious immune reactions. Stem cells cultured from embryos are the best. They are completely undifferentiated. The problem is, aside from bone marrow transplants and using stem cells for a few other things, like spinal cord injury, heart disease, and Parkinson's, there's very little research that uses stem cells as a therapy for Alzheimer's disease in humans. Most studies are being done on model organisms, like mice. But I did find a Phase 2a clinical trial being conducted in South Korea. They're delivering stem cells obtained from umbilical cord blood to the brain ventricles of Alzheimer's patients using a catheter system. The study is ongoing, so the results haven't been published yet."

"I think this is all very interesting, Liya. But how would this help your dad? You aren't doing research anymore, and Jamaica certainly isn't a hotbed for cutting-edge scientific research."

"Well, as a med student, you could start working in a clinical Neurology research lab. A lot of students conduct research while they're in school. In fact, they're encouraged to, right? It looks great on a resume to be an author on a scientific publication. And teaching is pretty easy for me. I have a lot of extra time. I could get a part-time job in a lab. There is a fertility center in Kingston that does IVF that's affiliated with the university."

Aaron stopped dead in his tracks. He was baffled. "What on earth are you suggesting?"

Aliya gave him the most pleading look. "KRISPR Cas is not destroyed. I have the entire protocol on a jump drive. I just couldn't bring myself to throw out all my years of hard work. And before I burned down the lab, I took the tank with the human embryos from Russia and put it in an unused storage closet in another building at ARC Labs, where it would be safe. I told Edwin to keep it filled with liquid nitrogen so that the embryos remain cryopreserved. At the time, I did this because I didn't want to kill innocent human embryos. Maybe someday they could be returned to their rightful parents. My guess is they were stolen. Women can be super-ovulated with hormones to produce many eggs that can be fertilized in vitro. It would be easy to lie to someone and say they had three viable embryos when they really had eight. I'm guessing that is how these embryos were stolen. But, in reality, I don't see any way these embryos will ever be returned to their rightful owner." Aliya took a deep breath before continuing. "So why not use them?"

Aaron blinked as his mouth fell open. "What? What are you talking about?"

"I want to culture embryonic stem cells from the human embryos. Then I'll use KRIPSR Cas to upregulate the expression of the healthy genes in the stem cells that are known to be mutated in people with early-onset Alzheimer's, such as the amyloid precursor protein gene and the presenilin genes. I'll also upregulate the *Arc* gene. The *Arc* gene is known as the "memory gene" because it enhances synaptogenesis in the hippocampus and has been shown to restore memory in mouse models for Alzheimer's. I'll also increase the expression of the genes that mimic the current drugs prescribed to Alzheimer's patients. Like, I'll upregulate the gene that makes a protein that inhibits the breakdown of acetylcholine, which would basically mimic the action of a drug called Aricept. Then I'll transform my KRIPSR Cas engineered stem cells into neurons, and you can transplant them into Dad's hippocampus in a similar manner to how it's done with Parkinson patients, where they transplant dopamine-producing neurons."

Aaron shook his head in disbelief. His eyes were wide. "You're fucking out of your mind. You of all people should know you can't just do non-reviewed, uncontrolled, unauthorized studies on humans. Aliya, you can't use your dad as a guinea pig. So many things can go wrong. You could make it worse. You could kill him for God's sake! I will not be a part of this."

Aliya's voice quivered. She was shaking. "Jesus Aaron, look at him! He's got nothing to lose. Not a God Damn thing to lose. He's already lost himself. If I have a chance to reverse this miserable curse, I've got to try."

Aaron took both of Aliya's hands in his own and looked deep into her teary eyes. In a calming voice, he said, "Liya, listen to yourself. You're acting no different than Lux. You want to do exactly the kind of thing you went to great lengths to keep Lux from doing. What has gotten into you?"

Aliya pulled away. "Maybe I am like Lux. We both felt like outcasts when we were young, me with my height, he with his weight. We were both driven by our life experiences. When I modeled, I loved the attention. It was intoxicating. Lux was the same way. He needed accolades and recognition to sustain him … to thrive. We are two of a kind. Maybe it was wrong of me to kill him."

"God no, Liya. You are not like Lux! Lux was evil. His ideas were twisted. He had Dr. G and your mom killed. He would have killed us all if he could have. If you didn't prevent him from learning how to make KRISPR Cas work, he would have sold it to criminals who would have used it for everything that is wrong in this world. You did what you had to do. Never regret it. But you can't do this now. It's crazy… and wrong for so many reasons."

Aliya looked steadily and intently at Aaron. Her gaze was piercing. "You don't get it, Aaron. It's different when it's someone you love."

Aaron dropped his head into his hands and closed his eyes, letting out a deep sigh. When he looked up, Aliya was running down the beach, away from him.

CHAPTER 50

Promises

"Hey," Aaron said to Sara and Mark as he entered their shared home.

"She's in your bedroom. She didn't want to talk," replied Sara. Aliya's sunken expression, bloodshot eyes, and the fact that she had returned without Aaron told Sara that things did not go well on their walk. Sara went to her room to offer support, but Aliya asked to be left alone.

Aaron's sadness was written all over his face. "Maybe I'll give her some time to herself."

He went to the sunroom, where he too could have some personal time. He sat gazing through the full-length windows at the night sky for a very long time, trying to make sense out of things. He recalled his exact thoughts when they were reunited in Key Biscayne, when he felt so much love for Aliya as he watched her in her peaceful slumber in the fort. She had been through so much, more than enough pain for one lifetime. She would need time to heal. He vowed then to do whatever he could to bring her happiness for the rest of their lives.

Aaron picked up his laptop and opened the google search engine. He typed in "stem cell therapy." Articles from the International Society for Stem Cell Research appeared on his screen. He read that human stem cell therapy was indeed, very promising, but that it was in its very early stages and would likely take many years of careful and labor-intensive FDA-approved research in order to develop safe and effective treatments for disease. He read about how stem cells were essentially immortal because they could self-renew—divide into copies of themselves, and that once a stem cell line was established in the laboratory, it could be used practically indefinitely.

Aliya was already skilled at establishing embryonic stem cell lines from mouse embryos. She had learned how to do this expertly when she was at ARC Labs. Aaron knew from a developmental biology course he had taken that human preimplantation embryos at four to five days post-fertilization were virtually identical to the mouse embryos that Aliya worked with. She would have no problem developing human embryonic stem cell lines, provided she had the right laboratory equipment, equipment that would be readily available if she worked in an in vitro fertilization clinic.

He read that exposing stem cells to particular factors would cause them to differentiate into specific cell types, such as cardiac tissue, skin cells, and neurons. In fact, there was quite a bit of research currently being conducted using dopamine-producing neurons that were made from embryonic stem cells to treat Parkinson's disease. Human research trials implanting such neurons into the brains of Parkinson's patients were already in full swing in Japan and Singapore. Aaron read a recent publication that described exactly how the transplantation procedure was done. A small needle was used to inject stem cell-derived neurons in a liquid suspension through a tiny burr hole in the skull. MRI guided stereotactic apparatus was used to accurately position the needle to ensure the precise delivery of the neurons to the specific regions of the brain damaged in Parkinson's patients. The doses of local anesthetic and prophylactic antibiotics given to the patients were also reported. Aaron knew there was an excellent Neurology Department affiliated with the medical school he attended. It likely would be equipped with the apparatus needed to make precision injections into the brain's memory center, the hippocampus.

As he should have known, Aliya's plan was not that far-fetched at all. It was very, very well thought-out. She had, of course, already immersed herself in the scientific literature, scrutinizing every accessible scientific study, research publication, and commentary on stem cell therapy, especially as it related to neurodegenerative disease.

It was late into the night when Aaron finished reading and joined Aliya in bed. He gazed at his beautiful wife, the love of his life, in her peaceful slumber, knowing he would keep his vow to do whatever he could to bring her happiness.

CHAPTER 51

Allies

Julie drove her rental car down the tree-lined, winding dirt road until she reached the driveway of the bright yellow farmhouse. Its white trimmed windows and columns, the large white banister porch that extended across its front, and the wooden swing hanging from a large oak in the grassy yard gave it a warm and welcoming feel.

Edwin smiled and waved as she pulled up, excited to meet LeeLee's good friend that he had heard so much about. As Julie got out of the car and approached him, Edwin took a good look at her, comparing her to a picture on his phone. He wanted to be sure she was really Julie. He smiled when he realized she was.

"Hello. You must be Edwin."

"Ayuh."

He was exactly as Aliya had described him, a great big teddy bear. She smiled and moved to embrace him, feeling as if she knew him already. He shied away, uncomfortable with hugging a woman that wasn't a family member. Julie realized her mistake and moved out of his personal space, holding out her hand for his brief handshake.

Julie glanced at the cell phone he was holding. "Oh. You have a picture of me."

"Ayuh. Not just you. All of you. LeeLee missed you all so much. She showed me all of your pictures. Then she sent them to my phone so I could look at them whenever I wanted. Do you want to see them?"

"Yes. I'd love to."

Edwin pointed to some lawn chairs. "Do you want to sit with me, and I will show them to you? It will be just like when LeeLee and I sat on our bench in the quad."

Julie nodded and followed him to the chairs. She could see how Aliya could befriend him. He was a gentle giant.

"Would you like a cold drink?" asked Edwin, trying his best to be a good host to Aliya's best friend.

"That would be lovely, Edwin. I am a bit parched," replied Julie, excited for a nice strong cocktail after her full day of travel.

Edwin returned with two ice-cold cans of Moxie. Julie had never heard of this beverage before, but was always willing to try new things, especially things in the drink category. "Cheers," she said as she took a very big gulp. As she swallowed, her eyes became wide, and she began to cough.

Edwin shrunk in his chair. "Sorry. I guess not everyone likes it. Especially people who come from away."

After Julie recovered, Edwin swiped the screen on his phone to show a group picture from Aliya and Aaron's wedding. "See, that is you and Aaron's brother. I forgot his name. That is Sara and Mark, Matthew and Ellie, Aaron and Aaron's parents, but I don't remember their names either."

His face softened. "And there is LeeLee." He smiled tenderly. "I miss her."

"She misses you too. She'll love your surprise for her."

Edwin looked up from his phone. "Do you like Christina?"

"Uh, Christina who?"

"The pretty lady singer. The one LeeLee likes?"

"Oh, you must mean Christina Carlton. Yes, I do. LeeLee and I used to listen to her music when we lived together in college."

Edwin beamed. "I got to see her. LeeLee sent me a ticket. It was so great. There were a lot of stars out too." Edwin was lost in the memory of that wonderful night. "I wish LeeLee was there. Please tell her I miss her very much."

"I will. I know she misses you too. I'm sure she will call you as soon as she can."

"I would like that. Maybe I can sit on our bench when she calls." His eyes met Julie's. "Tell her not to worry. I will always keep her secret." Then he put his hand to his mouth and giggled. "Everybody thinks she is dead."

"Yes, I know. It is very important that you do keep that a secret. Aliya needs you to."

"Ayuh. I will," he said solemnly, nodding his head.

Julie handed him a piece of paper. "LeeLee said to be sure I tell you thank you for helping her again. She really appreciates you doing this favor for her. Here's the shipping address."

"It's no problem. I know how to ship specimens on dry ice from ARC Labs. It's one of my jobs. I have to do it a lot for the researchers, so I am really good at it. I will make sure it is done the right way."

Julie stayed and visited with Edwin for most of the afternoon. He showed her around the farm, taking her to their lighthouse and to the pasture where their sheep were grazing. The property was beautiful, a pastoral green oasis set along the rugged, granite coast of the North Atlantic.

Julie drove back down the winding road with a full heart and a smile. What a wonderful day it had been, she thought. She did not notice the car that sat on a nearby turn-off, nor did she realize that this car had followed her from the airport to Edwin's farm.

CHAPTER 52

Ian

Aliya recognized the familiar meow right away.

"Oh my God. He survived! I was afraid to contact Edwin about him. I figured the police would question Edwin like everyone else, and that it was better if he honestly hadn't heard from me."

Julie placed the carrier on the floor and gave Aliya a huge hug. "Ayuh. This is Edwin's surprise for you. He took great care of Krispr and nursed him back to health."

Aliya took Krispr from the pet carrier, stroking his fur and rubbing under his ears as he purred, elated to be reunited with him. He certainly had helped her get through many lonely nights in Bar Harbor. "I bet he's sick of being cooped up. How did he do on the trip?"

"He did great. Edwin's vet prescribed some medicine for him that made him sleepy, and he slept in his carrier the whole way."

"I'm sorry I couldn't pick you up at the airport. I had to work."

"That's okay. Aaron was an awesome chauffeur. He gave me a nice little commentary about Jamaica on our way here. This is a really nice house, by the way."

Aliya took Julie's hand. "Come on. Let's sit in the sunroom. We get a nice breeze through the windows."

"Are you ready for a drink, Jules?" asked Aaron.

"Why not? One more won't hurt. I had quite a few Jamaican Welcomes on the plane. Do you have rum and punch? I'm getting too old to mix my liquor. My body can't handle it as well as when we were in college, when we welcomed the challenge of mixing a variety of beverages when we imbibed!"

Aaron brought drinks out for them all. "Where's Cassie? I'm sure she'll be happy see her feline brother."

"Sara and Dad took her for a walk. She'll get to meet up with him later," replied Aliya as Krispr jumped onto her lap and made himself comfortable.

"How is your dad?" asked Julie.

Aliya frowned. "It's progressing, Jules."

"I'm so sorry, Liya."

Aliya shrugged slightly. There wasn't much else to say about that. "So, you got to meet Edwin! How is he? I miss him so much."

"He misses you too. Told me all about the Christina Carlton concert. And his farm and lighthouse are so cool. He's exactly the way you described him. But enough about that. I've got to tell you all about the incredibly gorgeous guy I met on the plane. So, he's sitting in the seat next to me, by the window and he just kind of looked up and smiled when I sat down. Then he paid absolutely no attention to me. So, I'm thinking, I don't want to be annoying, but the flight is only like five hours, so I don't have much time."

"Wow, it only took you five hours to fly from Maine to Jamaica?"

"No, Krispr and I had to change planes in NYC, so it took a little longer. Anyway, I'm trying to get this gorgeous dude's attention as nonchalantly as possible. But he's pretty engrossed in the book he's reading, and he's got his AirPods in. So, then the flight attendant announces that they will be serving Jamaican Welcomes for two dollars. Clearly, the flight was filled mostly with vacationers who were ready to start partying. When she came to our row, we both ordered one. Well, that's all I needed to break the ice. I said, 'cheers.' He said, 'cheers' back, then, 'Wah Gwaan?' I had absolutely no idea what that meant."

Aaron spoke up. "Oh, I've heard that before. It's Jamaican for 'What's up?' or 'How are you?'"

"Right. That's what he told me. So, we started chatting, and the drinks kept coming. I told him how I'm a financial consultant for Goldman Sachs in Chicago, and he thought that was really cool. But he's the one that's totally cool. He's an engineer for Tesla. He works at Giga Texas in Austin. Well, most of the time. Sometimes he travels to Shanghai, or Berlin—like how cool is that? So, then he says he plays guitar, loves to rock climb, skies Tahoe, and goes to Napa every chance he gets. And I'm like, 'Oh my God, I was just in a wedding at Lake Tahoe!' So, we talked all about how awesome Lake Tahoe is. Then he's like, 'so you're a cat lover, eh? What's your cat's name?' I had completely forgotten that I had Krispr in the carrier because he was so quiet. So, then I told him how Krispr wasn't my cat, that I was just bringing him to you. He got a big kick out of how we came up with his name. Remember when we burned the lobsters at your apartment in Bar Harbor?"

Aliya laughed. "Oh Yeah. How could I forget? That's so awesome, Jules! What's Mr. Studly's name?"

Julie looked dreamy. "Ian."

"So, what brings Ian to Jamaica? Maybe he's got a hot girlfriend here?" teased Aaron.

"Well, if I can swing it, the only hot girlfriend he's gonna have here is me! He's here for a conference, and he said he'd text me to meet up with us the first chance he gets. I was hoping you guys would know of a cool bar we can all meet at."

Aaron answered, "Ya, mon. I've got that covered. I know just the place."

CHAPTER 53

Sidestep

Bob Marley's "Three Little Birds" played in the background as the four relaxed on the outdoor patio, drinking and singing along. The less stressful and slower pace of life in Jamaica was starting to sink in, and Aliya and her family were beginning to really flourish in their new surroundings.

Julie raised her glass. "Too bad Mark isn't here. I bet he'd have the balls to try one of these beasts! Read the description out loud again, Aaron."

Aaron looked at the thick liquid in his glass. "Are you sure you want it repeated? Not sure I want to be reminded right before I take a drink of it."

"Go for it," said Sara.

"Easy for you to say. You aren't drinking it. Okay. So, a 'sea cat' is slang in Jamaica for octopus. This specialty drink, sea cat punch, is made with rum cream, white rum, molasses, peanuts, malt powder, and Supligen, which is a protein supplement, and I quote: 'the milky white liquid produced by boiling octopus.'"

Aliya drained her glass without hesitation. "I am so glad I'm sticking with rum runners tonight. That sounds so gross."

"When in Rome…" Julie said, as she took a big gulp of her sea cat punch, immediately chasing it down with a full glass of water.

Aaron followed suit. "Okay. That was wretched."

Aliya glanced at Sara. "Feel free to drink, Sara. I'll get up with Dad tonight if he wakes up."

Sara smiled widely, barely able to contain her excitement. "I know. That's not why I'm not drinking."

Aliya tilted her head. She had a huge smile. "There's one, and only one reason that I can think of as to why a sane woman would choose not to drink."

Aaron looked confused. "What would that be?"

Aliya and Julie jumped out of their chairs to hug Sara. "Congratulations!"

Aaron lifted his hands and shrugged. He still couldn't decipher what the rapture was all about. "What? What is so great about not drinking?"

Julie smiled and shook her head. "Men are so dumb. She's expecting!"

Aliya rolled her eyes. He's so book smart, she thought. But sometimes he can be so clueless.

"Thanks, guys. Mark and I are really happy."

"So, give us the run down. How are you feeling? When are you due?" Aliya said as she waved her hands with genuine excitement.

"I feel pretty well most of the time. Sometimes I get morning sickness, though."

"I've read that getting morning sickness is actually a good sign. It's a normal occurrence in early pregnancies," said Aaron.

"Yeah. I read that too. It's been okay. Since Mark is working from home, he can hang out with Dad if I'm not feeling well. And Dad still takes a lot of naps, so I rest then too. I'm just really glad that the Jamaican government bought our story that we lost all of our official documents and issued us new ID cards, so I was able to get a good OB/GYN. And Mark's job provides excellent benefits."

Aliya nodded in agreement. "Yes, it has been helpful that the government here doesn't ask too many questions about Americans. I think they like having us settle here. I had very little problem getting my job. And Aaron got into med school pretty easily—just had to pay the tuition. Thank God for your parents, Aaron, who could throw money at our problems to resolve all our issues."

"Yep, thank God for Mitch and Jen. And the exchange rate helps a lot too. The US dollar is really strong. I can buy a Red Stripe for only a couple of bucks here."

Julie took another big swig of her sea cat punch, now getting used to it and feeling its effects. "Y'all are freakin' outlaws! I'm damn proud to be in your presence and call you my friends."

"So how far along are you, Sara?" asked Aliya.

"I'm just over thirteen weeks. I'm through the first trimester. If Mark's job continues to go well, we'll be able to get our own house before the baby arrives. We plan to get an extra room for Dad. I'll be a stay-at-home mom and can take care of both of them. And we can look into getting a home health care aide for Dad if necessary."

Aliya agreed. "Absolutely. We can definitely look into getting more help." If need be, she thought, optimistically.

Julie cell phone chimed. "Ah! He's here. He's out front. How do I look?"

Aliya, Sara, and Aaron all spoke at the same time. "Awesome, beautiful, gorgeous…"

"What? I don't care about that. Do I look hot? Sexy? Irresistible?"

All three nodded in agreement. "Yes, yes. Of course. That too."

Julie saw Ian first, as her chair was facing the patio entrance. Her face lit up. She jumped out of her seat and went to greet him, holding onto his arm like they were old friends as she led him to their table.

Julie beamed. "Hey, everyone. This is Ian."

Aliya turned in her seat, excited to meet Julie's new heartthrob. He looked to Aliya first, extending his hand in an offer to shake hers. "*Enchanté, mademoiselle*. You may remember me as Étienne, eh?"

Aliya's mouth dropped open. Her face became ashen. She nearly fainted.

Julie was astounded. "What? You two know each other?"

Special Agent Michael Conrad saw that Aliya was paralyzed with fear. "Aliya, it's okay. I'm not with the people who were after you in Paris. I'm not going to hurt you. I'm a special agent for the CIA. I'm going to reach into my pocket and take out my badge to show you."

Aaron and Sara were wide-eyed and speechless. Aliya nodded slightly as if to say "Okay." Aaron took charge and picked up the badge, inspecting it closely. It seemed official, he thought, although he didn't really know for sure.

Sara spoke authoritatively. "Why are you here? What do you want from us?"

Julie looked at Ian and did a double-take. She was incredulous, speechless. She sat back down and drained her glass. Then signaled the waitress for another round, ordering herself a double.

Agent Conrad put his hand on the empty chair. "May I?"

Still in shock, Aliya slowly nodded her head.

Agent Conrad folded his hands on the table and looked directly at Aliya. "I'm here for answers. Let's start at the beginning. What is it that you have that others want so badly?"

Aliya knew she had a split second to make a decision. Was he who he said he was, a legitimate federal agent? His badge did look official. Her gut told her to trust that he was. Her nerves began to calm a bit. She fully expected that this day would come, and just as she always thoroughly thought through a protocol before beginning a new experiment, she had thoroughly thought through what she would say to the authorities, if she were ever found to be alive.

"It's not what I have. It's what I know."

Agent Conrad leaned back in his chair. "Go on."

"When I was at Franklin University, I worked with Dr. Charles Gustaffason. He was a well-respected bacteriologist, one of the top in his field. As funding agencies became more interested in clinical research, it became harder for him to secure grants for his work. I used to think this was a shame because so much of what we know of today we have learned by studying very simplified systems in organisms such as bacteria, that we can then translate to mammalian systems and even human conditions. But I guess not everything is translatable."

Aaron gave Aliya a confused look, unsure where she was going with this. Aliya had already proven her technology was translatable to mammals (and therefore highly likely to work in humans). But he decided not to say a word.

Aliya continued, "Dr. Gustaffason and I discovered a novel system in bacteria that was a mechanism for precise, efficient, and inexpensive gene editing. With it, any gene could be manipulated. Bad genes could be fixed. Good genes could be inserted and upregulated. It was revolutionary and had tremendous promise for studying, developing treatments, and even curing human disease." She paused to take a deep breath. "That's when we met Dr. Andrew Lux. At the time, he was a world-renowned researcher at the National Institute of Neurological Disorders and Stroke. He recognized the promise of our work and offered to collaborate with us. Dr. Gustaffason's funding had just about dried up. In order to continue with this promising research, we needed to collaborate with Dr. Lux."

"And does this revolutionary technology have a name?"

"Yes, of course. It's just kind of long. It's called: Clustered Regularly Interspaced Short Palindromic Repeats/Cas enzyme gene-editing technology. I call it KRISPR Cas for short.

Agent Conrad smiled. "Crisper … like your cat."

Julie was impressed. "Good memory!" she said, with a goofy smile, now fully feeling the effects of the alcohol.

Aliya continued, "It was Dr. Lux's idea to move the research to ARC Labs. I now realize it's because he wanted to carry out a clandestine operation in a remote part of the nation. He wanted to use our technology not only for unethical experiments in human embryos, which are shunned by the scientific community, but also for criminal activity. If our technology could be made to work in human embryos, it also would have the potential for diabolical uses, such as eugenics. Now that the entire human genome is sequenced, and if you can easily manipulate any gene with our new gene-editing technology, you can also make designer humans: blond hair, blue-eyed, athletic, highly intelligent (even geniuses), for example. Or super soldiers. Or a class of simpleminded people that could be exploited and used as slave labor. The possibilities are endless."

She took a deep breath before continuing. "This past summer, Dr. Gustaffason found a liquid nitrogen tank filled with tubes of cryopreserved human embryos from Russia in Lux's lab. This led us to believe Lux was colluding with criminals in Russia, probably to sell genetically engineered human embryos on the black market. But they couldn't get my technology to work. They thought I was withholding information, that I had some special secret that I wasn't telling them. I had no secret. I realized that the problem was that they were trying to get it to work in human embryos, not bacteria. And mechanisms that work beautifully in bacteria don't always work in mammals. This makes sense. Organisms adapt to their own particular situations and develop unique biological mechanisms accordingly. This is the underlying principle of evolution."

She placed her hand on her chin and shook her head ever so slightly. "I had no idea how ruthless Lux and his accomplices were until I arrived in London for a conference and learned that my apartment had been ransacked and that Dr. Gustaffason and my mom had died suspiciously. I was scared. I knew then they were after me and my family, that they must have arranged for Dr. G and my mom's deaths and likely had taken my dad. I decided the only way out of this was to go back to ARC Labs, get my protocol, and hide someplace where I couldn't be found, hoping they would give up on my failed technology."

"As you know, I was able to connect with an old friend, Hai Pei, in Paris. He is a high fashion designer who has a private jet. He was able to take me back to ARC Labs. It was late when I went to gather my files. When I entered my building, I smelled smoke. As I approached the corridor leading to my lab, I saw the blaze. It was so intense. I turned and ran to the parking lot where Hai Pei was waiting. We drove back to the airport, and he flew me here to Jamaica. Julie helped get my husband, sister, and brother-in-law here."

Aliya paused, then looked directly at Agent Conrad."The fire was a gift. Everyone believed that I had died and that the 'secret' to my technology died along with me. But I'm worried now. If you can find me, I'm afraid they can find me too."

"So, you never saw Andrew Lux that night?"

Aliya shook her head. "No."

"Why would he be at ARC Labs that late?"

"Lux was a workaholic. He often worked well into the night. Sometimes he would even sleep on the couch in his office, like if he were writing a big grant with a deadline looming."

This was in agreement with what others had told Agent Conrad when he questioned Lux's coworkers and the security officers at ARC Labs. It wasn't unusual for him to go into the lab at any hour, especially if he felt he had a brilliant idea that couldn't wait. But Agent Conrad still asked because he wanted to see how Aliya would respond.

"Why didn't he attend the research conference in London?"

Aliya rolled her eyes and smirked. "Because he was so egotistical. They didn't invite him to be keynote speaker, and it pissed him off."

For a few moments, Agent Conrad sat quietly with a wrinkled forehead, resting his chin on his folded hands. He was pensive, taking in all he had just heard before he spoke. "Well, first of all, I'm very sorry about the loss of your loved ones, Dr. Gustaffason and your mother, and your father. Since he's never been found, it is likely he has been killed. Please accept my sincere condolences."

Aliya didn't reply, rather just nodded quietly to accept his sympathy.

"Second, Russians were not after you in Paris. Members of the most notorious drug cartel in Mexico were. My guess is they got the embryos from Russia because IVF is frowned upon in Mexican society and it was just easier and cheaper to get them on the black market from Russia. They probably brought them up the coast from Mexico, likely by boat. And lastly, I wouldn't worry too much. The CIA hasn't picked up any intelligence lately that indicates that the cartel is still interested in you. Hopefully, they believe you died in the fire and have given up on this project. They have plenty of lower hanging fruit to keep them busy, like heroin trafficking, gun-running, and moving illegal immigrants across the border."

Agent Conrad rubbed his forehead and thought for a moment. "Still, they are pretty ruthless. And they certainly don't like to be outmaneuvered, especially by a young woman. It would damage their reputation. I could put you all in protective custody, but it seems you have already done as good a job as we would do reinventing your identities and establishing yourselves in a new environment. Starting over would just risk leaks and could put you in danger. This may be the best option now."

He leaned forward and looked Aliya directly in the eyes. "Aliya, if I'm going to go along with this and let you all hide out here in

Jamaica, I have to trust you. You have to be completely honest with me. It's for your own safety and the safety of your family. Have you told me everything? Is everything you have just told me the full truth? And are you absolutely sure that your gene-editing technology was completely destroyed in the fire—that there is no possible way anyone else could have access to it?"

Aaron bit his lip. His stomach sank as he waited to see if Aliya would tell Agent Conrad the truth—that she had burned the lab down and intentionally killed Lux. That KRISPR Cas technology worked perfectly in mammals, and that she still had the protocol.

Aliya's face dropped. She sighed deeply. "No. No, I haven't told you everything."

Agent Conrad nodded in satisfaction, thinking what a skilled profiler he was. He knew he had an uncanny ability for knowing when people were not being fully truthful, and for getting them to concede. Aliya McKenna may have been resourceful at escaping detection, but she couldn't fool the CIA for long.

"My dad is alive. He is here with us. Our friend Ralph Simpson found him in Cleveland and brought him here. We all live in a home not far from here. But aside from that, everything else I have told you is the absolute truth."

Michael Conrad was still suspicious. There was something about her story that didn't add up. He just couldn't put his finger on it. This investigation was far from over, he thought. But it was not necessary for them to know that. If they believed it was over, they may let their guard down as time passed and things settled.

"I'm glad you are now being fully honest. Of course, I've come by your home already, after I followed Julie there from the airport. And I've seen your dad. He seems to be doing pretty well. In the past few days, I've learned you are a teacher, Aaron is in med school, Mark works as a computer science engineer, and Sara takes care of your dad. Obtaining new identities, jobs, and a lovely home, in a period of only a few months, is an admirable feat. Your resourcefulness is very impressive."

Agent Conrad stood up and handed Aliya his card."Well, my work is done here. I'll write up my report and submit it to the director. For all intents and purposes, this case is closed, at least for the time being. But be vigilant. Trust your gut. And be sure to contact me right away if you notice anything suspicious."

As he turned to leave, he gave Julie one last gorgeous smile. "Nice to meet you, Julie. I enjoyed getting to know you on the plane." And with that, he left.

As he climbed into his rental car, he heard a car alarm sound nearby. He looked to see the owners promptly shut it off, satisfying him that there was no burglary occurring. As he pulled away, he thought…alarm. Of course. If his memory served him correctly, the report he read from ARC Labs stated that only one fire alarm was pulled and this was done by a security guard in another building, who saw the flames coming from Building #5 after the blaze was well underway. Why hadn't Aliya pulled the alarm? There were fire alarms in every corridor, and she would have had to pass right by one. If she had indeed pulled it, the fire would have likely been contained and would have been much less devastating.

CHAPTER 54

Foolproof?

The shipping container arrived as expected on the typically hot, sunny Jamaican day. It was marked with phrases that were not unusual for a package sent to an IVF facility: "Fragile - Handle with Care," "Biological Specimens," "Keep Refrigerated."

Aliya had kept track of its journey en route from ARC Labs to the Wexner Fertility Management Clinic at Kingston University Hospital. She wanted to ensure it did not get delayed along the way and that she would be the one to receive it when it arrived. Aliya knew the embryos would be packed in dry ice, but she was still a bit worried that they might have begun to thaw if they were held up at the border. She cut through the packing tape and opened the box to find a thick white styrofoam cooler. She put on her cryogenic gloves and lifted the lid. Edwin had done an excellent packaging job. She could tell he took extra care.

The insulated royal blue steel storage containers harboring the tubes of embryos were submerged deeply in the dry ice pellets. She carefully removed them from the cooler, unscrewed the lid, and inspected each tube to be sure it was completely frozen and that absolutely no thawing had occurred. Then she interspersed these tubes with the other specimens she was in charge of and immersed the entire metal holding rack back into the liquid nitrogen cryopreservation tank, hoping they would not be noticed. She reached her gloved hands into the dry ice pellets, moving them around to make sure she had retrieved everything. She felt something hard, with a unique solid form. She pulled it from the pellets and recognized it right away. The small, plastic baby Jesus figurine. Edwin must have placed it there. He was returning the one she gave him in the king cake that was with the concert ticket. It was his sweet way of connecting with her. Her heart warmed. She was so grateful to him for his unconditional friendship and constant support.

"*Wah gwann*?"

Aliya was startled. She hadn't heard anyone come in. She turned to see her boss, Savannah, standing behind her and smiled pleasantly. "*Mi deh yah, yuh know*—I'm doing well." Aliya thought very highly of Savannah, a native Jamaican who had worked hard to earn her position as one of the clinic's most respected staff scientists.

The feeling was mutual. Savannah was very fond of Aliya. She recognized right away how bright, skilled, and hardworking Aliya was. Aliya fit in perfectly and got along very well with her co-workers. She was a model employee, and Savannah would have been happy to have her full-time if Aliya didn't already have a job teaching. The clinic had just undergone a fifty-million-dollar expansion. Business was booming as a lot of foreigners came to Jamaica for IVF treatments. The price was right—about three times cheaper in Jamaica than in the U.S.

Savannah and Aliya chatted for a few minutes until Savannah received a call that she needed to take. "See you later, Aliya. Keep up the good work."

Aliya was done for the day and looked forward to returning home to tell Aaron and the others that the embryos arrived safely. She was both relieved and excited to begin working with them.

Her first step would be to establish a stem cell line from the cells of the inner cell mass of the embryo. This could be tricky as she needed to be sure to isolate only the cells she needed and not include any nearby cells. In a recently published journal article, she had read about a new methodology that utilized a highly successful culture system known as MTP: minimized trophoblast cell proliferation. The embryos would be thawed and placed in a solution containing an enzyme that would destroy the zona pellucida—the thick, transparent, protective outer membrane of the embryo. Then she would aspirate the cells of the inner cell mass into a pipette and re-suspend them in a nutrient-rich broth before adding them to tissue culture plates.

She would need to prepare the plates in advance by adding live fibroblast feeder cells which would adhere to the bottom of the plate, yielding the perfect biological matrix for the embryonic stem cell colonies to grow upon. Next, she would add more fresh nutrient broth to the plates and place them in the warm incubator. Soon thereafter, colonies of human embryonic stem cells would grow. From these, she would establish healthy embryonic stem cell lines, in which she would edit her genes of choice using KRISPR Cas. She knew the whole process by heart, as she had done it so adeptly many times before with mouse embryonic stem cells at ARC Labs.

Aliya and Aaron relaxed in the sunroom, discussing their progress toward their goal of helping Matthew. The chief neurosurgeon in the clinical lab where Aaron worked recognized immediately what a quick learner Aaron was, as well as the tremendous potential he had to become a fine physician. He took Aaron under his wing and was a superb mentor to him, allowing Aaron to participate in as many surgeries as possible to gain valuable experience. Aaron was particularly excited to partake in a neural stem cell transplantation surgery for a patient with Parkinson's. He learned how to perform this type of procedure by witnessing first-hand how it was done, from the initial brain scans that were carried out to mark the appropriate location of the injection site and determine the depth of the injection, to the anesthetizing procedure, to setting up the stereotactic apparatus, to the actual injection of the transplanted stem cells.

Aliya sipped her tea as she sat comfortably with her feet resting on the coffee table. She had her laptop open, perched on a pillow on her lap.

"Aaron, could you explain to me again how stereotactic surgery works? I'm not sure I fully get it."

"Happy to. Basically, any point in space can be determined by the intersection of three planes: the X, Y, and Z-axis in the Cartesian coordinate system. I'll use the MRI scans of your dad's brain to determine the specific location and record the coordinates of the transplantation site. I'll use fiducials, or reference points, on the images for accurate targeting. The coordinates will be converted to exactly match the coordinates on the stereotactic frame that will be fixed rigidly to your dad's head. And I'll use the stereotactic frame coordinates to accurately place the needle with regard to the three axes—horizontal, vertical, and depth—to ensure the precise injection of the cells."

Aliya nodded. "Very cool."

"But one thing I'm still really worried about is the rejection of the transplanted cells by your dad's immune system, since we are not using his own cells to make induced pluripotent stem cells, but rather are using embryonic stem cells from a donor. There is a real possibility that he could have a massive, hyperactive immune response that could kill him."

Aliya took a deep breath and shot Aaron a worried glance. "I know. I've read those studies too."

Aaron frowned. "Standard treatment would be to give him immunosuppressant medications before the procedure, but then he'll be immune-compromised and, at his age, he could easily get sick and die of something else."

"There is another option."

Aaron couldn't help but smile. Of course, his brilliant wife had already thought about this potential complication and had already found a solution.

"I could use KRISPR Cas to knock out the genes that enable a cell to be recognized by the immune system."

"You mean the MHC genes?"

"Well, actually they're genes that enable the MHC, Major Histocompatibility Complex, genes to work properly. Researchers in California have already done this successfully in mice. But they also determined that in order for the transplanted cells to escape recognition by the recipient's immune system, another gene, CD47, has to be activated. If it's done correctly, it seems pretty foolproof. Weighing the risk and benefits, I think it's the best option for Dad. But I'd still like you to read the paper about this, just to make sure I'm not missing anything."

"Sure. I've always loved learning about Immunology." Aaron paused, thinking deeper about their plan. "Once you've edited all the genes you want in the embryonic stem cells, what will you use to convert them into nerve cells?"

"Great question. There are a couple of checks I'll need to do before I even transform them into neurons. First, I'll use standard molecular biology techniques, like PCR, to make sure my edits precisely target the intended genes, and that there are no 'off-target' effects. Then I'll need to screen my cell lines to ensure they haven't become aneuploid while they were being cultured, which sometimes happens because, as the cells are dividing and multiplying in culture, there can be errors when the chromosomes segregate into the newly produced cells, resulting in a cell having an abnormal number of chromosomes. But, to answer your question, once the stem cells are precisely edited and karyotyped, I'll use a reprogramming factor called neurogenin-2 to convert them to neurons."

"Okay. So, let's assume the neurons that are transplanted survive and work the way we expect. Is there a possibility for transplant overgrowth, resulting in too many cells, which could disrupt normal processes or even lead to tumorigenesis?"

"Yes. That is a possibility. But it wasn't seen in the previous studies done with Parkinson's patients. We'll follow their protocol as closely as possible and transplant the same amount of cells they did."

"Wow. You've really done your homework on this."

Aliya's expression was serious. "I had to. We have to. He's my dad."

"That's what scares me. It's your dad. Not some model organism in a lab." The concern in Aaron's eyes was pronounced. "Sometimes I really have second thoughts about this, Liya. I know we are trying to think of everything and that all we are doing is based on solid research, but…" Aaron's voice trailed off.

"But what? We've got to try, Aaron. If we never try, he's no better off. He's got nothing to lose."

"Maybe he does. What if we make it worse? What if something goes wrong? What if we turn him into a vegetable?"

"Oh, for Christ's sake, we're not doing a lobotomy on him. The transplant is no different than what has already been done with Parkinson's patients. The imaging and stereotactic apparatus will allow you to make a precise injection so that no other brain tissue will be damaged. And it's such a localized procedure, the risk for infection is nearly non-existent. But we'll give him prophylactic antibiotics just in case. The only other significant concern is an uncontrolled immune reaction, and we have a way to keep that from happening."

Aliya paused and brought her hand to her forehead, lost in thought. "It's got to work," she said confidently before looking away. She sighed deeply and returned her gaze to Aaron. "It's just got to work," she whispered.

CHAPTER 55

A Beginning

"He's so beautiful," Aliya said, overcome with heartfelt emotion at the sight of the precious, hours-old infant.

Sara's exhaustion was surpassed by the immense sense of tranquility she felt as her newborn son nuzzled her breast. "It's just so amazing. I never knew I was even capable of loving something this much."

Aliya smiled and stroked her nephew's soft skin. "You did a great job, Sara. You already are a wonderful mother. You have a beautiful family."

Sara lifted her gaze from her child. "I wish Mom were here."

Aliya's heart sunk. She too had wished Ellie was with them all, many, many times before.

"Would you like to hold him?" Sara said, as she finished feeding him.

"I would love to."

Aliya began to gently sway as she held him.

"You're a natural," Sara said. "You automatically rock back and forth, just like Dad did when he held babies." She frowned. "But Dad

… well, he'll never really know his grandson. It such a shame. Both Mom and Dad would have given him so much love."

"There's still hope for Dad to get to know him," Aliya said softly, as she carefully placed her new nephew in the clear plastic crib next to Sara. "You should get some rest now," she said, as she gently squeezed Sara's hand.

"Yes, I think I will. The nurses told me I should sleep when the baby sleeps."

"Sweet dreams to you both. Love you."

"Love you too."

As Aliya left the hospital, she could not stop thinking about how much she wanted her dad to get to know this beautiful child, to feel the same intense love she had felt, to hold him on his lap while reading to him in his animated voice, to teach him how to build, to impart all his wise sayings, just like he had done with Sara and her. Her experiment *had* to work.

CHAPTER 56

Unforeseen

Shrill, piercing screams penetrated the night's silence. He was having yet another horrific nightmare. Aliya and Aaron ran to his bedroom to find him dripping in sweat, crying in anguish. It was a heart-wrenching sight. Aliya spoke to him in a calming and reassuring tone while Aaron went to get him some water.

"It's okay, Dad. It'll be all right. You're safe."

Warm tears rolled down her cheeks. She could barely stand to witness him in such agony yet again that night. His eyes met hers, but they were confused. He didn't know what was happening … what was real. Aaron brought him a sleeping pill, and he gradually settled, falling back to sleep, still grasping Aliya's hand.

Aliya recalled the exact evening some time before this very night that she, Aaron, Sara, and Mark had sat quietly together in the sunroom, lost in their thoughts, with both Krispr and Cassie cuddled on the couch next to them. Many months had gone by since she had devised their plan. Her meticulous work in the laboratory had paid off. She was able to accurately edit the genes she had targeted and successfully establish cultures of healthy neurons. Aaron had gained abundant experience in the clinical neurology lab and was confident in his ability to perform the transplant. It was the day of truth. Should they really go through with it? Aliya weighed all the pros and cons again. The pros won. But even more importantly, she felt compelled to follow her heart. How could she not use her knowledge and skill to try to help her dad?

Sara and Mark still felt much trepidation. Mark let out a sigh and shook his head. "I know we're not scientists. I'm just a computer guy, and Sara's forte is business. You're the experts. And I know you have no intention of hurting Matthew. But, frankly, we're worried."

"Yeah. Really worried. Beyond worried," Sara said, as her eyes grew wide. "I mean, it's freakin' brain surgery, right? And neither of you are brain surgeons."

Aliya just looked at Sara but didn't respond. Aaron gave a slight nod. They all sat in silence for a while.

Finally, Sara took a deep breath. "Well, I guess we'll just have to trust you. I really do want Dad to be better, even if only a little bit. And he's only getting worse."

Aliya thought more about it. She had previously decided to give up her teaching job and continue to work part-time at the IVF facility. This enabled her to take care of Matthew, as they all had decided it was best that he lived with Aliya and Aaron, in the home he was now familiar with and somewhat comfortable in. Sara and Mark had moved to a house nearby and were very busy with their new little one. As Matthew's primary caregiver, Aliya became acutely aware of his worsening dementia but also recognized that his physical health remained strong. If they were to go through with their daunting experiment, now was the time.

Aaron had managed to get Matthew in for an MRI during daytime hours on a holiday, when the census was low and no one questioned his taking a patient in for the non-invasive imaging procedure. He would use the information from the MRI for the presurgical planning: to determine the correct stereotactic coordinates that would ensure proper placement of the injection. Late one Saturday night, Aliya and Aaron brought Matthew to Aaron's clinical lab in the Department of Neurology.

"Here you go, Dad," Aliya said, as she dropped the sleeping pill in his palm and handed him a paper cup filled with water.

He looked at her and smiled, recognizing her as a friend, perhaps connecting her familiar face to that of his beloved wife's. He swallowed the pill without a problem. Aliya and Aaron helped him under the starched white covers of the hospital bed and pulled up the railings. He drifted off into a peaceful slumber.

Aliya picked up the cloth restraints and hesitated. "It just feels so, so … unsettling to have to tie him down."

"I know. But we have to. Want me to do it?"

"Could you?" Aliya said.

Aaron took the restraints from her and slipped them around Matthew's wrists and ankles, attaching the opposite ends to the bed frame.

"Let's gown up," Aaron said, in the serious tone of a medical professional. For the next few hours, he intended to view Matthew objectively, as his patient, not as Aliya's dad, so that his emotions would not affect his crucial task.

Clink, clink.

Aliya watched intently as Aaron placed the sterile metal tools on the shiny stainless-steel tray: a razor, scalpel, forceps, hemostats, a handheld drill. On another sterile tray, he placed betadine and gauze, a syringe filled with a local anesthetic, an empty syringe, and black surgical stitches.

Aaron powered the bed to move Mathew to a more upright position and draped the area, making a sterile field. He picked up the razor and bent over Matthew, squinting.

"Liya, could you please adjust the overhead light to illuminate the area better?"

She grabbed the long arm of the light and adjusted its location to his liking.

He shaved a small patch of Matthew's hair, wiped the area thoroughly with the rusty red colored betadine, and then carefully injected the local anesthetic just under the skin. He turned to another nearby table and removed the sterile sheet covering the meticulously designed stereotactic head frame, then paused to examine it.

Aliya felt her knees weaken as she gasped. To her, the frame looked like a piece of macabre equipment from a torture chamber in the Dark Ages. It was slate gray with moveable posts that could be adjusted to fit snugly on each side of the head. Attached to the posts was a metal arch that had a scale of ruler-like gradations marked with white numbers and hatch marks.

Aaron was too focused on his task to notice Aliya's reaction. He carefully placed the stereotactic frame on Matthew's head and securely tightened it into place. He compared the placement of the frame with the MRI scans hanging on the nearby lighted wall panels.

Aaron took a deep breath as his eyes met Aliya's. She bit her lip and nodded slightly. Aaron made an incision and drilled a small burr hole at a precise location in Matthew's skull, using the stereotactic coordinates to guide him. Aliya's shoulders tightened and her teeth clenched upon hearing the high-pitched whir of the drill.

Aliya had prepared the neuronal cell suspension right before they came to the hospital and kept it in a sterile tube on ice. Aaron aspirated 2.5ul of the suspension into the syringe. He held it upright and flicked it with his finger to remove any air bubbles, then moved towards the hole in Matthew's skull.

He stopped.

He looked to Aliya, his eyes meeting hers, and ever so slightly nodded "No".

"I can't do it," he whispered.

Aliya's face dropped in shock and disbelief. She felt irritated as she moved toward him intending to grab the syringe. Before she took it, her eyes again met his. She realized that what he was about to do went against ever fiber in his body. She paused, took a deep breath, then gently took the syringe from him and moved it toward the hole in her father's head. She hesitated for one last moment, contemplating what she was about to do. Then she positioned it in the hole and steadily depressed the plunger, carefully injecting the genetically engineered, neuronal suspension it into her dad's brain. They repeated the procedure four times, at various locations in the hippocampus known to be essential for memory. When they were finished, they both breathed an enormous sigh of relief, hoping the worst was over.

Throughout the night, Aliya constantly glanced at the monitors that reported blood pressure and heart rate, as well as the pulse oximeter, which indicated the oxygen saturation of the blood. Matthew's vitals were good. He was stable and had no apparent issues. She held her dad's hand as he rested peacefully. She watched his chest rise and fall rhythmically. Thank you, God, she thought.

About an hour before dawn, Mark joined them to help move a groggy Matthew to a wheelchair to transport him out of the medical facility before staffers showed up for a new day of work. There was a gentle breeze that night, and the sky was full of stars. Cassiopeia was as prevalent as ever. Matthew looked so peaceful. Aliya felt a warmth and optimism swelling inside her.

A few weeks after the procedure, Aliya and Matthew were enjoying breakfast at the table in the sunroom. Bright sunshine flooded the room. Matthew reached for the local newspaper and looked at it for a moment.

“Do you need your glasses, Dad?”

“Yes. But I can get them. I left them on the nightstand in my bedroom.”

Aliya’s mouth dropped open as she watched him get up from the table and head to his bedroom. She fell back into her chair and brought her hands to her mouth as she smiled, almost in disbelief. Could his short-term memory really be returning?

As time went on, they all began to notice subtle changes. Matthew was congenial again, pleasant and helpful. He was more verbal and would make small talk about safe subjects that weren’t confusing to him, such as how lovely the flowers smelled, how refreshing the breeze was, how good the dinner tasted. Aaron noted that it was a positive sign that his olfaction had returned, as losing one’s sense of smell was associated with Alzheimer’s. His confusion and disorientation were gradually lifting. His glances changed from being empty and distant to being alert and curious. He no longer appeared to be just going through the motions of daily life, but rather was showing signs of experiencing true joy.

"Would you like some lemonade, Dad?" Aliya asked from the kitchen.

"Not right now, honey," Matthew replied. "I'm kind of busy."

Aliya cocked her head as she peeked into the family room.

"Ahh. Nope. Now it's here," Matthew said with a huge smile, as Krispr furiously chased the elusive beam Matthew made jerk, jump, and climb up the wall with the laser cat toy. "Oh, are you jealous? Needing some attention too?" He picked up the tennis ball Cassie had dropped at his feet and threw it across the room, watching her grab it before it ricocheted off the bottom of the couch.

When Sara entered with Matty, his namesake, Matthew's eyes twinkled. "Bring him to Papa," he said as he gestured to his lap. He took Matty's hands in his own. "You may have your mother's eyes, but these hands … well I can tell, these are the hands of a carpenter."

Aliya was convinced that her experiment had worked exactly as she had hoped. Aaron remained cautiously optimistic. He very much wanted to take Matthew in for follow-up MRIs to observe how the transplanted cells were progressing. He was concerned about overgrowth and the potential for tumorigenesis. But it was too much of a risk. There was a new technologist in charge of the MRI facility, and she kept a meticulous accounting of all the scans that were performed. And, if it was ever found out that he performed brain surgery on a patient as a med student, he surely would never become a doctor. Hell, they'd probably all go to jail. They had risked not only Matthew's well-being, but also their own futures.

But then the nightmares began.

At first, they happened gradually. Then they became nightly occurrences. This was totally unexpected. Aliya and Aaron scoured the scientific literature and found nothing about night terrors—or any sleep disorders—as potential side effects of stem cell transplantation into the brain. As the nightmares progressively worsened, Matthew's pleasant demeanor during the daytime started to diminish. He seemed skittish, anxious, and fearful. He grew quieter. Aliya tried in earnest to communicate with him, to learn what was causing him such deep-seated anxiety. But he couldn't tell her. The words wouldn't come to him.

Aliya and Aaron sat at the table in their dimly lit kitchen. She was distraught. Tears streamed down her cheeks as she held her head in her hands and her body trembled."Dear God. What have I done? You were right, Aaron. We've made it worse. He had memory loss, was confused, but he never had all this mental anguish. What are we going to do?"

Aaron rubbed his temples and looked downward. He found it almost impossible to think clearly. He too was overcome with guilt. They never should have been so reckless, so rogue, especially with a loved one. They were arrogant to think that they, a couple of amateurs, should even consider trying something so unprecedented and risky. They had no experience, no formal training, no credentials. What were they thinking? He looked to Aliya, the love of his life. It pained him, even more, to see her so upset.

Aaron took a deep breath. "We need to get to the bottom of this. He cries out in his sleep, but by the time we get to him, he is already so upset it's hard to determine what he is saying. Tonight, I'll stay up with him while he sleeps and hopefully hear what he says at the start of his nightmare. Maybe that will give us a clue as to what is causing him such distress."

Aliya brightened. It was a good idea. "I'll stay up too."

CHAPTER 57

Baffled

"Mount the plows! BFVs first. Vulcans follow." Matthew waved his arms as he shouted authoritatively in his sleep. Then he paused for several moments, before his face became tortured. "Stop! Stop!" He thrashed and screamed, tormented by a nightmare that was all too real. He awoke abruptly.

After some time, Aliya was able to quiet him enough for Aaron to give him a sleeping pill, and he drifted back to sleep.

Aaron followed Aliya to the family room. "I have no idea what any of that means."

"Neither do I," said Aliya, as she grabbed her laptop from the coffee table and powered it up. Aaron joined her on the couch. She typed 'BFV' into the google search engine. She squinted and nodded her head in confusion. "BfV stands for Bundesamt für Verfassungsschutz, the domestic intelligence service of the Federal Republic of Germany."

Aaron thought for a moment. "That makes no sense. What does 'vulcan' mean?"

Aliya didn't look up from her laptop. "Vulcan is the God of Fire in Roman Mythology."

Aaron thought deeply as he spoke. "What could those things possibly have in common: plows, the German CIA, and a Roman God? And why would they make him so agitated? He kept screaming 'Stop!'"

"I don't know. But we have to find out or else we'll never be able to help him."

Aaron stood. "He'll be out for the rest of the night now, Liya. Let's go to bed and sleep on it. Tomorrow is a new day."

"You go ahead. I'll come soon. I want to look into some other things."

He gently kissed her forehead. "Okay."

Aliya sat in silence for some time, watching the shadows from the swaying branches of the Blue Mahoe tree in their yard bounce off the sunroom wall. She typed "memory retrieval" into the PubMed Search engine. She read several abstracts before it dawned on her. Of course, she thought. Such a simple thing. Retrieval cues can facilitate recall. Why didn't I think to try this sooner?

CHAPTER 58

A Hope

"By door 2" read the text.

"K" Aaron typed, before maneuvering his way to the curb in the pick-up zone of the baggage claim area. When he spotted Ralph dragging two large suitcases through the exit door, he hurried out of the car to help him.

Aaron grabbed a suitcase."Hi. Let me give you a hand with those." The two friends loaded the heavy luggage into the back of the SUV and climbed into the front. Aaron's smile was genuine. "Good to see you, man."

"Nice to be here. The weather in Cleveland sucked. Overcast, cold, and windy. The Jamaican sunshine and heat are awesome."

Aliya and Matthew were sitting in the sunroom when they arrived. Aliya smiled warmly, hugging Ralph affectionately. "Thank you so much for coming. And for doing this for us. We really appreciate it."

"Happy to. Don't mind getting away from all those damn iguanas once in a while. They're taking over Key Biscayne." Ralph looked to Matthew and smiled, giving him a pat on the shoulder. "Good to see you, old friend. You're looking well."

Aaron entered with a Red Stripe for each of them. "Thought you all might be ready for a cold one," he said, handing them each a bottle of his favorite Jamaican lager. "Speaking of iguanas, we've got a few different kinds of lizards here too. Although you usually don't see them too much. The island cats keep the smaller ones in check. Krispr has become a pro at catching them and leaving them by the door for us. And a lot of the locals aren't real fond of the larger, bright green ones. Apparently, some folks think they are the ghosts of dead people. They call them 'duppies,' and you don't want to mess with a duppie or else serious harm, even death can come to you."

Ralph took a big swig of his beer and smiled. "No pissing off the duppies, eh?" Then he turned to Matthew. "How're you feeling today, Matt? Up for looking through some old photo albums? I brought a bunch."

Aliya watched her dad reply in his usual manner— by just shrugging his shoulders. "Actually, Ralph, I was thinking it might be better to do that tomorrow. He gets tired out by the end of the day and is so much brighter in the morning. Plus, it will give me a chance to go through the albums and select some pictures that will hopefully jar his memory and maybe even help us figure out what his nightmares are about. Sara is coming over tonight to help." She paused and her face softened. "Again, I can't thank you enough for going to the storage unit in Cleveland and bringing all this stuff down here."

Aaron glanced at Matthew and Ralph. "While the ladies are going through the old photos, I was thinking the guys could do a little fishing. Does that sound good to you both?"

Matthew looked up and smiled. Ralph smiled too."Only if you have more of these," Ralph said, holding up his beer bottle.

CHAPTER 59

Sisters

"Hello?" Sara called as she entered her sister's home.

"I'm in the kitchen," Aliya replied. Sara joined her and placed a bag on the counter. "I brought some pretzels and cream cheese."

Aliya was mixing colorful cocktails. "Perfect. That will go great with these fresh rum runners." When Aliya finished, they took their snacks and drinks into the sunroom, where the two large suitcases that Ralph had brought sat. Krispr was curled up in a ball on the top of the couch, fast asleep.

"Where's Cassie?" asked Sara.

"I sent her with the guys on the fishing trip. I figured she could help keep Matty occupied. Besides, she loves the beach."

"Great idea. The fresh air and exercise will tire them both out."

They sat cross-legged on the floor and began to look through the many photo albums. The sisters were filled with emotion and nostalgia. It was obvious that Ellie and Matthew had lived a rich and fulfilled life.

"Aww. Look at these," Sara said as they flipped through the pages of the albums.

Ellie had saved so many pictures, documenting all the wonderful occasions throughout their family's entire lives. She clearly was very content in her roles as both a mother and a wife.

The photo albums were all ordered, starting with the most recent occasions, such as Aliya and Aaron's wedding, their college graduation, the Christmas holidays, Thanksgiving, birthdays, and summer holidays. There were albums of Sara and Mark's wedding, Sara's college graduation … all the way through the girls' younger days—of special occasions as well as the extra-curriculars they participated in during their adolescence and childhood. There were also several albums with pictures taken from their many vacations to national parks and scenic settings all over the U.S. and Canada: Yosemite, Sequoia, Glacier, Yellowstone, the Grand Canyon, Sedona, Olympic, Banff … even Hawaii, where they snorkeled with sea turtles.

"My God, look at you, Liya, in your yellow Belle dress. I think you wore that dress every day for a year."

"I think I did too. After I met the 'real' Belle at Disney World, I couldn't stop thinking about how wonderful she was. Mom just played along and let me wear the dress every day. It was even her idea to have us all dress up as characters from *Beauty and The Beast* on Halloween."

"I remember that! Dad was the Beast and Mom was Mrs. Potts. Dad convinced me to be the wardrobe. He said it was very fitting for me. But I forgot her name."

Aliya burst out laughing. "Madame de la Grande Bouche," she said in her best French. "Mistress of the Big Mouth!"

"Oh, great," Sara said, rolling her eyes. She picked up another album. "God, Liya, these modeling pictures of you are stunning. I guess I was off at college when you were doing all of this and kind of missed it."

"Well, it was short-lived."

"Has Aaron ever seen these?"

"No, I don't think he has."

"You should show him. You were freakin' gorgeous!"

"What do you mean 'were'?"

Sara and Aliya laughed, feeling the effects of their potent drinks as they reminisced.

"Even though I knew you were doing some modeling, I guess I just always thought of you as my gangly kid sister."

"Well, that's basically what I was. All the professionals, the make-up artists, hairstylists, and photographers, just transformed our look. It was so superficial. But deep down all the models were the same inside—super young and super naive."

Aliya opened another album. "Oh my God. Look at these pictures!" She moved closer to Sara to show her.

Sara was taken aback. "Okay. Now that's really stunning. Look at them. What a striking couple."

Ellie was wearing a full-length, white satin gown with exquisite brocade that was trimmed with small pearls and shiny sequin. It was long-sleeved, off the shoulder, and tightly fitted to accentuate her perfect figure. She wore her luscious chestnut-colored hair up, styled into a French braid, which highlighted the symmetric features of her comely face, enhancing her natural beauty even more. Matthew looked ever so young and handsome in his tailored black tuxedo—lean and fit, sporting an attractive suntan. Aliya's heart filled with warmth. They looked so incredibly happy on their wedding day. So in love, she thought.

Sara took another sip of her drink. "I haven't seen these pictures since we were kids. Dad's mustache is hysterical!"

"I know, right? I guess mustaches were really cool back in the early nineties. You've got to admit, it did look good on him."

"Remember how we would take turns putting on Mom's wedding dress, complete with her high heels and veil, and would prance all around the house in it?"

"Not just the house. I even wore it out to the fort, which Mom was not happy about."

"That's right. Because then she had to get it professionally cleaned, which was very expensive. She wanted to make sure it was in good condition in case either of us decided to wear it on our own wedding day."

Aliya sighed. "She was such a great mom."

Sara's smiled slightly. Her expression was tinged with sadness. "She was. And she would have been an awesome grandma." Sara looked at her phone. "Mark just texted. They are on their way back. I should head out soon so I can meet them at home and help get Matty to bed. Which pictures should we show Dad tomorrow?"

"I was thinking we should show Dad more recent pictures of him and Mom first. Then we can look at the vacation pictures, and pictures when we were little kids. I hope looking at pictures of Mom doesn't make him sad."

Sara got up to leave. "Sounds like a plan." She and Aliya embraced for a long moment. "It was a great night, Liya. I'm so glad to have you as my sister."

Aliya smiled. "Same. See you tomorrow."

CHAPTER 60

Mick

Aliya handed Ralph a mug of strong, locally grown coffee as she joined Aaron and him at the kitchen table for breakfast. "I was so busy getting Dad settled when you got in last night, I forgot to ask how the fishing went."

Aaron devoured the last of his cornmeal porridge before answering. "Not too bad. We caught a few. But they were small, so we just threw 'em back."

Ralph sighed and gave Aliya a troubled look. "LeeLee, you're right. There's something about your dad that just ain't the same since I last spent time with you all. It's more than his Alzheimer's. He's skittish and fearful, like an animal that's hiding from a predator. And at times yesterday when we were fishing, he would just look off into the distance, mesmerized by his thoughts. But his face would look so pained. Whatever is bothering him, it's really rough on him. I can tell."

Aliya's heart sank. "I know. We've got to get to the bottom of this. I don't think it's related to his Alzheimer's. I've read that people with Alzheimer's can become depressed and can get agitated due to being disoriented and frustrated. I also read that they may have restlessness or wakefulness at night. But Dad's symptoms, like what you've just described, and having all-out horrifying nightmares, are not generally associated with Alzheimer's, so it makes me think his awful nightmares and intense anxiety are related to the transplant. But I can't figure out why they would be." Aliya sighed. "Well, I guess I should go check on him. He's probably awake by now."

Sara arrived a short time later. "Hey. Sorry I'm late. Mark had to finish up some work before he could take over watching Matty."

Aliya gave Sara a hug. "No worries. Dad just finished his breakfast. We're heading to the sunroom now to start looking at some of the photos."

Matthew took his usual seat in his comfy recliner while Cassie perched on the floor at his feet. Sara crouched next to him so she could look over his shoulder at the photos that Aliya passed to her, handing them to her dad. Aliya, Aaron, and Ralph sat across from Matthew, focusing intently on his reactions to each photo.

For what seemed like forever, Matthew showed absolutely no reaction to any of the pictures. He was disinterested. Bored. Clearly, he didn't recognize anyone.

"Flat affect?" asked Aaron.

Aliya shook her head in disappointment. "It seems so. He's very … apathetic."

Ralph moved closer to Matthew and viewed the pictures with him. He smiled and spoke with enthusiasm. "Hey, Matt, look at this one! Who is that good-looking young guy with the beautiful wife? That's you, man, and Ellie! Look how happy you two are! Look at the nice house you had. And your girls, Sara and LeeLee. What little cuties!"

Matthew produced a slight smile. But his eyes were still vacant. It seemed to Aliya that he was reacting to the enthusiasm in Ralph's voice, rather than to what Ralph was actually saying or to the photos he was viewing.

Aliya quickly looked up and addressed Ralph directly. She practically shouted. "Ralph!"

"Yeah?" he answered, a bit alarmed by her sudden outburst.

"I saw that you brought old music albums and CDs from when you were younger. Did you happen to bring a player too?"

"Um no. I didn't think to bring a player."

"Then why did you bring them?"

"Oh, because back in the day, the artwork on the covers was all the rage. The designs were every bit as cool as the music. If they were really good, posters would be made, and teenagers would hang them on their bedroom walls. When I found a crate filled with your mom and dad's old music albums and CDs in the storage unit, it brought back such awesome memories for me. So, I thought I'd bring a few along for ol' Matt to see too."

Aliya was excited as she grabbed the albums and handed Matthew one. "Hey Dad, take look at this."

Matthew brightened a bit. Ralph now understood what Aliya was trying to do."Here, show him this one. It's called 'Versus' by Pearl Jam. There's a great tune on it called 'Daughter.'"

Aliya's thoughts raced. "When was it released, Ralph. Do you remember?"

"Um. God. Probably in the early '90s. Yeah, actually, it was '93 'cause that was the year I got married, and Breyona and I went to see them in concert. They were on tour, promoting the release of this album."

Aaron watched closely as Matthew examined the album. "He's taking a lot of interest in it. Seems like he might recognize it."

Aliya looked at the stack of albums. "Give him another one, Ralph. Pick out another good one. From when you were young."

"Okay. If I remember correctly, this one came out a few years earlier. It's called 'Nevermind' by Nirvana. It has a totally awesome tune, 'Smells like Teen Spirit.'" He handed Matthew the album. The cover design had a baby swimming in a pool toward a dollar bill attached to a fishing line. Matthew's face lit up.

Aliya grabbed her phone. "Ralph, you're a fucking genius! We don't have a way to play these, but we do have Spotify. It came out in 1991," she said, as she touched the play button on her phone, which was connected to their home speaker system. She turned up the volume and flooded the house with music. As soon as the guitar started, Matthew came to life, moving his body as if he was experiencing the music live. When the drums kicked in, he really started to jam. Ralph began playing the air guitar and singing the words from memory. Matthew joined in on the verse, singing his heart out like a teenager at a concert.

Sara and Aaron didn't quite know what to make out of all of this. Aliya jumped up and danced wildly to the music, throwing her arms into the air and whipping her long hair around. When the song ended, she grasped each of Matthew's hands and bent down to look directly into Matthew's exhilarated eyes.

"Dad?"

"It's Mick. My name is Mick."

Sara's mouth dropped open. Aaron was stupefied. Ralph whispered under his breath, "WTF?"

Aliya tilted her head. She smiled and gave him a pleasant, agreeable look, not wanting to offend him. She spoke slowly, hesitantly. "Mick. Oh, right, Mick."

Matthew looked around at the stunned faces staring at him. "Hey all. That's a great tune. Love to hear more, but I'm beat. Slept like hell last night. Okay if I get some shut-eye?"

They all looked at each other dumbfounded.Aaron answered, "Uh, sure. We'll just, uh, head out so you can nap," he said, as he glanced toward the sunroom doorway.

The four went into the kitchen. Sara plopped into a chair and threw her arms in the air. "Mick? Mick who? Who the hell is Mick?"

Ralph rubbed his forehead. "I've never heard anyone call him Mick. And I've known him for a long time."

Aliya felt like she had just seen the word "Mick," but she couldn't remember where.

Sara shook her head in dismay. "Could he have some sort of mental illness? Like a split personality?" Aaron sighed and shrugged. He had nothing to add.

The rest of the day went pretty much as usual. After Matthew awoke from his rest, he regressed back to being his quiet, but noticeably anxious self, frequently shooting nervous glances around the room and listening intently to even the slightest sound. Aliya and Ralph decided to take Matthew and Cassie for a walk on the beach while Aaron worked at home. They felt awkward and kept their conversation light, not knowing whether to call Matthew "Mick" or

"Dad" or "Matthew." The long walk tired him out, and he turned in early.

Ralph, Aliya, and Aaron sat in the sunroom that evening, talking through the events of the day. They tried in earnest to make sense of it all, hoping to come up with a plan for what to do next. But they were at a loss.

Ralph looked to Aliya then to Aaron. "You two look spent. You've been getting up with your dad so much at night, and still working and going to school full time. No wonder you're exhausted. You guys sleep tonight. I'll stay up. Besides, I want to hear what he's saying during these reoccurring nightmares. Maybe I'll pick up on something. Just show me where the sleeping pills are kept so I can give him one if he needs it."

As night fell, Ralph reclined in the comfy chair they had put next to Matthew's bed, covering himself with a blanket. Sure enough, late into the night, Matt began to cry out. Aliya had warned Ralph that Matthew thrashed around, tormented by his dreams. Ralph thought he was prepared, but witnessing his good friend in so much distress was unnerving. What he shouted was similar to what Aliya had told him: "Mount the plows. BFVs first. Vulcan's follow. Let's roll." Then, "Stop, Stop! Fall back!"

Ralph had no clue what was meant by "Mount the plows." Or what the words "BFVs" or "Vulcans" meant. But he had seen this type of intense trauma before, and he recognized "Let's roll" and "Fall back" as military jargon. "Smells Like Teen Spirit" was from 1991. Ralph thought about what he was doing in 1991. He had met Breyona but wasn't married yet. What was Matt doing in 1991? A light bulb went on in his head. The Gulf War was in 1990-91.

CHAPTER 61

The '90s

Aliya was busy at the stove when Ralph entered. "Good morning. I thought you might like to try a traditional Jamaican breakfast."

Ralph smiled and took a seat at the table. "Love to."

Sara had joined them too, hoping to somehow figure out what was going on with their dad.

"Hey," Aliya said. "No offense, but you look like shit."

"I'm exhausted. Matty was up most of the night. I think he might have strep. Mark's taking him to the pediatrician."

"Have some breakfast. It'll make you feel better."

Aaron poured the coffee while Aliya served the cabbage and saltfish accompanied by dumplings, bananas, and yam slices. It was a feast.

Ralph took a bite. "Mmm. Delicious." He glanced at Aliya and Aaron. "Well, you two look rested."

Aaron sipped his coffee. "Oh man, it was so great to sleep through the night. I guess I didn't realize how much it was wearing on us, having our sleep interrupted so much. Thanks again for taking care of Matthew last night."

"How did things go?" Aliya cowered a bit, afraid of the answer that might follow.

Ralph frowned. "Well, he had a helluva nightmare. He was flailing about and sweating profusely. His face was all red and contorted. I felt really bad for him. It took me a while to quiet him down. But then he settled a bit and took the sleeping pill. After that I never heard a peep out of him. I take it he's still sleeping now. I'm sure he could use the rest."

Aliya was disheartened. "I'm sorry you had to see him like that, Ralph."

"He's a good man. Just going through a lot. There's something I've been thinking about, and last night really drove it home. You mentioned he said things like 'Mount the plows, Line up the BFVs and the Vulcans,' but did you ever hear him say 'Let's roll' and 'Fall back'?

Aaron looked to Aliya. "No. I don't recall hearing him say that. But sometimes his speech would be pretty garbled, and it would be hard to make out what he was saying."

Sara spoke next: "That reminds me of something someone in the military would say."

Ralph nodded in agreement. "That's what I thought too. Do you think Matt could have PTSD?"

"I suppose it's possible. How long was he deployed?" asked Aaron.

"Well, he would have been in the Gulf War. And that only lasted two years, 1990-1991," replied Ralph.

Aaron looked a little embarrassed. "What was the Gulf War about? I know I should know this, but I kinda forgot."

"The Gulf War was when the U.S. and coalition forces fought against Iraq because Iraq invaded Kuwait then occupied it. It was all about oil and Iraq wanting to control the region. Our president, George Bush—the first George Bush that is, not his son, who was the president during 9/11—and the U.K. Prime Minister, Margaret Thatcher, sent troops to Saudi Arabia and got a bunch of other countries to form a coalition with them. First, we just bombed the hell out of the Iraqi military from our planes and ships. Then we sent in our special operation forces—these are our badass ground soldiers. But Saddam and his boys didn't give up without a fight. They started firing the Scud missiles they had gotten from The Soviet Union, targeting our friends in Israel and Saudi Arabia. The Scuds pretty much sucked—didn't hit their targets—so they hardly did any damage. Plus, we sent our superior Patriot missiles to shoot 'em out of the sky. There were some ground battles with tanks, but we kicked their asses in those too. I know we lost soldiers, but not nearly as many as they did."

As Aliya listened intently to Ralph, she became totally consumed by her thoughts. Sara waved her hand in front of Aliya's face. "Liya, you with us?"

Aliya looked up. "Of course." She paused. "That's how Alzheimer's works. You forget recent things, like where you left your car keys, but remember older things. The engrams that encode the more recent memories must no longer work in Dad because those neurons have died off, so they can no longer synapse with other neurons. Even the transplanted neurons can't help to regenerate these memories because they are gone. But if the engrams from the older memories are still viable, then the new neurons we transplanted can synapse with them, strengthening their connections and bringing back these memories. We must have hit the region in his hippocampus that encoded for memories in the 1990s. And apparently, some of those memories are from a bad experience he had during the Gulf War, because, as you said, Ralph, he seems to be suffering from PTSD, and it's severe."

Sara held up her hands. "Okay, wait. Let's back up a bit. You lost me a long time ago."

"Me too," agreed Ralph. "How about explaining that in laymen's terms? Like, what's an engram?"

"An engram is a memory trace. It's the neurons that connect to, or form synapses with, other neurons that make up the memory. Basically, it's the particular neurons that fire, or are activated, when a specific memory is formed."

Once again, Aaron was duly impressed by his wife's vast knowledge, and how she could readily apply it. "It makes sense, Liya. That would certainly explain your dad's behavior."

Sara listened closely to Aliya's explanation then shook her head, her face reddening with anger. "So how can we help him? Are his thoughts just going to be stuck in the early '90s, focused on the traumatic experiences he had during the Gulf War? So, he'll just be like this until he gets really old and dies of something else? That's a shitty way to live! Much worse than when he just had Alzheimer's. At least then he didn't have horrific nightmares and he wasn't freaked out all the time." She looked directly at Aliya. "You and your goddamned 'revolutionary' technology. It's your fault that Mom's dead, and now, well, you fucked up again, LeeLee!" Sara banged her hand loudly on the table and stomped out of the house, slamming the door as she left.

Tears streamed down Aliya's face. "She's right. She trusted me, but look what I've done. KRISPR is a curse. I should have let it burn with Lux."

Aaron embraced her and spoke softly. "No. No, Liya. It's not your fault. You had no way of knowing. Sara's just upset now. She'll settle down. We were only trying to help."

Ralph buried his head in his hands for a long while, trying to take it all in. When he looked up, he asked, "How do you treat PTSD? Is there something we can give Matt to help with his anxiety?"

Aaron thought for a moment. "Well, medications for PTSD are usually the same ones used for anxiety disorders in general. The standard meds are SSRIs, like Prozac, Paxil, and Zoloft.

Aliya began to regain her composure. "There's also one called propranolol. It's a blood pressure medication. But it also is able to block receptors located on cells in the amygdala, the part of the brain that's activated when you are fearful. I learned about it in a Neuroscience course I took in college when we were covering the section on memory. When you make a memory, it gets consolidated—kind of like cement hardening. When you recall a memory, it gets reconsolidated—that is, the memory becomes malleable again, like wet cement. Propranolol can be given during the reconsolidation period to alleviate PTSD." She grabbed her phone and typed into the Pub Med search engine. "Yes. Here's the paper we read in class. It gives the correct dosage: 20mg/dose. Four doses daily for ten days for sustained improvement. But they report positive results even after the first dose."

Aaron looked confused. "I'm still not getting the connection between propranolol, a standard beta-blocker, and PTSD. To treat

PTSD, you'd have to erase the bad memories. How could propranolol do this?"

"Well, it doesn't erase the memory. It detaches the fear from it. So here's how the treatment works. First, the patient has to be re-exposed to the traumatic event. They have to recall it, think about it, talk about it. As they do this, their memory will be undergoing reconsolidation, making it open to change—like wet cement. Then they take propranolol, which blocks the activation of the amygdala, so no fear is associated. This enables the memory to be reconsolidated without being connected to fear. The next time they think of the traumatic event, they will remember the details of it, but it won't cause them distress. The memory will no longer be pathological. Dad's nightmares and anxiety should subside. There are studies that show that this treatment works."

Aaron folded his hands across his chest. "Hmm. So how are we going to get propranolol? It's a prescription drug, and your dad doesn't have high blood pressure."

Ralph perked up. "I do."

Aliya got excited. "You have high blood pressure, Ralph?"

"Yep. Doc says is probably due to my crappy diet, too much cholesterol, blocks the blood vessels to my kidneys and that somehow causes the high blood pressure."

Aaron nodded. "Yes. Right. It's called 'renal artery stenosis.' It certainly can cause hypertension. Are you taking anything for it?"

"Nope. Why should I? I feel fine. Why take something if I feel fine? But I don't have to tell the doc that. I could tell him I'm worried about my high blood pressure and ask him to prescribe some of that stuff. I can be very convincing when I want to be."

Aaron thought for a minute. "I've heard of some not so 'upstanding' doctors here in Kingston. We can probably get you to one who will prescribe it for you, especially if you tell him you've been diagnosed in the States with hypertension due to renal artery stenosis and you're out of your medication. Maybe you can make up some story, like your doctor died unexpectedly and a computer glitch caused your files to be lost, so you can't get a hold of your medical records. Lots of people take blood pressure medication, and propranolol is a pretty standard prescription. It's been around for a long time and has a good safety profile. I don't think it would set off any alarms. When you ask him for it, don't call it propranolol. Call it Inderal. That's its brand name. Oh, and be sure to mention you also get anxiety. It's given to people for that too. I hadn't heard that it was being used during memory reconsolidation until Liya brought it up just now. But it totally makes sense. I think it's certainly worth a try."

"Sure. Or I could just do it the old-fashioned way and bribe the guy. But even if … when, I get the drugs, how the hell are we going to get Matt, I mean Mick, to talk about his trauma? He hardly talks about anything during the day. Are we going to wake him up from a nightmare and give him the drug?"

Aliya shook her head. "No, that wouldn't work. He has to be reminded of the traumatic incident in a controlled setting, a place he perceives is safe. The treatment is based on the principle of exposure therapy. We talk about the trauma to Dad, so he recalls it in a safe setting, like our house—so he isn't so worked up about it that he's experiencing intense fear, like when he has nightmares. Then, right after he has recalled the traumatic memory, and while it is being reconsolidated, we give him the propranolol, which will disassociate the traumatic event with the emotion of fear."

Aliya paused, deep in thought, cocking her head. "Mick. Mick. Where did I just see that?" She got up and walked into the sunroom. She pulled a tattered old photo album from the bottom of the stack. She brought it back to the kitchen where Ralph and Aaron were and began to look through it. It was so old that its pages had yellowed. She found a picture of young soldiers dressed in tan army fatigues, arm in arm, outside a barracks. Names were written in black marker under each soldier: Bo, Jack, Andy … and Mick. Her dad was Mick! It must have been his nickname. Why Mick? Mick is usually short for Michael, not Matthew, thought Aliya.

CHAPTER 62

Forgiveness

"She's still not answering my calls. I figured she'd need a few days, but I thought by now she would be willing to talk with me. It's been over a week. I just want to tell her how sorry I am. She's right. It's all my fault. I should have apologized to her a long time ago. I miss her, Aaron."

"I know, Liya. She'll come around. She must just need a little more time."

Aliya was sick about the falling-out with Sara. They had always been close, but after all they had been through lately, they had grown even closer. Even though they were getting used to Jamaica and making the best out of it, it was still very foreign to them. Try as they might, it would never feel like home, like the USA. They relied on each other, not just for sisterly support, but for companionship. Aaron wasn't around much these days, devoting a great deal of time and effort to medical school. Mark worked a lot too. Aliya often brought Matthew to hang out with Sara and Matty during the day, going on walks, to parks, to the beach, even going shopping in town with them. When the guys were available, they all spent so much enjoyable time together, gathering on the weekends for picnics, dinners, and regular euchre games.

Aliya picked up her cell phone and sent a text."Hey. Got a minute? Could use some of your sage advice."

Julie texted back. "Sure. My multi-million-dollar client can wait. I'll call ya."

Aliya answered. "Hey."

"Do I need to get a drink for this conversation?"

Aliya laughed. "Well, to quote my best friend, there's never a bad time for a drink!"

"Hmm, perhaps I should refrain as I am technically working. What's up?"

"Sara is still not talking with me. Aaron says I should give her more time."

"You guys haven't made up yet? What's it been, like a week? OMG. Go over there. Go see her. Talk to her. Do it today. Do it now."

"You're right, Jules. You're always right."

"Of course I am. Call me later with an update. Love you."

Aliya walked into her backyard and cut some fresh hibiscus and orchids, arranging them into a colorful bouquet. She put Cassie on her leash, and the two walked in the warm sunshine to Sara's house.

Sara was holding Matty when she answered the door. "Hey," she said, tersely, without returning Aliya's smile.

"I brought you a peace offering," Aliya said, handing Sara the bouquet. "Do you have some time to talk?"

Sara rolled her eyes. "I guess. We can sit out back."

They followed Sara and Matty to the patio, where Cassie found a cool spot in the shade to rest and Matty played in his sandbox. Aliya and Sara sat across from one another, both feeling dejected.

"If I could do it all over, if I could take it back, I would."

Sara looked off into the distance, still agitated, then looked back at Aliya. "I know you would, Liya. And I know your intentions were always good. It just got to me—all at once. I really miss Mom. I'm so worried about Dad. And I'm sick of Jamaica. I'm sick of living like this. Of hiding. I want to go home. I want my life back. I want a different life for Matty and for Mark. For all of us."

Aliya looked at Sara in earnest. "I miss Mom too. We never really had a chance to grieve her death. And Dad, well …" Her voice trailed off. "I can't tell you what to do, Sara. I know, this sucks. You and Mark worked so hard. You had incredible jobs in Chicago. You were both rising stars in your professions, with nowhere to go but up. It sucks for us too. Aaron was set to get his MD training from one of the most prestigious institutions in the world. Graduating from Columbia Medical School would have catapulted his career. It would have paved the way for him to land a top-notch residency. But instead, he's here, at a med school that's barely mediocre. And I had dreamed of getting my Ph.D., which will never happen now. It's not fair. None of it is. But if we go back, we risk losing everything. Even that CIA guy Julie brought thinks it's best to stay hidden here."

Sara's face softened. She began to laugh. "I'm sorry. I know this is a serious conversation. I just had a flashback of Julie's face when she realized he wasn't into her at all, that he had just made up everything he told her on the plane and was using her to find us."

Aliya laughed too. "Oh God, her expression was priceless. Then she ordered a stiff drink!"

Sara looked over at Matty then back to Aliya. "I'll be okay, Liya. We all will be."

Aliya gave her sister a heartfelt hug. "I love you, Sara."

"I love you too."

CHAPTER 63

Reconsolidation

Their spirits might have been lifted by the beautiful weather that warm sunny afternoon, but instead, Aaron, Ralph, and Aliya sat together at the kitchen table, feeling considerable trepidation. Aliya sat next to Matthew, holding a stack of photos.

"Mick, I wanted to show you this picture. These are your army friends, right?"

Matthew took the old picture from Aliya and smiled broadly. "Yeah. Great guys! My buddies. Always got my six. Well, we all had each other's backs."

Ralph smiled, knowing how strong the sense of brotherhood was in the military. "Just curious, why'd they call you Mick?"

Matthew glanced at them all, a bit surprised by this question. "Mick. Short for McKenna, my last name."

Aaron looked at Aliya as if to say, "Of course, why didn't we think of that?"

Aliya spoke with deliberate calm. "Mick, this isn't going to be easy to talk about. But first, I want you to know that you're safe now.

Look around. We're not in Desert Storm now. It's over. The coalition won."

Matt flinched at the words "Desert Storm." Aliya smiled gently and looked around. He followed her gaze and nodded.

"I want to talk about the Bulldozer Assault."

Matthew's eyes grew large, and his breathing quickened. He became greatly distressed.

"It's all right, Mick. We're not there now. We're here, where it's safe. Can you tell us about it? About what happened that day?"

The pain in his eyes did not go unnoticed. It was agonizing. At first, he hesitated to speak. He looked around the room. For some reason, he knew he trusted the faces he saw. He spoke quietly.

"It started on February 24, 1991. Jack, Andy, Bo, and I were all in the 1st Infantry Division. They called us 'The Big Red One.' The Iraqis were defending the Saddam Line on the Kuwait border. The enemy had dug a large network of trenches, some seventy miles long. We began at zero dark thirty. We were ordered to mount anti-mine plows on the tanks and the combat earthmovers. The plows looked like giant teeth. We lined up our BFVs, Bradley Fighting Vehicles, and Vulcan armored personnel carriers and straddled the trench lines."

Matthew paused. He was completely lucid. His memory was crystal clear. He took a deep breath and looked away. His eyes were now filled with tears.

"We were all inside armored vehicles. Their small arms fire couldn't touch us. We fired on their guys and just kept plowing through, covering them with mounds of sand … burying them alive."

Aliya winced at the thought of soldiers being buried alive.

Matthew continued, "When the Iraqis in the trenches ahead saw how quick it was all going down, they jumped out of the trenches, screaming that they surrendered. I yelled 'Stop, Stop. Fall Back!' But we just kept going." Matthew looked up in earnest, shaking his head. His face was pale. "We didn't have to do that. They were surrendering. We had won. But we didn't stop. We didn't stop. When it was over, we drove back down the line. All we saw were arms and body parts, sticking out of the dirt … for seventy miles. We buried them alive. All of them." He slumped in his seat, placed his head in his hands, and cried.

Ralph wept too. "It's okay, Mick. You tried to stop it, but you weren't in command so you couldn't. It's not your fault. It was never your fault. You wanted to do the right thing. But they wouldn't allow you to. It's over now. You're safe now. You've got to move past it."

Matthew started to calm and breathe easier upon hearing Ralph's reassuring words. They all sat quietly for several moments, horrified by the acts of war.

Ralph spoke first. "Hey, let's have a beer and some lunch and then go fishing. I hear they're biting in the bay. It's too beautiful of a day to waste inside. Matthew nodded slightly. Aaron grabbed the bottles from the refrigerator, slipping the small white propranolol pill into the bottle he gave to Matthew.

Later that night, Aliya awoke automatically. Her body had become accustomed to being aroused in the middle of the night. The house was quiet. She peeked in on Matthew. He was asleep, ever so soundly. Her shoulders dropped, and she smiled warmly, feeling both relief and a sense of contentment. But she knew that this was only the beginning. They would need to continue his propranolol treatments and if necessary, give him anti-anxiety medication. Still, it was a wonderful beginning.

CHAPTER 64

A Lesson

Aliya sat with Ralph in the sunroom long after Aaron and Matthew had turned in for the night, each enjoying their refreshing Wray and Ting drinks. Krispr was curled up next to Ralph, and Cassie rested her head on Aliya's lap.

"Thanks for staying with us all this time, Ralph. It has been so great to have you here. We're all going to miss you, but I know Dad and I will miss you the most."

"Well, I wanted to give Matt some time … make sure he didn't regress. And it looks like he's doing fine. Your experiment worked, LeeLee."

"This one did. But Sara was right. I fucked up everything else. Royally."

"We gotta just live in the moment."

Aliya laughed. "You sound just like my yoga teacher."

"Must be a smart gal. But think about it. Your dad is doing fine. He's happy and content. He's such an easy-going guy, so nice to be around. Seems like even though he doesn't recognize us, he still feels like he fits in. He's comfortable here. He knows in his heart that this is where he is supposed to be. He knows he's loved. What more can you ask for?"

Aliya looked up at her friend. "You're a good egg, Ralph."

"I try," he said. Then Ralph went to the suitcase that was still sitting in the corner of the sunroom and took out a well-wrapped package. "I brought this back from Ohio too. It's your mom's ashes. I thought you might like to give her a proper burial. It might give you all some closure. Some peace. Because of the circumstances, you were never able to properly mourn your great loss. There's a beautiful little cemetery on the hill that overlooks the bay. Matt, I mean, Mick, and I have taken some early morning walks up that way. I think he likes it there. It's a great place to see the sunrise. Your mom and dad always did like the sunrise. They used to tell me the dawning of a new day meant a new chance."

Aliya felt a lump swell in her throat. She nodded as her eyes filled with tears. She had no words.

Ralph took a deep breath. "I've been thinking, LeeLee. What would you say if I decided to close up shop in Key Biscayne and move down here? Get a little place of my own. Even though Matt is doing much better, he could still use someone to hang out with, and that would give you and Aaron a little breather, some time to yourselves, to do the things you want to do." He paused before continuing. "And to be honest, I haven't been a part of a family for a long time. I feel like I am now. And it's a good feeling."

Aliya smiled, overcome with emotion. "That would make us all very happy."

The two sat in silence for a long time, enjoying the peaceful evening together, lost in their own thoughts.

Ralph broke the quietude. "I guess you learned something really important from all this, LeeLee."

Aliya cocked her head, waiting for what he was about to say next.

"Just because you can, doesn't mean you should."

"That's for damn sure."

CHAPTER 65

Over

Michael Stipe's distinctive voice resonated through the wireless speaker as REM's hit from 1991, "Losing My Religion," enlivened the mood. Matty handed his Grandpa a toy nail from the tool belt he wore over his white carpenter overalls. Matthew smiled and thanked him kindly. Ralph grabbed a two by four and began to pound it in, completing the door frame.

Aliya entered the backyard on the warm May afternoon, looking ever so radiant in her bright yellow sundress. "The fort's looking good, guys."

Ralph wiped the sweat from his brow. "Yep. Right on schedule. Mick runs a tight ship. It will be a great playhouse for Lil' Matty and will be done before the weekend, when all the guests arrive."

Aliya could hardly wait for the weekend. It was Aaron's graduation from medical school. His parents were flying in from California, and Julie was coming from Chicago. Aliya had brought her plant clippers with her and proceeded to cut some beautiful fresh flowers from her colorful garden, making a lovely bouquet. She chose one of the bright red hibiscus blossoms to put in her hair. She walked up to the cemetery on the hill and placed the flowers at her mother's grave.

She gently touched her stomach then walked to the edge of the hill, overlooking the bay far below. She took out the sturdy clippers that she had placed in her pocket along with the jump drive she had used to back up her laptop from ARC Labs. It had the only remaining copy of her protocol for her KRISPR Cas technology. She used the clippers like pliers, to bend and twist the jump drive until it snapped into pieces then flung the pieces over the cliff into the water below, knowing the tide would carry them far out into the ocean.

CHAPTER 66

Old Friend

"Arriving a little later than expected. Don't want to disrupt the festivities. Will Uber. No worries."

Aliya responded to Julie's text, "K. Thx. C u soon," then she joined Aaron, who was decked out in his cap and gown, complete with his green hood, traditionally worn by medical school graduates, for pictures by the flower garden. Aliya looked into Aaron's eyes and smiled warmly—her love as strong for him on this day as it had ever been.

"You did great, Aaron."

"We did great, Liya."

Their kiss was heartfelt. They were oblivious to those around them, as if they were the only two on the planet.

As the festivities continued, family and friends mulled about the patio and lush yard, enjoying the happy occasion, great food, and beautiful weather while Bob Marley's "Is This Love" played in the background.

When Aliya saw him walking toward her, her mouth dropped. Her eyes filled with tears of joy as they embraced.

"Edwin."

"Surprise, LeeLee! Julie brought me all the way from Bar Harbor to see you. Oh, but I won't tell anyone."

"Thank you so much for coming, Edwin. It's wonderful to see you."

"Ayuh," he replied, grinning from ear to ear, delighted to have pulled off such an incredible surprise.

"Come, let's sit down. We have so much to catch up on." She took his hand and led him to a bench seat on the patio, glancing over her shoulder at Julie, giving her a grateful smile.

Julie grabbed a drink and went to congratulate Aaron, hugging him warmly while whispering in his ear, "Got any hot single classmates you can introduce me to?"

Aaron's dad quieted the crowd so he could propose a toast, congratulating Aaron for earning his degree and thanking Aliya for supporting him. It was then that Julie realized something was off.

"Liya. WTF? You're not drinking."

Aliya smiled and rubbed her hand on her stomach. "Nope. I'm not."

"Ah! Congratulations! I'm so happy for you guys!" Edwin looked confused as Julie continued, "Do you know if it's a boy or a girl?"

"She's a girl." Aliya looked to Edwin. "I'm going to have a baby girl."

Edwin smiled. "Will you call her Christina?"

"Hmm, that is a really nice name, but we were thinking of calling her Ellen, after her grandmother."

"That's a nice name too."

CHAPTER 67

Some years later

India Bourne's cello resonated throughout Aliya's whole being. The brilliant morning sun emerged in the golden sky, rising above the tranquil, cerulean water. She laid in savasana, as a corpse, in the purest serenity, breathing slowly, deeply, as the chords from the so aptly titled song "For Grace" gently permeated the quietude.

She thought of her wedding vows, taken as the morning sun crested majestic mountains. She thought of her children, each born at dawn. She thought of the Cadillac Mountain sunrise and of the many acoustic sunrises. She thought of her dad. In her mind, she could hear his gentle voice saying: "The early bird gets the worm, LeeLee."

Yes, she thought. *Le monde appartient à ceux qui se lèvent tôt*; the world belongs to those who rise early.

The music gently transitioned to Debussy's Clair de Lune, taking her back to that warm spring day in Washington Square Park in New York City, when she was with her mother, touring colleges. She smiled as the image of her mom on that splendid day filled her mind. She thought about her mom's unyielding support, enduring optimism, and unconditional love. How her own life had changed so dramatically since that day. It hadn't turned out as she expected. She didn't see it coming. She thought of the daunting decisions she had faced and the choices she had made. And she was still plagued by the question: Is it ever justified to do the wrong things for the right reasons?

When the song finished, her teacher bowed, saying, "Namaste."

"Well, girls, how did you like your first yoga class?"

"It was okay. The music was nice, but it's really early!"

Aliya couldn't help but smile as she looked at her two beautiful young—and yes, lengthy—daughters on either side of her.

"Yes, it is early. It's the dawning of a new day."

CHAPTER 68

KRISPR

One-thousand, four-hundred and thirty-nine miles away, Agent Michael Conrad took his seat at the large conference table, waiting for the briefing to begin. Although a few hairs at his temples were now a bit gray, it in no way detracted from his handsomeness. Director Delaney arrived and seated himself at the head of the table.

"Good morning. I'll get right to the point of this special meeting. Our intel has become aware of a data breach at one of our nation's most prestigious research laboratories. For both security and proprietary reasons, ARC Labs has a longstanding policy of automatically backing up all of their employee's computer systems to a secure iCloud server. Most employees aren't made aware of this. Only high-level administrators are privy to this practice. Regarding this breach, we are picking up an unprecedented amount of chatter from our foremost foreign adversary, suggesting there is something of profound interest to them, which of course, causes us to have great concern." He paused and took a look at his notes. "Has any of you ever come across the notation: K, R, I, S, P, R?"

ACKNOWLEDGEMENTS

To my mom, one of the first to read this story, I owe my eternal gratitude for a lifetime of unconditional love and support…and for bequeathing me with her love of stories from great authors like Agatha Christie, Mary Higgins Clark, and many, many more. Most importantly, for showing us all how to be the consummate caregiver when my dad suffered from Alzheimer's.

To my children: Noah, Rin, Christina, and Tom: the true loves of my life. There's a little piece of each of you in this story.

To my brothers and sisters, with whom I experienced the pure joy of family life.

To Amy B. and the YaYa's, the best friends a girl can have, who I came of age with and who were models of the endearing friendships in this book.

To Miss Anne, who kept me going with her Irish wit and New Yorker candor.

To the WLP-our neighborhood book club, who drew me back into the world of literature and motivated me to keep reading and discovering new worlds.

To The Fellowship, lifelong supporters who helped me navigate the sea of life.

To my Posse, who taught me all about the wonders of NOLA!

To my students, who were constant reminders of what it's like to be a college student in the 21st century.

To my professors and mentors, who inspired my deep love for science.

Of course, my heartfelt appreciation those who dedicated the time to read this story. I hope you enjoyed it.